Also by Meg M. Robinson

<u>Chloe Chadwick Series</u>
Finding Salus
Waking Salus
Remembering Salus
Saving Salus

Megaverse Series
<u>Immortal Love Series</u>
Seeking Eternity
A Fury's Heart
The Last Lemurian
Grim Favors
Dance With Death

<u>The Athenaeum Series</u>
Legacy

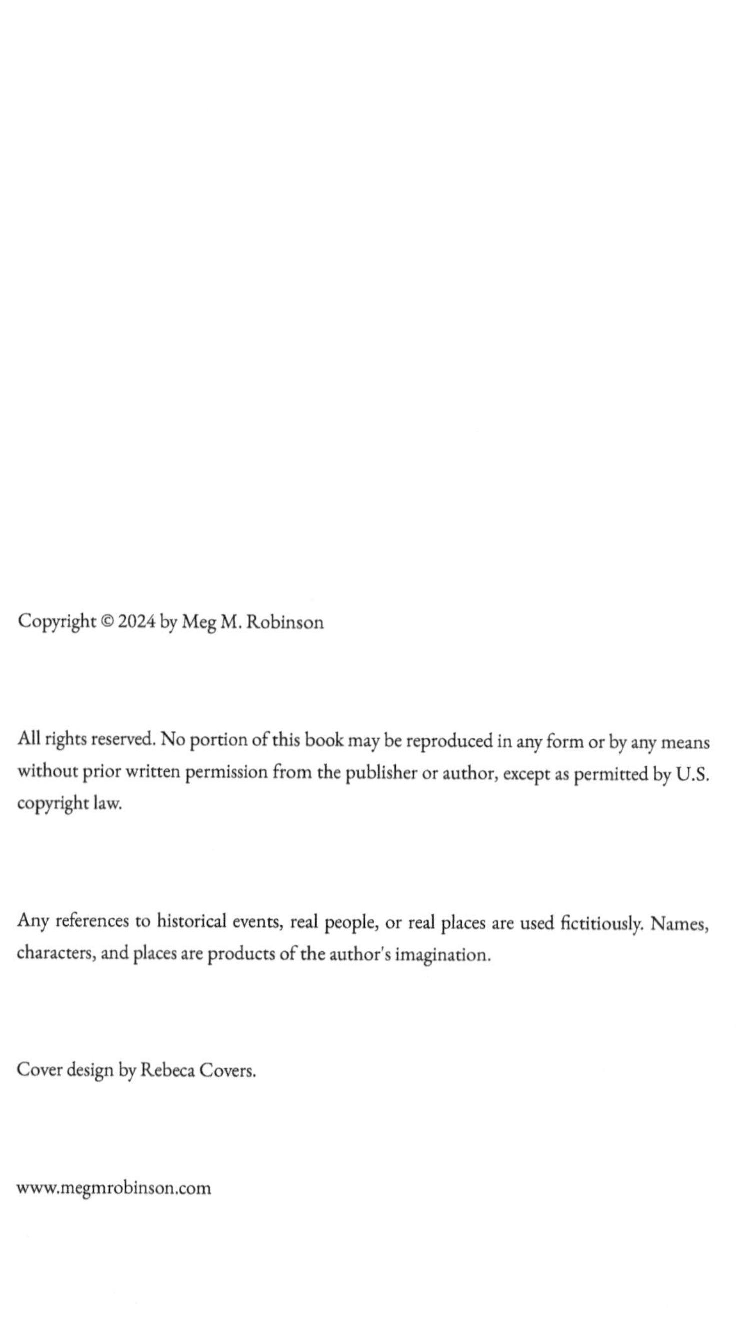

Anarchy

Meg M. Robinson

Dedication

This one is for Sherri and Carol, two women who help remind me that
I can do this.
Thank you!

Chapter 1

Sophia groaned as she clung to Lucas, an arm wound around his neck as he pinned her to the wall and thrust into her. She hadn't expected him to pull her into an empty storage room just before dinner, but she sure as hell wasn't going to complain about it, either. Especially not when his lips were doing wonderful things to her throat and she was only moments away from climax. This man was absolutely amazing, both in and out of bed. Amazing and gorgeous. He was tall and built like a viking, with short dark brown hair, just long enough for her to grab hold of. And his eyes. She loved his eyes. They were pale green and beautiful when he was calm, but she adored when he lost control and they went the color of stone like they were now.

Her release was almost on her when both her phone and Lucas's went off with text alerts. For a second she was tempted to ignore it and chase her orgasm, but there was only one reason why they would both receive messages at the same time. Something was wrong.

Lucas drew out of her with a low curse, and she couldn't quite contain a whimper. She had been so close. There had better be a fire or flood or some other catastrophe. Still, knowing her responsibilities as head of the Athenaeum, once her feet were on the floor, she retrieved her phone and pulled up the message.

Farid*: Lachlan's gone crazy in the common room!*

"Shit." Lucas's reaction mirrored her own thoughts, and they exchanged a regretful and concerned look. It only lasted a second before they hurried to get their clothes back on. Lucas only had to tuck himself back into his black cargo pants and zip them up, but Sophia had to find her jeans before she could put them back on. As soon as they'd gotten dressed, they hurried out of the storage room and started running. Since Lucas was almost a foot taller than her own five foot four, he quickly pulled ahead of her, but that was okay. He was much better at subduing people than she was.

While they rushed down the hallway, then down the stone stairs to the next level of the Athenaeum, she tried to recall what she knew about Lachlan. Scottish originally, tall, with a swimmer's build and bright red hair. Friendly, though she hadn't had much time to talk to him. She knew he was a curator, but not precisely what he did. She did remember seeing that he was a vampire, though. Not good. As a gargoyle, Lucas was strong and sturdy, but vampires were known to be exceptionally powerful and unbelievably fast. As a half-elf, half-owl shifter, Sophia couldn't compare with either if it came to a physical fight. At least not yet.

They were halfway down the stairs when Sophia heard the sounds of a fight. Someone was roaring, others were screaming, and something crashed. She lost sight of Lucas as he raced down the last few feet of stairs and out the doorway. She was worried about what she'd see when she caught up with him. Those fears weren't unfounded.

The common room was a collection of couches and chairs, with several tables, chairs, and TVs. It was where all the members of the Athenaeum could go to relax and hang out or play games. Which explained why there were so many people there, as she saw at least a dozen. Lachlan was at the center of everyone's attention, especially when he slammed Jericho—one of the guards—onto the pool table, hard enough that she heard wood crack even from across the room. Farid grabbed him from behind, but the tall redhead slammed his head back, cracking the nose of the slightly shorter guard. Carla darted in and Sophia fought not to yell at her to be careful. Yes, Carla was a woman, and not much bigger than Sophia, but she was one of the nasaru—the guards of the Athenaeum—and all of them were more than capable. Carla proved it when she slammed her fist into his nose, hard enough to make him roar as he stumbled back a few steps. Lucas, along with two others, leapt at him, tackling him to the ground.

It really did look like he'd gone crazy. Sophia had spoken to him a couple of times and he'd always seemed like a nice, controlled man. Yes, he drank blood on occasion, but all vampires did. It was no weirder than when she shifted into an owl or how her mom had pointed ears. All the Arcane had their unique traits, but it was rare that a vampire lost control and attacked people to feed, not when there were so many willing to be bitten. So for him to be acting so animalistic was extremely out of character, not to mention concerning.

Though she had thought Lachlan being tackled by three guards would be the end of it, she was shocked when he knocked them all off of him, and with enough force that one of them actually went flying. Lucas might have as well, but his skin turned gray as he assumed a partial gargoyle form, making him heavier and harder to fling. Faster than she could process, Lachlan turned to the pool table and plucked Jericho up, one arm wrapped around his chest to hold him tight. He struck, his fangs sinking deep into Jericho's neck with enough savageness that the seasoned guard screamed. Ice began to creep across the floor, radiating out from Jericho's feet, reminding Sophia that he was an ice elemental. Which meant if they didn't stop this fast, the entire room could end up coated in ice. And while she'd love to help, she hadn't yet learned enough sorcery to do much, and her fighting skills were still next to non-existent.

Some boss she was.

Carla, Lucas, and an Amazonian looking woman with blonde hair streaked with pink and blue didn't have that problem. All three chanted at once, though the spells used were all different. She wasn't sure who did what, but Lachlan's body went rigid, the ice started to recede, and the vampire was carefully pulled away from the elemental, all at the same time. As soon as Jericho was freed from Lachlan's hold, Farid, nose still bleeding, ran forward and pulled the other guard further away, one hand clamping over the wound on Jericho's neck in an attempt to slow the bleeding.

"Keep holding him," Lucas directed. "Melissa, get me a pair of cuffs?"

The pink and blue-haired woman spoke another few syllables, causing a pair of engraved handcuffs to appear in her hands. She held them out to Lucas, while keeping her eyes firmly on the enraged Lachlan.

"I can't release just his arms," Carla informed Lucas. "It's all or nothing."

He looked less than pleased, but nodded. "Can you hold him until Sergei gets here?"

"I should be able to," she answered, but Sophia wasn't sure how confident she was in her answer.

"What the hell is going on?"

Sophia half turned and saw her mom and another guard named Ray, both holding luggage. They really had perfect timing. Her mom wasn't a demigod like Sergei, but she was a skilled enough healer. "Mom, you can put people to sleep, right?" she asked, ignoring Ray's question. "Without touching them, I mean?" Sleep was a common enough skill of healers, but doing it without physical contact was another level she wasn't sure her mom was at.

"I can..." Heather answered, her eyes wide as she stared at the wreck Lachlan had made of the room and its inhabitants.

Sophia pointed to the vampire. "Put him to sleep. Now. I'll explain later." It was weird giving orders to her mom, but she really wanted Lachlan immobilized before Carla's hold on him wore off. Or before he broke free of it.

Heather frowned but nodded, setting the luggage down and hurrying over. Just as Sophia was about to warn her not to get too close, she stopped and held a hand toward the vampire. In moments, his eyes went unfocused, then slid shut.

"You're sure he's out?" Carla asked.

"He is, though I can't say for how long," Heather admitted as she took a few wary steps back.

"Do it," Lucas told Carla. She released the spell, causing Lachlan to collapse. As quick as he could while still in gargoyle form, Lucas pulled Lachlan's arms behind his back and cuffed him.

"Will those hold him?" Sophia asked.

"They're enchanted," Melissa assured her. "They dampen magic and physical strength. He's little more than a human right now."

"Oh gods. Jericho, what happened?" Heather asked when she caught sight of the guard, who still had Farid holding his throat, though it didn't hide the blood.

"Lachlan," was all Jericho said, his eyes closed. Sophia could understand why. It looked like he'd lost a lot of blood, and that bite probably hurt like hell.

Heather rushed over and laid a hand beside Farid's, working on healing the two ragged gashes. In general, vampires left two neat punctures, but Lachlan had torn the side of Jericho's throat open.

While Heather worked and Lucas made sure Lachlan was secure, Sophia looked around. A few tables had been smashed, a TV looked as though something had been thrown or slammed into the middle of the screen, and more than a few chairs were overturned or broken. Then there was the damage to the people. In addition to Farid's nose and Jericho's throat, Sophia's friend Josie was cradling her wrist and Ellie—the goth conservator—had a bite on her forearm, though not as severe as Jericho's.

Sophia pulled out her phone and sent a message to Sergei. Heather could absolutely help these people, but there was no reason for anyone to wait when they had another healer. That done, she focused on the next most important thing. She hated being the center of attention, but pushed her nerves away to do what had to be done.

"Okay," she called, raising her voice to carry to everyone in the room. "Who was here when this started?" Multiple people answered in the affirmative or raised their hands. "Everyone else can clear out unless they need healing. We don't need a big crowd right now."

Though most of the rest did start to leave, one woman lingered. Sophia had seen her before, but didn't think they'd been introduced.

She was slim, with hair a little darker than Lachlan's red, and pale blue eyes that had a darker ring around the irises. Pretty, but she looked determined and a little annoyed. "I'd like to stay. Someone needs to start cleaning this up," she said, gesturing to the destruction.

"Curator?"

The woman nodded. "I am. Olivia."

"Nice to meet you, Olivia. And you're right. When we're done, we'll get some others in here to help get everything put back to rights."

"Thanks." But she didn't wait for any others, just started righting furniture.

When the room had emptied, Sophia checked and saw that Sergei had slipped in and was taking care of Ellie's bite, while Heather had moved to dealing with Farid's nose. Half a dozen people besides the guards and injured parties lingered. Lucas, Carla, and Jericho were picking Lachlan up off the floor, though he was still out cold. "I'll be back after we get him secured," Lucas told her before the three of them left the room with the vampire.

Blowing out a breath, Sophia turned back to the rest. "Okay, what happened?" Three people started speaking at once and Sophia shook her head and pointed to one—Jeremiah, she thought his name was. "You first."

"I'm really not sure," he admitted. "Some of us were just hanging out like we always do. A couple watching TV, a couple playing pool, a couple talking. The usual, you know?" She did know, so she nodded. "Lachlan came in, but he didn't look right. He was sort of...I don't know. Twitchy?" he said, looking around at the others, and several nodded in agreement. "He also looked kind of...not angry, but agitated. He was also flashing his fangs, which he doesn't normally do."

"Yeah, I've noticed that. I didn't realize he was a vampire when I first met him," Sophia said.

"Right? He's like the most easy going vampire I know," Jeremiah said, nodding. "Someone—I don't remember who—asked him if he was okay, but he didn't answer. He just grabbed a little statue and flung it at the TV," he said, pointing to the damaged screen. On the floor near it was a foot and a half tall stone statue. It was probably meant to be one of the gods, but the face was smashed beyond recognition. "Then he grabbed Josie and just picked her up by her arm and flung her across the room." That explained the wrist. "Fortunately, Ellie caught her before she hit the wall or she'd be hurt worse than she is."

"So no one said or did anything to provoke him?" Every single witness shook their head or said no. "Has anyone noticed him acting odd in the last day or two?"

"I had a late lunch with him today," another guard, Kirk, said. "He was acting like normal then. Laughing, joking, nothing out of the usual. And nothing the last few days either. Until he came in here twenty minutes ago, nothing was wrong. And I have no idea what could have triggered that. I've never seen him acting like that."

"Has he been feeding normally? Or fed on anyone new?" Sergei asked, now finished healing Ellie.

"Pretty sure he's not lacking in the blood department. As far as new people...not that I know of? I mean, he doesn't exactly give me a list or anything. I know he's got a couple people here in the Athenaeum that he feeds on regularly, but he doesn't brag about it. It's personal, you know?"

"I do," Sergei agreed, "but if he fed on someone new, it might explain his reaction."

"I'll see if we can find out," Sophia said. "Anyone have anything else to add?"

"Just that I've known Lachlan for almost a century, and I've never seen him react like this. Even in a fight he's not this...savage," Ellie called from across the room. "Sergei's right, though. There are things that can be done to essentially poison a blood source. It's the only thing I can think of."

"Okay. Thank you. You can all go, but let me or Lucas know if you think of anything else."

"I'm going to stay and help Olivia," Kirk said, and a few others chimed in, saying they wanted to do the same.

Sophia smiled at them. She wasn't all that surprised. Everyone in the Athenaeum shared two traits; they loved knowledge, and they loved the Athenaeum. Of course they'd want to set it to rights. "Appreciated. Sergei, Mom, everyone patched up?"

"They are," Heather said, walking over toward her. "And I think we need to talk, if you're done here?"

"Let me just check with Lucas, but then I am." She gave both her mom and Ray a faint smile as she pulled out her phone. "It's good to see you two back in Greece, by the way." And she meant it. She'd been in the country for a month, and her mom had been gone for the last few weeks. It was hard enough adjusting to being in an ancient, hidden library without her mom being across the world in the United States.

She shot off a message to Lucas, who responded within a minute.

Lucas: Lachlan's contained. Did you get the story from the witnesses?

Sophia: I did. No apparent cause for his outburst, but we'll talk later. Mom wants an update.

Lucas: Be safe.

Sliding her phone back into her pocket, she exhaled deeply. "All right. Your room? I know you need to put your luggage away, anyway."

"Sounds good. Just tell me it hasn't been this exciting the whole time it was gone," Heather said as she returned to her luggage.

Sophia didn't say anything as they started for Heather's room. Her mom might know about Agatha's murder and Dion's subsequent death, but only Sergei and Lucas knew that Sophia was still chasing a murderer. Then again, only those two knew that Sophia's grandfather had been poisoned. And Sophia wasn't sure those deaths would be the last. She could only hope she was wrong.

Chapter 2

Once in Heather's room, they set her luggage down and Heather turned to Sophia, her hands on her hips and a stern look on her face. "Okay. You're going to give me a hug, then tell me what the hell is going on," she said before wrapping her arms firmly around her daughter. She might be baffled and more than a little concerned, but Sophia knew she'd missed her. Missed her and been worried. Which was why she was home a week earlier than intended. When Heather had gotten a call that two people have been killed within days of her departure, she'd immediately compressed everything into a much shorter timeline. She'd had to cut some corners to get their things shipped from Georgia and their old house put up for sale, but Heather was nothing if not effective. And with that kind of motivation, she made it work. Sophia was both relieved and resigned. On one hand, she didn't mind having her mother—someone familiar and support-ive—close. On the other, she wanted her mom out of the line of fire. She'd already lost her grandfather. She didn't want Heather to end up on a funeral pyre, too.

"It's a mess," Sophia admitted against her mother's shoulder.

"To say the least," Heather agreed. She drew back, then urged Sophia to sit on the bed. "Did Dion really kill Agatha?" she asked, sorrow in her eyes. It reminded Sophia that her mom had known Dion for decades longer than she had. While he'd been her cousin, too, Sophia had only known he existed for a few weeks and didn't have the same emotional attachment.

"It seems like it." Sighing, Sophia flopped back, her arms stretched out to her sides as she stared up at the stone ceiling. One of these days, she might get used to living in what amounted to a small underground city, but she wasn't there yet. For now, it still struck her as odd. Amazing and full of fantastic things, but odd. "I woke up that morning and didn't find Agatha in the kitchen, even though it was past the time she was normally in there. Told Lucas, and the two of us went to her bedroom. She was already dead when we got there," she murmured, shaking her head. "I called Sergei, and he confirmed it was a death spell. That's when I called the meeting and told everyone."

"I'm so sorry you had to be the one to find her," Heather said softly, rubbing Sophia's arm. "How did you find out it was Dion?"

She closed her eyes, which was a mistake as she saw the memory of Agatha's body. It hadn't been a gruesome sight—it had been a bloodless death—but her lifeless eyes haunted Sophia. Quickly opening her eyes, she answered her mom. "After the meeting, Peter wanted to talk to us. Told us he suspected Dion. He had a couple of reasons for that, but I won't go into those now," she said when Heather opened her mouth. "They were mostly circumstantial, nothing that really put a flashing 'I did it' sign over his head, but when we went to see Dion, he attacked us." She rubbed at her eyes. "Peter had to kill him," she whispered.

"Oh gods," Heather said, covering her mouth with her fingers. "That poor boy. How's he doing?"

Sophia's hands dropped to the bed. "He was forced to kill his own dad in self-defense, so...not good. He's better than he was, but when he thinks no one's looking, you can see it on his face. It's not an easy thing to bear, killing your own dad, no matter what the reason."

Heather nodded, her eyes full of sympathy. "No, I don't imagine it would be. I'll have to go see him. I know I haven't seen him since he was a child, but with his mother not in the picture, maybe I can help."

Sophia nearly smiled. Of course her mom would only think about comforting him. But she wasn't done. Taking a deep breath, she added, "And that's not all."

Heather frowned. "Not all? Did someone else die?"

"No." Sophia pushed herself up onto her elbows. "This next bit is not to be shared. Sergei and Lucas know, but it can't go any further." She probably shouldn't even be telling her mom, but she felt too guilty about keeping the truth of Erasmus's death from her. Besides, Heather was the one person in the Athenaeum she knew, without a doubt, that she could trust. Not only had Heather absolutely not been in Greece when Erasmus was poisoned, she simply wasn't the sort of person to be involved in anything...evil, for lack of a better word.

"You're hiding something from the rest of the Athenaeum?" Heather asked, surprise in her tone and on her face.

"Yeah, I am," Sophia said with a nod. "You were around when Erasmus was aspida. You had to know I'd have to make tough decisions once I got chosen to lead after him. Hell, there are going to be things I can't tell you! But while I didn't choose to be leader of this place, I'm going to do the best I can with it. I owe him that."

"I know," Heather said, rubbing Sophia's arm lightly. "It's just odd to see my daughter as head of the Athenaeum."

Sophia laughed. "How do you think I feel? A month ago, I lived in Georgia and was a grad student. Now I'm in control of the oldest surviving library and repository of relics in the world. It still hasn't really sunken in. Not sure it ever will."

"No, I don't suppose it would have," Heather murmured. "And again, I'm so sorry I didn't let you grow up here."

Though Sophia wished she had grown up with this, had gotten to know her grandfather before he'd died, she just said, "I know, Mom." The past couldn't be changed, and nothing good could come out of making Heather feel guilty for the choices she'd made in the past, choices she'd made when she'd been full of grief for her husband.

Heather smiled weakly. "To address your concern, though, I won't speak of whatever you have to say with anyone but you."

"Thanks." Sophia pushed herself fully upright. "So after Agatha and Dion died, Sergei took their bodies to the clinic. To examine them, I guess, and prepare them for the funeral rituals. But before he could...they disappeared."

"What do you mean? Someone stole the bodies?" Heather asked, shocked.

Sophia shook her head. "No. Well, I guess, yeah, but not in the way you're probably thinking. I mean, they literally disappeared. Like right in front of Sergei. And we haven't been able to find them since."

Heather's mouth opened, closed, and she frowned. "Who would steal their bodies? And why?"

Sophia smiled wryly. "And you have just hit on the questions we've been looking into."

"Have you found anything?"

Sophia sighed and let her head fall back. "Not really. We know powerful magic was used to steal the bodies, but we don't know where they were taken to or by whom. Sergei recognized the spell used to kill Agatha, and though it's forbidden to be used, it's definitely sorcery. Because of that, we're thinking it was probably sorcery that was used to steal the bodies rather than witchcraft. And of course that means it could be literally anyone in the Athenaeum who took them. Hell, maybe it isn't even someone in the Athenaeum. That spell could have been cast from the South Pole, for all we know." That was the reason that sorcery was both loved and despised—and often feared—within the Arcane community. Those like shifters or gargoyles who had no true magic of their own could learn spells, but it also meant that absolutely anyone—including humans—could use all manner of magic. In some cases, extremely powerful, extremely dangerous magic. And sometimes it was extremely hard to track.

"What kind of spell?" Heather asked, voice soft. "Agatha, I mean. What kind of spell was used on her?"

"It stopped her heart." Sophia had learned within days of being named aspida that beating around the bush did little good, and was quickly becoming blunt when it came to bad news. It still felt a little wrong to say terrible things without softening them at all, but if she was going to keep her sanity, she needed to get over that.

Her mom's face was pale and her eyes wide as she nodded. "Do you think whoever stole Dion and Agatha's bodies was...involved...in Agatha's death? Someone working with Dion?"

Not just that, but Sophia thought he or she was involved in Erasmus's poisoning too, but she had promised her grandfather not to tell anyone about that, even her mom. She'd already broken that promise once with Lucas, but she didn't want to worry her mom anymore than she had to. "I can't say for certain, but I will say that other than Lachlan's…outburst…things have been normal. Or as normal as they can be while everyone's mourning three people."

"Yes, it'll take time for everyone to get past that," Heather murmured. "Erasmus was part of the Athenaeum since the moment he was born and was aspida for quite some time. He was beloved by everyone here, and quite a few who aren't directly associated with the Athenaeum. Agatha used food to ensure everyone was taken care of, and was just as adored. Even Dion—before all this—was well liked. No one's going to get over any of that quickly."

"No, they're not," Sophia agreed. "I only knew Erasmus—Grandpa—for a few days, but I wish I'd had centuries. And Agatha? That woman made me feel more welcome than just about anyone else. And that's including Peter."

"She was good at that." She patted Sophia's knee. "On to happier news, though. How are you settling into being aspida?"

Sophia laughed humorlessly. "Shall we recap? In the space of two weeks I learned the Athenaeum existed, met my grandfather and watched him die horribly, was forced to take his place as head of the Athenaeum, then had two people die on my watch, and a vampire went crazy and attacked half a dozen people. I'm starting to understand the job, but the first impression of me as aspida doesn't really have people trusting that I can do my job."

The smile Heather gave her was meant to comfort, but it did little good. "That'll pass, just like the worst of the grief. Like you said, it's only been a few weeks. No one can be expected to do a job perfectly after such a short time."

"Maybe. I'm doing one-on-one interviews with everyone, to get to know them better and get a better handle on my job, but it's kind of weird. Especially since I have to find a replacement for Dion since he was head curator. At least one of the other curators has stepped up to fill Agatha's shoes. As much as he can, at least. Everyone knows he's no Agatha, but he can cook."

"No," Heather said with a faint smile, "it's impossible to fully take her place. I'm sure whoever it is will do well, though."

"So far, so good," Sophia agreed. "Now if I can find out what's going on with Lachlan, things might get back to calming down."

"I'm sure you will," Heather said before she yawned.

Sophia rubbed her mom's knee. "You've been traveling for hours. Why don't you get some sleep?"

"I think I will. After I shower off the flight."

"Good." She kissed her mom's cheek, then got to her feet. "Sleep well."

"I will. But Sophia?"

"Yeah?"

"Be careful."

"I will. I'm using that threat sensing spell Erasmus taught me. And I've been quickly learning more sorcery." Lucas insisted, and she wasn't arguing. She liked not dying.

"Good. Now go. Be aspida, but don't forget to get some rest and have some fun, too."

Sophia's lips twitched as she remembered what she'd been doing when she got the message about Lachlan. "I'll do my best." And that memory meant her mood was slightly improved as she left her mom to sleep. Just so long as she could find Lucas and finished what they'd started.

Chapter 3

Sophia had only taken a few steps away from her mom's door when she ran into Sergei.

"Ah, Sophia. I was just about to text you," he said, his Russian accent more noticeable now that they weren't surrounded by a dozen people all talking at once.

She immediately feared the worst. "Everyone's okay, right? I mean, you and Mom healed all the people Lachlan hurt?"

He smiled—which for him meant his lips barely curved upward. "Sorry, I didn't mean to worry you. Yes, everyone was healed and has been cleared to resume their days. But walk with me?"

Something in his tone put her on alert. Not like something bad was about to happen, but more like he didn't want to talk around others. She was getting entirely too used to hush-hush conversations. For weeks now, she'd been speaking secretly with both Lucas and Sergei, trying to figure out who had poisoned her grandfather. There was no sense in tipping the killer off that they knew it hadn't been natural causes. They needed every advantage they could get. She nodded slowly and followed him as he led the way back to the stairs and down, past the level where the crypt was, and down multiple levels of the library until they reached the door to level six—the level that only the aspida and heads of the three factions could get through. Since Dion had been one of those heads, it meant only Sophia, Lucas, and Nick could get through it. Nick—the head of the venatores, the ones who retrieved books and relics—wasn't likely to come down here, which made it the most private place for them to speak. Even in her room, someone occasionally knocked on her door. No one would be knocking here.

Sophia set her hand on the palm scanner and entered her PIN, then led the way through the door. Once they'd gone down the stairs and turned left to enter the half of the level reserved for books, they stopped. Lucas was already there, waiting for them. "What's going on?" she asked both men.

"About which problem?" Lucas asked dryly.

"Whichever one has us meeting down here?"

"About which problem?" Lucas repeated blandly.

She rolled her eyes but almost smiled. He had a point.

"Lachlan first," Sergei decided.

"Did you find out what caused him to freak out?" she asked.

"Yes and no." Before she could make a comment about how unhelpful that answer was, he continued. "I don't know the exact cause, but there's something foreign inside him. I don't, however, know if it's a substance or if it's magic. It almost feels like both," he admitted. "I don't even know if it's natural or not."

"So it could be...what, like an enchanted substance?"

His head wobbled back and forth, a look of uncertainty on his face. "Unsure. Possibly? I really don't have any clue as to its identity, and that concerns me. I learned to heal from a great many people, including some from my father and brother."

Sophia blinked. "Apollo and...Asclepius?" She was certain about his father, but he'd never mentioned siblings before, so could only guess at which one he meant. But if it involved healing, then the Greek god of healing and his son, the god of medicine, were pretty good guesses.

Sergei nodded. "Part of my training included being able to identify any manner of foreign presences in people's bodies. What's inside Lachlan is something I've never encountered before."

She groaned and sank down to the floor, careful not to bump the bookshelf behind her. They were all heavy and looked secure, but since she'd accidentally touched a cursed book on this level once, she wanted to be careful. "Okay, so we start researching, just like we did to identify the Achlys poison. We can do that."

"I'm more concerned about the now," Lucas said, studying the slightly defeated and extremely stressed look on Sophia's face. "Is he still a danger, or has whatever he was given or encountered cleared out of his system?"

Sophia's eyes closed, further proving just how stressed she was. Lucas would have to ensure he distracted her later.

Sergei sighed. "He's still a danger, unfortunately. He's currently secured and sedated in the clinic. As soon as I let him wake, he tried to attack me, so I had to put him under again."

"Keep us updated? And if you figure out anything we can use to narrow our search parameters, let us know."

"I will. And to add to the bad news, I still haven't been able to pin down anyone who might have had the knowledge to use the spell that killed Agatha."

"I've been looking into how the bodies could have been stolen," Sophia said, opening her eyes. "I know we've basically ruled out witches and think it's sorcery, so I've been looking, and I did find a spell that could have done it. Problem is, I found it on level five, so pretty much anyone could have found and used it."

"There still might be a way to trace it," Lucas said, but he doubted they'd manage it. They'd need to find some other way of discovering the body thief. "And when we find out what was used on Lachlan, we'll trace who's responsible for that, too."

"A couple of people agreed that he was fine at lunch," Sophia said. "We should check the security feed, to see if there's anything suspicious before then and when he went nuts."

"That's my next stop," Lucas assured her, but he didn't hold much hope that he'd see anything. He had a funny feeling that whatever had been done to Lachlan had something to do with the deaths that had occurred not that long ago. There was nothing obvious linking them, but the moment he'd processed that Lachlan's outburst wasn't normal, his gut had just told him they were all connected. The question was why. Erasmus's death? Maybe someone had wanted his job. Agatha's? Maybe she'd learned something about Erasmus's poisoning. Lachlan? He could only speculate, and that wouldn't help them.

But the fact remained that prior to Erasmus's poisoning, nothing like this had happened in the Athenaeum for decades, maybe centuries. It couldn't be coincidence that this was all happening within just a few months. He was also absolutely fucking positive that Lachlan's episode wouldn't be the last issue they ran into. If they were very, very lucky, there wouldn't be any more deaths, but he had a feeling they'd be burying at least one more friend.

"Good. Maybe between that and whatever tests you can run, Sergei, we'll figure something out," she said. "And if we can't identify whatever was used on him, maybe we can find something to counteract it." She paused, then her brow furrowed. "Didn't you say there was some super antidote here? Could that work?"

Sergei made a noncommittal sound. "Doubtful, unless this is a poison, but if I can't find something else, I'll try it. We do have some—it's called mithridate—but it isn't as commonly available as other antidotes. From what I gathered from Erasmus, it was actually very difficult for the healer—Suni—to make it."

"Is it something that could work through his system?" Lucas asked.

"Normally I'd say yes, that anything introduced to a body will metabolize unless it continues to be introduced, but with the magic I sensed, I can't say anything for certain," Sergei admitted. "I do plan on closely monitoring him, though, regardless of what treatments I attempt."

"Keep us updated, please," Sophia said.

"I will."

"Anything else?" she asked, looking between them.

"How are the interviews going?" It wasn't just an attempt to get her mind off Lachlan for a moment, he was genuinely curious. When she'd had the idea to sit down with each member of the Athenaeum, he'd supported it. She was new to the organization and since she was now leading it, she needed to know the people in it. But he'd also had concerns. The fear that Dion's co-conspirator would harm her, of course, but he also knew there were several who were less than thrilled to have someone so new as their boss. With all she'd been through in the last month, he wanted to keep her from reaching her limit.

Sophia wasn't a weak woman, but the last month would have put a strain on anyone, and he hated seeing that stress on her face. A face he was coming to be very fond of. Not just because she was beautiful—though she was certainly that. Glossy hair the color of chocolate. Eyes that were bright green and filled with intelligence. A warm smile, even when she was in an unfamiliar situation. And a body he loved to touch. Curvy and soft, though she was losing a bit of that softness with the training he insisted she do. Not that he minded. Her skin was still sensitive beneath his fingers and sweet against his lips, no matter what shape it held.

"Informative?" He cocked a brow and she sighed. "They are informative. Peter's files on everyone were helpful, but it's so clinical. Actually talking to these people gives me a better sense of who they are and what they want, not just what they know or are good at. Lots of people are good at stuff they don't want to do for a living, and I'd like to balance happiness with efficiency." She paused, then added, "But the interviews are hard, too."

Sergei frowned. "Are people giving you a rough time?"

She bobbed her head from side to side. "A few are less than friendly, and some are hesitant. A couple have been...quietly sullen, is the term I've been using in my head. But no one has been outright antagonistic. Unfortunately, no one's been giving off any guilty vibes, either."

Lucas smiled inwardly. She might be young for her position—only twenty-four—and she might still be getting her feet beneath her, but she was smart and rarely seemed to have only one purpose for everything she did. "Is that the real reason for the interviews? You were hoping to find whoever was working with Dion?"

"I wouldn't say the real reason, but I figured that if I was going to be talking to everyone anyway, I should keep an eye out for anything suspicious. But so far, the most suspicious thing has just been people not knowing if they can trust me." She ran a hand through her hair and lifted her gaze to the ceiling. "I really wish the patrons had some idea of who was behind this."

"How do you know they don't?" Lucas asked curiously, and his brows lifted at the instant look of guilt on her face. "Sophia…"

"A week or two ago, when I was alone, one of them showed up," she confessed.

"Which one?" Sergei wanted to know.

"The young one. Seth."

"And he said they didn't know?" Lucas pressed.

"He said there was something dark keeping them from…" She trailed off and straightened, a smile creeping onto her lips as she yanked her phone out. "They couldn't see what was going on, not even who killed Erasmus, but I've got an idea," she told them as she tapped on her phone.

"What idea?"

She just shook her head and watched her phone. When it dinged in her hand, her smile grew. "He'll be here in a minute," she said, putting her phone away.

Sophia had been speaking to the divine patrons? That was interesting, and he felt a pang of hurt that she hadn't shared that fact with him. He squashed it, as he knew she was dealing with a lot, and tried to focus on the more important fact. Even the gods didn't know what was going on in the Athenaeum. While he knew they weren't truly omnipotent, it was still concerning. Very concerning. Gods did tend to know more than mortals, at least regarding their areas of expertise. The divine patrons should be able to know everything that happened in the Athenaeum.

A low, brief rumble echoed through the room as a man appeared before them. He was a few inches taller than Lucas's own six two, with black hair gone just a little shaggy. His golden eyes were cool as they looked at Lucas, over Sergei, then settled on Sophia. The power that radiated from the man made Lucas's bones ache. Seth was a god of mountains—of stone—and since Lucas was a gargoyle with a stone form, he had power over him, even if Lucas wasn't in his gargoyle form at the moment. It was a good thing he'd known Seth before he'd become a god and knew he could trust the man. He only had to hope divine power didn't change him too much.

"Sophia, are you okay?" Seth asked, his voice softer than his gaze had been.

"Okay's a good word for it," she agreed, scrambling to her feet. "And thank you for coming."

"You know I'm as invested in the Athenaeum as you are. Has something else happened since Dion's death?"

She let out a wry laugh. "Yeah. We had a curator go crazy a little bit ago, but that isn't why I texted."

"Okay? I do want to know about this curator, but what's the problem?"

Sophia shook her head. "It's not actually a problem. Not sure if you're aware, but this is Sergei, our main healer, and Lucas, the head of the nasaru," she said, motioning to Sergei and Lucas in turn as she spoke. "Sergei was the only person here besides myself that knew Erasmus was poisoned until I brought Lucas in on it. The two of them have been helping me. Trying to keep me safe, teaching me, and helping me try to figure out what in the hell is going on."

Seth turned and studied both men for several long moments. "I do know of them both. Have met them," he told her before addressing them directly. "You were always a hard-ass, Lucas, but Erasmus spoke highly of you both. While it's clear someone here betrayed him, I do think he was a good judge of character. And I can't say I know Sophia well yet, but she's smart. Don't make her regret her trust. Or mine."

"I have no intention of losing another aspida, nor another friend," Lucas said, refusing to refer to her as anything else. Yes, they were lovers, but now was hardly the time to try to consider anything more than that. And that was if either of them even wanted more than a friendly sexual relationship.

"Neither do I," Sergei added. "I like Sophia, and I loved Erasmus like another father. I also thought of both Agatha and Dion as friends. I want to get to the bottom of this as much as anyone."

"Good." Seth turned back to Sophia. "I don't get the impression that you just wanted to introduce them to me, so why did you ask me to come?"

"No, that wasn't it, though I also didn't know you already knew them." She shrugged and worked up a bright smile. "I was hoping you could give them the same gifts you gave me."

Seth arched a brow and gave her a curious look. "You trust them that much?"

She smiled at Sergei, then turned it onto Lucas. Again, he regretted that they were interrupted earlier. He'd have to make sure to get her alone so they could finish later. Thoughts of that almost prevented him from wondering what gifts she was talking about. "I trust them more than anyone here besides my mom, and I do *not* want her getting involved in this. Too many people have already died. I don't want her to be the next. I don't want these guys to be next either, but...Well, my mom isn't a fighter." He appreciated the confidence, however weakly it was expressed. He knew what she meant, though, so wasn't offended.

Seth nodded. "Very well." Turning again, he offered a hand to each of them. After exchanging a look with Sergei, Lucas took the offered hand, then Sergei did the same. It took only a second before a warm blast of magic flooded his veins. His eyes widened slightly, but he clenched his jaw to prevent any sounds from escaping. Almost as soon as it had begun, it was over.

"What did you just do to us?" Lucas asked when his hand was released. He trusted Seth, but 'gifts' was a little too vague for his liking.

The god looked amused and looked at Sophia. "Want to tell them?"

"The patrons worked together to give me gifts from all of them," she began. "He just shared them with you. They were..." Her gaze went unfocused and her brow furrowed as she thought. "Wisdom, so I could see through deceptions and make good plans. Healing, which is sort of self-explanatory. Magic, to help what I already have. And...crap. There was one more."

"Hecate," Seth prompted.

"Oh! Right, some protection from poisonous plants, since she's got skill with them."

"Hopefully we won't need any healing, not even my own skills," Sergei said. "But I do appreciate it. Sophia's already dealt with one illusionary attack, so we can expect more. And making good plans will certainly come in handy."

"Yeah, thanks," Lucas said, rubbing his hand discreetly against his leg. It felt like it was tingling, but he had a feeling it had more to do with Seth's powers than the gifts he'd just given them. "Do you know anything that might help us? Something Erasmus might have said?"

All Seth's amusement drained away. "I've told Sophia everything I know, and it wasn't much. It sure as shit wasn't as much as I would have liked. Something or someone here is blocking us, and it takes a lot to prevent six gods from seeing like that. Me? Okay, possible. I've been a god for a year. But the others?" He shook his head. "It's something powerful, because not much gets past Isis or Hecate, much less the others. If you can find the source of the block, we can probably help more, but as it stands, I've done all I can."

"What could block gods from seeing into the Athenaeum? Especially since your power is literally in its walls?" Sophia asked.

"If I knew, it would already be gone," he said dryly. "Let me know if you find out anything," he added before he disappeared.

With the god gone, two sets of eyes turned back to Sophia and she smiled weakly. "It's something, anyway?"

"Normally I'd say you should be careful of the gods," Sergei warned, "but the patrons do tend to be more lenient with the aspides. And Seth really is a young god. He hasn't learned the…arrogance most of the older gods have."

"Yeah, I think I'm still going to be careful, but I really do think he wants us to solve this as much as we do. He seemed pretty pissed that Erasmus had been poisoned. He's the only god I've ever spoken to, but I think he's a good guy."

"I agree."

"I think we just need to continue as we have been," Lucas said, and it came off a little abrupt, which surprised Sophia. He hadn't been so blunt lately, at least not with her. Did he not like interacting with the gods? If so, she couldn't blame him. It was a little nerve-racking. "Sophia will continue her interviews and learning sorcery. Sergei, can you keep an eye out for any other suspicious injuries or illness? If this happened to Lachlan, it could happen to others."

They both nodded and Sophia asked, "What will you do?"

"First, I'm going to check the security footage. Then I'm going to be watching everyone, training you, and seeing if I can locate the source of this block. And keeping you safe."

He said all the right things, but something was clearly bothering him. "I'm definitely all for keeping me safe. I'm going to add in research, though. We found the poison used on Erasmus. We might find whatever was used on Lachlan, too."

"Poison..." Sergei's thick brows lowered. "Sophia, have you interviewed a woman named Olivia yet?"

She thought for a second, then shook her head. "No, but I think she's on my list for tomorrow. I met her earlier, too. She was the first to start cleaning up. Why?"

"We mentioned two others that were poisoned before Erasmus, yes?"

"Yeah. One of them died, right?"

"Thomas did, yes. Olivia was the other. If you can get the subject to come up organically, maybe you can get something from her," he suggested.

"It's not a bad idea," Lucas agreed. "The poisoning should be in her file."

"I'll check, and if it is, I'll see if I can bring it up." She smiled. "Thanks, Sergei. Anything we can figure out could be that last little thing we need."

"Exactly. Now, I have about an hour before I want to wake Lachlan and check on his status. Would you mind if I stayed on this level for a bit to research? Something like this isn't likely to be found on the upper levels. It might not even be on this level, but we have to start somewhere."

"I've got zero problem with that. If you need down here later, just let me know. As for me, I think I need some sleep. I'm really not used to excitement like this."

Sergei smiled and patted her arm. "Hopefully we'll have less of this excitement soon."

"I hope so," she said. To her relief, despite Lucas's odd behavior since Seth's appearance, he followed her out of the library to her room. He'd taken to sleeping with her most nights—and not just to keep her safe. It was a happy side-effect, she knew, but not the main reason. But tonight he went right to the computer, pulling up the security feed while she showered and got ready for bed. Unfortunately, he found nothing suspicious surrounding Lachlan, at least not for the two hours prior to his attack.

Perhaps because of that, when they slipped into bed, all he did was hold her. While a small part of her was disappointed, she was entirely too exhausted to have truly enjoyed finishing what they'd begun earlier.

If she was lucky, tomorrow would be a great deal calmer. But her luck since arriving in Greece had been nothing but crap.

Chapter 4

Sophia's first interview the next day went okay. Manny was one of the venatores—the men and women who went out and obtained texts and relics for the Athenaeum—and a former MI6 agent. She was a little surprised he'd gone for retrieval instead of protection, but figured having venatores who could take care of themselves only made the guards' jobs easier.

The second interview was much worse. Morgan was one of the few female nasaru and looked almost as young as Sophia. Because she was one of the few women, she went into the interview expecting someone like Carla—badass, blunt, and a little arrogant. She was wrong. While all the notes in her file said she was indeed badass, she was more than a little arrogant. A lot more. Morgan acted as though she was the best guard in the entire history of the Athenaeum. Sure, as a water elemental she had access to some extremely versatile powers, especially if she was as strong as indicated, but she spoke over Sophia, tried to push her into reorganizing the nasaru, and badmouthed Lucas with every other sentence. And while Sophia was sure there were better fighters than Lucas, she had a feeling the woman across from her wasn't one of them.

By the end of the interview, Sophia was half-wondering if kicking people out of the Athenaeum happened often, and how long she'd need to wait before doing so. Except they needed good guards, especially now, and aside from the arrogance issue, Morgan's file said she was a very good guard. She would, however, let Lucas know he should keep an eye on her, just to be safe.

The third was a calmer interview. Boring, really. She'd already met Valerie, the woman who was in charge of all the Athenaeum's finances, so there wasn't really much to it. Still, Sophia wasn't going to single anyone out or exclude anyone, so she spent fifteen minutes with the woman before Valerie retreated to her office.

After a quick break for a coffee refill, Sophia got to the interview she'd been looking forward to since the conversation with Sergei and Lucas the evening before. Olivia.

The woman was waiting at Sophia's door when she got back. Sophia couldn't have placed her face before yesterday, but now realized she'd seen her quite often over the past weeks. Inevitable, really, since they all lived and worked together, they just hadn't been properly introduced. She was about Sophia's height, but that was where the similarities ended. Where Sophia's hair was brown, Olivia's was red, a little darker than Lachlan's and just brushing her shoulders. Her eyes were much more interesting than Sophia's ordinary green; a pale blue that was ringed by a much darker shade of the color. And while Sophia was on the slender side, Olivia was truly petite in stature. Sophia did have to wonder if the woman was cold, though, as she was wearing a long-sleeved tee-shirt and thin black gloves to go with her charcoal pants. It was cooler down here than outside, but not enough to be truly chilly, but it could just be a fashion choice. The Athenaeum did seem to attract a wide range of people. Not all of them would be considered normal to the outside world.

What truly fascinated her about the woman was her species. Sophia had never met a nightmare before. They weren't as common as witches or elementals, and they tended to have a bad rap. Mostly because people were scared of their powers. Maybe not as much as necromancers or demons, but they were still feared. Since it was rumored that they could control people's dreams and kill with shadows, Sophia couldn't really argue the fear, but she was trying to judge people based on how they acted rather than what they'd been born as. After all, Dion had been a mer—who were thought of as mostly harmless on land—and he'd killed his own great-uncle. And before yesterday, Lachlan had been a mild-mannered vampire.

"Olivia?" Sophia asked with a smile as she stepped into her office. "Come on in." Olivia followed and, when Sophia gestured to a chair, sat. "Thanks for coming. I'm sure you've heard I'm doing these interviews with everyone?"

"I have," she agreed. "It surprised a few people, but shouldn't have. It makes sense. Even if you'd been here for years, it would have made sense to talk to us since you'd be boss instead of coworker."

"I think you're the first person to say that," Sophia said with some surprise as she took her seat.

Olivia shrugged. "Not my fault if some people lack common sense. It's even worse here sometimes, since everyone worries about being book smart."

Sophia's lips twitched. "That's not exclusive to the Athenaeum," she pointed out.

"Believe me, I know." Clearly Olivia had dealt with more than a few people who lacked common sense. Sophia also decided that she liked this woman.

"So I've got everyone's files, and they're thorough, but they're also kind of...impersonal. And I'll admit, yours is a little unusual. It says you're both a curator and nasaru? It also doesn't specify what curators duties you deal with. Is it just the library?" To be honest, Olivia's file was fascinating for a number of reasons. And as far as she could tell, Olivia was the only person to have dual roles within the Athenaeum.

"What can I say? I'm an individual," Olivia said dryly. "But yes, I'm a part-time guard, a fight instructor, and a curator. I'm good at all three, but I prefer staying close to home most of the time. As for my curator duties, they are mostly in the library. Cataloging and translating, mostly. None of the other roles really fit me, and honestly, organizing and research are where my strengths lie. And I like it."

"Honestly, it's the same for me," Sophia said with a wry smile. "But at least organizing suits my new role."

"Herding would be better."

It took Sophia a moment before she laughed. "Because it's like herding cats?"

Olivia nearly smiled as she nodded. "Sometimes, yeah. The people here get hyper focused sometimes and forget basic stuff. Goes back to the common sense thing."

"I'll keep that in mind. So you're content with where you are? I've had a few people request reassignments, and I do want to make sure people are happy whenever possible."

Olivia shook her head. "No, I don't want to move. Besides, I promise it's where you want me. I don't think anyone else here can read as many languages as I can, which makes me the most valuable when I'm available to translate the more difficult languages. Though I will say," she added after a second, "I have been asked to go on site now and again when something immovable needs translating, especially before smart phones were a thing. Being a part-time nasaru helps in those situations, too."

Sophia nodded. "Makes sense. And I'm fine leaving you where you are." And she truly was. With one little exception. "How are you with teaching? Beyond fighting, I mean. Obviously you're good there if Lucas still has you doing it, but have you taught more academic subjects? Are you comfortable with it?"

That stumped the curator for a moment. "I...don't know," she admitted. "I've never tried to teach anything but combat, though I can't say I'm against new things in general. I'll try anything once. What sort of teaching did you have in mind?" Her eyes narrowed slightly. "And who would I be teaching?"

Grinning, Sophia tapped a finger on Olivia's file where it listed her known languages. It was extensive enough that she didn't doubt her claim about knowing more languages than anyone else in the Athenaeum. "Me, and some of these languages. I'm fluent in four—including English—and can muddle through a few more with trouble, but it's quickly becoming obvious that I need to know as many as I can."

"Depends on the ones you're fluent in, but no, it couldn't hurt. And I'd be willing to try. An aspida who knows what the fuck they're doing is a benefit to everyone in the Athenaeum."

Sophia studied Olivia's face for a moment, but while she saw some uncertainty, she didn't see reluctance, so nodded. "Thank you. Now, all that said, is there anything you're concerned about? Or questions you have for me?"

Olivia shrugged then shook her head. "Not really. Any questions I had you basically answered when you addressed us right after you were chosen as aspida."

"Good. If you do think of anything, let me know." Now came the part she wasn't looking forward to. She was second-guessing whether to bring the subject up at all, but it *was* in her file, and she thought anyone doing interviews like these would bring it up. "I just have one last thing...It says here in your file that you were poisoned a few months ago?"

The woman's face hardened. "Yes, I was," she said in a clipped tone. "Me and one other. He died, and I only barely survived."

It was obviously not something Olivia wanted to speak about, but Sophia made herself push. She nodded, genuine sympathy staining her features. "Are you fully recovered from that?"

"Seem to be. Sergei gave me a clean bill of health. So did this other healer they brought in from the outside. No trace of the poison, and they repaired the damage it did to my body." But they hadn't been able to heal her bitterness. Sophia really couldn't blame her, though. She'd be pissed if she'd been poisoned, too. Hell, she was pissed Erasmus had been poisoned. And having someone nearly kill her with a book wasn't all that dissimilar.

"I'm sorry to ask you about it, but it was so recent, and I want to make sure everyone's safe. Do you know how you were poisoned? If it was intentional? Accidental? Or maybe it was a relic?"

The shake of Olivia's head was immediate and definitive. "It definitely wasn't something on any relic or text I handled, and I didn't eat, drink, or inhale anything suspicious. I also looked and didn't find any puncture marks. Believe me, if I knew how I'd been poisoned, I would have let Erasmus and Lucas know immediately. It might have been after breaking someone's nose and sending them screaming into the night, but I would have told him."

Despite the topic, Sophia felt her lips curving. "No one could have blamed you. I take it that means you have no idea who—if anyone—might have wanted to hurt you?"

"You mean who wanted to kill me? Because let's say it like it is. Whoever was responsible didn't want me hurt, they wanted me fucking dead. I got damn lucky that the other healer had some magic potion or I'd be ash, just like Thomas."

There was no arguing that, so Sophia inclined her head to Olivia.

Olivia started to speak again, but stopped, visibly hesitating. "How much like your grandfather are you?"

That wasn't something she'd expected to be asked, so took a moment before speaking. "That's not an easy question to answer. I only knew him for a couple of days, and he was far from at his best. I will say I'm smart, and while there's no way in hell I know everything he did, I'm not a slow learner. I also plan on doing what I can to do this job in a way that would make him proud. Does that help answer your question?"

Olivia made a noncommittal noise. "And are you as able to keep a secret as he was?"

She wasn't sure where this was going, but was just curious enough to let it continue. "I like to think I am, yeah. Especially if it's something important, or something personal." She leaned forward, resting her forearms on her desk as she took a guess. "I have no right to share anything about you that you don't want shared, if that's what you're worried about. Unless it's something that needs shared because it's life and death or affects the safety of those in the Athenaeum," she added.

"Fair enough. This shouldn't be anything you need to share, and I really don't want it getting out. In this case, this needs to be *not* shared because it's life and death."

Sophia frowned, her head tilting as she studied Olivia. Whatever was on her mind, she was absolutely serious about this being life or death. It might be an exaggeration, but nothing in her file suggested she was the excitable sort. "Like I said, unless I have to share it, I won't."

Olivia nodded slowly. "Have you heard of the Ogham? And I don't mean the writing."

"Then no. I'm not even sure what the writing looks like anyway, but it's some sort of Celtic alphabet, right?"

"It is, and that's actually related. The Ogham is also a bloodline. A rare one. Centuries ago, they were blessed by Ogma—the god responsible for creating the Ogham language. I won't go into all the specifics, but basically it gives them a genetic photographic memory. They can remember anything they see or hear, and they can pass that knowledge down."

"Really? That sounds fascinating, and extremely handy. How do they pass the knowledge down? Is it a ritual? A magical transfer? Can they pass the knowledge to people outside the bloodline?" Sophia asked, immediately sinking into nerd mode.

Olivia blinked, then her lips twitched. "That's a hell of a lot of questions. First, no, it can't be passed to people outside the bloodline. That's required, no matter how the knowledge is passed on. As for the how? There are exceptions, but generally a tattoo is given to the Ogham receiving knowledge, and magic is used to...imbue it, I guess is the best word, with the information the other Ogham wants to pass on. So a little ritual, a little magic, and the right blood."

"Huh. That sounds both painful and very much worth it. But I'm not sure why you're telling me this." She could guess, but had been surprised too many times since hearing about the Athenaeum to just assume.

Without a word, Olivia pulled her gloves off and drew one of her sleeves up to her elbow. Beneath the cloth and leather, the woman's skin was covered in colorful and elegantly drawn symbols. They were all made of a straight line that had short dashes or swirls drawn through it. It sparked a hint of recognition in Sophia's memory, but something about it was off. It could just be the decorations around the main lines and swirls, but she wasn't sure. She knew Greek, not Ogham. "Clearly you're one of these Ogham, and I'm guessing that's the Ogham writing you were talking about?"

"I am and it is. Well, sort of. Think of it like a secret dialect," Olivia answered. "And this is actually why I'm so good at my current position. My bloodline means I remember things without having to study or even try, and I remember everything my ancestors knew. It's how I'm fluent in so many languages. You get two languages from two people, that's nice. You get five from twenty? Makes it harder to find an ancient language I don't know."

"Makes sense, but it doesn't explain why you're telling me about it. I already agreed to leave you in your current jobs."

"No," she agreed with a nod, "but it might explain why I was targeted. Not a lot of people know about us, and I try to keep it that way—hence the long sleeves and gloves," she said, tugging her sleeve back in place and replacing her gloves. Just like that, all her tattoos were hidden. "I said we were a rare bloodline, but it isn't because we don't have a lot of kids. It's because most of the outsiders who know about us want us enslaved or dead. They don't want someone who can remember things they'd rather be forgotten, unless it benefits them. We tend to not respond well to shackles."

Unfortunately, that made sense. It made even more sense, given that Sophia knew Erasmus had been poisoned. Not only could Olivia have been a guinea pig for Dion and his associate, they might have wanted her out of the way because of her memory powers. If they were trying to take over the Athenaeum, they wouldn't have wanted anyone around who knew so much ancient lore and could put all the little clues together. For all Sophia knew, Olivia had a wealth of forensic knowledge in her head. Or she might have known the antidote. There was no telling what all she knew. If she had as many tattoos as Sophia suspected, even Olivia might not know exactly what had been passed onto her. Not until it became relevant.

"I get it. And I'll keep your secret unless absolutely necessary. Thank you for telling me, though." Not only did it give her another insight into this whole mess, she might have just found Dion's replacement. A head curator who never forgot anything would be extremely useful. And she really did like the woman, nightmare or not. "I won't keep you, but let me know if you need anything, okay?"

"I will. And thanks," Olivia said, getting to her feet. "And for the record? I think you're going to do a good job as aspida. Anyone else says different, tell them to fuck off."

Sophia smiled. "Thanks." But as Olivia left, she had to admit to herself that Olivia was one of the few who thought that way. Sighing, she shifted Olivia's file to the bottom and prepared for the next interview, hoping it would be as helpful as this one.

Chapter 5

THE NEXT FIVE INTERVIEWS weren't anything special. Two guards, a curator, and two venatores who did their jobs well enough and seemed content in their current roles—even if three of them hadn't seemed very thrilled about her role. She was trying not to get offended.

With all the interviews for the day done, she went back to her room, changed, then headed to the clinic. Sergei wasn't there, but Heather was, keeping an eye on Lachlan. He was still sedated, and according to Heather, there was no change. Worse than that, they hadn't identified the substance affecting him.

After giving her mom a hug, Sophia went down the hall to the gym. This was no longer her least favorite part of the day—the interviews had stolen that—but it still wasn't her favorite. She wasn't a guard, nor was she exceptionally athletic, but she couldn't deny Lucas's reasoning that knowing how to defend herself might save her life. Considering that within a week of arriving she'd been locked in a closet, had some-one try to scare her with illusionary fire, and had a sniper try to kill her, she needed every edge she could get. At this point, it might be only give her a few seconds, but that could be the difference she needed. Though she prayed to all the gods that she never needed to use it.

The gym was split into two sections. One—the side she pre-ferred—was full of equipment like treadmills, weight benches, and other things found in any gym. The other had mats where people could spar. To her dismay, sometimes they sparred with weapons. Not always practice weapons, either. She'd seen more than a few sharp swords and knives, and even a battle axe, once. She'd been relieved when Lucas had told her the days of her using any of those were quite a ways away. Since she was more likely to lop off a foot than hit her opponent, she hoped that day remained far, far away.

Lucas had beaten her there, and she wasn't sure how she felt when she saw him standing with Steven—a former guard who now trained other guards—Carla, Jericho, and Joshua. Normally it was just her and Lucas or Steven, sometimes both, but there had never been any-one else involved. The presence of the other three guards made her nervous. Then again, they could all be talking about the issue with Lachlan. Trying to convince herself that was it, she approached the group with a smile on her lips, ignoring the ten or so other people in the room. "Hi guys."

The guards murmured greetings to her as Lucas turned toward her. When she caught a glimpse of his face and the devious smile on it, she stopped and narrowed her eyes at him. She might be sleeping with him, but knew he wasn't against putting her in uncomfortable situations if it meant it could possibly help keep her alive. "Nope," she decided, turning to leave. She didn't need to know what he had planned to know it wasn't something she'd like. Since this was fight training, it would probably also hurt.

"Catch her," Lucas said, and she felt someone's magic wrap around her, pinning her arms to her sides before she was lifted off her feet.

When she was turned around and pulled back toward the group, she glared, focusing it solely on Lucas. It was clearly one of the others—Joshua, she thought—using magic on her, but he'd ordered it. That made him responsible.

"You're an ass," she told him as she was set gently down and released.

"I am," he agreed without hesitation, "but it's going to keep you alive."

"Maybe." She wasn't willing to commit, especially since no one had come at her head on. Whoever was working with Dion seemed to prefer working from the shadows. Folding her arms across her chest, she tried for a serious and stern expression. "What torture do you have in mind for me today? And don't try to pretend like it's not going to be torture."

"Depends on your definition," he said while Carla and Steven grinned. "You're sparring today. And not with me or Steven."

That was sort of what she'd been thinking, and hated that she was right. "Which one of you is the lucky torturer's assistant?" she asked the other three. She definitely didn't want to spar with Carla, not when she knew how strong a fighter the woman was. Then again, she had no idea how good either Jericho or Joshua were. When she'd been in the gym in the past, she'd always been focused on the instructions from Lucas and Steven than what the others were doing. Odds were all of them could wipe the mat with her. They were trained guards, after all.

Carla's grin widened and there was a glee in her eyes that doused all of Sophia's hopes. "All of us."

Sophia narrowed her eyes at Lucas and settled her hands on her hips. "I've been barely sparring with just you or Steven, and now you want me to fight three people? Three guards?"

"Not at once," Steven assured her. "But he's right. It's time you fought someone besides the two of us. We don't want you to get complacent. Fighting different people with different styles can only benefit you," he promised. "The more you've experienced, the less likely you are to be caught off guard or freeze."

"I really hate this," Sophia said, but she nodded. "All right. Who's first?" she asked as she walked to the center of the nearest empty mat.

"Oh, that's absolutely me, *koukla*," Carla said brightly as she followed.

"Of course it is," Sophia muttered, but she wasn't really upset. She'd initially found the guard irritating, but Carla had grown on her. She still wasn't sure why. "Normal sparring rules?" she asked, directing the question to Lucas without taking her eyes off Carla. She wouldn't put it past the woman to start the fight without warning and point out that warning rarely came before a real fight.

"Yep. Though this time I won't be stopping you to correct your form. You go until one of you yields," Lucas answered.

Sophia was nervous. She knew full well that both Steven and Lucas had gone extremely easy on her, and they had stopped often to offer suggestions or corrections, which gave her a minute to breathe. These three wouldn't. She couldn't say she knew Joshua at all, and Jericho was definitely not impressed with her, but it was honestly Carla she was most worried about. Carla did seem to like her, but she was also the sort to push people to the edges of their limits. She'd proven that on day one. It was probably good for her, but it didn't mean it would be fun.

She was right.

Carla didn't exactly sucker punch Sophia, but neither did she give any warning before throwing a fist toward Sophia's face. Only the hours upon hours of drills allowed Sophia to jerk back and throw an arm up to block. It was clumsy, and her forearm stung from the contact, but she managed to keep the fist out of her face. Even better, she avoided falling on her ass. She'd done enough of that for a lifetime. The second punch slipped through her defenses and hit her ribs, but while it hurt, Sophia knew Carla had pulled the hit. She'd be bruised, but wouldn't have a cracked rib. At least there was that.

"Tell me Lucas taught you better than that," Carla taunted as she drew back a step. "Even you should be able to throw a punch, not just catch them."

A few weeks ago, the jabs might have gotten to her. Hell, they still stung a little, but Lucas and Steven had used similar tactics on her and warned her against reacting to them. She mostly listened, but the punch she threw wasn't quite as good as her usual. Carla also dodged it easily, but the woman had been training for decades while Sophia had only been at it a few weeks, so she didn't expect anything more. The second punch was cleaner, and she almost clipped Carla's shoulder. Then she took a kick to her side and gasped as the air tried to rush out of her lungs.

"Faster," Lucas called from the side, and she wanted to glare at him for his lack of sympathy. It was laughable, putting someone with as little training as she had with one of the senior nasaru. But she didn't want to make a complete fool of herself in a gym full of people, and she wasn't about to get a rep for being a whiny aspida. So she pushed her body, trying to move faster, put more precision behind her attacks. Carla slapped away a punch, ducked around a second. When Sophia dared to try one of the kicks Lucas had been trying to teach her, Carla actually caught her leg. It surprised her enough that she didn't react quickly enough, and the practiced move Carla did landed her squarely on her face.

It wasn't the first time Sophia had found herself in this position, and she found she hated it just as much now as she had the first dozen times it had happened. Embarrassment heated her cheeks as her hands planted on the mat and she began pushing herself up. A hand appeared in front of her face and she looked up to see it belonged to Carla.

"You're doing better," the smiling woman said when her hand was accepted and she pulled Sophia to her feet.

"That's better?" Sophia asked, rubbing her aching ribs. "I ended up on my face in under a minute."

"True," Carla agreed without hesitation, "but when you started, you wouldn't have lasted ten seconds. You *are* improving, so give yourself a break." She leaned in then, dropping her voice so it was only for Sophia. "And if it helps, these two aren't as good as me. You should last at least a minute and a half."

"I'm not sure if I should laugh or be offended," Sophia admitted as Carla walked to where the guys stood.

"Laugh. It's always the better choice," Carla called over her shoulder. "Good for the soul or some shit."

Sophia only shook her head and looked at Joshua and Jericho. "Okay, which of you is next?"

"I am," Jericho said as he strode toward her.

Great. The guy who thought she was a joke as aspida was next. Carla's prediction was probably going to be wrong. This guy really wouldn't hold back, but she just nodded and forced her body to relax. "Okay. Let's go," she told him. Unlike with Carla, she didn't wait for him to make the first move, but attacked as soon as he was in range. To her shock and delight, it connected, her fist slamming into his stomach. Of course, it was rigid beneath her knuckles, but he still let out a little oof. Then he promptly backhanded her, which she was definitely not expecting in a friendly spar. Especially not right off the bat.

Her head whipped to the side, and she tasted blood from where her teeth cut open the inside of her cheek. It wasn't really the sort of fighting Steven and Lucas had been teaching her, but she wasn't going to stop and complain. If she was fighting for her life, her attacker wasn't really going to hold to any sort of code of honor. But not complaining didn't mean she wasn't going to prove that she wasn't weak. The Athenaeum had chosen her as aspida. The people of the Athenaeum might not all like it, but it wasn't their choice. She *would* do this job well, if for no other reason than to honor her grandfather's memory. And to prove her naysayers wrong.

She glanced up at him through her lashes, noted the smug smirk playing over his lips, then moved, taking advantage of the ten-inch difference in their height. Ducking under his arm when he threw another punch, she stepped into him and brought her knee up hard. Yes, he might say it was a girl move, but backhanding was a dick move, so she thought it was only fitting. The fact that it connected just as she intended pleased her, but not as much as when his face went red and he dropped to one knee.

"Bitch," he wheezed, looking as though he might be sick.

"Don't," she warned, surprised to realize she was more angry than anything else. "You wanted to ignore normal sparring rules and try to prove how tough you are and how weak I am. Not once in all the weeks of training has anyone backhanded me, or even tried to, because this is *training*. And yet that's the first thing you did. So if you want to fight dirty, then why in the hell would I not follow suit?" she snapped before turning toward Lucas. "I'm not sparring with him again," she said, and it wasn't a request. "And he needs to learn the difference between training and a drunken bar fight."

It was unexpected when Lucas smiled, but he nodded without even a pause. "Understood, Aspida."

Straightening, she blinked at him. Had including Jericho been a test? She'd had a hard time adjusting to being the boss and hesitated to give orders unless she had to. Lucas had been encouraging her—as her mom and a few others—but it wasn't natural for her. Telling Jericho off and giving Lucas the order had been a step in the right direction. It had to be, because no one had ever referred to her by her title like he just had. She kind of liked it.

"Thank you," she said after a moment. Movement had her looking back to Jericho, but he did nothing more than pull himself up and walk off the mat.

Joshua took his place and smiled faintly. "You won't get dirty tricks from me," he promised. "Just an honest spar."

"Fair enough. That's all I ask," Sophia said as she worked on making her muscles relax after the confrontation.

Joshua might not be looking to fight dirty, but he also wasn't willing to wait for her to get ready, attacking quickly like Carla had.

Unfortunately, it made sense. A real fight wouldn't give her time to get her head in the right place. She blocked the first attack, but he followed it with a second, a third, pressing forward. They were stopped as well, but each one was blocked more clumsily than the last, until finally one got through, his punch skimming along her jaw. Refusing to give up, though the side of her face exploded with pain, she lifted a foot and kicked at him, managing to knock him back a few inches. Unfortunately, it knocked her off balance even more, and she stumbled back a couple of steps.

Joshua only gave a second to recover before going for a roundhouse. Her eyes widened, but it wasn't the first time she'd had a foot coming at her face and she ducked, his foot scraping over the top of her head. When she came up, she led with her fist, shoving it into his ribs. He grunted, but it didn't stop him. Instead, he grabbed her, much like he had with his magic earlier, turned, and slammed them both down to the mat. He caught some of his weight on his arms, but it knocked all the breath from her so she couldn't do anything but lie there with his body pinning her.

"Do you yield?" came an impassive voice. Lucas's, she thought, and she wanted to hate him a little.

Sophia tried to speak, but nothing came out, so she nodded and slapped the mat with her hand. Immediately, the weight lifted from her and she was able to suck in her first lungful of air. Like Carla, Joshua offered a hand, but he stopped when she was in a sitting position, giving her time to recover. "Are you okay?" he asked, sounding sincere in his concern.

"Will be," she assured him with a weak smile.

"Good. That was a nice move, that last hit," he told her. "Next time, throw the punch, then circle around so you can't get grabbed."

"Being small can be an asset," Carla agreed, though she was almost half a foot taller than Sophia, "but only if you're quick, too. But he's right, it was a nice move."

"You did well," Lucas added, reaching down to pull her gently to her feet. "And because of that, you're done for the day. No more training today. Go see Sergei if you need to, then relax," he said, smiling and brushing his thumb over the back of her hand. The gentle tone now was far different than when he asked if she yielded and she wondered as to the why. They hadn't exactly been advertising their relationship, but neither were they hiding it, so was he trying to prove that he wasn't showing favoritism? Did the reason matter? He was never mean or cruel, just hard to figure out sometimes.

"I'm not going to argue," she said before smiling at Carla and Joshua. "Thanks for helping out," she told them. Jericho? He got a glance, but she wasn't going to thank him for using it as an opportunity to try to knock her down a peg.

"Anytime, *koukla*," Carla said with a grin.

"You're welcome. And you are doing well," Joshua told her.

Offering one last smile to Lucas and Steven, she turned and left the gym. She debated going to see Sergei or her mom, but decided she could probably handle her injuries. Besides, she mostly wanted a shower now, so headed back to her room.

The moment she was inside the room that had once been her grandfather's, where no one could see her, she slumped against the door and blew out a breath. She really hated training, and Jericho had made it extra unpleasant today, but she did believe them when they said she was improving. It might even be enough, especially if she had a few more months before needing to use any of what she was learning.

Pushing away from the door, she stripped her clothes off as she headed to the bathroom, grimacing when she took in the bruises starting to blossom. They were going to be truly fantastic colors, which was why she really loved how the room came with an attached bathroom. And the shower? It was absolutely fabulous. Better than any she'd seen, even in normal houses that weren't built beneath a mountain. So when she stepped beneath the hot water, she sighed with pleasure and thought she could feel the bruises disappearing beneath the heat. To her surprise, when she was done and was drying herself off, she noticed that some of them were actually gone. The ones that remained looked paler than they had. Seth's blessing really was no joke, and she reminded herself to thank him next time she spoke to him. Him and the other patrons.

But though the training was done, her day wasn't. Being the boss wasn't just ordering people around, it was work. She needed to go through her emails—which included several mission briefs from Nick, the head venator—study the sorcery that was required of her as aspida, and try to figure out the Lachlan issue. All she could do was take things one at a time and pray nothing else dropped in her lap.

Chapter 6

AFTER SHOWERING, SOPHIA HEADED to her office. It still seemed odd to her that a large part of her job as head of the Athenaeum involved sitting behind a desk checking emails. True, they were emails approving acquisitions of relics and old texts, or requests for her to research something obscure—and usually pretty damn cool—but a magical library should be more than emails. Still, it wasn't actually bad, even if she did hold some envy for the venatores and nasaru who were leaving the Athenaeum to do retrievals. She knew aspides were allowed to do that themselves, but she could admit that she wasn't the right person for that. Yet. First she needed to learn more, and she needed to get the issues within the Athenaeum sorted out.

She'd been at it for nearly an hour when Alicia—one of the guards—stepped into the open doorway. "Sophia?"

She glanced up and smiled before she caught the shaken look on the woman's face. "Alicia? What's wrong?" she asked, rising from her chair.

"You know how we can't teleport inside the Athenaeum? How we have to leave before we can teleport anywhere?"

"I do..." It was one of the many protections the divine patrons and former aspides had placed on the Athenaeum, but the fact that Alicia was asking probably meant someone had just appeared or managed to leave.

"Well, a man and a woman just teleported in. They're demanding to see Erasmus, and while the woman seems pretty powerful, the man is..." She shivered, hard enough for Sophia to see from across the room. "He's scary powerful and seems pretty pissed. You should get up there."

Shit. It really never stopped around here. Not for the first time, she wished she could step down as aspida. "Do you know who they are?" she asked as she shot off a text to Lucas.

"No idea, but the man definitely isn't human. I'm not even sure he's Arcane. His eyes are white. Like nothing but white and the pupil."

White irises? It could be a mutation, but in all the reading she'd done since assuming her new role, the only beings she'd found who had eyes like that were demons. If a demon was inside the Athenaeum, then today was going to be a very bad day. "I take it there are other guards there?" she asked as she shoved the phone in her pocket and walked around the desk.

"Oh yeah," Alicia agreed as she started leading the way upstairs. "As soon as they appeared, the call went out to all the guards."

So Lucas was probably already there. Good. Someone powerful enough to get through the protections meant she wanted the nasaru on alert. Sophia still took a moment to cast two spells—a spell shielding her from physical attacks, and one to sense nearby threats. She wasn't sure whether to be relieved or not when the latter just covered in her the now familiar tingles that indicated someone wished her harm but wasn't close enough to do anything.

They were silent as they hurried down the hallway and into what she thought of as the foyer. It was the first main room of the Athenaeum and empty but for a few stone columns and two eight-feet long sphinx statues standing guard just outside the doorway to the stairs. Normally there were just a few people here, standing guard or pausing to chat as they passed through. Today, there were a full dozen people inside, and that didn't count the couple standing in the middle of the room. A quick glance told Sophia most of the dozen were guards—including Lucas, who stood a few feet in front of the two strangers.

They hadn't yet noticed Sophia, so she took a moment to study them. The woman was tall and slender, with straight, jet black hair and pale eyes. She was pretty, but in an unassuming way. And, if Alicia was to be believed, powerful. The man, however, was striking in every way. He was tall and muscular, with hair as dark as his companion's and eyes even paler. They did look white from this distance, but they could simply be an extremely light color. And while the woman wore black cargo pants and a tee-shirt, he was wearing leather pants and a snug shirt, both also black. But the most noticeable thing about him was that he radiated enough power that even Sophia could feel it without a problem.

Steeling herself, Sophia inhaled deeply, exhaled slowly, then started toward them, trying to look like she was more confident than she really was. "Hello. I hear you're looking for Erasmus?"

The man turned his gaze on her and Sophia froze. She couldn't help it. There was something about having his attention on her that filled her with a cold dread. "I am. Where is he?" His voice was deep and she swore she could feel it vibrate through her, though that could be his power, too. Scary powerful was a good way to describe him. So was plain scary.

Where the man looked irritated, the woman looked oddly delighted. Lucas, on the other hand, looked serious, and when she reached his side, he gently laid a hand on her arm to prevent her from getting any close to the couple. Not that she needed such precautions. She didn't want to get an inch closer to him than she had to. "I'm sorry, but he died a month ago. I'm his granddaughter, as well as his successor. And I hate to be rude, but who are you two, and how did you get in here?" Her voice was steady, and she was proud she'd managed to avoid sounding as frightened as she felt.

The irritated was replaced by confusion, and Sophia couldn't understand what she'd said that could be misconstrued in any way. Before she could dwell on it, the woman spoke. "I'm so sorry to hear that," she said, sounding genuinely sympathetic. "Erasmus was a good man, and one I considered a friend, though I never met him in person. I'm Blanche."

"It's nice to meet you," Sophia said politely. "And yes, he was," she agreed, her gaze continuing to flick back to the man. His eyes looked unfocused, and she had to wonder what he was doing. The fact that he'd shown up inside the Athenaeum worried her, too, but she had to step cautiously. She had a feeling that if she spoke wrong, he could decimate them.

"I want to speak with you alone," the man said abruptly.

Beside her, Lucas stiffened and shook his head. "Not happening."

The man smiled, and it was just as dangerous as his stare had been. "Yes," he corrected, "it is. I asked as a courtesy, but I can make it happen if you want to be difficult. And don't even think about trying to attack me. It won't do any good."

"Maybe I should introduce my husband," Blanche interjected quickly, though she looked more amused than worried. "This is Death. And yes, I mean the Death you're thinking of. Not a death god, but *the* Death. Trust me, you really don't want to piss him off. Being dead when you've pissed off the guy who rules the underworld isn't fun."

That explained a lot, including how they'd gotten in here. She didn't imagine there were many places where Death couldn't go. She also really, really didn't want to talk to him alone. In fact, she didn't really want to be around him at all.

Blanche nudged Death and he sighed. "I should add that I don't mean her any harm. I want to talk."

"Doesn't change the fact that you're not talking to her alone. I'm her head guard. I'll be there or it isn't happening," Lucas insisted stubbornly. She wanted to kiss him for that.

"Fine. Lead the way."

Sophia frowned, as she hadn't agreed to this, but reasoned that if she gave him what he wanted, he might go away. "Very well." Blanche gave her an apologetic smile before she turned and started back down the hall to her office. No one spoke until all four were in the office with the door closed. To get a little bit of distance between herself and Death, Sophia stood behind her desk, though she knew it wouldn't protect her if he did decide to attack. "Why were you looking for my grandfather?"

"Several months ago, he gave a summoning spell to another woman, who gave it to Blanche. A spell to summon me."

"He gave it to Suni," Blanche supplied.

"Yes," he agreed with a nod. "And I want it destroyed. There is no reason for anyone to be summoning me before their demise. More, I refuse to have people summoning me every single damn time they lose someone they care about."

Sophia had never heard of such a spell, though the name of the other woman sounded familiar. She mouthed the name as she tried to place it. Lucas must have noticed because he leaned in and helpfully whispered, "She's the healer who gave us the mithridate and helped save Olivia."

That's right. She was used to people just referring to the outside healer. Sophia nodded slowly and tried to meet Death's eyes, but couldn't quite manage it. She did manage to see enough to realize his eyes weren't actually white, just an extremely pale blue. "I can understand not wanting to be summoned, but I'm afraid I don't know where the spell is. I didn't even know it existed," she admitted. "I may be Erasmus's successor, but I'd only known about the Athenaeum for a few days before that happened."

Death really didn't like hearing that, and his eyes narrowed as she spoke. Blanche rested her hand on his arm and he seemed to calm. Sophia had to admire the woman who not only didn't fear Death, but had married him, though she had to admit that the thought of Death being married hurt her head. "We get it," Blanche assured her. "Getting dumped into a position you didn't even know existed isn't easy. Do you think that you could look for the spell and destroy it when it is found?"

"I don't know how much either of you know about the Athenaeum, but there are...I don't even know how many books, scrolls, tablets, loose pages, and other forms of the written word within these walls. There's no telling what form the spell was in or where it is, so I can't promise how easy it will be to even find it. Not to mention that some of our materials are spelled to be difficult to destroy, so I can't promise anything there, either." Death started to get worked up again, so she hurried to add, "That being said, at the very least, I could put it in a place where only I can access it, and make a note to never use it."

That didn't reassure Death, but Blanche leaned into him and he sighed before subsiding. "You do know that if it weren't for that spell, I never would have found you again," she told him quietly. Sophia was curious about that, but she knew better than to butt into their personal business.

"Fine," Death said reluctantly.

"Good. Now, how about you give me your number?" Blanche asked, smiling at Sophia as she pulled out her phone. "I really did like Erasmus. A lot. He also helped me. I wouldn't be married to Death now if it weren't for him. I just wish I'd been able to meet him in person."

"Oh. Sure." Sophia gave Blanche her number, unsurprised when her phone vibrated with a text a minute later. She wasn't sure how she felt about being phone buddies with Death's wife, but it couldn't hurt to have that connection. Surely there were items in the Athenaeum that hadn't been identified, and Death had to be one of the oldest beings in the universe. Maybe it could work out well. Then she realized it might pay off right now, if Death would agree. "I am sorry that I couldn't help you right away, but there are some...issues...in the Athenaeum right now, and..." Her courage faltered a bit. Asking

Death for a favor when she had just refused his demand probably wasn't smart, but maybe she could spin it to helping them both. Lucas rested his hand on her shoulder, and she drew in a slow breath. "These issues are taking up a lot of my time, which is honestly preventing me from doing anything new, such as looking for that spell."

"Why are you telling me?" Death asked bluntly.

"Because there is a way you could possibly help me to resolve those issues, which would free me up to look for that spell."

Death cocked his head and actually smiled a little. Blanche just grinned. "What's that?" he asked.

"A man was killed a few days after Erasmus, and all evidence points to him being Erasmus's killer. We also have reason to believe he wasn't working alone, but we don't know who his accomplice was. If we could speak to him, that would help considerably." She gave a weak smile. "I actually wished that I knew a necromancer so we could speak to him. I just had no idea I'd be speaking to Death himself." Honestly, she'd prefer to speak to Erasmus, but that wouldn't help her find his killer, not when he'd admitted to not having any idea who it might be.

"Death and a necromancer," Blanche said smugly.

"Oh? Well, yeah, that makes sense. Do you think either of you could help me then?"

"It really would help," Lucas chimed in. "Three people have died in the Athenaeum in the last month, and we'd like to make sure not to add to that number."

"Death is natural, though," the man himself said.

"Yes, but not when it's murder."

"And Erasmus did help us. I think we should help his granddaughter," Blanche told her husband.

Death inclined his head, conceding the point. "Fine. What was his name?"

"Dion. Erasmus was actually his great-uncle."

Death nodded and a moment later, a shadowy version of Dion appeared in front of him. Dion looked startled and confused, turning in place and taking in the four faces. When he seemed to realize where he was, his expression went frantic and his focus landed on Sophia and Lucas. "Tell me you're not dead," he begged in Greek, though when he'd been alive he'd stuck to English with her.

The words baffled her, and a quick look at Lucas told her he was equally surprised. "No," he answered slowly, also in Greek. "We're alive. Death was kind enough to summon you to speak with us."

Dion frowned and looked back to Death, but dismissed him quickly. "Good. When I saw you, I was worried that you had died, too."

"Why would you care if we died? You killed Erasmus," Sophia said, not able to wrap her mind around his behavior.

Dion stepped back, expression shocked and hurt. "I would never hurt him! I loved Erasmus. He was more like my father than my great-uncle. I never would have had any part in his death."

His words sounded sincere, but if he hadn't killed Erasmus, then why had he attacked them after they'd discovered Agatha dead a few weeks ago? "Can the dead lie?" she asked Death.

"They can, just as easily as the living, but this one isn't," Death answered without hesitation. "I'll let you know if he speaks an untruth."

She nodded slowly, contemplating what this could mean.

"Do you know who was responsible, then?" Lucas asked.

Dion shook his head. "I don't. I had only just realized that his death hadn't been natural when I died. I was looking into it."

"Partial truth," Death said, voice bored.

Dion shot him a glance, then sighed. "I don't know for certain who was involved, but since dying, I have been wondering why Peter attacked me when the three of you came to speak with me."

Sophia frowned. "But he didn't. You attacked, and Lucas and Peter responded."

"No, I didn't," he insisted. "I didn't use any magic that day. And while I love my son and want to protect him, he is the one who attacked first." His voice went quiet, filled with sorrow. "He's the one who killed me."

Though Death again verified Dion's truthfulness, Sophia didn't need it. There was no mistaking the honesty in Dion's words. But while it was good that her cousin hadn't murdered her grandfather, it opened up an entirely different set of problems. Had Peter been involved instead? Or was it whoever had stolen the bodies from Sergei's clinic? It felt like they'd taken several very big steps back instead of forward.

Lucas laid his hand on Sophia's shoulder and squeezed comfortingly. "Is there anything you do know that might help us?" he asked.

Though Dion's expression went even sadder, he took the time to think before shaking his head. "I've had little to do but pick through everything I knew, but like I said, I'd only just realized Erasmus had been killed when I was killed. I'm truly sorry, Sophia, but I don't know anything that could help you."

Except he had. Not in the way she'd expected or wanted, but he had helped. Being able to know for certain that he had nothing to do with Erasmus's death was information they hadn't had the day before, and it changed things. It also put the suspicion firmly on his son.

Because of that, she worked up a smile for him. "I know, Dion. And thank you, for telling us everything you do know."

"It is good to know that you had nothing to do with it," Lucas agreed. "If it eases your mind any, no one knows Erasmus was murdered, so no one blames you for his death."

"Just Agatha's," Dion murmured. Unfortunately, Sophia couldn't argue with that and just smiled at him again.

Kindly, Death said, "Thank you, Dion. Rest well, now," before he sent Dion back to wherever his soul resided.

"And thank you," Sophia said to Death. "That changes things a lot for us."

"And not all for the better, it sounds like," he said, not quite sounding as bored as he had before.

"No," she agreed, "it answers a few questions, but created several more."

"Call me if you need more spirit summoning," Blanche added. "He's not the only one who can manage that," she said, grinning mischievously. "Or just to talk."

"I will. Thanks, Blanche."

On those words, Death nodded, then he and Blanche disappeared. When they were gone, Sophia realized she was able to take the first deep breath since she'd been in their presence. Here was hoping it was the last time she'd see Death for a very, very long time.

Chapter 7

Lucas had seen and dealt with a lot in his life, despite being younger than at least half of the Athenaeum. Meeting Death wasn't something he'd ever expected to do until he'd died. He couldn't say he was happy to have met the man, but surviving that meeting? Especially since he'd pushed back at the man's demands? He was surprised, and not unpleasantly so. He could also privately admit to being shaken after the experience. That was one being he wouldn't have been able to protect Sophia from, though he would have done his damnedest to try.

But as much as the private meeting had thrown him off, Sophia looked worse. Her face was pale, and it looked like there was a fine trembling in her fingers. Not anything that most people would notice, and he could admit that she'd held up better than most would have, especially with all the stress she was under. It was admirable how she'd handled herself, and he felt his heart soften just a little more toward her.

"You okay?" he asked, rubbing her shoulders, which had turned to stone almost as completely as he did.

"I could really go for a drink right now," she admitted, resting her head on the desk.

It was the first time he'd even heard her mention wanting alcohol, including right after Erasmus's death, so it surprised him. But honestly, he couldn't think of a better time for someone to get a little drunk. He grinned and bent to kiss the top of her head before heading for the door. "Be right back."

When he returned a few minutes later with two shot glasses, two bottles of water, and one of tequila, she laughed, some of the color returning to her cheeks. "Really? We're going to get drunk in my office?"

"We can go to your room if you want," he offered as he set them on the desk and pulled one of the chairs closer, so he was sitting across from her. "Honestly, though, I'd just consider it one of the perks of being boss. If you think any of them wouldn't need one after not only realizing Death is real, but having a private conversation with him, you're wrong."

"What do you mean realizing he's real?" she asked as he opened the tequila and filled both glasses.

"Most people know of the death gods associated with the different religions. Hades, Hel, Osiris, all of those. But an actual Death is more like a myth. There's the Horseman for the Christians, and the whole Grim Reaper myth, but most people—even Arcane—don't think there's a separate Death. Now we do, and sounds like Erasmus knew, too. And we are going to get a little tipsy and revel in the fact that we met him, survived, and you even made friends with his wife."

"It's weird thinking of Death as being married," Sophia admitted as she picked up her glass. She sniffed it and wrinkled her nose, but when he lifted his own and extended it to touch hers, she smiled then downed the first shot with him. "Oh gods, that's horrible," she said immediately. Setting the glass down, she opened one of the waters and took a deep drink.

Lucas chuckled and refilled the glasses. "First time having tequila?"

"Yeah. Not much of a drinker. Back in America, I was too focused on school," she admitted.

"No college parties?" he asked, surprised. Yes, she was focused and determined, but she wasn't uptight. She was social and liked having fun, so he'd honestly expected her to have gone to plenty of parties.

"No college parties," she admitted. "Well, there was one, but it was pretty boring for me."

An idea popped into his head. "So no drinking games?" She shook her head. "Then we'll fix that now. For each shot we take, the other person has to tell something about themselves."

Her eyes narrowed. "What sort of thing?" she asked suspiciously.

"You can't go with the completely obvious, like you have green eyes or went to the University of Georgia. More personal stuff than that."

She continued to watch him as she considered it. "Okay. But you go first," she said, grinning impishly at him.

He'd had a feeling she'd insist on that but hid his smile. He pushed her now full glass to her and studied her face. One shot and the promise of a game, and a little of the strain had already slid away from her. Some of the tightness around her eyes had lessened and her shoulders didn't look quite so heavy. If nothing else happened, that made this worth it. The fact that he was curious to see what kind of drunk she was didn't hurt. Sophia wasn't an overly controlled person, but she had been holding herself in check since he'd met her. It was clear enough to see, even to a stranger. Not that he blamed her. Since the moment she stepped into the Athenaeum, she'd been dealing with more than most could handle, all while being under a microscope.

"I was almost married once," he told her once she took her shot, complete with a grimace. "Back when I was twenty-one." Her eyes narrowed and he fought another smile.

"Why didn't you go through with it?" she asked, her fingers tightening slightly on her now empty glass.

"Mmm. Turned out she didn't care who she married, so long as it was a Marine who was likely to be deployed. She wanted to be a military wife, to not have to work, and to have the freedom to do whatever the hell she wanted when her husband was overseas."

The irritation faded, replaced by sympathy. "I'm sorry, Lucas. And glad you realized that before you actually got married."

He laughed as he refilled her glass. "Oh, me too. Kicked her to the curb," he said, leaning back in his chair and downing his own shot. "Your turn."

"Well, I can't say I was ever married, or even almost married." One corner of her mouth turned up in a wry smile. "Was honestly more focused on school than guys, so I haven't even had what most would call a long-term relationship before."

"What do you consider long term?"

She blew out a breath. "Four months is my record," she admitted.

That surprised him. "I know you said you were working on school, but why only four months?"

Sophia started to answer, then narrowed her eyes. "That sounds like a second fact," she teased. "You want to ask that question, then you need another shot first."

Lucas chuckled and toasted her with his shot. "Fair enough," he said before tossing back the tequila. They were already out of order, but that wasn't the point of this little game. Not only did he want to relax her, he found that he wanted to know more about the woman who was in his bed. Or more specifically, whose bed he was in. He liked her and had a feeling he could like her more. A lot more.

She grinned at his lack of hesitation. "There were a couple of reasons," she began, smile fading. "Some of them just..." Her expression shifted a few times like she was hunting for the right words. "Bored me, I guess is the best way of saying it, but I can't say they were really boring." She reconsidered, smiled slyly, and added, "Well, most of them. There was one who seemed okay, but when we were alone was probably the dullest person in existence."

"And the others?" he prompted.

"Apparently, I bored them," she answered with a shrug. "We were in college. They wanted to go out, go party, just go. And that was fine now and again, but I wasn't going to waste my tuition money by blowing off my classwork and partying all the time."

"Just means they were fucking morons," he assured her. "But for a lot of people, college is just a party. Getting out from under the parental thumbs, exploring, having fun. And for some people, learning and working for their future is fun."

"I think that does make me sound boring."

He laughed and shook his head. "You're not. How could you be? You're a beautiful woman who can transform into an owl, who is the head of the oldest and most secretive library in the world, who speaks multiple languages and knows sorcery. Add in that you're sleeping with a sexy gargoyle, and how could you be considered boring?" he asked, only partially teasing.

She smiled and reached across the desk to brush her fingers against his. "Thanks, Lucas. But I think it's my turn?" He silently gestured toward her glass. This time she took a steadying breath before she took the shot, but there was no unhappy expression this time. Clearly the alcohol was working its way through her blood. "Okay, spill," she demanded.

"I've got a brother and a sister, though I'm not sure if that's news since it's in my file," Lucas told her after a moment.

"No, it's not," she confirmed, and he smiled a little when he realized she was starting to slur her words. It was subtle, but there.

"I'm not sure it's in my file that we're fraternal triplets."

She blinked and straightened in her chair. "No, it isn't. Seriously?" He nodded. "That's kind of cool. I've never met triplets before. I couple sets of twins, but no triplets. Who's the oldest?"

"I am, by a whole six minutes."

"Do you get along with them?"

"I do, yeah. I haven't seen them in a few years, but they both do a lot of travel for their jobs, so it's kind of expected." He grinned and poured tequila into his glass and lifted it. "And now it's my turn," he said, lifting his brows in challenge.

She only laughed and made a 'go ahead' gesture as she slumped back in her chair. "Go for it." When he had, she leaned her head to one side and studied him while she thought. Her brow wrinkled cutely as she struggled to think past the tequila. "You know, ever since I found out you're a gargoyle, I've really wanted to see you in your gargoyle form.

And can you actually fly? I know gargoyles are always portrayed with wings, but it doesn't seem plausible than a stone person can fly."

Her rambling was also adorable, and he liked that she was so curious about him. It might not quite be a revelation about herself, but he wasn't going to argue. "Yes, I can fly. Are you wanting to have someone to fly with?"

"Yes," she said wistfully. "I've only been flying once since I got here, before we went to Delphi. I miss it. I hate going this long without flying, but I know it isn't safe. Especially since Dion had nothing to do with Erasmus."

"I'll fly with you."

"Really?" she asked hopefully.

"Really. And if you want, I'll shift now so you can see me in my gargoyle form."

She beamed at him and nodded. "That'd be great. I've never met a gargoyle besides you. I've always wondered how you really look."

"Don't get too excited," he warned as he rose and moved around the desk so she'd be able to see him. "I mostly look like myself."

"That's okay. I love how you look."

It was said casually and without thinking, and he felt his attraction for her bump up a notch. It was always nice to be appreciated, if it was minor as far as compliments went. He bent down and kissed her lightly, one of the few times they'd showed real affection to one another outside of sex. She seemed surprised, but returned the kiss before he straightened and pulled off his shirt. With her eyes a little darker than they had been, he allowed his gargoyle form to rise.

He hadn't lied. He didn't look that different, not really. He didn't become some grotesque monster or anything. His skin transformed to a tough, flexible stone, and though he could hide his bat-like wings, he allowed them to show now, too. Even his features were essentially the same, though his nails elongated into claws and his canines lengthened into fangs, hidden now by his lips. Some people were afraid or disgusted by a gargoyle's true form—or the alternate form of anyone in the Arcane—but not Sophia. He wasn't sure if it was because they were lovers or her innate desire to learn everything she could, but she was obviously delighted.

"Oh gods. You look amazing!" She pushed out her chair and wobbled, extending her arms so she didn't fall over. Chuckling, he caught her waist, helping her catch her balance. He had to smother a laugh when she lifted one hand and poked at his exposed arm. In this form, he barely felt it, even when she repeated the poke, harder this time. "Wow...You really do turn to stone," she breathed, now trailing her fingers along his arm. He wished he could feel the sensation, but having her touch him like this, so intrigued by his real form, was almost as good. Then she lifted her hand to his wing—which had much more sensation than the rest of his body—and he fought a shiver.

"I don't understand how you can fly," she murmured as she explored the textures of his body.

He smiled and drew her in closer, so her body was lightly pressed to his. "The same way winged horses fly. The same way you can turn into an owl. Magic."

"Oh. Right," she said, nodding solemnly at him, her hand stilling as her eyes lifted to meet his. "Do you remember how we got interrupted yesterday?" she asked, her hand sliding over his wing, to his shoulder, and down to his bicep.

"Trust me, I'm not likely to forget," he said, still regretting that they hadn't been able to finish.

Grinning, she pressed closer, and he slid his arms fully around her waist. She really was adorably drunk, and he was surprised Seth's gifts hadn't prevented it, but if she wasn't a drinker—and this was the first time he'd seen her have so much as a drop—then it made sense. "It's about dinner time. What do you say we go back to my room and pick up where we left off?"

Lucas loved the idea, and though he transformed back to his human form, one part of his body remained rock hard. "You sure?"

Sophia laughed, and the way she rubbed herself against him made him groan. "Definitely."

Not caring at the moment if they made a spectacle, Lucas scooped her up into his arms. "Get the door," he ordered as he turned her toward it. It took two tries, but she got it open. He wished her bedroom wasn't down on the next level, but his long legs covered the distance quickly. They passed few people, since most were at dinner, but he noted those who saw them did give them curious looks. He didn't give a damn.

By the time they reached Sophia's bedroom, she was giggling and kissing on his throat, making him desperate to get inside and get her out of her clothes. He kicked the door closed behind them and strode over to the bed, dropping her onto it, which made her laugh. "Clothes," he demanded, finding he was as eager as he'd been in his teens.

"Impatient?" she teased as she kicked her shoes off and clumsily worked her shirt off. She got stuck once, and he grinned, pausing to help her out of the garment.

"With you? Definitely," he said, unbuttoning his pants as he toed his boots off. The moment his pants loosened, he breathed a little easier, now that it no longer felt like he had a vice around his cock. Then she removed her bra and he throbbed with need for her. Quickly shoving his pants down and off, his hands found the fastening of her jeans, undoing them and yanking them down with enough force that she slid a few inches down the bed. The moment they were off, he dropped them and let his eyes move over her body.

"You are impatient," she said breathlessly as he used a knee to nudge her legs open, then rested it on the bed.

Lucas leaned forward, elbow beside her head, his hand sliding into her hair and gripping it firmly. "Yes, I am," he agreed before he lowered his mouth to hers. He wasn't gentle. He couldn't be. She didn't seem to care, either, meeting the kiss with the same intensity. Her arms lifted and wound around his neck, pulling his chest against hers. She wrapped her legs around his hips, but he didn't give in to her, not yet. It would be so easy to just ease inside her, but while he wanted her, he desperately wanted to see her writhing, hear her crying out his name, feel her body trembling as she came for him.

Sliding his free hand between them, he found her, middle finger brushing teasingly over her clit, making her gasp. He nearly smiled, but wasn't done. His finger slid down and into her, pleased to feel how wet she already was. It was one of the things he loved about being with her. She was responsive as hell, gave everything she had, and took what she wanted. In bed, she allowed herself to stop worrying, to stop being aspida, and just *be*.

Sophia moaned against his mouth and bucked her hips against his hand, her legs again trying to pull him closer. "Now who's impatient?" he asked as he trailed his lips across her cheek to nuzzle her throat.

"Me. Stop teasing," she growled.

"But it's so much fun," he said, slowly thrusting his finger in and out of her.

"Not for me," she complained, but her body was on edge, primed for her first climax. Then she did something that shocked and thrilled him. She used some of the sorcery he'd taught her to push him back. With more agility than he'd thought her capable of in her current state, she sat up, grabbed his arm, and pulled him to one side, quickly enough that he was off balance. When he landed on his back on the bed, she climbed on top of him and grinned, her hands on his chest. "Now we'll have fun," she purred as she slid one hand down his chest until she could wrap her fingers around his cock. Positioning him at her entrance, she pressed down onto him, groaning as he slid into her slick heat.

He grabbed her hips, and in the back of his head he barely remembered not to hold her too tightly. The last thing he wanted to do was hurt her when she was making him feel so good. And he was loving her taking control, which should have surprised him, since normally he liked being the one in charge. But he wasn't going to complain, not even a little. And while it took a bit of effort not to take over, he managed it. Instead, he held onto her while she moved, thrusting up to meet her each time her hips pressed down against him.

"Touch me," she said, her voice an erotic mix of plea and demand. Since the words were accompanied by her grabbing his wrist and guiding his hand to her breast, she left nothing open to interpretation.

He was also more than happy to oblige. Cupping her breast, he stroked the nipple with his thumb, and she sighed, holding his hand more firmly against her.

Smiling, he released her hip and slid his hand inward until he could rub her clit. That was all she needed. Her head fell back as she sucked in a breath and her body clamped down around him as she came. Groaning, he arched up into her, at the same time she ground down against him. It was too much. The way she felt coming around him undid him. It always did. His fingers gripped her hair, pulling her down for a kiss. The moment her lips parted to allow him to deepen the kiss, he lost the fight against his control, pouring into her.

As the rush of pleasure began to ebb, the kiss gentled, but didn't end. The trembling of her body gradually stopped and she relaxed atop him. After several minutes, she lifted her head and gave him a sleepy but content smile. "That was better than the tequila," she said, her voice soft.

"Always wins for me, too," he told her, fingers loosening in her hair so he could smooth it back down.

Her head lowered to rest on his shoulder. "I'd thank you, but I think I already did."

He chuckled and reached a hand out, grabbing the blankets and tugging them over her. The cold didn't bother him, but he knew she'd start feeling it soon. "And then some," he agreed. "Sleep now."

"Okay," she mumbled. It took only a minute before the sound of her breathing changed, and he knew she was out. Smiling, he reached for a pillow and carefully tucked it beneath his head before he closed his eyes and joined her in sleep.

Chapter 8

WHEN SOPHIA WOKE, SHE did so without any confusion or the hint of a headache. While she had never been a big drinker, the few times she'd had more than a few sips had led to a hangover. Apparently, Seth's gift was good for more than just keeping her alive. In fact, she felt so good that she wanted to start her day on a high note, especially since it was likely to go to crap afterward. They still didn't know what was wrong with Lachlan and they now had to find Erasmus's real killer, since Dion was innocent.

So she kissed Lucas gently on the lips, then along his jaw, down his throat, and over his chest until he woke. Last night he'd let her take control, but this morning she found herself getting flipped over and thoroughly loved. It was definitely the best way to start her morning. Her mood stayed up through breakfast, though it had become a somber affair since Agatha's death. The new guy was a good cook and tried to take care of people, but he wasn't Agatha. No one could truly replace her and they all knew it. She could sympathize with the new cook though, as she had also had to step into someone else's shoes.

After breakfast, they parted ways, with Sophia going to continue more of her interviews. Lucas, though, spent a few minutes checking with the guards before he headed to his own office. Sophia needed to focus on being aspida, but looking into the problems in the Athenaeum actually fell right under his job description. Okay, it fell under hers as well, and if she wasn't new to the job he'd include her more, but he wanted to take something off her shoulders. Or try to, anyway.

To start, he pulled up personnel files. They were more thorough than most employers bothered with, but the Athenaeum wasn't a traditional employer. Which meant he should be able to use those files to further narrow down their list of suspects. Dion's confession from literally beyond the grave had changed things, but not as much as Sophia seemed to think. They could still be looking for one person, or they could be looking for an accomplice as well, just not Dion's accomplice. Either way, they were looking for the person who had engineered three deaths.

Before he started any searches, he mentally ran through what they knew.

Whoever it was needed to be able to get to level six of the library. That was just Erasmus, himself, Dion, and Nick...as far as official permissions went. But Erasmus was clearly innocent. Dion had been cleared by Death himself, and he sure as hell hadn't killed the man. It would be easy to point the finger at Nick, but Lucas's gut leaned against it being the head of the venatores. Not just because he liked the guy, but he wasn't sure Nick had the skills to do everything that had been done. Not to mention it would be difficult to hide something like that from his wife. No one pulled anything over on Carla, and she was loyal almost to a fault. She never would have stood for anyone murdering Erasmus.

The person they were looking for also needed to be able to find and combine the ingredients to create the Achlys poison that had been used, steal the bodies of Dion and Agatha, create an illusion of fire, and do all of that while simultaneously blocking the *gods* from being able to see what was going on. That was honestly the most scary part of it. The patrons weren't just gods, they weren't even just powerful gods, they were gods who were intimately tied to the Athenaeum. Each one of them had put some of their power into the very stone of the place, which meant whatever was blocking them had to be extremely powerful. Was the murderer in league with another god? If so, why? Which god? Whoever could hide something like this from two goddesses of magic and two gods of knowledge was not someone Lucas wanted to be going up against. He hated that he already was.

Shaking his head, Lucas began his search. It didn't take long for him to find three people who were documented as having skills that might allow them to bypass the Athenaeum's digital security. Peter was obvious, since he was the one who had set up the tech side. Penny was another, as she had tried for Peter's position before he'd been chosen for that role. Then there was Jericho. The last one surprised him, as he couldn't recall ever seeing Jericho with a computer, but that didn't mean anything. The man was also a hothead who didn't approve of Sophia as aspida. Except all this had started before she'd ever stepped foot in the Athenaeum. And Penny was personable, but that didn't necessarily mean she was innocent, either. Peter, however, was the one he was most suspicious of. If Dion hadn't used magic the day he died, then it was either Peter or someone who had been invisible. Not that he could rule out invisibility. Sorcery was a very potent and versatile tool and the Athenaeum was full of spells. Most weren't even hidden away from general members. Some were, but invisibility was a useful tool for the venatores, so it wasn't. Right now he wished it had been, even if it was a spell that he actually knew as well. Gargoyles weren't exactly subtle, and not all jobs favored strength over discretion.

Two of the three suspects also knew Old Persian, which was what the antidote to Achlys had been written in. It didn't necessarily mean anything, but it was another weight tipping the scale toward guilt.

There might be others, people who didn't have the necessary skills listed in their file, but he had three names to start with. Clearing the search and closing the program, he left his office and made his way down the stairs through the levels of the library. He stopped in front of the security panel for level six when he heard the distinct sound of a foot over stone. Now, people being on this level wasn't rare, but to be so close to the door for the next level and trying to be sneaky about it? That was suspicious.

His skin turned to stone and his muscles expanded, though he kept the wings hidden. The rows between the shelves weren't exactly ideal for a large set of wings, especially if he wanted to move quickly. As he started toward the sound, he cast a spell to sense magic and nearly stumbled mid-step. Someone had just cast a powerful spell, but it didn't feel like anything he was familiar with. He did know it had been cast in the last few seconds, though.

Rushing around the shelves, he sought even a glimpse of who might be down here with him, but despite searching for a solid ten minutes, he didn't see any sign of another person, nor did he hear any other noises. Frowning and letting his skin transform back to human, he stalked toward the nearest computer. Pulling up the security log, he saw no one but he and Sophia had logged into level six in the last few days and there were no failed attempts. Though if they'd gotten down there once, they might have perfected their methods months ago. Or when they hid the book containing Achlys and set up the cursed book for Sophia to find.

He still wasn't sure how they'd managed that, as Dion had been alone with Sophia when she had touched it. Probably. Or a compulsion might have been used to encourage Sophia toward that particular book.

Acting on a hunch, he looked up all failed attempts for any levels below him. There was one a few days after Sophia had arrived, but he'd noted that weeks ago—and had confirmed with her that it had, in fact, been her giving it a shot. Prior to that, he found an attempt three months ago, but it was followed just a minute later by a successful entry by Dion. Mistypes happened, but it could have been someone using Dion's PIN, or maybe even his palm print somehow. Two weeks before that was another, with one last attempt a week before that.

Oddly, all the incorrect credentials were for level six. He couldn't find a single instance of someone trying and failing to get into level seven. Since that was the level fondly referred to as the Vault, and accessible only by the aspida, wouldn't it make sense for whoever was doing this to try to get down there? As dangerous and powerful as some of the books on level six were, they had to pale next to the ones in the Vault. Not that he knew for certain. Unless Sophia had been down there, he wasn't sure anyone alive had stepped foot on that level. Then again, level six could have been a test to get into the Vault.

Maybe Lucas should encourage her to check it out. He'd feel better if he went with her, but he'd even be okay if she went alone and he stayed by the door to ensure no one tried to ambush her in a place where she should be safe. But if he truly wanted her—and the rest of the Athenaeum—to be safe, then he needed to figure out who amongst them was a killer.

Once again clearing his search, he went back to his office, this time to focus on the sorcery section of the personnel files.

He was still there two hours later when his door opened. Head snapping up, he relaxed minutely when he saw Sergei shutting the door behind him. "Hey. Glad you're—" He broke off when Sergei held up a hand, then spoke several hissing syllables. "Okay...what was that?"

The healer smiled. "Do you remember how Sophia let me stay on level six to research?"

"Yeah?"

"I didn't find anything that directly helps us, but I did find a useful spell. I call it a bubble spell, because while we're inside it, they shouldn't be able to see, hear, or otherwise sense anything we do. Unless they're more powerful than I am, in any case."

Since Sergei was the only demigod in the Athenaeum, there were few—if any—who could match him in pure power. Which meant they could finally speak securely. "Nice one."

"What about you? Did you find anything?" Sergei asked, sitting in front of the desk.

"Actually, yes." He told Sergei about Death summoning Dion, and the research Lucas had done that day.

Sergei slumped down in the chair. "I can't say I'm not relieved to find out that I didn't misjudge Dion so badly, but it's concerning that we're back to square one. And that his son is on the short list of suspects."

"Not necessarily." Lucas nodded at the monitor. "I can't say that one of these three is one hundred percent our guy, but it's definitely a place to start. I'm also wondering if what had happened to Lachlan is related. Have you been able to identify the cause of his behavior yet?"

Sergei sighed and shook his head. "There's definitely a trace of something foreign in his system, and it's definitely magical in nature, but I have no idea what it is, how it got into him, or how to remove it. I've tried dozens of things—including mithridate—and nothing is doing anything to this...whatever it is. I will say the effect doesn't seem to be fading, and he doesn't seem to be metabolizing the substance."

"Is there anything else that doesn't metabolize?"

"Yes and no?" Sergei said after tilting his head side to side for a moment. "Generally, if the levels of something remain steady, it's because it's still being ingested in some way. Since either Heather or I is always in the room with him, there shouldn't be any way for anyone to be slipping him something."

"Shit. So he's still sedated?"

"He has to be. If he's awake, he tries to attack one of us. I could survive—probably—but I don't know how well Heather would fare. She's a strong healer, but I don't recall her ever being good in a fight."

The door opened again and both men looked over. Sophia glanced around, didn't seem to see them, and sighed, grabbing her phone from her back pocket.

"I think that's proof your spell works," Lucas said. "How do we get her in the bubble?"

Chuckling, Sergei rose and crossed to Sophia, even as she started to tap on the phone. Grabbing her arm gently, he drew her into the room. She let out a squeak of surprise and her eyes went wide as she looked from one man to the other. "How'd you do that? Where were you two?"

Lucas laughed as she dropped into the chair. "Right here. Sergei found a spell. Keeps us hidden while we talk."

"Really?" she asked, twisting to look at the demigod. "That's cool! And very handy. Does that mean one of you found something?"

"Unfortunately not," Sergei told her. "No change on Lachlan and no idea what's wrong with him."

"And I've narrowed down potential suspects to Peter, Penny, and Jericho, but there could be others," Lucas added.

"Oh," she said, deflating. "Well, I don't have anything on that front either, but I did want to ask what you two thought of Olivia."

Lucas shrugged. "She's okay. Good at her job, smart. Steven loves her because she's as good at training as he is."

"Strong, too," Sergei added. "Why do you ask?"

"Because I liked her, a lot. And from her file and the sense I got from her, I have to agree about her being good at her job. I'm thinking that she might make a good head curator. Since I'm still getting to know people, I wanted some other opinions, especially since she's a guard some of the time. But I haven't found anyone else who has struck me as capable of doing Dion's old job."

Lucas hadn't considered that, but from what he knew of Olivia, he thought Sophia might be onto something. The woman had a fantastic memory and seemed to know a little bit about a lot of things. "I think she'd be good at it."

"As do I," Sergei decided after a minute. "I was impressed by her after the poisoning incident."

Sophia smiled. "Good. Then that's at least one problem crossed off my list. Onto another—though it's not really a problem—how's my mom doing? I know she officially started working in the clinic yesterday."

Sergei smiled. "She did, and she's doing fantastic. She's a very knowledgeable healer. Maybe not the best I've met, but I've met hundreds over the years. We're planning on starting the first healing and medicine classes next week and she's going to be running them."

"She is? Not you?"

"Not me," he agreed. "I've helped a few people learn magical healing, but she has actually learned medicine in a classroom setting. While we'll be teaching a few sorcery spells, most of it will be mundane first aid, at least to begin with. I think she'll be fine."

"I'm sure she's excited about that."

"She seems to be, yes."

"Good. I know she missed this place, and she was a little worried about helping you since you're the son of Apollo and she's an elf, but it sounds like she's found her spot."

"While I'm happy about your mom," Lucas interrupted, "I think there's another avenue you should try in the next couple of days."

"What do you mean?" she asked, focusing on him again.

"Have you been down to the Vault yet?"

The only reason he noticed her cheeks going a little paler was because he was watching her so carefully. "No, I haven't," she admitted. "With all the trouble we've had with level six, I've kind of been avoiding it. It's probably awesome, but..." She could only shrug instead of finishing the thought.

"I think you should go. It's the one place we haven't looked, and you're the only person in this entire library who can. And," he continued when she started to protest, "if you're that worried, I can go with you or stay just outside the door and make sure no one tries to get to you."

She looked down, picking at the hem of her jeans while she thought. He didn't say anything, not wanting to rush her into a decision. He could understand her reticence. The first time she'd gone to level six she'd nearly died, and the Vault was said to have even more powerful books and relics.

"You're right," she said, looking up. "And I would feel better if you guarded the door. At least there shouldn't have been anyone in there messing with things like they did on six."

He wasn't so sure about that, but he just nodded. "Let me know, and I'll clear my schedule to make it happen."

"Thank you."

They talked for another hour, rehashing the same thing from different angles, but by the time they headed to dinner, they hadn't come up with anything new. If they didn't find anything in the Vault, they really would be back to square one, just like Sergei feared.

Chapter 9

Dinner was the single meal that almost everyone in the Athenaeum shared. Breakfast was mostly buffet style, with people wandering in and out as they woke, and they basically fended for themselves when it came to lunch. But dinner reminded Sophia of how American Thanksgiving was always portrayed in movies. A lot of food, a lot of people, and a lot of conversation. It would have been wonderful if she wasn't busy surreptitiously studying Lucas's three suspects.

Jericho she could easily believe. He'd been an ass since before they'd officially met. Penny was harder to wrap her mind around, as the woman was always friendly and had been extremely helpful. But Peter? He was the one she just couldn't comprehend. In all likelihood Jericho was their killer, they just needed to find proof. Somehow.

Sophia forced herself to eat, though her appetite lately had been almost nonexistent. Still, her body needed the fuel to keep up with Lucas's training regimen. She also participated in the conversations around her, though she couldn't really remember what had been said on either end, not until Josie—one of the guards as well as Sophia's friend—leaned forward and called her name.

"Yeah?"

"You work too hard. Movie and popcorn after dinner? You, me, Peter, and whoever else wants to watch hot superheroes without their shirts on?"

It was tempting, but Sophia was about to say no, that she had too much to do, when Lucas whispered, "You should go. She's right. You do work too hard. You deserve some fun."

"I thought that was what we did last night," she whispered back to him. "And again this morning."

His deep chuckle made her fight off a shiver of desire. "It was, but you deserve to hang out with your friends, too. I'll be waiting in your room when you're done."

Spending some time relaxing, then finishing it off with some world-class sex? It was definitely tempting. Responsibilities tugged at the back of her mind, but she pushed them away and smiled at Josie. "Sounds good, but I pick the movie."

Josie thought about that for a moment before she nodded. "Fair enough. You've got good taste. Normally. Still not sure what your deal is with disaster movies, though."

"Hey, I like them! And are you saying superheroes causing destruction to save the world isn't a disaster?"

Josie wrinkled her nose. "Fair point."

With two things to look forward to, Sophia was actually to eat with a little more enthusiasm. It didn't hurt that Lucas's hand settled high on her leg beneath the table. But though she enjoyed the contact, the last thing she wanted was to be wound up while watching a movie with her cousin and friend.

Soon enough, dinner was over. Some started clearing away the food, while Sophia was half-dragged out of her chair and to the common room, with Josie on one side and Peter on the other. Not that she put up much of a fight. It had been a while since she'd just relaxed—other than those times with Lucas.

Josie playfully pushed Sophia onto the couch. "You pick a movie, I'm grabbing popcorn and drinks."

"Popcorn? But we just ate," Sophia argued.

"Yes, but you can't watch a movie without popcorn," Josie huffed.

Hard to argue with logic like that, so Sophia just grinned at her retreating back.

"She's right, you know," Peter told her as he settled on her other side. "You do work too hard," he said, bumping her shoulder with his.

"Not like I have a choice," she pointed out as she scrolled through the available options. "I'm sure aspida isn't always an all-consuming job, but since it's not only a new job for me, but I'm also learning about the Athenaeum and the people in it, it pretty much takes up my entire brain."

"Valid points," he agreed easily, "but if you don't take time for yourself, you're going to burn out. Can't say I've seen it with an aspida since I've only been around for two, but I've seen it with other people. And isn't there a saying in English about all work and no play?"

"Makes Jack a dull boy, yeah. And I'll work on it," she promised. "I don't mind the research and spending time with the books and relics, but the rest can be exhausting."

"So take the time. Hang out with Josie and me sometimes, even if it's just playing a movie. Go on another picnic. Go flying. Go see some more sights. Nothing says you have to be chained to the Athenaeum."

Sophia really did want all those things, but she was still a little anxious about the idea of leaving the Athenaeum after being shot at when they were at Delphi. Part of her brain reminded her that Peter had known where they were going that day, but it hadn't been a secret, not really. Jericho could have easily heard about it, too. To avoid thinking about it, she changed the subject. "So, is there anything going on between you and Josie? Seems like if you're not hiding in the computer room, you're with her."

To her delight, he blushed a little and shrugged. "I don't know. Maybe? We haven't really talked about it."

"Maybe you should," she teased as she decided not on a superhero movie, but one that had been a favorite since she was a kid; Indiana Jones. Who didn't like watching him kick ass and save not just relics, but the world? In fact, she was pretty sure she'd been wearing an Indiana Jones shirt when she first arrived at the Athenaeum. Fitting, really.

"Maybe," he mumbled, carefully straightening his bright blue mohawk. It was, she'd noticed, one of his nervous gestures, along with toying with one of the several piercings on his face. She'd never understood the desire for lip or eyebrow piercings, but they worked for him, along with the sleeve tattoos. And yet, despite his punk appearance, she'd always thought of him as a puppy dog. Sweet, friendly, and happy to help. That was why she couldn't believe he was the culprit they were looking for.

Josie returned with a huge bowl of popcorn, several bottles of water, and a Coke, which she knew was Sophia's favorite drink aside from coffee. The popcorn and Coke got passed to Sophia, one of the waters to Peter, then she plopped down beside Sophia. "Indiana Jones, huh? You know you're supposed to be taking a break from work, right?"

she asked, plucking a piece of popcorn from the bowl and tossing it at Sophia's head.

"I like it! Even before it was work," Sophia protested. "Besides, you agreed I could pick."

"Fine," Josie said, drawing the word out, though she followed it with a grin. "But we're doing this more often."

"I just promised Peter I would. Not just movies either."

"You didn't actually promise," Peter corrected, "but I'll take that as a promise, so it still works."

Sophia rolled her eyes, but couldn't prevent the smile. "Can we watch the movie now?"

"Sure." Josie curled her legs beneath her and grabbed a handful of popcorn. Peter was more polite with it, but he too got comfortable.

The next two hours were some of the most relaxing she'd had since Erasmus's death, and she decided that no one who could care so much about her mental health could possibly be responsible. But starting tomorrow, she'd begin coming up with a way to prove Jericho's guilt. Because she knew these two were right. She couldn't keep working like she was. Except burning out wasn't her biggest fear. Dying and letting Erasmus's killer go free was.

Lucas had fallen asleep twenty minutes ago, but Sophia's mind wouldn't stop working. She slipped out of bed and got dressed, surprised he never woke when she snuck out in the middle of the night. It wasn't something she had started off doing that often, but in the last two weeks, she'd done it more nights than she didn't. Casting both her shield and threat spells, she quietly left her room, doing what she could to remain unnoticed as she went down a level. It might not be smart to secretly visit the hidden room she'd discovered a few days after Erasmus's death and her subsequent promotion to aspida, but it was full of so much knowledge she couldn't resist. And she kept hoping she'd find something that might help her with the current situation. Or make being aspida easier.

Walking down the hallway she thought of as the Hall of Death, where the urns of past aspides rested, she went straight for the last one, waiting until the wall shifted to admit her into the room beyond. It closed after her, but it no longer scared her to be locked in this room full of books and jars of spell ingredients. Three of the four walls contained shelves of those two things, and the single desk currently held three of those books. One was a grimoire—a book of spells the previous aspides had deemed too dangerous to be kept anywhere but in here—the second was a journal written by her predecessors, and the last was a book on the Athenaeum itself written by those same predecessors.

For the most part, she'd been focusing on the grimoire, trying to find something that could help her find the murderer—and memorizing what she thought might be the most important spell in the book; a failsafe that would destroy the Athenaeum should the worst happen. Since it wasn't something she could practice, she read through it several times whenever she was in this room. It was ingrained in her brain, but she couldn't risk misremembering if she ever needed to use it. She hoped to all the gods that she never needed to use it, because the simple thought made her sick to her stomach.

Tonight, however, she opted for the journal. Since she hadn't asked Death to let her talk to her grandfather, this was the closest she could get to getting advice from the aspides who had come before her. She'd flipped through it before, but had never really read it. It probably meant she was slacking in her duties, but she doubted the previous aspides had dealt with a situation like hers. Only a few pages in, she forgot all about her shortcomings and the danger surrounding her, caught up in the story of how the Athenaeum had come to be. Sophia had been told that the Athenaeum had been born as the Library of Alexandria had died, but little more than that. This book held the missing information.

Eugenios, a human and the first aspida, had been in Alexandria when the library had been in the process of being destroyed. As a lover of knowledge and seeker of anything magical, he'd risked himself by going into the building and saving as much as he could. Scrolls had been his priority, but he'd also managed to save multiple relics, though at the time he'd thought they were nothing more than important or expensive mundane artifacts. Afterwards, with the way things had been in the city, he'd secreted them back to his homeland of Greece. He'd come to Mount Parnassus, discreetly guided by the gods to choose a cave halfway up the mountain. He'd hidden the scrolls and relics, then began to carve a home out of the rock. Over time, others had been led to him, and a few he'd recruited to help. He'd even been approached by the first of the divine patrons, Athena. She had admired what he'd done and what he was trying to do, and offered to help.

Within a decade, the natural cave had become a huge room full of things he and his associates had saved, one patron had become three, and almost a dozen people called the Athenaeum home. They had agreed to keep what they were doing secret, knowing that not everyone would agree with their chosen purpose. Many would try to use what they'd saved for ill, as they'd done throughout history.

Then the patrons had offered him an opportunity many would have killed for; the chance to be immortal. He'd actually refused, though, saying that it was better if the Athenaeum was headed by new blood now and again. That otherwise they would stagnate, that the excitement and drive of the Nasaru would fade. Nasaru, she learned, was the name for the people of the Athenaeum as a whole. It had come to mean the guards specifically later on.

Over the next few centuries, protections were placed on the Athenaeum, by its members as well as its patrons. And while aspides were chosen at first by popular vote, that hadn't worked well. They quickly discovered that popular didn't always mean most qualified, and more than once, they'd had to remove someone from power and replace them. Instead, with the help of the patrons, the current system of the Athenaeum and patrons choosing had been put into place.

Important, since as the years passed, the Athenaeum became bigger and more people gravitated to it. A bad aspida leading thirty people could be much more dangerous than one who led a dozen.

By the third century, five of the patrons had imbued their magic into the Athenaeum, and at times the number of people working in and for the Athenaeum had swelled to over a hundred. It had changed from a small, natural cave into something resembling what it was now; a mini city full of wonder.

A quick glance at her phone showed her that she'd been there for more than two hours. She needed to get back. Not only was her mind mush, she didn't want Lucas to wake and find her gone. He'd worry, and he tended to get cranky when he worried. She'd learned that early on, when she'd touched the cursed book and gotten yelled at. He'd been forgiven, but she didn't want a repeat.

Marking her place, she closed the journal and left, being just as cautious returning to her room as she'd been sneaking down there. It was a little disappointing that she hadn't found anything immediately useful, but she was happy she'd learned exactly how the Athenaeum had started. And something in that journal might give her insight into why Erasmus had been killed. It no longer made sense that he'd been killed for his job, not with the way the selection process worked, so it either had to be something personal or for something the aspida had access to. She was leaning toward the latter, because why else had Agatha, Thomas, and Dion died?

Quietly, she opened her door and stepped inside. After changing back into a tee-shirt and sleep shorts, she slipped back into bed, but the moment she did, Lucas rolled over to face her, his eyes open and alert. Busted.

"Where were you?"

Sophia hesitated. She didn't want to lie to him, but everything she'd found said that the room was meant to remain known only to aspides. As much as she trusted him, she couldn't bring herself to break what felt like a sacred trust. "I can't tell you," she said miserably. "It's an aspida thing."

He searched her face in the dim light. When he'd woken and discovered her missing, he'd been worried, of course. How could he not be? Before he'd been able to get out of bed to text her or go searching, she'd come back. And while his concern was strong enough that he wanted to press, he could see the true regret on her features, hear it in her voice. He might be a guard, but everyone in the Athenaeum was innately curious, and this was no different. Still, he had to trust her. They might not have defined their relationship, but it was a relationship, and she was smart and capable—not to mention his boss. And he did believe that if she could tell him, she would.

Reaching out, he trailed the back of a finger along her cheek and nodded. "Fair enough," he told her. "But you don't need to wait until I'm asleep and sneak out to go wherever you go. Just tell me and go. That way, I don't have to worry that something's happened to you."

Her whole body relaxed, and she nodded. "I will."

"But make sure you're safe, okay? We can't lose you." *He* couldn't lose her.

"I will. I cast the threat and shield spell every time," she promised.

"Good." He drew her closer, and she automatically rested her head on his shoulder and curled an arm around his waist. His arm slid around her, holding her to his side. Kissing her temple, he murmured, "Now sleep. We can worry about the rest tomorrow."

Chapter 10

LUCAS WASN'T SURE WHAT he'd dreamed of, but he woke frowning, with something tickling at the back of his mind. The frown shouldn't have been possible, not with Sophia still in his arms, warm and soft against him. On a normal morning, he would have woken her, but not this morning. Now he just wanted to chase the thought that was eluding him.

Carefully pulling his arm from beneath Sophia, he climbed out of bed and went into the bathroom. By the time he was done, he was more frustrated than he'd been when he walked in, and Sophia was just stirring.

Yawning, she rolled onto her back and stretched. A stirring of desire pushed against his thoughts, but then her eyes opened and she smiled at him.

"Morning," he said, crossing to the bed so he could bend and give her a kiss.

"Morning," she murmured sleepily. "Ever have a dream that feels like it's important, but you can't figure out what's so important about it?" she asked as she sat up and ran a hand through her hair, yawning again.

He frowned again and sat on the edge of the bed. "Yeah, though now I'm...intrigued. I'm not sure what I dreamed, but it's got something stuck in my head. Just don't know what the fuck it is. What was your dream about?"

She cocked her head and looked confused. "What, like when you've got a word on the tip of your tongue?"

"Basically, yeah. So distract me so I can get it out. What was your dream about? Maybe I can help you figure out what was so important about it."

"Before coffee?" she complained, but she did so while smiling.

"Before coffee," he agreed. "You know dreams fade."

"True." She twisted on the bed so she could lean against him, her head on his shoulder, an arm going around him. Content to hold her, his arm went around her as well, and he kissed the top of her head. "It was weird. Kind of chaotic, which is why it feels weird that it's important. Like, you know sometimes on TV shows or movies when they're moving the camera all around and it's hard to focus on any one thing? Up is down and you're spinning and all you get from it is a sense of chaos?"

"I do," he agreed.

"It was like that. And I got the sense that I was in the past. The clothes, you know? Couldn't really see more than glimpses, but I didn't spend all those years in school and not learn something. They looked like they came from ancient Greece. I think."

She stopped, so he said, "Go on."

"I think I was in the middle of some war, but couldn't tell you which one. There were a lot of wars and battles back then. But there was definitely fighting. Swords and armor."

"Okay." He thought for a moment, but nothing came to him. The sense of something poking at his mind grew, though. "Ancient Greece isn't my area of expertise, so you're going to have to help me here. What were some big battles or wars back then?"

She blew out a breath. "Not asking for a lot, are you? Well, there was the Peloponnesian War, the Battle of Thermopylae, Marathon, of course, the Trojan War—"

His arm tightened around her as he realized what had been nudging at his subconscious since he woke. "The Trojan War, that's it," he breathed.

"That's it? That's what?" she asked, confused.

"The Trojan War. Or a book about the Trojan War."

Some of her confusion faded. "The book that nearly killed me?"

He rubbed his hand over her arm as she nodded. "I think we need to go check it out. Carefully," he added when she tensed.

"Can't say I have any interest in seeing that book again, but...why?"

"I'm not sure," he admitted. "It's been circling in my head for a couple of days now. I think it has something to do with what Seth said about the block preventing the patrons from seeing what was going on in here."

She stiffened. "How could the book have anything to do with it?"

"I don't know, and I could be wrong, but it feels like it's important. Maybe it doesn't have anything to do with the block, but there's got to be a reason why someone put that book where you'd find and touch it."

She didn't say anything for a long minute, then she nodded. "Let's grab coffee on the way down," she said as she pulled away and went into the bathroom.

After they'd both changed, they stopped by the kitchen for the coffee, and she gulped down her first cup then refilled it. She was kind of cute with her coffee addiction. Not that she really seemed to need it to think clearly.

When they had descended the first level of stairs, they left everyone else behind. The Nasaru might be a dedicated group, but they also weren't really morning people. Very few people started work before breakfast had been served. They said nothing as they went down to the sixth level of the library and Sophia opened the door to allow them access, then turned left to the library side of the level.

Though Lucas had been on this level dozens of times, and despite being a guard rather than one of the curators, he loved this place. Since it was reserved for dangerous texts, it was less crowded that the upper levels of the library. There were floor to ceiling shelves spaced out, each one holding multiple books, scrolls, tablets, and boxes—the ones which spelled books were placed inside to protect the Nasaru from their magic.

Sophia started to head for where the book had been moved, but he caught her arm. "Let's start at the beginning," he suggested. "Just so we can make sure we don't miss anything."

Nodding, she changed direction, moving to a different shelf. She placed a hand on an empty spot about eye level. "I was standing near here when Dion told me I could check out one of the books. The one on the Trojan War was here."

"And it wasn't in a box, right? Just on the shelf like the other books?"

She nodded. "Right. I touched it, and as soon as I did, it...attacked me. I've never felt pain like that, and it was basically instantaneous."

There was a pause as she stared at the shelf, her fingers moving lightly over it. "Dion saved me," she murmured.

"He did," Lucas agreed. "I know we were suspecting him, but knowing what we do now, I think we can safely say he didn't just call for help in time. He probably broke your contact with the book."

"Yeah." She dropped her hand, and he wished he could wipe the sad look off her face. Since he couldn't, he just took her into his arms to provide what comfort he could. "I'm okay," she said softly, though she clung to him for a full minute. "Anyway. When I came down here after Sergei healed me, the book had been moved."

He reluctantly released her, and she went to another section of the library and pointed at one of the protective boxes. She kept her distance from it, but he didn't blame her. He wouldn't want to get too close to something that had almost killed him. He opened the box and verified the book on the Trojan War was still inside, then stepped back. "I wish one of us was a witch."

"Why's that?"

"Because they could examine the magic on the book better than either of us could. I can tell if there's magic or not, but not what the magic was."

"Could Sergei? I mean, I know his main power is healing, but he's a demigod. He's got to have more than just healing. Especially since his dad is Apollo. Not like the guy is the god of just one thing. He's...what, the god of the sun, music, archery, plagues, and a dozen other things, right?"

"He is, and he might," Lucas agreed, pulling out his phone. It only took a moment to send Sergei a text. "He's definitely our best bet, since we don't want to bring any of the witches in on this."

"We don't," she agreed, nodding slowly. "I know we think it's either Penny, Jericho, or Peter, but we could be wrong, and I'd hate to tell the wrong person and give the killer a heads up."

"No, I agree," he said, nodding. His phone vibrated and he glanced at the screen. "He'll be down in a few minutes."

"While we wait, why don't you tell me why you think this book is so important? Why it and not the illusion of fire or poison or any of the other things this person has done?"

"Don't get me wrong, the poison is important," Lucas assured her, and she looked so worried that he stepped closer and drew her into his arms. She came to him easily, her arms going around his waist, her head resting against his chest. "Everything this guy—or girl—has done is. But the poison? I don't know that we can track it. If we encounter it again, we can give the antidote, but as of right this second, we can't do anything about it. The illusion and locking you in the closet? Also can't track it. And we've done what we could to find out who hired the sniper, but since they used your account..." He shrugged without releasing her. "That still just narrows it down to our three suspects, as it would have taken hacking—or Valerie's direct access."

"And the book?"

"I know I said the book had killed before, but I honestly don't know much about that book. I'm a guard, not a curator. And sure, I like books, but I don't handle them like the others do. But it wouldn't be on this level if it wasn't dangerous. That said, we need to find out if the pain you experienced was from the known danger, or a separate spell placed on it. I'll be honest, I'm hoping it's a separate spell, because then we have something to track, and something powerful. And knowing if it was just intended to hurt you or do something else might give us an idea of what this bastard wants. What he hopes to gain from all this bullshit."

"I never thought I'd be hoping someone was trying to kill me," Sophia said dryly.

Lucas smiled, but his phone buzzed before he could answer. "Sergei's here." He kissed her before pulling away and going to the door to admit the healer.

"Is everyone okay?" he asked, looking Sophia over, then Lucas.

"We're okay," Sophia assured him. "Lucas had a thought about the book that nearly killed me, and we were hoping you could help."

His thick brows furrowed. "Of course I'll do what I can, but what do you need me to do?"

"We're not witches, and I don't know the sorcery I'm sure Erasmus did that could help him identify spells and curses and stuff, but we need to know what exactly the book did to me. Or what it was supposed to have done."

"Ah." He nodded, glancing at the box beside Sophia. "I can certainly do my best. I'm not as skilled as some, but I should at least be able to give you an idea of what the spell was meant to do. And even without seeing the book, I can tell you that it drained you, rapidly and forcibly. That's what caused the pain. I estimate if you'd been allowed to remain in contact with it for just another fifteen or twenty seconds that you never would have made it to me alive."

Sophia paled, and Lucas guessed she hadn't realized just how close to death she'd come. Yes, she talked about nearly dying, but knowing it and *knowing* it weren't the same thing. Before he knew what he was doing, he was walking over to her and taking her hand, giving it a squeeze. Comforting wasn't really his thing—the tough love he'd shown her when she'd first arrived was more his speed—but he hated that she was dealing with so much instead of enjoying learning about the Athenaeum

"I'm really glad Dion got me away from it, then."

"We all are," Sergei assured her. "Now, is the book in there?" he asked, pointing to the box.

"It is," Lucas answered when Sophia remained quiet.

Sergei nodded and pulled the box down, moving it to a lower shelf. He studied the writing on the outside of the box, turning it in a full circle to see them all, then frowned. "Lucas, your thoughts might be right."

"What does it say?" It wasn't a language he knew, and he hadn't had time to translate it.

"Well, it does verify that a book on the Trojan War should be in here, so that part is accurate, but according to this, touching the book shouldn't have caused any harm."

"What? Why? What makes it dangerous, then?" Sophia asked. "It was put in a box on this level for a reason, right?"

"Reading the book is the trigger. You would have to open it and actually read the words. If this level wasn't restricted to you and the faction heads, and if Lachlan didn't have a foreign magical substance in his body, I'd think that he read this book."

"It causes violent behavior?" Sophia asked.

"Warlike behavior, yes," Sergei confirmed. "So whatever caused it to hurt you just by touching it is something that was added after the book was placed in this box."

Lucas was expecting that, but it still pissed him off. "Shit. Hopefully, we can trace the additional spell."

Sergei grimaced. "Hopefully I can identify it."

"Just be careful," Sophia warned.

"I will." Drawing in a deep breath, Sergei lifted a hand and let it hover over the book, clearly being careful not to actually touch the cover. Like when he healed, his hand glowed faintly. After a few seconds, his fingers started to twitch a little and his brows lowered in concentration.

It took several minutes before he drew his hand back and frowned at the book. No, not just a frown. He looked deeply disturbed, which had Lucas fighting not to let his skin turned to stone. "What is it?"

"The spell was placed on the book long before you touched it, Sophia. Centuries ago, if my guess is correct," he said as he walked quickly away from the book and to the only computer on this level. He opened the lid only to stop and look back at Lucas and Sophia, who had followed him. "Can one of you look the book up? Since it's on this level, I don't have access."

Sophia stepped forward and pulled up the correct program, doing the search. "What are you looking for?"

Instead of answering, Sergei gently pushed her out of the way and scowled at the screen before he nodded. "Like I said, it had to have been put there centuries ago. According to this, the book was brought into the Athenaeum in 906. The spell isn't that old, so someone did the spell after it we brought it here. I also don't see any notes about the spell, so either no one triggered it before you, or someone stupidly forgot to notate it."

He sounded angrier than Lucas had ever heard him, but he understood. That book was like a time bomb, and Sophia had set it off. "Do you know what the spell was?"

"To an extent. Like I said before, it drained her," he began, turning to Sophia. "But now I can tell you that it focused on your magical essence. Your life force was pulled with it, but that's what it targeted So yes, if you'd touched it for a little longer, it would have killed you. And the entirety of your magical self would have been held within the book."

"So it's a death spell?" Sophia asked.

Sergei shook his head as he began to pace. "No, the death is a side-effect. Probably an intended side-effect, but I think collecting the essence was the point."

She frowned. "But why? What can someone do with my essence? Or anyone's?"

"I don't know who the spell was originally intended for, but if someone took your essence, it could be very, very bad."

"That's a major fucking understatement," Lucas muttered. "Remember how you're connected to the Athenaeum? Magically connected?"

"I need to sit down," Sophia said, voice shaky as she sank down to the stone floor. "They could have taken control of the Athenaeum?"

"I'm not entirely sure they don't have some measure of control now." And he wanted to kick his own ass. He was head of the nasaru. He was supposed to prevent shit like this from happening. "You said it would have held her essence within the book. Could you tell if it was still there?"

"I could. It wasn't."

"So the person who killed Erasmus, who has done all this other bullshit, has part of my magic and can use it to influence the Athenaeum?" Sophia asked, sounding like a kid who'd just been told the monster under the bed was real. It didn't stop her from acting like the aspida she was becoming, though. "What exactly can they do with my essence?"

"I honestly don't know," Lucas answered, crouching in front of her. "The fact that they didn't get it all is good. It may be that they have to have it all to do anything. And we're looking for him. We know he's out there, so we've got the advantage there."

Sophia nodded slightly, and though she was pale, her expression hardened. "You said it's possible someone touched the book before, right? It just wasn't recorded?"

"Anything is. A lot can get lost in a thousand years," Sergei answered.

"So, is it possible that they've gotten the essence of another aspida, and that's the source of the block? The one keeping the gods from seeing in?"

That was something he hadn't considered, and a glance at Sergei said he hadn't either. "I...don't know. I mean, I guess it's not outside the realm of possibility. Though I'm not sure any aspida has the power to block the patrons, since their magic is in the Athenaeum, too."

"Yeah, but if the patrons give the aspida control over the Athenaeum, wouldn't that mean over the entire Athenaeum, including the magic of and within it?"

"The fact that you have a point terrifies me," Sergei admitted.

"Same here," Lucas admitted as he straightened. "Mostly because, if that's true, I'm not sure how we could undo it."

"Maybe we can't," Sophia said as she pushed herself to her feet, "but Seth and the other patrons might."

"It's certainly worth a shot."

Sophia nodded and pulled out her phone. "At this rate, he's going to get sick of hearing from me. Not really in my plans to piss off a god," she said with a touch of a smile.

Sergei shook his head. "You're working to resolve a problem that is as much his as yours. He might get frustrated, but not at you."

The faint rumble in the air and in Lucas's bones alerted him to Seth's appearance even before he saw the god. "You know what the block is?" he said without bothering with pleasantries.

"No," Sophia corrected, looking calm despite her concerns. "We *might* know what the block is, but I think we need you to verify it."

Seth's brows drew together. "What do you mean?"

"You want the long version or short version?"

"Let's start with the short and you can fill in details after if I need them."

"There's a book that took some of my essence about a month ago, and we think it might have done the same to another aspida in the past. Would it be possible for someone to use that to manipulate the magic of the Athenaeum and use that to block you and the other patrons?"

Sophia looked like she was both anticipating and fearing his answer, so Lucas stepped closer and rested his hand on her back. He wanted to hold her, but didn't want to derail her confidence.

Seth, on the other hand, looked like he was fighting back fury. Lucas felt it regardless, but doubted the others did. Most days he loved being a gargoyle, but it definitely had its downsides when Seth was around.

"I'll admit, shit like this isn't my area of expertise, but based on what I know? I won't say it's impossible. If they had taken the essence of a former aspida, and use it to tap into the magic when that person was still aspida, *and* if they were strong enough and skilled enough, then yes, I do think it's possible."

"If that is how they did it, would you be able to detect it? Or counter it?" Lucas asked.

"Me?" Seth shook his head. "Not a chance. But give me a second."

"Isis or Hecate?" Sergei asked.

Seth actually smiled. "You'll get to see your cousin."

"Cousin?" Lucas asked.

"Oh my gods. Is she actually the daughter of Asteria?" Sophia asked.

Lucas arched a brow. "Remember the guard? The one who doesn't know the family trees of every pantheon of gods, past or present? Little lost here."

"She is," Sergei told Sophia before looking at Lucas. "Hecate's mother is Asteria, who is sister to Leto. Leto is my grandmother. So that makes Hecate my cousin."

"Indeed I am. And it's good to see you again, cousin," Hecate said on the heels of Sergei's words, smiling at the man and giving him a warm hug.

Lucas had never met the goddess before, though he recognized her instantly thanks to the statues and the glimpses he'd gotten over the years. She was tall and bordering on skinny, but ethereally beautiful, with long, straight black hair, skin as pale as moonlight, and pale blue eyes ringed in a dark blue-violet color. And she looked like the stereotypical witch in her black dress and multitude of rings and necklaces. It suited the goddess of witchcraft, though.

"I'm just sorry it's under unfortunate circumstances," Sergei replied as he released Hecate.

"Not unfortunate if it means we can finally lift the block and truly see what's going on in our library."

Sergei inclined his head, conceding the point.

Hecate turned to Sophia, studying her for a moment. Lucas nearly smiled, because while Sophia had gotten used to Seth—at least to an extent—she had instantly gotten nervous when the goddess had appeared. "You think the essence of yourself and another aspida are being used?"

"Maybe? It's a theory."

"And you said it was a book that was responsible?"

"Yeah. Well," she corrected herself, "it definitely took my essence. Sergei confirmed that much."

"Show me."

Sophia, Lucas, and Sergei all pointed to the culprit, which made Hecate laugh. Even Seth smiled. Hecate stepped closer and examined the book. After a minute, she looked at Seth and arched a brow. He nodded, and she turned back to the book before she rested a single fingertip on the cover. She stiffened and jerked her hand back. "It definitely drains the essence of a person." She cocked her head and narrowed her eyes. "And stores it. Whoever took your essence had to have come back to collect it afterward." Making a beckoning gesture with one hand, Lucas swore he saw a shimmer rise up from the book and sink into her skin. "Give me a moment to see if I can prove or disprove the rest of your theory."

No one spoke while Hecate worked, and she didn't seem to mind having four sets of eyes fixed on her. Sophia shifted from one foot to the other, but calmed herself even before Lucas could offer her a comforting touch.

Hecate had looked serene when she arrived, and even when she began working, but a frown was starting to form on her perfect brow. When she opened her eyes, she looked disturbed. "Your idea about your essence—and a former aspida's—being used to warp the magic of the Athenaeum may have some merit, but I can't confirm it. I'm not sensing any of your essence within the Athenaeum—or at least no more than is normal after someone has been aspida for a while. But there is something…unusual. Not something I can really sense. More like when you see something out of the corner of your eye that you can't quite make out."

"Could it be what's blocking you guys from seeing everything?" Sophia asked.

"It's possible, but without being able to get a grip on it—so to speak—I can't verify that. That said, based on what I do know, I don't think that just having your essence could have done this. They would need more."

Lucas wasn't sure if this was good news or not. On one hand, it was definitely good that Sophia's essence wasn't being used against the Athenaeum, but on the other, they were back to square one. Or close enough. And it never boded well when the goddess of witchcraft was stumped on a magical issue. Gods might not be omniscient, but they tended to know most everything about their spheres of influence. Hard not to, when most were tens of thousands of years old and some were far older. "More how?"

Hecate shook her head. "If I knew that, I could unravel the spell. It may be that they combined multiple things to achieve this block, or used a spell even I'm unaware of. But there is one thing I can do before I leave." She held her hand flat over the book and a faint charge entered the air, like static before a lightning storm. Her eyes narrowed at the cover, but after a minute passed, she began to smile. Reaching in, she closed her hand around the book and lifted it out. "Catch," she said, tossing it at Sergei.

A laugh slipped out of Lucas when the normally stoic healer jumped back like he'd just had a spider thrown at him. The book landed on the floor with a thud, the cover flying open. "What in the name of all that's holy did you do that for?" he yelled at his cousin, his accent thicker than Lucas had ever heard it before.

Hecate laughed, the sound low, pleasant, and a little eerie. "It's harmless now, cousin," she told him as she closed the book and picked it up. "Or at least it won't be drawing a person's essence from them anymore. Since it's down here, I'm sure it has some sort of downside."

Sophia stepped toward Hecate and reached for the book. She hesitated a moment, drew in a breath, then took the book from the goddess. Lucas saw the tension in her shoulders, just as he saw it ease when the book did nothing but sit in her hands. While he trusted Hecate as one of the patrons, it still took a lot of courage for her to willingly touch the thing that had nearly killed her. "Thank you, Hecate," she said, smiling at the goddess before she placed the book back in the box, then put both back where they belonged.

"You're very welcome. I need to go, but if you learn anything else, don't hesitate to call out to me again."

"We will."

"Be safe, cousin," Sergei said, earning a smile before Hecate disappeared.

"I need to get going, too, but let me know about any other theories. Remember, Sophia, the Athenaeum chose you for a reason," Seth said before he smiled. "And it wasn't because of who your grandfather was."

When the god was gone as well, Lucas was finally able to relax. "At least the day wasn't a total waste. We have a safer book and an idea to build off of."

"We do," Sophia agreed, running a finger along the carvings on the box. "And we're going to." She looked back at him and smiled fiercely. "It might be slow progress, but it's progress."

It wasn't hope on her face, it was determination. In Lucas's book, that was just as strong. And it was about time Sophia found hers.

Chapter 11

Nothing new happened over the next two days. In a way, it was a relief. It seemed like a new disaster occurred every other day, so to go two days without something going wrong was nice. But on day three, Sophia was waiting for the other shoe to drop, and when it did, she expected it to be a doozy. Still, she'd spent part of every day with Josie and Peter, forcing herself to take some downtime. She hadn't been able to bring herself to leave the Athenaeum, but that was okay because they'd watched the rest of the Indiana Jones movies. Sophia had only gotten her way after she promised Josie could pick the next movie, which meant she was probably due for a rom-com the next time.

Lachlan's condition was no different, and Sergei and Heather were no closer to finding out how to reverse whatever had been done to him. They were also no closer to finding out who had actually killed Erasmus, Agatha, and Thomas.

Sophia had finished the last of her interviews the day before, and the people who didn't live in the Athenaeum had gone home or off on assignment. It was a gamble, but she had discussed it with Lucas and they'd decided it would look odd if she'd held them over with no reasonable explanation. Besides, most of them were innocent—unless there was a huge conspiracy, which didn't seem likely.

And she'd been visiting the aspida room every night. She no longer snuck out, but kissed Lucas and told him she'd be back every time. And every time when she got back, he was still up. It was sweet, though she was glad there hadn't been cause for his worry.

Her visits had been more informative than anything else, though she couldn't really call them productive. They were helping her as an aspida, just not helping her figure out what to do about the here and now. She read more about how the physical structure of the Athenaeum evolved; how they used both magic and manpower to carve out the hallways and stairways she knew so well. How magic had been placed on the rooms which held the texts to ensure they were preserved, and how the patrons had put protections into place, one by one. The labyrinth was originally the work of Isis and Hecate, but Athena had later added her own magic to it, which she found cool. When the goddess of warcraft invested some of herself in a labyrinth, it was a sure bet there was plenty of strategy involved.

Then she read about how a sloppy venator had almost revealed the existence of the Athenaeum to the human world and the measures that had been taken to clean it up. Unfortunately, it hadn't been a perfect solution, and the Ekklesia had learned about them. As the Arcane body who took measures—often extreme ones—to ensure that humans as a whole never learned about the Arcane, they'd been concerned. The Athenaeum had taken a hit for the near miss, and for a while the Ekklesia had tried to take over the Athenaeum and replace the Nasaru with their own people. If they'd known exactly where the Athenaeum was, they might have managed it. After some negotiations, which had included several of the divine patrons, they'd reached an understanding. What the Nasaru did actually helped the

Ekklesia. Keeping magical texts and relics out of human hands just made their job easier. So they backed off and even sent the occasional book or relic to the Athenaeum for safekeeping, though the aspida who had written about that was sure they kept much more than they sent.

She hadn't just read the older entries, either. It had occurred to her that Erasmus might have put something in the journal that might apply, but there was very little. Erasmus had been furious when Olivia and Thomas had been poisoned, and extremely grateful to the witch Suni for bringing the antidote that had saved Olivia. He, Sergei, and Lucas had investigated back then, but had come up with absolutely nothing. Not long after, Erasmus had started feeling ill, and it hadn't taken long for him to realize he'd been given the same toxin that had killed Thomas. The effects weren't as strong or as immediate, but he hadn't had any doubt it was the same poison, not after a single thorough examination by Sergei. He'd been disappointed that one of the people of the Athenaeum, people he thought of as family, could do such a cold and calculated thing.

Sophia had looked beyond that, but it was strangely the last he'd written of any of the poisonings. After that was just comments on the day-to-day goings on. Dull, really, and she couldn't figure out why he hadn't said anything else. Detailed the progression of his symptoms or what they'd tried to do to help him. She knew they'd given him the same antidote that had saved Olivia, but he hadn't written that down. She had no idea why it had worked for Olivia but not Thomas or Erasmus, especially since Erasmus seemed to have gotten a smaller dose. Then again, toxicology was far from her specialty.

Today though, as she left breakfast, her mind was on the passages she'd read the night before. With Lucas going to train with the guards, and since she had no interviews to conduct, she kept herself in public places. Not only did it allow her to observe the other Nasaru, it lessened the chance that the resident murderer would try anything. Yes, magic could be sneaky, but there were multiple witches around who could track it down, not to mention all the various sorcery spells essentially everyone in the Athenaeum knew. They'd have to be extremely ballsy to try something in public. Then again, they had to have been ballsy to kill their aspida.

She visited Nick's office to ask his opinion on Olivia replacing Dion, and he didn't seem as certain as Lucas and Sergei had. Olivia had kept a low profile so he didn't know her well, but he couldn't deny she was qualified, so conceded to Sophia's decision. They took a few minutes to discuss upcoming retrievals, but he sounded like he had everything in hand, so she left him to it.

Next, she went to the gym and sparred with a few people under Steven's supervision. It was rough on her body, but it was rougher when she realized that a few of the people she trained with were going harder on her than they had previously. At some points, it felt like they weren't sparring, they were fighting, much like it had been with Jericho. If it weren't for the patrons' gifts, she'd have left there and had to go straight to Sergei. As it was, she took a minute to clean up, then headed to the common room. That was when she was certain there was something weird going on.

Sophia hadn't exactly made many friends since arriving at the Athenaeum. Not because she didn't want to or because she was inherently unlikeable, but because she hadn't had time. It was hard to really socialize when you were trying to learn the rules of a new organization, meet all its people, solve murders, and mourn a grandfather you'd only met a few days prior to his death. But she had made a few beyond Josie and Peter, and was friendly with several more people, so when she saw multiple people eyeing her with suspicion or even dislike, she started to wonder why. The suspicion—or maybe it had been caution—had been more common in the first few days she'd been aspida, but it had lessened in the last few weeks. At first, the new dislike was just baffling and a little annoying. Then Josie had given her one of those unpleasant looks. Given the time she'd spent with Josie, including over the last few days, it shocked her as well as hurt her. And she couldn't figure out what in the hell she could have done to upset the normally bright and bubbly venator. They'd met for a movie the night before, and Josie had even chosen the movie. It had been relaxing, friendly, and fun, and nothing had seemed off about her, her sister, or Peter.

Once Sophia started to really think about it rather than react to it, she realized it was something she might need to be worried about. If Lachlan could be contaminated by something and go nuts, what was to say that it couldn't happen to others? It could explain why a good dozen people were looking at her like she was something they had scraped off their shoes.

Needing a break from the tension, she left in search of Lucas. He was still in the gym and looked to be busy, so she went to find her mom. Today was supposed to be the first healing class, and they should be done or finishing up. They were doing these first few in the entrance hall, as it was a large central location.

People were starting to file out as Sophia neared the class, and she tried to ignore the few unhappy looks she got, waiting for them all to clear out. Peeking in, she saw her mom was alone and stepped inside. "Hey, Mom. How'd the class go?"

Heather glanced up from the papers she was flipping through and gave a faint smile. "Good. There's a lot more general knowledge than we expected, which is making it easier to teach. I don't think we'll need many of these to have most people up to speed on basic first aid. After that, we'll single people out for more advanced or magical healing."

"That's good. It'll be nice for everyone to be able to stabilize injuries. Had a question for you, though."

"Hmm?" was Heather's only reaction as she went back to the papers.

"Have you noticed anyone acting kind of...off?"

"What do you mean?"

Sophia didn't want to fully explain, not when her mom didn't know everything going on. She'd been through a lot, too, and Sophia didn't want to add anything else on top of that. "Just...not themselves. Distant or kind of standoffish, I guess?"

"No, can't say I have," Heather answered, but she sounded distracted. Very distracted, actually. But she had just taught her first class ever, so Sophia couldn't really blame her.

"Okay, just wondered. Glad the class went well."

"Thanks. Talk to you later, Sophia."

Frowning, Sophia stepped back, head cocking as she watched her mom, who had only looked at her once, and briefly. Her mom almost never called her by her name unless it was something important. Or when she was in trouble, but that had been when she was a kid.

Shaking her head, she turned and went to the clinic. It could be her mom had been more worked up and nervous about the class than

Sophia had realized. She might have confided in Sergei, especially since Sophia hadn't seen much of her mom in the last week. It might be that she was a bad daughter, but there just wasn't enough time in the day to do everything she wanted to do. Still, she made a mental note to try to spend more time with her mom.

Sergei was sitting at his desk, chair turned so he was facing the door, a book open in front of him. On the bed at the back was Lachlan, still in the same clothes she'd last seen him in, though someone had taken the time to clean him up. He was also still out cold. For a moment, she forgot about her own issues. What did it matter if people disliked her when Lachlan had been infected by something like this? Except she couldn't help him, not yet, and she needed to know if she was imagining things or if they actually had another problem. For the first time, she wished she was just imagining it.

She closed the door behind her and cleared her throat. He looked up and smiled a bit. "Sophia. How are you?"

"A little worried," she admitted.

The smile dimmed. "About what?"

"Couple of things, but we'll start with my mom. Was she acting nervous or anything earlier?"

"About the class?" She nodded. "No, she wasn't. She was excited more than anything. I'm not sure if it was just because she wanted to teach or because she believed like you do, that this will help save our people's lives, or at least lessen their suffering until full healing can occur. Why?"

Sophia drew another chair away from the wall and sat down. "I went to talk to her after the class because people have been acting weird today."

"Weird how?"

"Standoffish? Some of them were even…" She trailed off, searching for the right word. "Not hostile, not really, but I got a sense of distrust or dislike. Even from people I would have said were friends yesterday, like Josie."

Sergei's thick brows drew together. "Josie? Are you certain? She's the least distrustful person I can think of."

"Right?" Which is what had made it so much more noticeable in that case. "But yes, I'm sure. I take it you haven't noticed anyone acting weird?"

"I haven't, no. But what about your mom?"

"Oh, yeah. So I went to ask if she'd noticed anything, and *she* was acting weird. Not like she didn't like me, but she barely looked at me and didn't say much. And she has never acted that way with me, not when I come to her with something I'm worried about, not even when I just want to talk. Never. So after everyone else was being dismissive or whatever you want to call it, having her do the same just has me…worried."

To her relief, Sergei actually listened and nodded as he thought about what she'd said. "I truly didn't notice anything off about her behavior. Hers or anyone else's. That said, it doesn't mean it hasn't happened. I do tend to stay mostly here in the clinic unless I'm sleeping, eating, or researching," he admitted. "That means I don't interact with as many people as it sounds like you have today."

"I made a point of being seen," she told him. "Since I didn't have anything immediately pressing, I wanted to people watch. To see if anyone acted off, or if anyone else showed signs of the same thing that affected Lachlan."

As one, they turned to look at the vampire in question. "I can happily say I haven't seen anything else like with him. And as for the others? I'll be sure to pay attention at dinner and whenever I leave the clinic. No matter what I see or don't see, I'll let you know."

"Thanks. And if you see Lucas before I do, will you let him know, too? He was busy with training and I didn't want to interrupt."

"I can, yes. Just be safe, especially if people are starting to act suspicious of you."

"Trust me, I don't intend to be the next victim of whatever asshole is attacking the Athenaeum." In fact, it was quickly becoming her mission in life to root him out and see him punished for each and every one of his sins. She loved this place, and she was going to save it, one way or another.

Chapter 12

SINCE THE FIRST HALF of her day had been a total bust—and that was being generous—Sophia decided to do at least one productive thing. She shot off a text as she returned to her office. Breathing a little easier now that she was in her own space—and it was actually starting to feel like hers—she waited for the reply and smiled a little when it came in.

It only took a few minutes before Olivia appeared in the doorway. Once again, every bit of skin from the neck down was covered, though today her gloves were a deep red instead of black. "Everything okay?" she asked.

Far from it, but she wasn't going to burden Olivia with that information. Not yet, anyway. "I hope so. Come in, shut the door, please."

Olivia looked more curious than nervous as she did so and sat across from Sophia. "What's going on?"

Sophia smiled. "As you know, I've been interviewing everyone in the last couple of weeks. I need to know who I'm working with and understand who can do what. What role they belong in."

Olivia nodded slowly. "Yes, I remember. And I remember us talking about what job I did and if I wanted to keep doing it. Are you wanting to move me somewhere else? Because I really am happy doing what I'm doing."

That made Sophia question her decision. If Olivia turned down the job, she really didn't have any alternatives. No one else had struck her as someone she wanted to fill Dion's shoes. And they were big shoes. Of the three heads, Nick's might be the most obviously complicated since he had to work out whether it was worth retrieving a book or relic and, if it was, figure out a basic plan of how to get it. Lucas's might be the hardest, as it involved keeping people safe, even if there were others trying to kill them. But head curator? Sophia had learned that role was basically responsible for everything from the magically concealed entrance down to the aquifer beneath the library. Getting supplies, maintaining the armory and other equipment, keeping the texts and relics safe and organized. Everything. So while not complicated in the way of Nick's job, or difficult in the way of Lucas's, it had more moving parts.

She breathed deep, released it slowly, then smiled. "I'm glad. Because I don't want to move you out of the curators, I want you to be the head of them."

Olivia said nothing for a minute, just breathed and blinked as the words processed. "I'm sorry, you want me to be head curator?"

"I do," Sophia confirmed.

Olivia shook her head. "Nuh uh. I'm not qualified. I've only been a curator for five years. There are people who have been doing the job for a century—or more! They know this place better than I do."

Sophia laughed. "Okay, first off? I became aspida after being here for a freaking week. So if time spent doing a task is your criteria for whether someone gets a job or not, then I'm screwed."

Olivia almost smiled. "Fair point, though aspida is a little different," she argued.

"Is it? Head curator takes care of the Athenaeum, and so does the aspida. Except while the head curator handles just the people and things and rooms, the aspida also has to worry about what happens outside the Athenaeum to its people." Olivia made a noncommittal sound and Sophia continued. "Second, I've discussed this with several other people—including Nick and Lucas—and none of them have been able to think of anyone more qualified. And that's without any of them knowing about your special bloodline. Can you really say that anyone else here retains information the way you can? That anyone else can remember what books or relics that they've dealt with as easily as you can? That anyone else will be able to remember sorcery as well as you?"

"No, I suppose not," Olivia murmured thoughtfully. "This is a big step, though. Right now I'm a librarian who also sometimes teaches or guards people. You're talking about adding a fuckton of responsibility."

"I am," Sophia agreed. "Which is why I've not only thought about this, I've asked others who know more about the Athenaeum than I do. We all think you're the person to take on that responsibility."

"I'm not sure it's a responsibility I want. I do like my job as it is now." She hesitated and slumped down in her chair, rubbing her hands over her thighs. "Can I have a few days to think about it?"

While part of Sophia had hoped Olivia would have just said yes and taken the job, the rest of her thought more of Olivia for not just jumping in with both feet. It was a big decision, and she was treating it like such. She smiled and nodded. "Of course. Take the time you need and let me know if you have any questions. Hell, talk to Nick or

Lucas if you want the opinion of another head. Just let me know when you've made a decision."

"I will. And...thanks," Olivia said as she pushed out of the chair. "Not just for the time, but for thinking I can do the job."

"Hey, it was your fault," Sophia joked. "You were too good at your job, and then you add in a superpower almost no one else in the Arcane has? Made you the top choice."

Olivia grinned. "I can't be blamed for the superpower anymore than I can for having red hair."

"Fair enough, but you still have it. Take care, and let me know what you decide."

Olivia left and Sophia spent the rest of the time before dinner answering emails and doing some studying. When the alarm she'd set on her phone went off to tell her it was time to eat, she was reluctant to leave the solitude of her office. Would people be treating her like before? Or had it all been in her head?

Lucas noticed the tension around Sophia's eyes as soon as she walked in. And how her eyes scanned those already sitting at the table with wariness. Sergei had found him just half an hour ago and told him of her concerns. At the time he hadn't been able to think of any out of the ordinary behavior beyond Lachlan's, but he watched now and did notice a change.

It wasn't everyone. It wasn't even half, but there were a good dozen or so people whose demeanors changed when they spotted Sophia. One broke off mid-laugh to narrow his eyes at her. Another stared at her almost like Sophia had walked in covered in blood. The reactions were all different in how they presented, but the source was all the same. Something about Sophia somehow offended or irritated them.

And one of those was Josie, just like Sophia had told Sergei. Out of everyone he saw, Josie would have been the most jarring...if he hadn't seen Heather all but ignore her daughter when she sat beside her.

Sophia's face fell, then closed off as she put a professional smile on her lips. Lucas sought out Sergei, who had taken a seat at the opposite end of the room from Lucas, just so they had eyes on more people. The tight set of the demigod's mouth told Lucas he'd seen the same thing Lucas had. Something was definitely going on.

He continued to watch throughout the dinner and saw that all the weirdness, all the unhappy looks, were directed solely at Sophia. The people who were acting strangely would eye her like she'd rolled in garbage, then smile at the next person with genuine warmth. It made no sense. Even if someone had been spreading rumors—and the Nasaru weren't above gossip—it wouldn't explain this. It definitely didn't explain Heather's behavior. Before today, Heather had always been warm and loving toward her daughter, no matter what else had been going on.

When dinner was over, Sophia caught his eye, then Sergei's, and they followed her to her room, spread out so it didn't look odd that all three of them were going to her bedroom. Once inside, no one said anything until Sergei had cast his bubble spell.

"You were right," Lucas said the moment it was safe. "Not only were people acting weird, it was only with you. With everyone else, they seemed to be acting normal."

"Agreed," Sergei said, nodding. "It was extremely odd. I've never seen this group act like this. There are occasionally some arguments or bad blood that lead to two or three people being chilly toward each other for a little while, but nothing on this scale."

"Yeah, disagreements happen, but I counted at least thirteen people in there tonight who weren't happy to see you," Lucas added.

Sophia huffed out a breath and dropped down on the edge of the bed. "But why? I haven't done anything. I sure as hell haven't done anything in the last few days. Literally the only thing I can think of that anyone could be mad about would be Lachlan, and that's only if they were worried about him and making me the scapegoat."

"That wouldn't explain your mom," Lucas said quietly. "Or Josie."

"No, it wouldn't," she agreed.

"I'm going to speak to some people in the next day or two, see if I can find out why they seem to have that bad blood toward you," Sergei offered.

Lucas nodded. "Same. If there's something you've done or that they think you've done, we can work with that. If it's something else?" He shrugged. "Then we'll still deal with it, one way or another."

"Do you think it could be something like with Lachlan?" Sophia asked, her brow furrowing.

Sergei shook his head. "I doubt it. They're not showing any signs of violence, and he certainly was. And his condition is due to something in his system. While one person could be infected, it would be much harder to infect this many people without it being detected."

"Couldn't it be transmitted like a virus?"

Again, he shook his head. "I wasn't able to identify what it is, but I know it's a substance of some sort, not a virus."

Lucas wasn't sure of that. What if it was something they'd touched that had absorbed into their skin? Couldn't Lachlan have touched someone with it on his skin and passed it on? Except there was no proof of anything, nothing to suggest his theory had any merit whatsoever, so he kept it to himself. No need to put more strain on Sophia, not right now.

Sophia nodded. "Well, maybe one of you will figure something out tomorrow. In the mean time, I'll just keep doing what I'm doing. Oh!" Her shoulders, which had started to slump, lifted somewhat. "I talked to Olivia. Asked her to be head curator."

"Did she take the job?" Lucas asked.

"Not yet, but I'm hopeful. She wanted to think about it."

"I think she'll take it," Sergei said. "But you get some rest. Relax, try not to worry too much about the others, and...do whatever you do when you're not working," he told her, flicking a look to Lucas, his lips twitching. Clearly, they hadn't been as discreet as they'd thought. Not that Lucas really cared that Sergei had figured out they were sleeping together. Sophia did, judging by the blush, but she only nodded.

Sergei left and Sophia groaned, covering her face with her hands. "Were we really that obvious?"

"Depends on what you mean by obvious," Lucas said, crossing the room and sitting beside her. He slid an arm around her and pulled her in. She let her hands drop and tilted her head against his shoulder. "You have to remember that Sergei knows me well, and in the time he's known me, I haven't treated anyone like I have you. That's probably what tipped him off."

She smiled and her arm went around his waist. "That's kind of nice."

He chuckled. "Oh? You like knowing I had a dry spell before I met you?"

"I mean, yeah. It's kind of flattering that I was the one that made you break your sexual fast," she admitted, grinning up at him.

He gave her a squeeze and shook his head, but he was amused. Truthfully, he'd been too busy, too focused on learning everything he needed to know to do his job to worry much about sex. There had been a few flings, but nothing more than that. Sophia? She wasn't a fling. He still wasn't sure exactly what they were, but they weren't a fling. "You want to actually rest, or are you going back to wherever you sneak off to?" he asked. He hoped she would say she was staying for a while, because now that he'd gotten sex in his head, he was all too ready to participate in it.

Sophia smiled hotly and stood, turning so she could straddle his lap and wind her arms around his neck, her breasts pressed against his chest. "Neither. I think a distraction will work better than rest. Then I can sneak off," she told him before she kissed him.

He was more than happy to indulge her for the next hour.

Once Sophia was safely hidden behind the secret door, she pulled out the grimoire, done with history for now. The journal wasn't helping her find any insights, but there might be something in the grimoire that could help them identify the killer. That or how to remove whatever was blocking the patrons from doing their godly thing to solve it. She was aware it could be risky to use anything in the grimoire, but they were running out of options and she wasn't willing to risk more lives. The previous aspides had removed all traces of the spells in this book from everywhere else for a reason. Hell, some of the ones she'd seen terrified her. Not just the failsafe that would destroy the Athenaeum, either. Controlling time? Resurrection? Not just raising revenants, but true resurrection? Mass earthquakes? Nope, not for her, and she could absolutely understand why they'd been hidden away. Part of her wondered why some of these spells hadn't just been destroyed outright.

But if she couldn't find a way to find the murderer, maybe she could find other answers. Anything was possible, and she had to try, so she grabbed one of the notepads she'd brought down and opened the thin book, the leather spine creaking with the movement. She began turning the pages carefully, though it was in excellent shape for a book as old as it was. And she realized after a few pages that she was touching the paper as little as possible. It wasn't because they were fragile, it was that the ink covering them felt insidious. Which was silly. This wasn't a spelled book like the one down on level six. It was just leather, ink, and paper. Normal in everything but content.

Shaking her head and shaking off the paranoia, she made herself focus on the spells. Many she passed by without seeing more than the name of the spell. Teleportation she'd already learned, just in case the worst happened. Telepathy she knew could cause insanity, and she had no interest in controlling emotions, time, or the dead. But there were some spells that she noted, not because they gave her answers now, but because they might help if the worst happened. Stealing memories? On the surface it sounded monstrous—and it was—but if it came down to stealing the memories of a killer to prove they'd done the heinous and prevent further deaths, then it might be the lesser of two evils. And portal creation? The teleportation might save her, but what if something happened and the spell wouldn't get those she cared about to safety? Portal creation might, though it sounded complicated as hell.

Sophia turned to the next page then laughed, flopping back in her chair. This was where her grandfather had gotten the spell he'd given to Suni, the one to summon Death. Seriously? It had been right here? Well, at least it wasn't somewhere that anyone else in the Athenaeum could access, though she was surprised he'd given a spell in this book to anyone. Worse, destroying it wasn't really possible, as the other side held a spell, but she could do what she'd promised and make a note to never use it. Grabbing her pen, she took a deep breath, then made her first mark in any of the books down here, writing a warning at the bottom of the spell. Honestly, she was surprised the spell had worked, given how vague it was. But since she noted that Death hated this spell, hopefully it would never get used again.

Besides, she had Death's wife's phone number. She didn't need a summoning spell.

She spent another hour looking through the grimoire, but while some of the spells sounded interesting until she got to the downsides, most she felt belonged in this book, locked safely away. A few she wrote down just because she didn't understand what they were. She'd never heard of alkahest, so had no idea why it was so dangerous to make. It had to be dangerous or it wouldn't be in this book. There was also an unnamed alloy that was a mix of orichalcum and nalonium. It sounded like they were metals, but she'd never heard of either one before. So all of them got noted for later.

Marking her spot, she closed the grimoire and returned to bed, happily curling against Lucas's back, willing herself to not think, just long enough to sleep.

Chapter 13

AN HOUR AFTER BREAKFAST, Sophia stood in front of the door which would take her to the one place in the Athenaeum she'd never been; the Vault. She'd thought it would be more intimidating, but it looked like every other door in the library. Then again, there couldn't be anything more dangerous down there than some of the spells she'd found in the grimoire. At least she hoped not. Just to be safe, she'd just have to treat it like level six; touch nothing unless she was sure it wouldn't kill her.

"You ready to go down there?"

She turned and smiled at Lucas, lips twitching. Sometime since they'd parted, he'd changed into a tee-shirt that said "Rock Hard." But she nodded. "I am. And cute shirt. Little on the nose, though, isn't it?"

"Sometimes people need a reminder," he said, shrugging. "Besides, I thought it might make you smile. Now, am I going in with you or staying here to make sure you're not bothered?"

He was taking this well, considering she'd only asked him to come down here half an hour ago, but he was steady like that. "While I think you'd be helpful, I'd like to make sure that no one but me gets in there. Especially if there are people sneaking around upstairs."

Lucas nodded. "Yeah, that was my thought, too. But come get me if there's anything you need help with."

Smiling, she kissed him lightly. "I will." Placing her palm on the scanner, she entered her code. When the screen flashed green, she took a deep breath, opened the door, and went down the stairs into the Vault.

This level was vastly different from every other one in the library. With every other level, the stairs ended at a hallway, with a relic room on the right and books on the left. These stairs ended in a large, round room that left her stunned. Directly in front of her was a gorgeous mosaic of a map set into the floor. She didn't recognize the location, but the details were exquisite and the colors brilliant despite looking like it was centuries old. It resembled Roman mosaics she'd seen in books and she was tempted to seriously study it, but forced herself to look around the rest of the room.

There were freestanding shelves like on the other levels, though these were spaced further apart and nowhere near as cluttered as in other levels. The walls were filled with floor to ceiling shelves as well. There was also a hum of magic here that she hadn't noticed in any of the other levels. An extra level of protection, she assumed. Regardless, it was full of texts and impressive looking relics. She loved it at first sight.

One of the first things she saw after the mosaic was a full set of Greek armor. That alone piqued her interest, but then she wandered closer. After getting a look at the card for the armor, her jaw went slack. "Holy shit," she breathed as she let her eyes move slowly over the armor, taking in every detail. "The armor of Achilles," she said, lifting a trembling hand to rest her fingers against the bronze breastplate.

This was one of the sets of armor actually worn by the hero Achilles. The actual Achilles. The man she'd read about as a kid then studied as an adult. She could spend hours examining it, and really, really wanted to, but gave herself just a few minutes before she tore herself away. She was going to be in trouble if everything down here was as interesting as the mosaic and armor. Still, she entertained a brief daydream about seeing Lucas clad in the impressive armor. It certainly wouldn't fit her, but she had a feeling it would look amazing on him.

The items here were absolutely fantastic. There was a piece of Yggdrasil, which even she had heard of, despite not knowing much about the Norse gods. A large golden Egyptian tyet was placed upright on another shelf, and the card said it was the original, not one of the thousands of reproductions that had been made. She even found a single golden arrow set carefully on a stand. According to the card, it belonged to Sergei and had been given to him by his father, Apollo. When Sergei had joined the Athenaeum, it had been placed here for safekeeping. If she was remembering her lore correctly, that single arrow could heal or cause plagues, so she kept her hands firmly in her pockets and gave it a wide berth. She adored Sergei, but wasn't sure even he could fix her if she got his father's plague. He was good, but he couldn't be as good as his full-blooded god of a father.

Whenever the Vault had been mentioned, they'd always said it was the level with the most dangerous and powerful relics and texts. She couldn't say the things here weren't powerful, but some of what she was seeing wasn't just powerful, it was legendary. She'd wager money that some of the things down here weren't magically impressive or dangerous, just historically significant. And she really wanted to come back one day when the whole nasty murder business was put behind her, so she could thoroughly explore and spend as much time on each relic as she wanted.

The organization wasn't as clear cut in other levels, and texts were mixed in with the relics. Like the other levels, there were more books and scrolls she couldn't read than she could. She'd started to work on fixing that, but learning a language took time. There was a tablet she couldn't read that looked vaguely like it was in cuneiform, and the card said it was one of four tablets of destinies. It sounded vaguely familiar, but she couldn't place it. For now, she'd file it away in the back of her mind.

It took twenty minutes before she came across something that she couldn't pull away from, and it wasn't some mythical object she'd heard of. It was a scroll. What had drawn her attention to it was the fact that the scroll had been dyed. She'd seen scrolls in various tones of brown, even light enough to be white, but this one was a bright, warning shade of red. It probably wouldn't be anything she could use, but on the off chance it was, she had to look.

Carefully, she unrolled the scroll, letting her eyes skim over the ancient writing. This one she could actually read, since it was in Attic Greek. When the words registered, she could feel herself go pale, and she sank down to the cool stone floor. This wasn't just any scroll detailing a historical event or sharing a poem or spell, this was...primal. If what she was reading was true, then it was a secret no one in the Arcane knew. She doubted even anyone in the Athenaeum knew, not anymore. It spoke about the very creation of the universe, and not the creation stories that every religion had. This was something new and a little scary. And she had a feeling it was closer to the truth than anything else she'd heard. She blew out a breath and read through it again.

The creation of the universe had been a chaotic, messy process, and when it was over, there had been what the author referred to as primordial dregs left over. These substances couldn't be destroyed, and even if they could, they were vital to the universe. Despite that, in concentrated form they were extremely dangerous. Basically, too much of a good thing was still too much, so they'd been hidden away in secret chambers by what he called the Ethereals, the ones who had created the universe. Further down, the writer listed these five elements, but there wasn't as much information as Sophia would have liked. Then again, in this case, ignorance might be bliss, because she didn't know how she felt about knowing this.

Quintessence was the first mentioned, and was the essence of matter. It was literally what made up everything physical in the universe.

Then there was Chaos, and Sophia was surprised to read that it wasn't just the absence of order, it was part of what made life possible. It created the weather, evolution, and the spark of life. Basically, it was the 'what if' factor.

Miasma was the violence of change and emotion. Not just the negative emotions either, as even love and joy could be violent. Which made sense. Obsessive love was as dangerous as hatred. Maybe even more dangerous.

Oskila was Miasma's opposite; peace. But the author warned that peace could be as lethal as violence. The lack of forward momentum caused stagnation and death.

Last was something called the Wellspring. All that was said about it was that it was some kind of pool, which could mean anything. She had to wonder if the author hadn't known exactly what the Wellspring was, because why put all this other information in but leave the details of the Wellspring out?

The writer then warned that if anyone got control of any one of these elements, that it could be catastrophic. The amount of power they'd have, the carnage they could inflict, would change the world irrevocably.

That pushed this scroll from a little scary to full on terrifying, and Sophia had to wonder if this scroll spoke truth, or if it was a theory of some ancient man or woman. She kind of preferred to think it was the latter, but she was more certain now that it had at least kernels of truth. There was no way of knowing, as there was no card with this scroll.

Rolling it up, she placed it back where she'd found it and frowned at it for a minute. Shaking her head, she stepped away and continued searching for something useful. The problem was that while this section of the library might have fewer materials than any other level, it still had hundreds of relics and thousands of texts. So she poked, she skimmed, she read every card next to every relic. Then she came across a relic that she should have passed by.

The card said it was called Tefnut's Amulet and was in the Vault because it had been divinely created. All it did was prevent dehydration and create water, so it certainly wasn't powerful enough to be in the Vault. Honestly, it probably would have been perfect for the third level if it hadn't been created by the Egyptian goddess Tefnut. Sophia had to admit it was pretty. It was an Egyptian-style scarab, with an iridescent blue stone for the body and abalone shell laid into the wings. The front and back legs of the beetle each held another stone, with the one on top being crystal clear and the lower one a deep blue. The craftsmanship was exquisite, and Sophia couldn't resist picking it up from the stand and letting the amulet dangle in front of her eyes.

She traced a finger above the delicate details and felt her lips move into a smile. Jewelry wasn't something she normally bothered with. Her ears weren't even pierced. But something about this piece of jewelry was different. She found herself fixing the chain around her neck so the pendant settled between her breasts. Cupping her hand over it, she sighed and closed her eyes for a moment.

There was a moment of doubt and she nearly took it off. Wasn't taking a relic from the Vault to wear without purpose an abuse of her position? Then again, shouldn't there be perks to being the boss? So far she hadn't found any. Well, there was the bathroom attached to her bedroom. It was pretty sweet, but it certainly didn't make up for everything else she had to deal with as aspida.

After hesitating, she slipped it beneath her shirt. As soon as it rested fully against her skin, she gasped softly. It felt like she'd just gotten a burst of energy. The only thing she could figure was that it was the anti-dehydration properties kicking in. She'd probably been in the Vault for a good hour without anything to drink, so it was possible she was a little dehydrated. Or had been.

Smiling, she rubbed the heel of her hand over the now-covered pendant. Moving on, she continued looking, and though she found some texts that were intriguing, the most interesting by far were the mosaic, the pendant, and the scroll on the primordial elements.

Deciding that was enough for one day, she left the Vault and found Lucas leaning against the wall beside the door, guarding her, just like he'd promised. "Find anything?" he asked as he pushed away from the stone.

"That could help us find the killer or save Lachlan? No. Things I'd like to look into more later? Absolutely."

"Like what?" he asked as they started heading back up the stairs.

Despite her hesitation in telling him about the aspida room, she didn't even think for a second before telling him about the mosaic, scroll, and amulet. He asked to see the latter, and she tugged it out of her shirt long enough for him to study it. His response? "Pretty."

She was half expecting him to tell her to put it back, but his casual acceptance made her feel better at having taken it. "Yeah. Not sure why I took it," she admitted once it was safely hidden once more.

"Doesn't matter. I say keep it as long as you like, unless some weird situation comes up where someone needs it. And I can honestly say that I've never heard of Erasmus needing to pull any relics from the Vault for anyone. On occasions the relics on other levels have been used in a retrieval, but not the Vault."

"Why not? Given some of the things I saw in there, I could see how using them would make some of the harder retrievals much easier. Especially back when you guys were having to steal or fight for some of them."

"They are in the Vault for a reason," Lucas said, lifting a shoulder in a shrug. "If they're dangerous enough to be in there, then maybe the risk outweighs the rewards."

"But they're not all dangerous," Sophia argued, shaking her head. "The amulet, for one. Some of them didn't even seem all that powerful. Like I saw Heracles's club in there, and according to the card, it didn't have *any* power. It just happened to once belong to a demigod."

"A famous demigod," he corrected, "but I see your point. I also see why things like that would be a last ditch option. They're irreplaceable."

"So are people."

He smiled and inclined his head in her direction. "True, but if an alternative can be found, wouldn't you rather use that than a piece of history?"

He had a point. The thought of destroying anything in there was painful. "Yeah," she agreed.

"What's your plan now that you're done there?"

"Same as yesterday, basically. I'll get in some training, do some studying, hang out in public."

"You sure you want to do that after the way some of them were acting?" he asked, and she nearly smiled at the clear concern in his voice. For such a hard man—literally and metaphorically—he was surprisingly caring. Not just about her, though she did appreciate that, but everyone he considered to be under his care.

"None of them actually said anything to me. They sure as hell didn't do anything. It was just dirty looks. My skin isn't so thin I can't handle some dirty looks."

"Mmm." She expected him to say something else, but he didn't speak until they were back on the residential level. That wasn't really a bad thing, since they'd just climbed up eight flights of stairs. She might be in better shape now than when she'd first arrived, but the stairs were still a pain in the ass.

Still in the hallway, mostly concealed, he kissed her cheek. "I need to go, but enjoy your training," he said, giving her a cheeky grin before he walked off.

"Enjoy it, my ass," she muttered as she went to change into her training clothes. Everyone who trained her was a sadist, and they reveled in her misery. It had better be worth it.

143

Chapter 14

LUCAS WASN'T AS CERTAIN as Sophia that the weird behaviors would be limited to dirty looks. It might be for a while, but if they couldn't find the cause for the discontent, it could escalate. It *would* escalate. He wanted to stop it before it even came close to reaching that point. He also wanted to talk to his top three suspects. Someone who could kill four right under the nose of so many intelligent people was not only smart, they had to be devious, controlled, and skilled, so it wasn't likely they'd slip up in normal conversation, but all he needed was a sliver to grab hold of. Today, he was searching for that sliver.

Knowing Sophia would change before going to work out, the gym his first stop, hoping he'd beat her there. He did, but Steven was there, and Lucas beckoned him to the side.

"Is everything okay?" he asked.

"Yeah, it's fine," Lucas assured him. "Sophia's about to come in for training," he said, watching the man's face closely, but there wasn't a hint of the suspicion from the night before. Whatever was making people behave oddly, it wasn't bothering Steven. At least not yet. "She won't tell you, but her legs are tired, so go easy on the kicks." Thinking of how strong those looks had been, he added, "Maybe work on holds.

Her getting out of them, I mean, not her trying to put anyone into them."

"I can do that. She'll hate it," Steven said with a hint of a smile.

"She will," Lucas agreed, returning the smile, "but holds happen in a fight, and she needs to know how to deal with them when they do."

Steven nodded. "Very true. I'll take care of it."

"Thanks," he said, giving a friendly slap to Steven's arm before he started for the door. Before he could leave, he saw Jericho and paused. The elemental was alone at the weight bench, just lying back, which made it the perfect time for Lucas to try to get something out of him.

"Hey Jericho," he said when he approached the man. "Need a spotter?"

"Sure," Jericho answered as he lifted the bar off the rack and positioned it above him.

Lucas took his spot above Jericho's head, fully intending to do just as he'd offered. He let the guard work out for a minute before he started speaking. "How you doing? Lachlan wasn't exactly differentiating between friend and foe the other day."

"I'm okay. Had some bruises, but they didn't even need Sergei." The bar was lowered, lifted, then he asked, "Any word on why he went batshit?"

Mouth tight, Lucas shook his head. "Not yet. Sergei's still looking for the cause. Believe me, when we find out, we'll make sure the whole Athenaeum knows, because his actions that day weren't his fault."

"Will he be okay?"

There was concern in the tone, and while Lucas hoped it was genuine, he couldn't say for certain. "All I can say is I hope so. Sergei's doing everything he can, and so is Heather. Sophia's made it his top priority."

Since Lucas was still watching Jericho's face, he saw the change. It was subtle but unmistakable. Instead of focus and concern for Lachlan, it shifted to an expression like he'd just smelled something nasty. "I'm sure," he said, voice snappish, as he dropped the bar back in the cradle. Not something he normally did. "Gotta go," he said, pushing up from the bench and walking off.

Lucas would say the reaction was interesting, but it was just concerning. Jericho hadn't been Sophia's biggest supporter in the beginning, but this was on another level. But was he behind what was going on, or a victim like Lachlan?

Leaving the gym, he headed to the computer room. It was Peter's lair and where the young mer spent ninety percent of his day, including the hours when he was sleeping. He spent more time there than he ever had in the water, in fact. So it was no surprise when he was sitting behind his computer, his bright blue mohawk standing tall, light glinting off the eyebrow and snakebite piercings. His computer stood out even in a room full of the machines. Not only did it have multiple monitors, the computer itself was full of colored lights and had all sorts of accessories attached to it. Unsurprising, since Peter was the tech guy for the Athenaeum. He needed the equipment to maintain the security that he'd developed and put in place. Which is why he was high on Lucas's list, no matter how likable the man was.

"You busy?" he asked as he pulled one of the rolling chairs toward Peter's station.

Peter looked up and grinned. "Nice shirt," he joked as he spun his chair around to face Lucas.

"I'm getting a lot of compliments on it today," Lucas said as he sat in his chair and got comfortable.

"I'll bet. Makes me wonder how many gargoyles have a shirt like that."

"Probably a lot. See, people think they're funny and buy them for us as jokes. Only a few of us actually wear them."

Peter laughed and nodded. "I can imagine. What can I do for you today?"

"Just doing rounds. And with the trouble we had a few weeks ago, I wanted to check and make sure security is as tight as ever."

The puppy dog smile disappeared and Peter nodded. "Yeah, I get it. It wasn't really a security issue, not for the tech side anyway, but I can see how it would make you want to check any aspect you can."

Lucas nodded, though he disagreed that the tech side wasn't involved. "It was a tragedy. And I know Sophia's sick that it happened so soon after she took over."

The somber look remained as the tech nodded again. "I can understand that. She seems like the sort of person who would be blaming herself, even though she couldn't have any idea that my dad was..." He shook his head, eyes dropping.

Interesting. No reaction to Sophia's name, not like Jericho, but Steven hadn't reacted, either. And Peter was acting as though Dion had attacked first that day, weeks ago. But was it genuine or an act? "No, she couldn't have known," he agreed. "But yeah, is the security still tight? No holes, nothing that could use an upgrade?"

Peter shook his head. "Not that I've found, no. I mean, I'm always making small adjustments and improvements, but nothing that I'd call a true bug, and definitely not a hole. The system is solid, so you can put your mind—and Sophia's—to rest."

"Good. That'll definitely help her. She's still trying to get up to speed on everything, so having that off her plate is good," Lucas said, smiling though he knew the system wasn't flawed in some way. Either its creator had abused it, or someone else had gotten through it to get onto levels they weren't allowed on. "I'll leave you to it, then," he said, pushing out of his chair.

"Let me know if you need anything else," Peter called as he made his way out of the computer room.

"Will do."

For the next half hour Lucas wandered the ground floor, stopping to talk to people. In every conversation, he deliberately mentioned Sophia by name. Of the twenty he spoke with, thirteen had an adverse reaction. Not good. On the residential level, he only spoke to nine people, but four of them were apparently not happy with Sophia.

He really wasn't liking this, and worry for Sophia's safety was starting to build within him. Those who knew of the Athenaeum might think of them as just librarians, but none of these people were helpless. The guards were lethal, and most of the venatores weren't far behind them. The curators might not go out in the field much and so didn't have much reason to train their offensive skills, but they had more time to learn sorcery and practice using their powers. And a lot of them spent as much time with the relics as they did the books and scrolls. They knew exactly what was down there and what could be the most dangerous in their hands. Just because something wasn't on level six or in the Vault didn't mean it was harmless. A coffee cup was considered harmless, but in the right situation it could kill. Add magical powers to the cup, and it got worse.

His train of thought wasn't eased when he found Penny in the level five relic room, or when she displayed an obvious dislike for Sophia at the mention of her name. When he left her, he went right for Sergei. Heather was in the clinic as well, and they were both standing over Lachlan.

"Is there really nothing else you can think of that will get the contagion out of his system?" Heather asked.

"I'm still searching, but no, nothing yet has affected it in any way," Sergei confirmed.

"How long can we keep him like this?"

Sergei chuckled softly. "A few centuries. He's a vampire, so he won't age, and my stasis magic will prevent him from deteriorating. We might need to occasionally give him blood, but that's it."

"That's good. So he won't suffer while we figure this out."

"And you will figure it out," Lucas said as he stepped into the clinic.

"Of course we will," Sergei said, though Lucas saw the uncertainty in his eyes.

"Heather, could you give us a few? Need to talk to Sergei about something."

She smiled and nodded. "Of course," she said before she left the room, closing the door behind her.

Once they were alone, Lucas gave Sergei a pointed look. Understanding, he cast the bubble spell and nodded. "It's safe now. Has something else happened?"

"I don't know if I'd go that far, but I'm not happy with what I just saw. In the last hour, nineteen people have gone from happy to annoyed in the blink of an eye the moment I said Sophia's name. And that's including Penny and Jericho, who are on my short list of suspects."

"I know you told me you suspect them and Peter, but you didn't really tell me why."

"We know that whoever's responsible got onto level six, and those three have the tech skills to get past the security. There might be others, but on paper, those three are the only ones I could find. And yes, Nick could get down there on his own, but that's the only thing that comes close to pointing at him."

Sergei nodded slightly and frowned. "I can't see any of them doing this, but especially not Penny and Peter."

"Neither can I, but it wasn't Dion, which means it was someone else. Someone still here. Without something else to go on, this is where the facts are taking us."

"And you said Peter didn't seem to hold any ill will against Sophia?"

Lucas shook his head. "Seemed to be normal, but so were Steven and several others. Us included."

Sergei nodded slowly as he thought. "Unfortunately, I've noticed the same thing. It doesn't appear to be natural."

"No, it doesn't. It's like two different people in one body. I think next time it happens, we need to see if we can sense any magic or anything else unnatural on them."

"Agreed. And I'll see if I can do a more thorough look at someone. If there are guards on your list, then there will probably be a reason to heal them in the next twenty-four hours."

"That would be good." Lucas looked over at Lachlan's still form. "I really hope it's not a form of what Lachlan's got."

"I agree, especially not before we find out how to help him."

"And we need to keep an eye out for Sophia. I'm worried someone's going to escalate from dirty looks to an attack. She's making good progress, but she's still a novice, especially compared to the guards."

"I agree with that as well."

"Thanks, Sergei. I'm going to go find Sophia. Let her know she needs to keep her head on a swivel."

"Be safe. Both of you."

It wouldn't be that simple, and they both knew it. He found Sophia in her office, alone, with the door open. After closing it behind him, he moved around the desk to lean against it as she sat back in her chair.

"Everything okay?" she asked.

"I wish I could say yes. Just came from Sergei's."

Her shoulders tensed. "Lachlan?"

He shook his head. "No, not Lachlan. There's been no change there. While he's not better, he's not worse, either. But no, it's not that. It's those looks you were talking about. Both Sergei and I did some checking and saw it, too. The moment your name is mentioned, almost twenty people flip from pleasant to annoyed. Or worse. And I mean flip. There's no hesitation, no working up to annoyed, just instant distaste."

"But why?" she asked, resting her arms on her desk and dropping her head atop them. "I haven't done anything to these people. Why do they suddenly dislike me so much?"

"I'm not sure it's you," Lucas said, rubbing her shoulder. "At least not how you're thinking. Sergei and I are both going to check next time it happens, to see if there's some magic involved, because it does *not* come off like it's natural."

She turned her head so she could look up at him. "If it's not natural, what is it?"

"Not sure," he admitted. "One possibility is that it's a form of what Lachlan's infected with."

Sophia sighed and hid her face again. "It honestly feels like my tenure as aspida is cursed," she said, voice muffled.

Lucas couldn't really argue against that, though the curse had begun before she'd even known the Athenaeum existed. He also refused to lie to her, so stroked a hand over her hair. "We'll figure it out. Sometimes we just need one piece to fall into place, like Death showing up. Wasn't expected, we weren't looking for him, but now we know the truth about Dion."

"Yeah, true." She pushed herself up to a sitting position. "Except that doesn't really help us. We knew we were looking for someone who's still alive. And one of the people we're looking at is his son," she said, rubbing her face. "I've got to see if I can finally find some answers after dinner."

He really wanted to know where she was sneaking off to late at night, and how it could have any answers, but he'd been part of the Athenaeum for too long to not believe the aspides had secrets they didn't share with the rest of them. Probably a lot of secrets, actually. If they were all in the Vault—which they clearly weren't—he'd have been shocked.

"You really think you can find something there?"

"I don't know," she admitted. "I hope so, but there's a lot there and I can't read everything yet. Besides, there's only so much I can read in one night, and I'll bet I could spend a year there and not run out of things to read. But we're running out of places to look, so I have to try."

He really, really wanted to know where she was going to, now. It sounded like the Vault, which made him wonder why the aspides would split up their secret materials into two locations. Although it could be more than two locations.

"Then you'll look." The worst that happened is she wasted a little time. Unless someone caught her between her room and wherever this secret place was. But he wanted to take some of the stress from her face and get her away from their suspects for a little while. Glancing at his watch, he saw it was almost time for dinner, but afterward? He was going to put a smile on her face. Outside of the bedroom, this time.

Dinner that night was the most uncomfortable one Sophia had ever experienced. If the next one was this bad, she was going to start eating in her room. It might be cowardly, but she could only handle so much of the oppressive feeling being around so many people who were starting to hate her caused.

She intended to go to her room and try to relax while she waited for the Athenaeum to sleep, but Lucas caught her mere feet outside the dining hall.

"Come on," he said, linking his fingers with hers and pulling her toward the stairs.

"Where are we going?" she asked, unable to keep from smiling as they walked through the Athenaeum hand in hand.

"Somewhere you can let off some steam."

She arched a brow and teased, "Then why aren't we going back to the bedroom?"

He chuckled. "Is sex all you can think about?" he teased back, releasing her hand and wrapping his arm around her shoulders, pulling her closer.

"No, lately it seems to be either sex or trouble. I prefer thinking about sex, though."

"Fair enough. And we can always get naked and horizontal after, but we're doing this first."

"You're so mean to me."

"Let's see if you say that when we're done."

To her surprise, he guided her through the entrance and into the labyrinth. Though she could see the path now, he led the way through it and outside into the warm night air. Sophia had known it had been weeks since she'd been outside, but she hadn't realized just how much she missed fresh air and moonlight.

Leaning into Lucas, she wrapped both arms around him, closed her eyes, and tipped her face to the half moon that hung above her. She breathed in, smelling the unique scent of Greece, then exhaled, letting some of the stress slide out of her body. "This is wonderful," she murmured, "but is it safe?"

"It will be," he promised. "We're not staying here."

Opening her eyes, she looked up at him. "Where are we going?"

He smiled and lifted his free hand, index finger extended and pointed toward the sky. "Up there."

It took her only a second to grasp his meaning. "We're going flying?" she asked, excitement coiling in her belly.

"We are."

"I know we're a little ways from the neighbors, but don't you think a gargoyle flying around might attract attention?"

"It would," he agreed. "But I'm going to hide us from view. Remember, there's a spell for almost everything if you know where to look."

She wasn't about to argue. It didn't feel natural for her to avoid shifting for so long. She might be only half owl, but it felt like a larger part of her than the elf was. Not only that, but she absolutely loved flying. "Then make with the sorcery and the shifting," she told him, grinning as she stepped back from him.

"So impatient," he said with a laugh, but he followed it with a few syllables she didn't recognize. Still, she felt the magic settle over her. Pulling off his shirt, he shifted to his gargoyle form. His muscles thickened, his skin took on a gray hue, and his oddly beautiful wings stretched out to his sides. Before she'd met him, she'd appreciated gargoyles—the statue kind—but had never really thought of them as beautiful. Art, certainly, but they'd just been skillfully made statues. Lucas though? He was gorgeous, even with the fangs and claws. It still surprised her that his skin was tough, but didn't feel as unyielding as natural stone. She wouldn't want to cuddle with him when he was like this, but he was still oddly appealing.

"I could carry you like this, but don't you think it'd help if you shifted too?" he asked, which made her realize she'd been staring.

"It might," she agreed, hoping she wasn't blushing. If she was, the dim moonlight might keep him from noticing. Of course, if she was feathered, he wouldn't be able to notice anything, so she wasted no time in stripping then transforming. Her body shrank until Lucas stood more than four feet taller than her. Unconcerned by that, she stretched her wings out, inwardly sighing at the relief she felt assuming her animal form.

Lucas smiled as the owl replaced the woman. He'd never seen her shifted before, and noted that she seemed to be the same type owl Erasmus had been. Eurasian something. He'd never been able to re-member the name. Her feathers were a mix of tan, brown, and black, with a little orange thrown in. The same orange her eyes were, in fact. And though he'd never admit it, he found the feathered 'horns' she sported kind of adorable.

Crouching down, he lifted a hand questioningly. She took two steps forward and ducked her head enough to brush the top of her head against his palm. Though he knew shifters had the same mind in both forms, it still delighted him that she allowed him to touch the soft feathers. But this wasn't why he'd brought her out here.

Giving one last gentle stroke, he drew his hand back. "Ready to fly?" She let out a soft call and bobbed her head. He rose and stepped back, preparing to leap upward, but she beat him to it. Her wings spread, then beat downward, and he was struck by how silently she flew. There was a whisper of noise at first, but that was it. He'd have to be careful or he could easily lose her in the dark.

Taking off after her, he grinned, having to work to keep her in his sights. Their speeds were fairly well matched, so he wasn't concerned about that, but when she started dipping and twirling, he laughed. She was definitely more agile than he was in the air, but he'd expected that. A two foot tall bird versus a six foot two gargoyle? There was no contest. Which meant it turned into a game, with Sophia darting toward him and ducking beneath his wing, between his legs. Joining in, he tried to touch her when she passed by, but the closest he managed was a fingertip on the very edge of one of her feathers. Not that he minded. He was competitive, certainly, but not when it was something done for the pure joy of it like this was. He wanted them both to relax, to forget about the shit show inside the Athenaeum for a little while. It was working better than he could have expected, at least for him. Fun wasn't very high on his priority list, especially since he'd been chosen as head guard, so times like this were precious.

Lucas wouldn't have traded the hour they spent in the air for anything. The only reason he started to descend in a slow spiral was because his wings were getting tired. His wing muscles were strong, sure, but he didn't work them like he did the rest of his muscles. The best way to exercise them was by using them, and flying below ground just didn't work too well. Besides, if he needed to fly for more than an hour to save his life or someone else's, he was probably screwed anyway.

The landing wasn't quite as gentle as he would have liked, but he stayed upright. He looked up and caught a glimpse of Sophia flying across the moon. She let out a soft call he could barely make out, but flew for a few more minutes before she began gliding down toward him, using air currents rather than her wings. He expected her to land near him or shift and land on her feet, but she opted to land on his shoulder. It was a careful landing, and despite her size, she was surprisingly light. A house cat weighed more than she did right now.

Except cats didn't have claws as long as she did, not that he'd feel them with his skin still stone.

She nipped his ear delicately, pressed the top of her head against his cheek, then half fell, half flew off his shoulder and down to the ground. A moment later, she was a woman again.

Sighing, she stretched her arms out as she arched backward, unconcerned by her nudity. "That was amazing. I haven't flown that long in years."

"Why not? Owls are common enough in the States, and you fly quietly enough that you wouldn't have to worry about being spotted even if they were rare."

"No time," she said, letting her arms drop to her sides as she walked over to her clothes and started getting dressed. "Boring girl who always studies, remember?"

"Boring is the last word I think of when I think of you," he admitted.

"That's because you didn't see me when I was in school."

"Maybe." But he doubted it. "Ready to go back in? I know you wanted to go to your secret spot."

"Sure. But I want to do this again soon."

"Just say when." Because he was realizing he'd do a whole hell of a lot to see her this relaxed and happy.

Chapter 15

Sophia might have wanted to go research, but after the amazing hour Lucas had given her, she took the time to return the favor. Except instead of being in the sky, they were in her bed and naked. Which meant when she left him, her body was loose and relaxed, she was smiling, and he was happily dozing.

Again, she cast her protective spells before retreating to the aspida room. It was getting so bad that she only felt safe when with Lucas or here in this secret room. Feeling safe didn't mean she didn't feel agitated, though, as she was tonight, despite how much she'd enjoyed her time with Lucas. She hated thinking of Penny or Peter being a killer. Jericho was easier to see, but even he had never struck her as a bad guy. An asshole, sure, but not a murderer.

She sat down at the desk and looked at the various books previous aspides had collected. Pursing her lips, she finally chose the book on magic cast on the Athenaeum. It was a long shot, but maybe there was some kind of magical surveillance that had caught something. Which sounded silly, she knew, but anything was possible here. Magic could do damn near anything, so long as you knew how and had the power.

The book was interesting and definitely had information that she should know as aspida. A few she knew about, like the labyrinth, the spells to keep the books preserved, and a ward to prevent anyone from seeing the entrance. But not all the spells were big ones, and a few she should have guessed. They were underground and the only access she'd seen to the surface was the single entrance, so a simple but powerful spell had been cast on the Athenaeum to ensure air circulated and never went stale or had a buildup of carbon dioxide. And while they had a freshwater source deep within the mountain, there were spells to ensure it was clean and also to heat it.

Further on in the book, it changed. It was no longer talking about spells and protections, but the secrets of the Athenaeum. Her heartbeat quickened as a smile spread over her lips. She had known that this room wasn't the only secret here. How could it be? This place was too old and too magical to have a single secret within it. Something she refused to recognize as hope blossomed in her chest, though it was unlikely these secrets would be beneficial at the moment. But like Lucas had said, it only took one piece of the puzzle dropping into your lap. Maybe she'd just gotten that one piece.

The first section was a list of rooms, added as they'd been carved out of the mountain. Some had notes detailing that they'd been expanded or repurposed, but a couple had been blocked up for various reasons. One was listed as unstable and unusable unless a stone elemental was able to shore it up, and they'd been lacking such a person at the time. Another was marked as unnecessary, but she wasn't sure why it hadn't been turned into something else.

A few of the now unused and hidden rooms were on the upper two levels, but most were lower. If someone had been brewing up Achlys and stealing bodies, maybe they were using one of those rooms. It wouldn't have been smart for them to do it in their own room, especially with how infrequently people locked their doors. All it would have taken would be one person accidentally opening the wrong door. An easy thing to do since none of the doors were marked. Hell, she still occasionally opened the wrong door.

Grabbing her notebook, she flipped to a clean page and started marking down the rooms that had been hidden but not destroyed. Odds were they would be empty and uninteresting, but on the off chance they weren't...she had to look. Fortunately, the list didn't just include locations, but how to get into those rooms which had been sealed magically.

Tearing off the page, she folded it, stood, and shoved it in her back pocket. She considered, then left the room and started toward her bedroom. While she could go searching these rooms by herself, it wouldn't be smart. She was still a novice when it came to defense—or offense, for that matter—and if a murderer was using the rooms, she didn't want to surprise him or her when she was alone. Not only could they kill, they'd proven they would. She liked to think she was strong and independent, but she wasn't an idiot. She was taking one of her guards. Since Lucas had already saved her life once, she knew he was capable. Besides, there was no one in the Athenaeum she trusted more than him. Somehow he'd risen above her mom in that regard, and she wasn't sure why. Possibly because of the disinterested way Heather had been treating her the last few days? Even if that was the case, she felt a pang of guilt. Her mom had been there for every single day of her twenty-four years and she'd known Lucas for all of a month. But, she supposed, they were investigating something dark in the Athenaeum, and that had to bring people closer together.

Sighing, she tried to ignore the guilt as she made her way back to her room, hoping that tonight's excursion would result in them having a better idea of who was behind the deaths. And why.

As had become his habit, Lucas was awake when she got back. And to add to the evidence that he was a good guard, he instantly took in her expression, slid his legs over the bed, and stood up. "What is it?"

"I might have found something," she told him, smiling. "There's no guarantee, but it's a chance, and I know we need to focus on any possibility if it means finding this murderer."

"We do," he agreed. "What did you find?"

"First, I need you to swear that this doesn't go any further than the two of us, because it involves something that I'm pretty sure only aspides are supposed to know."

"Of course," he said without hesitation, and nothing in his tone or face told her didn't mean it.

Sophia pulled out the paper and opened it as she crossed to him, holding it out. "I found a list of rooms that have been sealed off and hidden. The way I see it, the killer didn't make the Achlys in their room or the lab because they wanted to keep it secret and their involvement hidden. They'd also need someplace to put the bodies when they stole them, no matter what they intended to do with them, so what better place than a room no one knows about?"

His brows lifted as he looked down the list of nine rooms. "I had a feeling there were one or two, but I didn't realize there were so many. And why hide them instead of using them for something other than what they were first intended for?"

"I thought the same thing, but sealing them off makes sense for a couple of them. This one," Sophia pointed to the third on the list, "they said was unstable. Basically, they were worried it would cave in unless they had a stone elemental shore it up, and at the time there weren't any in the Athenaeum. Shouldn't be a problem now, since I'm pretty sure Seth could fix it in a second. And we should be okay just to peek in."

"We should. And god of mountains...yeah, he'd be able to fix it up." Lucas's eyes lifted to meet hers. "I take it you want to go check on these now?"

"Yep. We can't really do it during the day. Even on the lower levels of the library, there tends to always be someone around. It would suck if we did end up finding where the killer's been working while they were nearby."

"Good point. Let me put my boots on."

In just a few minutes, with Sophia's threat and shield spells renewed, they left the bedroom and went to the location of the first room. It was on the ground floor, with the original door at the side of a supply closet. It took them five minutes of searching to find what remained of the doorway, and another three to get it open. Except when they stepped inside, the lights didn't glow automatically like in the rest of the Athenaeum. It was like it had somehow been disconnected from the rest of the convenience magic. They exchanged a glance and pulled out their phones, using the flashlights on them to investigate the room. It didn't take long, as it was only about fifteen feet by twenty and empty but for a piece of vellum. Even that only had some scratches on it, and no matter how hard they looked, they couldn't find any meaning in the marks. Which meant this room was a bust. Just to be sure, they did some checks, but there was no trace of magic and no hint that anyone had been in here for centuries.

The room off the gym was next and no better than the first, nor was the one off a now empty bedroom on the residential level. That was the one that needed shoring up, and Sophia made a note to talk to Seth when everything was settled. They weren't exactly hurting for empty rooms, but it was silly to have one unusable when one of their patrons could fix it.

The fourth room was better. It was off the relic room on the second level. Sophia thought the notes had said they were sealing it off to keep some materials safe, but gave no reason why they hadn't been moved later, when the lower levels were completed. There were both relics and texts here, long forgotten. Sophia and Lucas spent some time looking through them, and from what they could tell, they were a mix of things that should be on the fourth and fifth levels. Nothing earth shattering, but some interesting things. Sophia would have to talk to the curators and have them properly cataloged and moved to the appropriate levels and rooms. After she did a more thorough look. Then again, if Olivia did accept the job as head curator, she could help. The woman read more languages than Sophia and Lucas combined, so she'd be an asset.

Another one, down on level four had a few relics, but they couldn't figure out why they weren't on level one. Even Sophia could recognize that there wasn't anything outstanding about any of them. Then again, she'd quickly learned that looks could definitely be deceiving here, and it would take a witch to ensure these relics were ordinary.

But they kept looking, going down the list. On room seven, they finally found something worth hunting for. The doorway was hidden in the stairwell between levels five and six. It was also harder to open than any of the others, though they couldn't figure out why. The only magic either of them felt was the same magic that permeated the entire Athenaeum, but it was almost like there was some kind of blocking ward on it. Fortunately, Lucas knew a spell that helped get the door open and they looked into a hallway. Curious, they stepped inside, but they were cautious. Something about this hallway felt different than the other rooms they had checked, but Sophia couldn't put her finger on what it was. Given that Lucas's skin turned to stone, he clearly felt the same. She paused, quickly recasting her protections, and shuddered when the threat spell felt like pinpricks stabbing her entire body.

"Be careful," she murmured, though she knew it was unnecessary. Lucas was always careful, especially when it came to her.

He nodded and they moved forward. There was a short tunnel—she really shouldn't call it a hallway, not when it looked more like a natural cave—then it opened up into a room. Both of them paused at the opening and looked around. Unlike the other rooms they'd checked out, this one wasn't a dead end. The room itself was roughly fifteen feet square with a table holding a few relics, but on the far side was another door. Not a stone door like the one into this room had been, but one made of wood that looked like it was centuries old.

What was it about a mostly empty room that was making them both so skittish? Was it whatever was behind that door? The relics? Something here was triggering her threat spell, so it wasn't just them being paranoid. And the room really was bare. The walls were identical and a little rough. The floor was smoother, like it had been walked on for years before being hidden away. But there was nothing remarkable about it. No words or symbols, no discoloration anywhere. It was just a room with relics and it terrified her. Premonition had never been one of her gifts—and she hoped it never would be—but she knew that if they stepped foot in that room that something bad would happen. Except she couldn't let that stop her. Catching a murderer was rarely safe, and she would do anything to make sure no more innocent people died. Especially not on her watch.

She just prayed to the gods that Lucas didn't suffer for it.

Chapter 16

NEITHER OF THEM SPOKE for several minutes. Lucas was probably weighing the risks and searching for dangers. Sophia was gathering her courage.

"I don't see anything identifying those relics, so maybe we check out the other room first?" she finally suggested, inclining her head toward the door.

"Smart. Neither of us is equipped to identify relics," Lucas agreed.

Sophia had never grown up wishing she'd been born another Arcane race, but today she wouldn't have minded if she had been a witch. But if the next room was clear, there was no reason why these relics couldn't be cataloged like the others and moved to the appropriate levels. She'd figure out something to tell the curators so they wouldn't ask too many questions. Until she found out why these perfectly good rooms had been hidden, she didn't intend to share their existence with anyone but the three faction heads.

They started across the room, each step slow as they studied the relics. There was a statue of some kind of serpent, a small one of a mermaid, what looked like a torque, a sundial, and a round shield. They looked interesting, seemed innocuous enough, but she knew better than to assume anything. As they neared the middle of the room, Sophia felt her shoulders tensing, but nothing happened. She started to relax, to let a breath ease out, but four steps after, a crack echoed through the room. It wasn't loud, but it made the hair on the back of her neck stand up.

"Shit," Sophia whispered.

Lucas slowly nodded. "Yeah, that's probably not good."

They looked toward the relics and Lucas cursed when they saw the torque was snapped in half, despite looking like it was gold. It should have bent, not broken, not that there was any obvious reason for either to have happened. Hell, from what Sophia knew, a lot of torques had a core of iron or some metal harder than gold. Before she could do more than note that fact, water started pouring out of the jagged ends. It wasn't a trickle, though the torque was less than half an inch in diameter. No, this was more like a fire hose shooting out of both ends. Fast enough that the water reached their feet in seconds. Rather than draining past them, in only seconds it began rising. And the sound was insane. It reminded her of how people always described waterfalls, roaring instead of the gentle pouring sound she might have expected.

"We've got to figure out how to stop that," Sophia shouted over the roar of the water as she began making her way through it to the broken relic. There was no telling how much water the relic might shoot out. It could stop flowing at any second, or it could keep going and flood the Athenaeum.

Lucas reached the table before she did and picked up one half of the torque. It didn't stop the water, just changed the direction. It hit the wall hard, and he almost lost hold of it. The water rebounded against the wall and flooded the table, knocking the other relics onto the floor, though the second half of the torque remained in place as though held there.

Lucas tried to cut off the flow, but he couldn't get his hand close to it, despite his strength. Sophia's fingers barely brushed the other half before pain shot through her. She jerked her hand back, the tips of her fingers feeling like they'd been both singed and frozen at the same time. "I can't touch it."

He cursed and grabbed for the other piece and was able to hold it without trouble, probably due to his skin being stone at the moment. Getting the pieces close together was as impossible as just getting his hand to the end had been, but that wasn't the end of their trouble. The water was now up to their knees and Sophia glanced at the hallway they'd come through, only to see that the water stopped at the doorway, as though an invisible wall was holding it in. That was why the water had begun pooling so quickly; it had no where else to go. While that meant the Athenaeum wasn't likely to flood, it also meant that they ran a very real risk of drowning if they couldn't figure out how to stop the water. And if they couldn't, Lucas was definitely in trouble, as it was well known that gargoyles couldn't swim, no matter what form they were in. She couldn't let that happen. Not just because she was responsible for him, but because she couldn't bear to lose someone else. Not this soon, not ever. And definitely not someone she was coming to care for like she did him.

"Keep trying. I'll see if one of the other relics can help," Sophia told him as she bent to try to find the other relics in the water. The only good thing she could say about the situation was that the water was a comfortable temperature, but that was little relief.

The relics had gotten swept away from the table, and the water was moving so quickly that it was hard to see, so Sophia bent forward to feel around, but her hands had barely entered the water when something brushed her fingers. It wasn't stone or wood. It felt like...scales. Large scales.

Sophia jerked back and looked up to where Lucas was still struggling with the torque. "There's something in the water."

He didn't look up, his entire focus on his current task. "Yeah, relics."

"No, something alive. Something scaled."

"Fuck." He looked at the torque pieces, then dropped them on the table and shifted fully, so his nails lengthened into claws and his body bulked up even more. Only his wings remained safely hidden. "Shield spell on you, now. Be prepared to fight."

Sophia pushed to her feet and had to take a breath before she could speak the words, but she'd practiced this bit of sorcery so much that it only took one try, and it was just in time.

No sooner than the invisible shield formed around her, something dark, long, and thick slammed into her, knocking her back. She would have fallen into the water if Lucas's arms hadn't wrapped around her. Before she could get her feet under her, he spun them around, further disorienting her. The reason for it was clear when they were jolted forward a step, proving that whatever had attacked her had gone after him, too. He took a second to make sure she wouldn't fall, then roared and whirled back on their attacker. Sophia was only a moment after him, and her eyes widened. Lucas had pulled out a dagger, one she'd seen him carrying a number of times, and slashed at what looked like a life-size version of the serpent statue that had fallen into the water. The scales were an ombre blue, ranging from the crystal color of Caribbean seas to the navy of the ocean. It had fins where she expected its ears would be, and a long snout full of teeth as long as her hand. It was beautiful, in a lethal sort of way, she'd just prefer not to see it up close, especially since she couldn't tell exactly how long it was.

Lucas's first slash missed by a hair, but the second connected, opening a gash in the serpent's side. It let out a low shriek that hurt her ears and vibrated her bones before it whipped its long body about. It knocked into Lucas's hand, sending the weapon flying.

"Find that. I'll keep it distracted," Lucas ordered as he leapt at the creature. His claws had difficulty getting through the tough scales, which meant Sophia needed to find their only weapon, fast. She moved as quickly through the water as she could, took a deep breath, then dunked herself into the now waist-deep water. In another few minutes, it would be over their heads and Lucas would be screwed. She would *not* allow that to happen. She wasn't going to lose Lucas. No, she'd tear down the walls of this room before she let that happen.

She stayed under until her lungs burned for air, searching with both her hands and eyes for the dagger. Surfacing, she took only long enough to refill her lungs before she was under again. Just before she went up for air, she saw a glint of steel. It was too far for her to reach with this breath, so surfaced as she moved toward it. When she reached the spot she thought she'd seen it, she started to take another breath when one of the serpent's coils slammed into her. It didn't hurt, not with the shield spell, but it did knock her under the water and pin her face down against the stone floor.

Trying not to panic, Sophia squirmed, trying to wiggle out from under it or push it up enough that she could get free. It didn't budge, and she hadn't gotten a good breath before getting submerged, so her lungs were starting to scream with the need for air. The water above her was churning with the movement of the beast and Lucas, but it was impossible for her to tell what was going on, or if Lucas had even noticed what had happened to her.

As the seconds ticked past with the serpent acting as an anchor to keep her submerged, she started to lose her calm. Then she caught sight of the knife again. She stretched her arm toward it, but it was just out of reach. Straining, she pushed with her feet, her knees, anything to get just another few inches. If she could grab it, she could stab the serpent and possibly move it off of her. Hopefully before she drowned in the depths of the most fantastic—and potentially terrifying—place she'd ever seen.

The serpent shifted, its weight threatening to crush her legs despite her shield, and she gasped involuntarily, sucking in water. Rather than choking, instead of feeling the water burn her lungs, she felt as though she'd just taken a deep breath. Confused, she stopped struggling and attacking as her brain tried to figure out what the hell had just happened. Then she realized there was a gentle current near her chest. No, it was funneling directly *into* her chest. Into the amulet, specifically, which was weird. The card had said it would prevent dehydration and could create water from nothing, but it hadn't said anything about what it was doing now. Not that she was a hundred percent what it was actually doing, but she'd complain about the lack of information later since it seemed to be saving her life.

Taking a testing breath to see if the first had been a fluke, she smirked when no water reached her lungs. Now that she was at no risk of drowning, she resumed trying to reach the knife.

Red stained the water above her and she prayed to all the gods she knew that it was the serpent's blood, not Lucas's. Pressing her hands back against the coil pinning her to the stone floor, she drew in a deep breath—which felt beyond weird underwater—and did her best to speak a spell that would blast the serpent. With her palms in direct contact, it shifted the beast just enough to let her shove herself forward in the water. When it came down again, all of its body landed on stone, not flesh.

Sophia grabbed the knife and shoved herself up. To her shock, the water now came up almost to her shoulders. The amulet was still submerged, and she could still feel the flow of water spiraling into it. She had no idea what it was doing other than drawing water in, but she hoped it would keep helping them. Because otherwise, they only had a few minutes. If the water went above Lucas's head, she'd shove the amulet over his head. She, at least, could swim.

"Got it!" she called, but Lucas was now on the other side of the serpent from her and she wasn't sure how to safely get the knife to him. While she'd been taking self-defense classes from him and others, they had yet to move to weapons. They'd all agreed that she would need more than three weeks of training before doing that, but he definitely needed the knife sooner rather than later. While the serpent was bleeding from the earlier slash, it wasn't bleeding badly enough.

"Toss it!" he called, before slashing at the serpent's face. One of his claws managed to get through the scales, but it wasn't a lethal shot.

She wasn't sure this was a good idea, but threw the knife underhand, the way she'd seen people throw weapons in movies. Fortunately, Lucas was far more skilled than she was when it came to weapons, and snatched it out of the air. An instant after that, he had to backpedal several steps to avoid the foot-long fangs of the serpent. Then the knife lengthened in his hand. It wasn't a gradual or minor change, either. In just over a second, it went from a six-inch blade to one that looked four feet long. That was more like it! Without a real weapon, she hadn't been sure they'd stood a chance, but a sword in hands like Lucas's? The serpent was toast.

Lucas swung, the sword cutting through the scales a great deal easier than his claws had, causing the beast to let out another painful shriek. It was clear he had that under control—for now, anyway—but even if he killed it this second, they had another, arguably bigger problem. The water. She might have a plan to protect Lucas, but there was no guarantee the water would stop once it had filled this room. The barrier might be stopping it from going out into the hallway, but she knew water could crack stone, so it might still be able to flood into other parts of the Athenaeum.

Taking a breath out of habit, she submerged herself, searching for the torque that had started all this. She swam for the table, disheartened but unsurprised when she didn't find either piece on it. But since she didn't have to surface for air, she was able to stay down and hunt for the relic pieces. Still, she knew the clock was ticking and moved as quickly as she could through the water, wishing she was as good in the water as she was in the air.

It took thirty seconds for her to find the first piece, and when she grabbed it, she was surprised it didn't hurt as badly as it had the first time. Because it was underwater, maybe? It didn't matter. Wounds could be healed, and she had to keep looking for the other piece. After sixty more precious seconds, she saw it wedged into the corner. Shoving herself forward, she grabbed it, then pushed toward the surface. It was now deep enough that she had to go up on her toes to get her face out of the water. Taking just a moment to glance toward Lucas, she saw he'd made progress with the serpent. It was thrashing about in the water, bleeding from a dozen deep gashes. Then, as she watched, Lucas leapt out of water and lifted the sword above his head. As he came down, he swung the sword, and it sank deep into the serpent's neck. The creature let out a scream that vibrated through the water and echoed off the stone walls, making her wince. But its head quickly fell beneath the water, a moment before the water level suddenly dropped an inch.

She didn't have time to wonder at that. She had to figure out how to get the relic to stop spewing water before they drowned. Like him, she wasn't able to press the pieces together. Cursing, she studied one of the pieces, realizing that it had markings. It could be a language, but she doubted it. There were parallel wavy lines that clearly represented water, and a horseshoe shape that could be the torque itself.

Before she could further decipher the markings, she lost her balance and slipped beneath the water. It was murky with the blood of the serpent, but she could see just enough to keep desperately trying to shove the two pieces of the torque together again. To her shock, this time it worked. The seam sealed like it had never been in the first place and the flow of water from it stopped.

Sophia wanted to cry with relief. It didn't get them out of here, but with the serpent dead and the water no longer rising, their chances had gone from a snowball's chance in hell to a snowball's chance in the desert. It wasn't much, but it was something.

Strong hands grabbed her biceps and pulled her up so her head was out of the water. Lucas's face was full of concern and covered with blood.

"I thought you were drowning."

"The amulet saved me," she told him, touching it. "Seems it prevents dehydration *and* over-hydration. And I got the torque back together, so the water won't rise anymore."

"Good." He looked toward the hall they'd come through and scowled. Shifting his hold on her so she was pressed against his side, he pushed through the water, which reached the tops of his shoulders. To help make it easier, she wrapped her legs around his waist so she didn't trip him. There was no way she was going to risk him falling and not being able to get his head out of the water again.

He stopped just in front of the invisible barrier, still scowling. Reaching out, he poked the barrier. While it didn't seem to hurt him, it did prevent his hand from passing through. "Shit. We're stuck in here."

"Can't be," she said, shaking her head. "There's no way this torque has never broken before. There has to be a way of getting rid of the water."

"I hope so, because I have a feeling this barrier won't let us pass until the water is gone."

"This was a booby trap, wasn't it?"

He looked at her, gaze serious. "Probably, yeah."

"Then there definitely has to be a way of getting out of here. They wouldn't set a trap they couldn't escape."

"No, they wouldn't," he said darkly, eyes narrowing.

"If the torque caused the water, maybe one of the other relics can get rid of it?"

"It's possible. There was...what, a shield, sundial, and statue?"

"Yeah, but I'm pretty sure you just killed the statue."

He looked over his shoulder and smirked. "I think so, too."

Unwrapping her legs, she said, "Put me down and I'll see if I can find the relics?" She saw he was about to protest, so she smiled. "I'm not made of stone, and apparently I can't drown right now, so it has to be me. Besides, you know more sorcery than I do. Why don't you try to think of a way out of here while I go diving? Maybe there's something on here," she added, handing him the torque. It had stopped hurting her the moment it had repaired itself, but her hands were still tender. Tender and an angry shade of pink. Having them in the water eased some of the pain, but if Seth's gift didn't heal them, she'd have to visit Sergei later.

"Good point," he said, but before he released her, he kissed her hard and she gripped his shirt, wanting to continue, even though she knew they had more important things to worry about at the moment. He broke the kiss, saving her from having to make a decision. "Thanks for keeping the water from getting any higher. And for not drowning."

"And thank you for killing that sea monster," she told him before she slipped beneath the surface. With no more water pouring in, it was easier for her to move and navigate. Visibility still wasn't great, but it was improving. She was thrown at first because she didn't see the body of the serpent, and she should have. The thing had been massive. Then she found the serpent statue she'd first seen and realized why. The head of the statue was detached and lying next to the rest of it. That explained why the water level had dropped when it died.

There was less mass in the water because it had transformed back to its original state. Scowling, she left it there, annoyed that they'd been attacked by a relic. It made sense, but that didn't mean she had to like it.

The mermaid statue was the next one she found, but she was reluctant to touch it. The torque had caused the room to fill with water and the serpent had attacked them, so what would happen if she touched this one? Would it come to life and attack them, too? She opted to leave it alone for now and continued searching. The sundial was the next relic she found, and she hesitated with her fingers over it for several seconds before she let her hand brush it. At the contact, she got zapped and tried to pull her hand back, but she wasn't able to move it from the sundial.

Her pulse starting to quicken again, she twisted in the water to put her foot against the relic and pulled again, but it remained firm against her fingers. That was bad enough, as she didn't want to be permanently attached to some magical sundial, but she was also hit by a wave of vertigo that had her swaying in the water. It passed, and the relic didn't seem to be hurting her, but it also couldn't be a good thing that it was all but glued to her and physically affecting her.

Lucas's legs came into view and a second after, he reached into the water, wrapped a hand around her bicep, and hauled her to the surface. The sundial, of course, remained attached to her fingers.

Blinking the water out of her eyes, she looked up at him. "What? Did you figure something out?"

He frowned and shook his head. "I thought you did."

"What do you mean?"

"The water level dropped a good two inches a second ago. I thought you'd done something."

"I didn't." She lifted her hand out of the water and frowned at the sundial. It dangled from her fingers in a way that made it clear she wasn't holding onto it. "Not really, anyway. All I did was touch this."

"A sundial? Is that...stuck to your hand?"

"Yep," she said blandly as she studied it more closely. There was writing along the outer edge of the dial, partially obscured by her fingers, but what she could see she was able to read, as it was a form of ancient Greek. "Oh. I might have done something," she admitted.

"Oh?"

"Apparently, this can affect time in a small area."

"Affect how?"

"If I'm reading this right, it's basically like hitting rewind or fast forward."

"Which one do you think you did? Because I'd love it if you hit forward and this water is all draining somewhere."

She thought again about the current that led to the amulet. Could the relic be pulling the water into it and storing it? Could that be how it prevented dehydration? It sounded silly, even for a relic, but it did make a weird kind of sense. Magic didn't obey the laws of physics that humans believed ruled the universe, but there was a logic to it. A relic that drew water in to disperse it into the body of the one who wore it was logical. Strange, yes, but she wasn't going to bitch.

Closing her eyes, she focused on the sundial and mentally willed it to move them forward, hoping this was a relic that responded to mental commands. She could feel the water start to lower and pushed harder.

"That's it, Sophia," Lucas murmured, but she barely noticed his words. "Keep going."

She did, and although she was standing still, it quickly felt like she'd been running a marathon for several hours. When the water was mid-chest she nearly fell over, but Lucas wrapped his arms around her, pulling her in against his chest and keeping her upright.

It was only a few moments later that Lucas said, "The water isn't going down anymore."

No, it had to. They needed it to be gone so they could get out of here. Then she remembered her theory about the amulet. "Take off my necklace and put the amulet in the water. Make sure it's touching your skin."

He didn't ask questions, just did his best to support her while undoing the small clasp. She didn't open her eyes, not wanting to break her concentration. The way she felt, she might not be able to get it back.

"That did it," he assured her, and she only nodded slightly in response. She was relieved when his arms were back around her, as it felt like the sundial was sapping her vitality to speed up time. Not surprising. A lot of powerful relics had a cost to use them. If she was lucky, the water would disappear before the last of her energy did.

As the level of the water lowered, Lucas did the same for them, until he was sitting on the floor with her in his lap. She leaned into him and just kept focusing on keeping time sped up for them.

She wasn't sure how much time had passed—real or perceived—when she could no longer feel the water. Lucas gave her a gentle squeeze and whispered, "You can stop now. The water is gone."

Sophia opened her eyes, unsurprised when they felt heavy. She didn't remember the last time she'd felt this exhausted. Now she just had to figure out how to let go of the sundial so it didn't happen again. But when she opened her fingers, this time it dropped to the floor with a loud clatter.

"You were amazing," Lucas said, kissing her shoulder. "Rest for a few minutes while I put everything back where we found it."

"Serpent statue is broken," she murmured.

"I'll take care of it," he assured her, easing her off his lap. She half-fell, half-laid on the floor, and a moment later, her eyes slipped closed and she was out.

Chapter 17

LUCAS DIDN'T MISS HOW Sophia had pretty much immediately passed out. Using the sundial had taken more than expected out of her, and he'd seen it from the moment she'd started using it. Seen it, but he had also known better than to tell her to stop or give it to him. She was both stubborn and strong, which was a dangerous—and appealing—combination. But he let her rest now while he set about putting the room back to how they'd found it. She deserved it, even if it was only a couple of minutes. He might have been the one to kill the serpent, but if she hadn't dealt with the water, he would have drowned and they both knew it. Stone sank. Even magic didn't change that fact.

Sophia might not have realized it, but this room didn't look as untouched as the others. There was no dust, no trace of insects—which they occasionally had wandering in since there was no actual front door—which meant that the traitor might well know of this room. It might even be one he or she had claimed for themselves. If that was the case, Lucas didn't want to give them any reason to know someone had been here. When it came to guarding the lives of the Athenaeum, he always went with better safe than sorry.

He shifted back to his human form, as it was easier to move when he was flesh rather than stone. Unwilling to touch any of the relics again, he used sorcery to place them back on the table. And, just like Sophia had warned, the head was no longer attached to the serpent, which was trickier. While sorcery could do most anything, it still meant the sorcerer had to know the correct spell, and Lucas had focused on spells to keep him and his charges alive. That fact helped him now. In his human form he healed normally, but stone didn't, so he'd made sure he knew how to repair it in case something broke while he was in his gargoyle form. He didn't want to go through life without a finger or wing. The same spell should work here, though he was aware that working on relics wasn't quite the same as working on mundane objects or people. It took extra skill and power. He had to cast the spell four times before the head was firmly attached to the body once more. Now, if he could just be sure that it wouldn't come to life again, he'd be happy.

Fortunately, the amulet and sundial hadn't just gotten rid of the water, they had gotten rid of any trace of it, so he didn't have to do anything there.

Kneeling beside Sophia, he carefully put the necklace back around her neck before he shook her shoulder. "Sophia?" he said, voice gentle. "You can't sleep on the floor all night." It had only been twenty minutes, but it would have to do until he could get her back to her bed. He'd carry her if needed.

She let out an adorable little grumble, and he smiled, brushing her hair away from her face. "Come on, Soph. Time to wake up. Or do you need me to carry you to bed?"

Her brow furrowed and she worked her eyes open. She looked at him for a moment before those beautiful green eyes widened. "I can't go to bed," she told him as she pushed herself upright.

"Why not? I think you deserve it. You kicked some relic ass, and that sundial tried to kick yours."

"Yeah, but we haven't gone in that room yet," she said, nodding to the wooden door. "If we don't, then the serpent and near drowning and everything is just an annoying waste of time."

He didn't disagree, and doubted she'd relent, so sighed and took her hands, pulling her to her feet. "All right. But when we're done, you go to bed."

"I won't argue, but I want to see what's in that room. I want to see what all that," she waved a hand toward the table of relics, "was protecting."

So did he, but he wanted to make sure she was safe, too. Which meant the best option was to stick close to her. "Okay, but let me know if you need to stop. And though I'm sure it galls you, stay behind me when we go in there."

"Are you kidding? You're a gargoyle. I'm squishy compared to you. But I'm putting a shield on both of us before we so much as touch the doorknob."

"I was going to suggest the very same thing," he told her with a smile. "Shield us up," he told her, shifting back to his stone skin.

"You're good," she told him a moment later, after whispering the spell.

He nodded and they walked to the door. It looked ordinary, and a quick check told him there was no magic on it, but that didn't mean it was safe. Right now, he wasn't going to assume anything was safe until after it hadn't tried to kill them.

Gripping the knob, he slowly turned it and pushed the door open slightly. Nothing exploded, nothing slammed into the door from the other side, so he opened it fully. He was not expecting what he saw in the next room.

It looked like a cross between a mad scientist's lab and a witch's study. There were a few books, but more loose papers than bound volumes. Some of those were printed, but the majority were handwritten. There were shelves filled with jars, each one carefully labeled in a neat block print. A few Lucas recognized, like foxglove and lead, but some were mysteries to him.

Then there was something that looked like a chemistry set—or alchemy equipment, he wasn't sure which. Test tubes, a Bunsen burner, a set of scales, and multiple tools he couldn't name.

The most disturbing part of the room wasn't any of that, but the raised stone in the middle of the room. It could be a table, but to his eye, it looked like an altar. Now, several people in the Athenaeum devoutly worshiped one or more gods, and of those, many had altars to their patron deities. None of them looked like this. Those altars were respectful, full of love. This one? He wouldn't be surprised to find traces of blood over it. If anything was going to be a sacrificial altar, this was it. As it was, it was covered in something black, and without touching it, he could only assume it was soot.

"I think this is the creepiest place I've ever been, and Mom and I went on a couple of those ghost tours a few years ago," Sophia whispered.

"It's definitely not a cozy room," he agreed. "Be careful what you touch."

"Trust me, I've learned that lesson." Between the book that had nearly killed her and the sundial, he didn't doubt that.

They didn't stray too far from one another as they started to look for clues. Sophia focused on the jars and vials while he began sorting through the papers. Something about the handwriting was teasing at his memory, but he couldn't figure out what. It could be because none of them were written in any alphabet he was familiar was, so he decided to let it cook in the back of his mind, to see if something came to him later.

"Lucas?"

"Hmm?" he asked, using one finger to shift a paper so he could see the one beneath.

"Do you remember when we found that book that had the information about Achlys?"

That got his attention, and he looked over at her. "Yeah. Why?"

"Do you remember any of the ingredients?"

"A few. Hemlock, nightshade berries, asp venom...and I know there were a few others, but I can't remember them off the top of my head."

"Flax-leaved daphne was another. And all of those are here," she said, pointing out each one where it sat on the shelves.

"Shit. Might not be conclusive, but I'd bet this is where they cooked that poison up."

"That's what I was thinking, too." And she sounded pissed. Not that he could blame her. This was where the thing that had killed her grandfather had been brewed. *He* was just as pissed.

He rubbed her back, knowing nothing was going to help at the moment, but wanting to do something to soothe her. "Come on, let's see if we can find something to point to who this room belongs to." Or how they had discovered it. Erasmus might have known of its existence, but how had anyone else? He couldn't see Erasmus giving away Athenaeum secrets like this, not unless he trusted someone completely. Erasmus had seemed to trust all of his people, at least until his murder, but he'd also taken the responsibility of aspida seriously—just like his granddaughter did. Would he have told someone he trusted with his very life about something meant for him alone? It was doubtful. But that wasn't the only possibility. No one was asked to join the Athenaeum if they weren't smart and talented. A stone elemental might have been able to sense voids in the stone. Some witches might be able to do something similar. Then there was sorcery. He didn't know a spell to find hidden rooms, but it would make sense if the venatores were taught something like that. Ancient people had loved hiding rooms. But the many possibilities meant they couldn't use locating this room as a way of narrowing down the person using it.

The pages he could read were printed in modern Greek. One listed where Egyptian asp venom could be obtained from. Another looked like a layout of the Athenaeum, except it included some rooms he wasn't familiar with, like the one they were currently in, which was circled with heavy strokes. Then there was a printout of everyone in the Athenaeum. He skimmed down and noticed that neither Sophia nor Heather were listed, but Erasmus, Agatha, Dion, and Thomas were, so it had been printed before any of those deaths. Thomas and Olivia had their names circled, which confirmed to him that their poisonings had been targeted rather than accidental. He'd assumed as much, but confirmation was good.

Their names weren't the only ones circled, but the other circles had been drawn with a pen that had blue ink rather than black. His mouth tightened when he read those names; Lachlan, Agatha, Kaito,

Sergei, Valerie, Ray, Jericho, Dion, Nicolas. And himself. That pissed him off, even though he wasn't sure what he'd been earmarked for. But it did mean he needed to watch out for them. He wasn't part of the murders and his name was there, which meant they could all be potential victims.

Lucas pulled out his phone and took a picture before placing it back where he found it.

"Hey Lucas? I'm still trying to learn about everyone. I know Peter's merfolk, but what about the other two you suspect?" Sophia asked, her finger resting on a paper.

"Jericho's an ice elemental, and Penny's also merfolk. Why? Did you find something?"

"Yeah. Booby trap plans. Sort of."

"What do you mean?" he asked, walking to her and looking at the page.

"There's a list of relics here. A couple of them are crossed off, but look. That sounds like the torque the water was coming out of, that could be the shield, and that could be the serpent statue," she said, pointing to the three items on the list.

"Okay, I'm with you for that, but why did you ask about what the suspects are?"

She looked up at him. "Because the shield created a sort of force field to hold in the water, and the torque could have been triggered by the other statue. Which meant whoever set it up either had an easy out, or wasn't worried about drowning. Other than mers and possibly water elementals, who else wouldn't fear drowning?"

"Only someone who had a relic like your necklace," he said, voice low and dangerous. Jericho wasn't exactly ruled out by this information, but his powers wouldn't have saved him. No one did well when trapped in a block of ice, not even ice elementals. He'd have been stuck just like anyone else. He wouldn't freeze to death, but he might have suffocated. "Okay, let's make sure this is how we found it, then head to bed."

"No, let's check out the last room first. There's only one left, and it's just down one level."

Despite everything, he found himself smiling before he kissed her head. "Fine, just the one. Let's hope it's as boring as the other ones were."

"Screw that," she said as she started straightening up papers. "Let's hope it's full of relics and books that can be added to the general collection."

He chuckled. "You're really settling into being aspida, aren't you?"

"I guess I am," she said as they left the room and closed the door behind them. They carefully crossed to the hallway, and fortunately, the relics remained dormant.

They went down to the last room, but Sophia was disappointed when it was disused as the first room they'd found. Because of that, he was able to get her back to her bedroom, though he had an arm around her waist, half holding her up. She was so exhausted she was stumbling almost like a drunk by the time they reached her room. After collapsing on the bed, she fell right asleep. He carefully removed her shoes and socks and pulled the covers up over her. After stripping down to his boxers, he climbed in after her, body pressed against her back. She didn't even stir, and he was happy for it. She needed at least eight hours of sleep after what she'd been through. More would be better.

As for him, he just kept mentally going over the lists they'd found, trying to figure out what they meant.

Chapter 18

THE NEXT MORNING, SOPHIA seemed well rested and Lucas was pleased there were no lasting effects from using the sundial. Even her hands were fine, and she'd told him the torque had injured them. He gave both palms a kiss before they left her room. She went off for breakfast, but Lucas decided to skip it and find Sergei.

It was early enough that Heather hadn't yet arrived at the clinic, and even Sergei looked like he hadn't been awake for long.

"You coherent enough for a conversation?" Lucas asked, hand on the door.

"Mentally, yes. Physically, I'm still waking up," Sergei answered. "Has something else happened?"

"Not the way you're thinking, no," Lucas said, shutting the door and walking over to sit near Sergei. "How's Lachlan doing?"

"No change. Not sure if that's good or bad at this point. After a week I would have hoped he would start to show improvement, but he hasn't. At least he's not deteriorating."

"Any signs that anyone else has been infected by the same thing?"

"Actually...yes," Sergei said with a deep sigh.

"Who?"

"Two people have, both guards. Jericho and Ray."

That brought the list back to mind. Jericho and Ray had both been on it. "I think we can rule Jericho out as a suspect," he told the healer.

"Because he's infected? Accidental harm happens all the time with terrorists and the like, so it could be that he didn't mean to expose himself."

"No, it's not just that." He told Sergei about the nighttime excursion he'd had with Sophia—leaving out just how they'd found the hidden rooms—including the lists they'd found. "I can't see him putting himself on a list. He would have had no way of knowing that we'd find out that room existed, much less that we would get past the booby traps to his...lair."

"Lair?" Sergei asked, brow arching. "Little dramatic, isn't it?"

"Considering that four people are dead, three are infected with some mystery substance, and we're chasing our tails? No, I don't think so."

"Fair enough. So you've narrowed it down to Peter or Penny?"

Sergei looked about as happy about that as Lucas felt. Both were sweet people, each obsessed with their job—but in a good way. Or so he'd thought. Even with the evidence starting to add up, it was hard for him to picture either of them coldly dosing Erasmus with a lethal amount of poison or using a forbidden spell to kill Agatha. "Pretty much. I'm thinking of seeing if I can pinpoint where they both were when the bodies went missing, see if that can rule one of them out. I'm reluctant to bring it up with either until we have more, not with how capable at killing they seem to be. And how willing."

"Understandable." Sergei looked at Lachlan, considering him for a moment. "Heather should be here in a few minutes, then we can go to your office? I know I said there was no change, but I don't want to take any chances with Lachlan."

"I'll go now, but I'll wait for you before starting the feed."

"Thanks."

Lucas actually passed Heather in the hallway, so knew it wouldn't be long. True to his word, while he pulled up the program to view the security feeds and found the date and approximate time, he didn't hit play. Not just because he'd promised, but because two sets of eyes were always better than one, and he didn't want to miss even the smallest clue.

Fifteen minutes later, Sergei walked in and shut the door behind him. Before he spoke, he cast the bubble spell. "Sorry, I wanted to go over Lachlan's progress with her—or the lack thereof."

"Not a problem. I know you're worried about him, " Lucas said. "Pull up a chair." When Sergei had, he started the feed. It took some time to find either of their suspects. Eventually, they were able to follow Peter to his room. While normally somewhat unusual, his father had just died, so it could be said he wanted some privacy to grieve. But since there was no camera in his room, they couldn't rule him out. They'd already learned that the body theft could have been done from anywhere.

Penny was harder, as she'd been in and out of the library that entire day, but when the bodies had been stolen, she was actually outside the clinic, writing on a notepad. It could be seen as suspicious that she was so close, but it could also just be a coincidence.

"Can you go back further?" Sergei asked. "See if one of them was out when Agatha was killed?"

"I looked weeks ago, right after her death," Lucas said, shaking his head. "The time around when she was killed had missing sections. Whoever killed her also wiped the video."

"Damn. Is there any other time we can check?"

"We don't have an exact date for Erasmus's poisoning and I've already checked to see if someone was nearby when we confronted Dion, so unless you have a time frame for Lachlan's exposure to whatever made him overly violent, I don't think so."

Sergei sighed and shook his head. "I don't know enough about this stuff. He could have been exposed a few minutes before he went berserk, or it could have been a week. For all I know, he was exposed around the same time Erasmus was poisoned. I just don't have enough information."

"Then we monitor the Athenaeum, make sure no one else gets exposed to the same thing Lachlan was, and that those who have been exposed don't hurt anyone. And we keep a close eye on Penny and Peter. Discreetly, of course."

"Just be sure to keep me updated. I've been in the Athenaeum a long time, and I want it back to how it was. How it should be. It used to be we could trust every person here with our lives. We didn't just call each other family, we *were* family. Now to be suspecting our own of all this? It's heinous."

"It is. I do believe almost everyone here is trustworthy, but until we can get to the bottom of this, I know it won't feel like home again. And I don't just mean the murders. I mean everything. Including the why. Erasmus apparently believed someone might be trying for his job, but if that's the case, then why do everything else? Why infect Lachlan and the others? Why kill Agatha or terrorize Sophia?"

"It couldn't be that simple. Especially since there's no way to guarantee anyone the position. Not with the magical safeguards in place. And the fact that all the patrons show up for the choosing. It's not something they can tamper with."

"Exactly my point. Everyone but Sophia knew that was the case, so there has to be something else going on. I just don't know what. None of it seems connected. Erasmus, okay. He was the aspida, so could have stood in the way of a lot. Thomas? He could have been a trial run. Agatha? I don't know why she was killed. She didn't know a lot of sorcery because cooks didn't need it, and she was a mer, so while she was powerful for her species, she didn't have a lot of external power. Not to mention she was a sweetheart who was adored by the whole damn Athenaeum. And Dion? I think he was just a scapegoat."

"Don't forget Olivia was poisoned at the same time as Thomas," Sergei reminded him.

"I haven't. I just don't know why they would have targeted her. A second trial run? Maybe they were concerned about the poison affecting different species differently?" Lucas suggested.

"It's possible. And Lachlan?"

Lucas slowly shook his head. "I really don't know, but I'm going to find out."

While Lucas was doing his investigation, Sophia was continuing hers, except while he was watching security feeds, she was watching people.

Spending time out in the open was starting to feel about as safe as walking through the woods alone at night without a flashlight, which was why she was recasting her shield spell often. The number of people who were giving her dirty looks or outright snubbing her was growing. One of the curators had even gotten in her face and snarled at her to move when she'd accidentally gotten in his way.

None of that was as bad as when Sophia had sat next to her mom at breakfast, though. Heather hadn't snarled, but she had looked at Sophia with a look caught somewhere between dismissal and disgust. Then she had promptly ignored every single word Sophia said. It didn't matter what she did to get Heather's attention, her mother acted as though she didn't exist. Because of that, Sophia didn't eat much.

She had thought about what Lucas and Sergei had said about their theory and checked for magic, shocked to find it permeating the room. No, not the room, the people in it. All nine of them. Operating on another theory, she cast her threat sensing spell, dismayed but unsurprised when her skin felt like it was crawling. Even after leaving the dining room it persisted. Soon she discovered that everyone she encountered pinged as a danger to her, except for Sergei and Lucas.

At least there were two people in the Athenaeum who still didn't mean her any harm.

Unsettled, she retreated to her office and shut the door. The feeling subsided only a little, and she leaned against the door, closing her eyes as she tried to calm her breathing.

She couldn't live like this for too much longer.

Her head thunked lightly against the door and she tried to figure out what she'd do if one of those people actually attacked. No, they needed to figure out how they could get rid of whatever was causing everyone to act so aggressively before that happened.

Her phone buzzed in her pocket and she jumped, then immediately cursed herself for being so easy to startle. Pulling it out, she saw a text from Olivia asking to see her. Sophia told her to meet in her office, then drew herself together and sat behind her desk. If Olivia was acting like the others, then the desk would give her a second or two to react. And just to be safe, she renewed the threat spell. After a second, she added the shield spell, too, just in case.

Several minutes later, the door opened and Olivia peeked inside.

"Come in," Sophia told her.

Olivia did, closing the door and taking a seat across from Sophia. "Thanks for seeing me."

"Not a problem. Is this about the head curator job, or something else?" she asked before she realized that the threat hadn't increased when Olivia arrived. It was about as low as when she was around Lucas and Sergei. She could only feel the background threat that was omnipresent these days. That was a pleasant surprise.

"The job," Olivia confirmed, and Sophia saw she was twisting her hands. That sign of nerves almost made her smile. She got it. She'd felt the same way when she'd been chosen as aspida. Except she hadn't had a choice.

"What did you decide?" she asked, hoping she didn't sound as eager as she felt.

Olivia's shoulders lifted, then fell as she inhaled deeply. "I'll take it. I'm still not entirely sure there's not a better choice, but I think I can do it well and it'll be a challenge." She started to smile. "It might even be fun. Besides, if I do it, I don't have anyone else to bitch about, because it'll be my fault."

Thank the gods. At least one thing had gone right. Two, really, since Olivia wasn't a danger to her. Sophia smiled and nodded. "There might be someone else, but I haven't found them yet. Just don't expect me to be much help in learning the job," she said, only half joking. "I have no doubt that Nick and Lucas can give you some pointers, though, and I'm sure there are notes from...from previous head curators." She didn't want to mention Dion's name, not when she couldn't share that Dion wasn't a murderer. Not yet. As soon as they found the real killer, though, she fully intended to let the entire Athenaeum know he'd been innocent. She was going to do all she could to set everything to rights, and that included clearing an innocent man's name.

"I'm sure there are. And I think I can pick it up."

"No doubt. With your memory? I really envy you that."

Olivia smiled tightly. "It definitely has its benefits, but there are some downsides. Some really fucking bad downsides."

Sophia cocked her head curiously. "Like what?"

"You know how something bad or painful happens and you try to put it out of your mind, and eventually you sort of forget about it, at least until something brings it to mind?"

"Yeah..."

"I can't sort of forget without a *lot* of work."

"Oh. Yeah, I can see how that would suck," Sophia said sympathetically. "Well, back to the actual topic...did you have any questions for me? Concerns? Anything like that?" Olivia visibly hesitated and Sophia leaned forward. "Look, I know you don't know me well. I've been here for a month and haven't gotten to spend a lot of time with you, but I want to be the best aspida I can. I can't do that if I don't know what's bothering the people in the Athenaeum." That still didn't seem to convince Olivia, so she went on. "Whatever it is, unless it's something I need to inform the healers or head of the nasaru about, I promise it'll stay just between us."

Olivia glanced back to the closed door, then turned to face Sophia again. "Is there something going on around here?"

Everything inside Sophia stilled for a second. Carefully, she asked, "What makes you ask that?" According to the guys, people were only acting weird when Sophia was mentioned, so there shouldn't be anything going on that Olivia could have noticed. Or was there more that Sophia wasn't aware of?

"You know I'm a nightmare. Sometimes we slip into dreams or nightmares without meaning to, especially if they're really strong or..." She struggled for a moment to find the right word. "Bizarre. If they're magical, then they can even act as a kind of beacon."

"That makes sense. I think all Arcane accidentally do things now and again. I take it you've been slipping into some dreams?"

"Yeah, nightmares. And a lot of them. When I say a lot, I mean more than is normal unless we're in a war zone or near a lot of traumatized people."

"Okay." That kind of made sense. If a lot of people were under the influence of magic that was altering their personalities, then it stood to reason it could also affect their subconscious. "What kind of nightmares?"

Olivia's brow furrowed and she shook her head. "Strange ones, and I've been in a lot of nightmares. It takes a lot for me to call a nightmare strange anymore."

That also tracked. Sophia studied Olivia, debating how to proceed. Trusting Olivia was risky, but they needed another way of getting information, and she had to trust in her own spell and instincts. She didn't sense any threat coming off Olivia, so she decided to test the waters.

"I do agree that there has been some...weirdness, though I couldn't tell you why." Not a lie, even if it wasn't the whole truth. "I can't even tell you the full extent of it. Because of that, could you do me a favor?"

"Depending on what it is? Probably."

"How hard is it for you to intentionally enter or observe dreams of specific people?"

Olivia shrugged. "Not hard. I mean, it's harder if they're far away and I don't know them or have any connection to them, but if you're talking about anyone here in the Athenaeum, then it should be as easy as, well, falling asleep."

"Good. Okay, what I have to ask needs to stay just between us. I don't want it getting out in case no one I mention is actually involved.

There's been too much grief in the Athenaeum recently to add unnecessary suspicion."

"I suppose that makes sense. You want me to enter a couple of dreams and tell you what they're dreaming about?"

"I do, to see if you can narrow some things down for me."

Olivia's brows lifted in interest. "Such as?"

"I'm not trying to be vague, but I really don't want to say too much until I hear back, but basically I'm trying to narrow down the source of the weirdness. I *think*," she stressed, "I have it narrowed down to a couple of people, but I could be wrong, hence the discretion."

"That's fair. No need to accuse anyone prematurely, or start a witch hunt. The Arcane have had way too many of those. Normally I'd say no, because it is invading privacy, but I know something's wrong and I want it fixed. Whose dreams am I checking?"

Now was the last chance she had to change her mind, but instead, Sophia decided to cast the net a little wider. She wasn't an expert in dreams, so expanded the list from two to five. "Jericho, Peter, Josie, Penny...and my mom." Sophia knew that wasn't going to settle easily on Olivia's shoulders, and the immediate scowl proved her right.

"How sure are you?"

"Sure enough to ask you to look, not sure enough to really call myself sure. And I know it sounds improbable, but..." She shrugged. "I can only go where evidence leads me."

"I have to say I hope you're wrong, but I'll check and let you know. Might take me a couple of nights, though. Entering dreams is easy, but interpreting them is harder. I can probably hit two or three a night without any trouble, though."

"Thank you. And I'll announce your new role at dinner tonight." Not that Sophia expected anyone to care, given it was coming from her, but it was necessary for Olivia to have the authority she needed to do her job.

Olivia looked a little green, but nodded as she rose. "I'll be there."

Sophia felt the way about the upcoming dinner. But maybe Olivia would come up with something tonight and they could end this soon.

Chapter 19

After Olivia left, Sophia spent the next hour working. People might be treating her like a traitor, but she still had a job to do. The first few emails were pretty standard, but then she frowned at the screen. There were two groups that were supposed to have left that morning on retrievals, but they were still in the Athenaeum. Nor was there any reason given for the delay. No illness, no issues with the retrievals. They seemed to have just decided to stay. She shot Nick an email pushing for more information, but wasn't sure she'd get any logical response back. If she got a response at all, which was debatable at this point.

Her head was starting to throb, and she knew the stress was starting to reach a breaking point. She needed to do something to keep her head from exploding. While she popped a couple of ibuprofen, she debated. It was too early to fly, and as much as she'd like to drag Lucas away for an hour, she knew he was busy. Normally she'd text Peter or Josie, but Josie had already proven to be one of those acting weird, and while Peter hadn't yet, she wasn't looking forward to when he joined the hating Sophia bandwagon. She was still in contact—sort of—with some of her friends from the States, but she could hardly discuss anything going on with them. More than half of them were human, and those who were Arcane knew nothing about the Athenaeum. She could talk to Lucas or Sergei, she knew that, but both were busy and too involved. She needed someone who was distant from everything going on here, but who also could follow if Sophia started to ramble. It was pretty much assured she was going to ramble at some point.

Leaning back in her chair, she grabbed her phone and scrolled through her contacts. It only took a moment for a name to catch her attention; Blanche. The woman had actually been in the Athenaeum, and as Death's wife, surely she'd be able to give some insight. And if not, then having a conversation with her might distract Sophia for a few minutes. A week ago, she hadn't known Death was a real person, and while he wasn't the friendliest of people, Blanche didn't seem to mind socializing. Which meant Sophia could learn a lot from even a friendly conversation.

Before she could second guess herself, she selected Blanche's name and listened to the phone ringing. When it was answered, the first thing she heard wasn't Blanche's voice, but a bestial roar. Sophia yanked the phone away from her ear and blinked at it before she hesitantly drew it back. "Uh...someone with thumbs is there, right?"

Blanche laughed. "Yeah, I'm here. My pet cat was just protesting the interruption of his nap."

"Your pet cat," Sophia repeated, because that had *not* sounded like a tabby.

"Yep."

She'd never heard a pet anything sound like that, but wasn't sure questioning Death's wife would have the desired result for this phone call. "Oh. Is he going to keep protesting, or do you have a few minutes?"

"Nah, I've got a few. What's up? I've got to admit, I didn't actually expect to hear from you."

"I didn't expect to be calling," Sophia admitted. "Feels kind of weird, actually."

"It's the Death thing, right?" She didn't wait for an answer. "Look, before I ever knew he was real, I was just another witch. And a necromancer to boot, and you know how we're generally seen."

"I do." Like nightmares, they weren't generally trusted. And honestly, from what Sophia had heard, people would choose a nightmare any day of the week over a necromancer. She wasn't sure why.

"Right, so try not to think of me as Death's wife. I mean, yeah, I'm that, but I get being just a normal Arcane. And to tell you the truth, I'm getting tired of having most of my conversations with either souls of the dead or death gods. There's my family, but they're busy with their own lives so I don't see them as often as I used to. And my husband is fantastic, but the rest can get old. So it's kind of nice to have a conversation with not just someone who's alive, but another woman. This place is kind of heavy on dicks."

Despite everything, Sophia had to laugh. Most of the death deities she'd heard of were men, so she could see Blanche's point. "Glad I could help, then?"

"Good, because I may start calling you regular when I'm tired of the testosterone poisoning."

"I'd like that." And she would. She wasn't in the same position as Blanche, but it was almost like a change of scenery.

"Good," Blanche repeated. "And because of that, I'm going to tell you something I probably shouldn't."

Sophia frowned, not liking the sound of that. "What's that? Is it about what really happens when you die? Because I thought it really was true that we went to the underworld of whatever gods we worshiped."

"Oh no, that's true," Blanche assured her. "It's something Death told me when we got home after visiting the Athenaeum."

"About Dion?"

"No. About Erasmus."

Sophia sat up straight, her pulse quickening. "What about him?"

Blanche hesitated a moment. "Death isn't like the death gods. They rule over their own underworlds, but Death is in charge of all of them. He can generally sense any soul that's in any of them, regardless of what god is looking over them."

Oh, she really didn't like the sound of that. It was bad enough Erasmus had been poisoned and died a horrible death, but he should have been given a perfect afterlife. If he wasn't in the Elysian Fields, there was no justice. "Is Erasmus somewhere...bad?"

There was another pause and Sophia's mind started jumping to all sorts of nasty conclusions. "I don't know," Blanche admitted. "Death can't find him. And trust me when I say that doesn't happen often."

"What do you mean, can't find him? Like he's hiding?"

"No, you can't hide from Death. I mean, he's not anywhere in the underworld. Which could mean a couple of things, and I'm sorry, but none of them are good."

Sophia closed her eyes and felt the headache noticeably get more intense. "Like what?" she asked, rubbing her temple with her free hand.

"His soul could have been killed, but that's not an easy thing to do," Blanche said gently. "It's doubtful that's the case, but it is a possibility. Someone also could have taken his soul back to the land of the living."

"And is that more possible than...than killing his soul?"

"It is," Blanche answered. "And if that's the case, I'm going to find him. Like I said, I liked your grandfather. He was a good man and part of the reason why I'm happily married instead of dead, body and soul. I'll do what I can to help him."

Sophia let out a dry laugh. "I guess it's good to have a friend who happens to be married to the actual Death."

"I'm just sorry I can't do more. But I promise, as soon as I find something, I'll let you know."

"I hope you do. I've got enough trouble here without worrying that someone has...put his soul into servitude or something."

"The murder you mentioned?"

"Four murders," Sophia corrected. "It's actually partly why I was calling. I wanted to just have a normal conversation, but an outside opinion, too, because I'm sick of being scared in the place that's my new home."

"I get it." And something in those three words made Sophia believe Blanche really did understand. "Can't help that you're the boss, either. But I'll say this. From what I know of the Athenaeum—which admittedly isn't much—no one ends up in charge of it unless they've got what it takes to lead. And you've got all sorts of fantastic shit at your fingertips. You're the boss, so find what you need and use it. There's got to be some kind of upside to dealing with the stress of running a place like that."

Sophia lightly touched the amulet she'd decided to continue wearing. It had been one hell of an upside. "I will. Oh, and you can tell Death I found that spell."

"The summoning spell?"

"Yep."

"Please tell me you destroyed it. I swear, it turned out good for him, but he's so bitchy about it."

"I didn't," Sophia admitted. "Kind of can't without destroying something else. But it was someplace only I can access, and I wrote an impossible to miss note that he hates being summoned so to never use it."

"That's something. I'll pass it on. Maybe I can even talk him into letting the whole thing drop."

"That's be nice. I don't want to have Death pissed at me on top of everything else."

"I'll work on him. And if I can't convince him to drop it, I'll just distract him every time he thinks about it."

The tone told Sophia exactly how Blanche planned on distracting him, and she was momentarily distracted herself. Death having sex seemed like an oxymoron, but she wasn't about to say that out loud.

"Thanks, Blanche. Then I think I'll let you and your cat get back to napping, and I'm going to try to find something I can use."

"No problem. Take care of yourself, Sophia."

"I will."

She hung up and dropped her phone on the desk as she flopped back. Great. She'd been hoping to get answers and help, but instead she had something else to worry about. Blanche may have said it wasn't likely Erasmus's soul had been killed—something Sophia hadn't even known was possible—but with everything else going on, she couldn't discount it. Hell, when the best option was that his soul had been stolen, things weren't exactly looking good. Which was why she decided not to share this news with Lucas or Sergei, at least not yet. They all needed to be focusing on what they could fix, and none of them had any skill or experience with souls. The last thing they needed was a distraction, especially one of this caliber.

After forcing herself to do a little more work, she finally gave up and went to look for one of the guys. Sergei was the first she found, and at her request, he texted Lucas to join them. It took just a minute for Lucas to walk in, and before he could speak, Sophia signaled for him to wait and gave Sergei a look, one he interpreted correctly. After he'd protected them from being overheard, Sophia relaxed a little.

"What's wrong?" Lucas asked.

So very much, but she made herself smile and shake her head. "I don't know that it's wrong, or at least nothing new," she told him. "I spoke with Olivia a little bit ago. For the good news first, she took the job."

"Excellent," Sergei said with a nod. "She'll be a good head curator."

"I agree, but you said good news first, so what's the bad?" Lucas asked bluntly.

Sophia wiggled her head from side to side. "I don't really know if it's bad either. Olivia asked me what was going on because she's noticed a lot more nightmares than usual, and they're bizarre. Her word, by the way."

"What did you tell her?"

"Not a lot. That there was something weird going on, and I asked her to check on a couple of people's dreams, including Peter and

Penny's. If we're lucky, whichever one of them is responsible will be having guilt-filled nightmares. Preferably ones where they wake up terrified and drenched in sweat."

"That is definitely a new angle," Sergei said after a moment. "It could work."

"Yeah, it could help, though I'm not sure if psychopaths have guilty dreams," Lucas said thoughtfully.

Sophia shrugged. "Maybe they don't. I never studied psychology. And if she doesn't find anything, we're no worse off. But if she does…"

"Then we're one step closer to putting all this behind us."

"We can only hope she finds something to point us to the right person," Sergei said, "because I'm tired of looking at everyone with distrust."

Sophia wasn't going to put all her eggs in one basket, though. Tonight, she was going to find something to use, even if it meant she was putting herself at risk. Because the way things were going, every day she spent here with a murderer was a day everyone was at risk.

Chapter 20

AN HOUR LATER, THE three of them went to dinner, and this time they walked in together. Not because they weren't still worried about people figuring out they were suspicious, but because they were worried someone would take the aggressive looks to the next level. Lucas was the most vocal about that concern, but Sophia wasn't about to argue. Not when the Athenaeum was full of people with centuries of training in both combat and sorcery.

Sophia was happy they'd accompanied her because it looked like every single person in the dining room was unhappy with her—other than those two and Olivia. Even her mom, which really hurt. Peter wasn't there tonight, and she had to hope he was also immune to whatever was happening to the others. She needed at least one family member who still liked her.

And it seemed like the two retrieval groups weren't the only ones slacking off. Sophia had eaten a month's worth of dinners in this very room and she had to say that tonight's was the worst she'd had. It was even worse than when she'd been ten and tried to cook for her mom's birthday. The spaghetti had included ingredients that should never be put in any kind of Italian dinner, including chocolate. To Heather's credit, she'd eaten two bites before suggesting they order pizza.

After choking down a couple of bites, which tasted worse than the spaghetti had, Sophia rose to her feet. "Excuse me." Not a single person stopped their conversation, and the few that looked at her did so with disdain. "Excuse me," she repeated, louder this time. This time some of the conversations died off, and those people looked annoyed, but she didn't care. This wasn't them, she knew that. They'd fix this and they'd get back to normal. She had to believe that. "We have a new head curator."

That, at least, got their attention, and one annoyed voice asked, "Who?"

Sophia forced a smile on her face, refusing to let them know she was getting irritated by their behavior, and found the set of wide blue eyes at the other end of the table. "Olivia. She's our new head curator."

It came as no surprise when there was no celebration, but Sophia was relieved not to have anyone direct their hostility toward Olivia. Instead, she received apathy. It still wasn't normal or pleasant, not for this group, but it could have been worse. Much worse.

"Give her a few days to settle in before bombarding her. And Nick, Lucas, if you could help with that, I'd appreciate it."

"Of course," Lucas said without hesitation, while Nick only nodded.

The rest of dinner was just as uncomfortable and Sophia left as soon as she could, Lucas with her. They said nothing until they were in her bedroom. She set her phone on the nightstand and shook her head. "I'm getting so sick of this," she told him as she started stripping off her clothes and walking toward the bathroom.

"Which part?" he asked, and she heard the sound of his boots hitting the floor.

"All of it, but the way they look at me especially," she admitted, reaching in to turn on the water before she finished getting undressed. "I mean Josie? We were friends just a few days ago and now she looks at me like I'm something stuck on the bottom of her shoe. And my mom? My freaking *mom*. I wouldn't have thought anything could make her look at me like that, but she is. All my life it's been her and me, so whatever is doing this has to be strong, because nothing else could make my mom hate me."

"You're right," he agreed, running a hand down her bare back, his touch so light it made her shiver. "In the shower," he told her, patting her butt lightly.

Since she wanted to wash the day away more than anything, she smiled at him over her shoulder before stepping into the hot water. He joined her just a moment later, turning her around to face him and pulling her close. "Stop thinking, just for a little while," he told her before giving her a light kiss.

She scoffed. "Do you know how hard that is?"

He shrugged and leaned her back so the water ran over her hair, soaking it. After, he pulled her upright, then released her to grab the shampoo and pour some into his palm. "You're stubborn. I think you can do it. You can do anything you put your mind to."

When he started to work the shampoo into her hair, fingers rubbing over her scalp, she started to believe him. Her eyes slid closed as he washed her hair and she could only sigh as the tension began to ease out of her, swirling down the drain with the suds when he leaned her back into the water. When he'd finished rinsing her hair, he pulled her out of the water and repeated the process with conditioner. With each stroke of his fingers, she relaxed a little. The stress was still there, but it had been pushed to the back of her mind. For now, at least, but she'd take it.

When her hair was clean, she thought that would be it, but he turned her around again, so her back was flush with his chest. Now with body wash in his hands, he began to smooth the soap over her skin. It wasn't sexual, though it was highly sensual. Yes, his hands ran over her breasts, but he didn't linger on them. And sure, Lucas was absolutely seducing her, but it didn't feel like his goal was to get her into bed, just to take care of her for a little while. The seduction was a side-effect. She had to admit that she'd never felt so...cherished. It was also exactly what she needed after the day she'd had.

When he bent to wash her legs, he placed a kiss on the small of her back and she sighed. But though she half-expected him to make a move once she was clean, all he did was stand and shut the water off. Taking her hand, he tugged her out of the shower and spent just as much care drying her off.

"Lucas?" she asked when he was done.

"Yeah?" he asked as he started to dry himself off, movements brisk.

She waited until he looked at her before she stepped in close, her breasts brushing his chest. She cupped his head as she went up on her toes, kissing him. Though she was hot and needy from his tender treatment, the kiss only showed how much she appreciated being treated like she was precious. How much she cared for him. Not that she minded when a hand settled on her lower back and tugged her closer. Nor was she unhappy when she felt that he was far from unaffected by their shower.

"Take me to bed," she whispered against his lips before she sank back into the kiss. He was addicting, even more than the history and knowledge below her feet, and for so many years, that had been her first love. It was quickly getting knocked down to second place.

He lifted her into his arms, cradling her close. She'd always thought the bridal carry was overrated, but having him hold her like that while taking her to bed had anticipation pouring through her and heat pooling in her belly. Except, if he continued on his current path, he was going to continue taking care of her. She couldn't deny it would be spectacular, but she didn't want this to be one sided. Not this time. So when he laid her on the bed, she moved up onto her knees and faced him.

Hands moving back to his cheeks, she kissed him again, taking control. He groaned and buried his fingers in her damp hair, the tension in his arms showing just how hard it was for him to hold back and not wrest that control back from her. She loved it. Her hands trailed down from his cheeks, her fingers sliding teasingly over his throat, his chest, the flat, hard planes of his stomach. When the muscles there twitched, she drew back from the kiss and smiled. His body was the most amazing one she'd ever seen, and she could spend hours just touching and kissing him. Not that it happened often. Most of the time, they were either exhausted or stealing a few minutes when they could, which didn't lead to many lengthy lovemaking sessions. But this time, they weren't on a deadline, and she had the energy to savor him.

"Lay down," she whispered, pressing her mouth against his throat.

"I should be telling you that," he argued.

"Mmm. Not yet."

He growled but laid down as she'd asked, his muscles tense, his cock standing at attention. Oh yes, she was going to enjoy this. She straddled his hips, but kept her body above his. It was a tease for her as well as him, but if he so much as brushed between her legs, she was going to forget her plans and just sink onto him. She wanted that, but not yet.

Bending down, she lavished his chest with tender kisses, her hands resting on his belly. When it felt like he was getting restless, she began moving down his body, her breasts brushing over his skin. Reaching his lower belly, she almost decided to prolong the torment and continue her kisses down one thigh, but couldn't do that to either of them. He noticed her hesitation, saying her name between clenched teeth. Looking up at him, she smiled as she slid just a little further down his body. "Don't worry," she promised before lowering her head and taking him into her mouth. The sound he made had her pulse throbbing between her legs, but she was intent on showing him how she felt, even if she couldn't yet admit it, even to herself.

At first, she kept her eyes on his, but when they shifted to gray and he gave her an intense look, one so full of heat, she had to let them drift closed in order to maintain her control. That look did more to her than full out sex with other men ever had.

"No," he said the second they had closed. She opened them again, her mouth stilling on his shaft. He shook his head and reached a hand down, trailing the back of a finger over her cheek. "You want to take your time, then you keep your eyes on mine. Otherwise, I'm going to flip us over and return the favor."

It wasn't an idle threat, she knew that. She almost closed her eyes again, but she wasn't done. She wanted to bring him to the brink first. Holding his gaze, she drew him in deeper, then slowly pulled back until she could tease the head with her tongue. His hips twitched like he was fighting not to buck, but she only sucked harder on him until he let out a deep groan. She did it again, then a third time, and each time his groan grew more desperate. He was close, and they both knew it. While she could keep going until he came, that wasn't how she wanted the night to end. Lifting her head, she gave him a last, slow lick.

"Your turn," he told her as he sat up. Before she could move off him, he slid a hand behind her head and pulled her in for a long, deep kiss. As soon as she returned it, he slid his other arm around her waist and rolled them until her back was on the bed. His weight settled against her and she moaned, arching to rub against him. He felt so good, and she couldn't wait until he was inside her. But just as she'd wanted to savor him, he seemed to want to do the same with her.

Lucas took his sweet time working his way down her body. Cupping a breast, he flicked his tongue across her nipple and she gasped softly, arching against his mouth. His head moved, avoiding more contact, and he gave her another teasing lick before he kissed his way to her other breast to do the same. Before she could protest, he pushed himself further down the bed until his body was between her thighs and he could blow a warm breath against her damp sex. Groaning, as anticipation was becoming a torture, she tried to lift her hips, but he wrapped his arms around her thighs and pinned them to the bed. "Patience," he murmured in a voice deep and rough. It reminded her of his gargoyle form and made her shiver.

"Running out of patience," she admitted, stroking her hand through his short hair.

He flashed her a wicked grin, his gray eyes full of heated promise. "Good." Before she could even open her mouth to retort, his was on her and she was crying out in shocked pleasure. For a man whose job involved a great deal of violence, and who was often short-tempered, he was supremely talented with his tongue. He licked, he thrust, and he teased, until her body tried to writhe at the attention. When his thumb found her clit and pressed, stars exploded behind her eyes as the torture became release. Moaning his name, she held his head against her, but he wasn't going anywhere. His mouth loved her through the climax, but didn't stop, didn't slow, and began pushing her toward another.

Sophia whimpered when he didn't give her time to recover, only kept shoving more sensations at her. Just before they imploded again, he stopped, and she couldn't help the sob that escaped her lips. She was so close and wanted to kill him for stopping just shy of her second orgasm. Except he wasn't actually done.

In a movement too fast for her to track, he braced his hands on the bed and pushed up to his knees. Her legs were still caught on his arms, which spread them wide and lifted them toward the bed. The next movement had him thrusting into her in one hard, smooth slide. The sweet friction of it shoved her over the edge, hard. Her mouth opened, but she didn't have the breath to give life to the scream, so she grabbed for his arms, using her hold to keep her from floating away.

Only when the orgasm began to fade did she realize that Lucas was holding still. His arms were rigid with the effort it took him not to move and his jaw was clenched. But though her body was loose, having him buried within her made her greedy.

"More," she panted, grinding against him. She couldn't rock, not with the position he had her in, but she had to encourage him to move. It didn't take much.

He drew his hips back slowly, making her think it was going to be slow and intense, but then he slammed into her hard enough to make her gasp. Before the sound had faded, he started to pound into her, hard, fast, like he was trying to push her to yet another climax before he lost his battle with his body. She wasn't complaining. She wasn't a fragile woman, especially not after all the training he'd been putting her through, and she could handle his rough lovemaking. More than that, she loved it. Pushing his control to the limit always made her feel powerful and sexy, and no one had ever made her feel those two things so strongly.

If only she could kiss him, but she wasn't quite that flexible, so all she could do was stare into his wild, stone-colored eyes as he used her body in the very best of ways. There was little finesse, but she knew he was careful not to use his full strength. And she didn't need finesse, not this time.

He groaned deeply as his body's desires won out over his attempt to last, and the next few thrusts were almost feral before she felt him come, his hips pressed firmly against hers. Pushing her flexibility just a little more, he ensured he rubbed against her clit when he ground against her, giving her the last push she needed to find her next orgasm. Her eyes closed as her body trembled beneath his, but she didn't have the energy to so much as breathe his name, could only take the waves of bliss as they overwhelmed her senses and left her a weak, satisfied mess.

It took a moment before he moved, carefully untangling their limbs. His warmth disappeared completely, and she let out a soft whimper of protest. A minute later, she felt a warm washcloth as he gently cleaned her off. She smiled sleepily, realizing that maybe he did care for her as much as she cared for him. Every moment since they'd entered her bedroom showed her that. A minute after he tended to her, the bed dipped and she was pulled into his arms. Shifting to ensure she was touching him as much as possible, she let out a sigh of contentment and drifted into sweet, pleasure-filled dreams.

Lucas heard her breathing change and knew she was asleep. Before he joined her, he kissed her shoulder and whispered, "I love you."

Chapter 21

Hours later, something woke Sophia. Lucas was curled against her back, sleeping and unmoving, and she didn't hear anything out of the ordinary. Reaching for her phone, she frowned when she saw it was just shy of three in the morning. She never woke up in the middle of the night for no reason, so why had she now?

Carefully detaching herself from Lucas, she headed into the bathroom. After splashing some water on her face, she could only figure that her mind had been stuck on her plan to find something to use against the murderer. And since she was awake—wide awake—she may as well make use of the quiet hours. She got dressed and kissed Lucas's cheek. Knowing he would worry if he woke without her next to him, she wrote a note and left it on his phone to let him know where she'd gone.

She left her bedroom and made her way down the hall and to the stairs. She had only descended a few steps when something hit her hard in the back. Unprepared, she was knocked off balance. Her arms shot out, trying to find something to catch herself with, but her fingers only scraped against rough stone before she fell forward. The stone stairs were unforgiving on her body as she hit the first one then tumbled down the last few to the landing. It knocked the breath out of her and she could barely move. It felt like every inch of her body cried out in pain. Her head was the worst, as it had cracked against one of the stairs, but she wasn't sure any part of her body had avoided the stairs.

Struggling to fill her lungs and think past the pain, she barely noticed the shadowy figure before they stood over her. She didn't have a chance to react before a hand was on her throat. Weakly, she tried to shove at the arm attached to it, but her limbs didn't want to move.

Fingers squeezed her throat, making it so she could only get the slightest bit of air into her chest. Though she was looking right at her attacker, she couldn't make out a single detail about them. They weren't invisible, but the features seemed to shift, so it wasn't even clear if she was looking at a man or woman, much less anything more specific. That obfuscation carried to the voice when the person lowered their face to just inches from Sophia's and spoke.

"You're poking into things you shouldn't. I will give you a warning, but only one. Stop poking and leave the Athenaeum now. I don't care what reason you give, I don't care if you sneak out in the middle of the night. But if you're not gone in three days, I will kill you. I'm too close to let you ruin it."

"Why?" she croaked, and even the single syllable was a strain to get out.

The hand tightened for a second until she thought they were going to crush her windpipe and kill her now. Panic widened her eyes and made her attempt to struggle once more before it released and the figure straightened, looming over her in the dim stairwell. "Just be gone. Three days," they told her. They said something else she couldn't make out and disappeared. They didn't move away or hide, just vanished entirely.

Unsure if they were really gone or just invisible, Sophia forced her legs to move, pushing her to the wall. Painfully, she eased up until she was leaning against the wall. It wasn't much, but at least she couldn't be attacked from behind again. It figured the one night she forgot to cast her protection spells was the one night she was attacked. Coincidence? Or had they been watching her and waiting for a night when she had let her guard down? For that matter, did they know where she was going? And how had they found her? If she hadn't left her room, would they have attacked her there? Would they have hurt Lucas?

As she struggled to breathe normally, she leaned to one side and pulled her phone from her back pocket. The screen was cracked, but it still worked. Thank the gods. She needed help and wasn't sure she could make it upstairs by herself. Thanks to Seth's gift, she was sure she'd be okay, but only if she lived long enough for the accelerated healing to kick in. Which was why Sergei wasn't the one she called, Lucas was.

"What's wrong?"

His voice held no trace of sleep, which didn't surprise her. He woke up quickly. "I'm in...the stairwell. Someone...attacked me." Though she didn't want to worry him, she knew her voice was breathy and full of pain.

"I'm coming. Cast your spells and call Sergei."

He hung up, and she shook her head. How had it not occurred to her to cast the spells now? She was smart, so it should have. With her luck, she had a concussion. She cast them now, though the shield took a couple of tries. As soon as it settled around her, she called Sergei.

Like Lucas, he seemed to wake quickly, and for a similar reason, she expected. Both had jobs that occasionally required immediate action.

"Sophia? Is everything okay?"

"I was attacked...in the stairwell. Lucas is—" She cut off as she heard footsteps and glanced up. Closing her eyes, she sighed and said, "He's here. But I'm hurt."

"Tell him to bring you to the clinic. I'll be ready for you."

"'Kay. Thanks."

Her arm gave out then, just falling into her lap before she could end the call. Opening her eyes, she saw Lucas kneel in front of her. He was in his stone form, but his now gray eyes were hot with fury. He had been in such a rush to get to her that he hadn't put on any clothes but for a pair of sweatpants, but she felt too terrible to admire his bare chest.

Gentle fingers touched her cheek—no, wiped at it—and she saw blood on his fingers. She hadn't realized she was bleeding, but it didn't really surprise her. His silence did.

Lucas was silent because if he spoke right now, he was going to yell, and that was the last thing she needed. He'd never seen her looking so battered, physically or mentally. There was blood dripping from her forehead down to her jaw and scrapes on most of her exposed skin. Her jeans and shirt had small tears in them, and through the gaps in fabric he could see the abraded skin beneath. But the worst were the finger-shaped marks on her throat.

He wanted to kill whoever had done this to her, but first he was going to make sure she got to Sergei. Shifting, he lifted her into his arms as carefully as he could. He wasn't as successful as he wanted, because she let out a soft whimper, but it couldn't be helped. If he wanted her to stop hurting, he needed to get her to the healer.

Moving as quickly as he could without jarring her, he went up the two flights of stairs to the ground level, then over to the clinic. Sergei was waiting at the door, proving that Sophia had gotten in touch with him.

The demigod cursed in Russian before he pointed to an empty bed. Lachlan was still there in one of the back beds, still unconscious, but he barely registered on Lucas's radar. "What happened, Sophia?" he asked as Lucas gently set her on the bed. Unsure how injured she was, he helped her lie down.

"Got pushed...down the stairs...and choked."

Her voice was still rough, and Lucas felt his wings trying to burst free as his canines and nails lengthened. Gargoyles were known to be guardians, even the humans knew that. What most didn't know was just how protective gargoyles became over those they considered theirs, be it family, close friends, or their mates. Sophia had fallen into that last category for him, regardless of how informal their relationship might be. To see her like this, to know someone had done this deliberately to her, made him want to tear the Athenaeum down, stone by stone, until he found and punished the one responsible.

Sergei looked at least half as angry as Lucas felt. "How far did you fall?"

"Dunno...maybe half a flight."

"Just relax. I'll take care of you," he promised.

Sophia nodded, and her eyes flicked to Lucas. Though he felt like doing anything but smiling, he made his lips curve and took one of her hands in his, squeezing delicately. "You know you can't do better than Sergei, not unless you get his dad."

Sergei rested his hands lightly on her, one on her head, one on her throat. A soft glow emanated from his fingers as he began healing. Injuries sustained from sparring—especially with weapons—were common, and Lucas had seen them healed dozens of times. It normally took less than a minute. When Sergei took several times that, Lucas had to wonder just how badly her forced tumble down the stairs had hurt her. It had looked like it was all surface injuries, but had there been internal bleeding? Something worse?

The thought of everything that could have been done to her in that stairwell made him lose the last bit of control he had. His wings erupted, knocking a chair over, but he didn't care. He did care that the whooshing sound that accompanied his wings had startled Sophia, making her jump slightly.

"Sorry," he murmured, brushing his free hand over her hair.

When Sergei drew his hands back, he smiled kindly at Sophia. "How do you feel now?"

Sophia pushed herself to a sitting position then shifted a little, testing her body. "It doesn't hurt anymore, which is a major plus. How bad was it?"

The smile disappeared. "If you were human and didn't have access to healing, I would have been worried. You had a concussion, damage to your trachea, a few cracked ribs, and some internal bleeding."

"But you got it all?" Lucas asked.

"I did," Sergei assured him. "Sophia, before you get into sharing the details of what happened, I just have one question for you."

Sophia cocked her head. "What's that? And do you have some water in here?"

"I do." He turned and went to a cabinet, grabbing a bottle of water from it, which he opened and handed to her. "When did you two get serious?"

He asked the question just as Sophia was taking a drink, which resulted in her eyes widening as she choked lightly, the water going down the wrong pipe. "What?" she croaked.

"Bad timing," Lucas said dryly, but like Sophia, he hadn't expected Sergei to ask that question, so it calmed him enough that he could draw his wings into his body once more.

Sergei smiled a little as he stepped back and sat in his chair, arms folding over his chest. He almost looked pleased, though Lucas wasn't sure why. "I said," he repeated patiently, "when did you two get serious?"

"What makes you think we're serious?" Sophia asked, glancing at Lucas questioningly.

Lucas ran a hand lightly down her arm before he stepped back. He didn't want to. He didn't actually want any distance between them right now, but he needed to give her the space. It was serious for him, but he didn't want to pressure her into anything. He wanted her in his bed and in his life willingly. "Don't look at me. I haven't said anything."

"He hasn't," Sergei confirmed. "But I know Lucas, and I know gargoyles just as well. Never heard of one reacting like that just because their boss or charge was injured. Or even if a casual lover was hurt."

Her brow furrowed and she looked back at him. For a minute she just studied his face, which was still stone. It would probably be a few more minutes before he could take his full human form, so he just stood there and let her mind work through it. "Sergei?" she said without looking away from Lucas.

"Yes?"

"Can you give us a minute?"

He smiled and nodded. "Of course."

She said nothing until Sergei had closed the door behind him. Turning so her legs hung off the side of the bed, she reached for Lucas's hand and drew him closer, parting her knees so he could stand between them. "Is he right?" she asked quietly, her thumb rubbing in slow circles over the back of his hand. Not that he could really feel it, and he hoped his body allowed him to shift back soon.

"About what exactly?" He wanted to be very clear in this. He'd seen misunderstandings wreck otherwise perfectly good relationships before, and didn't want to be a casualty of that particular issue. Besides, with everything else she had on her mind, he didn't want to add to it if she didn't want the full truth.

She drew her lower lip between her teeth as she chose her words. "All of it? That we're serious. That you wouldn't have acted like you did if you didn't...if we weren't close."

Lucas wanted to smile, but didn't want her to think he was laughing at her, because laughter was the furthest thing from his mind. Easing a little closer, he lifted his free hand to her cheek and brushed his thumb over the lip she was biting again. "Whether *we* are serious is up to you," he told her. "A one-sided relationship can't be serious, even if one of the people involved is." She opened her mouth to speak, but he just pressed his thumb lightly over her lips to prevent. "But he was right about the way I reacted. I didn't like seeing you hurt. I hated it. Even though you're healed now, I still want to track down whoever did that to you and pay them back tenfold for every cut, every bruise, every hurt they caused you. I want them to suffer for daring to go after you. I want to rip them apart, then come back to you and promise that they'll never hurt you again before I kiss each and every spot you were hurt. But do you know what I want most of all?" he asked. She shook her head and his hand slid back into her hair as he bent his head so their mouths were only a breath apart. "I want to strip you down and keep you in bed for the next few hours, replacing the memory of pain with pleasure, all while assuring myself that you are whole and alive."

Her eyes had widened as he spoke, and he could hear her breathing coming in more rapidly. But it wasn't disgust at what he wanted to do to her attacker. Not even close. So he erased the space between them and took her mouth in a barely restrained kiss. Sergei might have taken care of the pain, but the fear Lucas had felt remained, as did the blood on her brow and cheek, which served as a visible reminder.

Sophia moaned and leaned into him, her hand clenching his, her other grabbing his shoulder to keep him close. Not that he was going anywhere anytime soon. She'd be lucky if he let her out of his sight for five minutes. But as much as he wanted to forget about the attack and lose himself in her, he was acutely aware of the unconscious vampire and very conscious demigod only feet away from them. And he wasn't used to kissing anyone in his gargoyle form and he didn't want to hurt her, either with his stone skin or his fangs.

Drawing back, he forced himself back to human form. "Did I answer your question?" he asked, smiling at the glazed look in her eyes. Oh, he liked that, and she certainly wasn't thinking about the attack right now.

"Um...yeah. Wait, no," she said, frowning and shaking her head. "I...Lucas..." She blew out a breath and closed her eyes for a few seconds. "That was probably more words than I've ever heard you say at once. Normally you're pretty blunt, and I appreciate that. Harder to misinterpret a blunt statement than a long one. Maybe I'm making this too complicated, but with everything in my head right now, I kind of need you to just tell me what this is for you. In fifteen words or less, if possible. Is this just sex and friendship for you? Or is it more?"

He chuckled as he straightened, toying with her hair as his fingers slid through it. She might be the most inexperienced aspida the Athenaeum had ever had, but she didn't lack for brains or courage. Or humor. In a place full of people who were mostly more than a century old, and with objects beneath them that could be thousands of years old, she made things new again. Especially for him. "You sure you want blunt?"

Squaring her shoulders, she nodded. "I do."

"And fewer than fifteen words?" She gave another nod. "Okay. How's this? I'm in love with you." He almost made a joke about only using a third of his allotted words, but now wasn't the time. The first time he told her that—while she was awake—deserved a bit of solemnity.

She smiled at him, warm and happy. "I was hoping that was what you were meaning," she whispered.

Lucas cocked his head slightly and arched a brow questioningly. "And?" he prompted.

"And...I guess that means this is serious, because it's definitely not one sided. Not sure when it happened, not with all the bullshit going on, but...I love you, too."

"Good. Don't get me wrong, the sex is great, but I want more from you."

"You've got it," she promised.

He kissed her lightly. "Then, in the interest of getting back to bed and getting you naked, should I get Sergei back in here so you can tell us what happened?"

Some of her light dimmed, but she nodded. "Yeah. I want to get it over with."

"Understandable." He went to the door and found Sergei just outside. The man looked at Lucas and one thick brow lifted. Lucas grinned. "She loves me, but also wants to tell us what happened so she can get some sleep."

Sergei scoffed as he pushed away from the wall. "Are you sure you plan on letting her sleep?" he muttered as he passed by Lucas.

Not really, but Lucas just closed the door behind them and went to stand by Sophia. "Whenever you're ready, love," he told her.

"I was going down the stairs where you found me," she began. "The ones from the second level to the crypt. I was...mmm...not quite halfway down when something hit me in the back, hard. I went down, of course. Couldn't really move once I hit bottom. Everything hurt too bad."

"Unsurprising, given all the injuries I found," Sergei murmured. Lucas didn't speak. He couldn't, not when her recitation was getting him worked up again.

"Right," she agreed. She seemed to recognize Lucas's irritation because she took his hand and smiled faintly at him. "A figure came down and stood over me, and I swear I couldn't tell you what they looked like."

"Were they wearing a hoodie or mask or something?" Sergei asked.

Sophia shook her head. "No, I think it was magic, but not magic I've ever seen before. Every feature was...blurred! I mean, that's not really it, but I can't describe it better. I couldn't tell you whether it was a man or woman, the color of their hair or skin, or even how tall they were. Hell, when they spoke, even that was disguised."

"I've heard of spells that could do that, but I've never seen them either," Lucas said.

"I'm kind of surprised I couldn't make anything out, though. Seth's gift, remember? Helps see through illusions? And that had to be some kind of illusion."

"Yes, but Seth also said something was preventing him and the other patrons from seeing what was going on," Sergei pointed out. "If they could hide from the gods, then a gift from the gods wouldn't help."

"Oh. Yeah, I hadn't thought of that." She was quiet for a minute, then went on. "Anyway. They grabbed my throat," she said, fingers brushing lightly where the tender skin had been marked. "Told me I was looking into things I shouldn't, and if I wasn't gone in three days..."

When the pause continued for too long, Lucas narrowed his eyes. "If you weren't gone in three days what?"

"That they'd kill me," she said, no emotion in the words.

In an instant, Lucas's skin was stone and his wings threatened to free themselves again. Attacking her was bad enough, but he had no doubt this person would follow through on his threat. Which meant Lucas had less than three days to find out who had done it and deal with the problem himself. Standard protocol was to imprison such a person unless they gave no other option but to use deadly force, but he knew he wouldn't be able to help himself.

"We won't let that happen," Sergei said, but Lucas got the impression he was trying to soothe him more than Sophia. "If we don't get to the bottom of this before the deadline, you'll leave, just until we do."

"Damn right," Lucas agreed.

"Now wait a minute," Sophia said, dropping Lucas's hand and standing up. "I can't just turn tail and run. I'm aspida. There *is* no stepping down, as I was told repeatedly when I got the job."

"You can and you will," Lucas corrected.

"No, I'm not," she argued. "If I leave, then what? This person just keeps doing what they're doing? The Athenaeum continues to crumble? Did you know that two teams were supposed to leave yesterday morning? They didn't. And dinner last night was the most half-assed meal I've ever had. Things are getting worse, not better."

"Sergei and I can keep working—"

Sophia cut him off. "Two heads are better than one, and three are better than two. Besides, you two don't have access to the Vault. And I know there's something here that can fix this fucking mess!"

"And you can't fix anything if you're dead!"

"Whoa," Sergei said, bravely inserting himself between them. "That's enough, both of you. I understand that you're both scared and angry, but we can't do this. There's time. Two days. If we haven't found the person terrorizing the Athenaeum by then, we can regroup. But there's no point in getting worked up now."

"Fine," Sophia said, folding her arms over her chest as she gave Lucas a stubborn look.

It took him a moment more, but he saw the wisdom in Sergei's words. "Fine."

"Good. Then you two go back to bed. In a few hours, we'll get back to work. Agreed?" Sergei asked.

"Agreed," Lucas said at the same time Sophia did.

She led the way, leaving the clinic without another word. He was only a step behind her and neither spoke as they went down the stairs and to her room. As soon as they were both inside, he closed the door and grabbed her arm, pulling her to him.

"I won't lose you," he told her harshly.

"You won't."

He wanted to believe her, but the odds weren't with them. For tonight, though, he could pretend. He lifted her into his arms and she wound her legs around his waist. As he carried her to the bed, he resolved to think of nothing but her until they had exhausted themselves.

Tomorrow was going to be hell, so he had to make sure tonight was heaven.

Chapter 22

Sophia woke a little sore, but it had nothing to do with her forced tumble down the stairs. She smiled and stretched before she rolled toward the warm body on her left. Lucas was lying on his side, head propped on one hand, watching her.

"How long have you been awake?" she asked, moving closer to him and tucking her head against his shoulder.

"Not long," he said, kissing the top of her head. "I was about to wake you up, actually."

Though she wanted nothing more than to stay in bed and thoroughly enjoy making love to him, she knew they had to get up. Still, she could take a few minutes, couldn't she?

She slid an arm around his waist and pressed closer, loving how warm he felt despite the fact that he was made of literal stone. At least part of the time. "After breakfast, I want to talk to Olivia, then hit the Vault."

"Olivia I get. You're hoping she learned something in the dreams, right?"

"Yeah."

"Mmm. Do you really think there's something in the Vault you missed before?"

She shrugged. "I have to hope. I wasn't able to get through everything. It's not as big as the other levels, but there's still a lot there. Worse, I don't know most of the languages the books and stuff are written in. At least the relic cards are all in Greek."

"You want me to help? I'm not really happy about the idea of not having an eye on you, and I know a couple more languages than you do."

Sophia considered that for a moment. "Couldn't hurt. And you might recognize some relics I don't, too. But if I'm breaking the aspida-only rule, I think I want to take Olivia, too."

He drew back enough to see her face. "Olivia? Why?"

"Because she knows more languages than both of us combined, then doubled," she answered with a smile. "She's a walking dictionary of a couple dozen languages. Besides, you're now both heads of your factions, so I think a little leeway can be given, considering the circumstances."

"Are you going to tell her about the threat?"

That was harder. "Maybe. I think so? Other than you and Sergei, she's the only person I've noticed who hasn't set off my threat spell."

"Yeah, but it didn't warn you last night, so it clearly isn't foolproof."

She winced and ducked her head. "Yeah...I kind of forgot to cast it and my shield spell," she mumbled.

The expected yelling didn't come, so she glanced up at his face. His jaw was clenched and his eyes were stone gray. "You can't forget again," he told her, teeth gritted. Probably to keep from yelling.

"Trust me, I'm not going to. I don't want a repeat of that."

"Good. You forget again, and we're going to have words."

"I expect nothing less."

He lightly smacked her ass. "Then let's get up and go. We've got a lot to do and not a lot of time to do it in."

She groaned, but got up and got dressed. Though Lucas had said he was staying with her today, she still cast her protection spells before they left the room. Peter was leaving the dining hall just as they were entering, and he stopped and smiled. "Sophia. Thought we were going to have another movie day or something. Instead, you've been hiding."

How could he be the person they were looking for? He was one of the few who wasn't treating her like a pariah. It had to be Penny—or someone they hadn't even considered yet. If only she could just come out and ask him directly, but it wasn't like the killer would admit to it.

"I know. Sorry. I've just been busy. And today isn't looking like it's going to be any better."

He pouted, again reminding her of a mohawked puppy dog. "Really?"

"Really. What with Lachlan and some of the venatores not doing their jobs, and me trying to figure out my job, it's just not leaving a whole lot of free time."

"You're supposed to make it, remember? But I understand. We'll do it again soon though, right?"

She smiled and nodded. "Of course."

"Good," he said, brightening. "You can join us, too, if you want, Lucas."

"I might just do that," Lucas answered.

"Great! See you later," Peter said before heading off, no doubt toward the computer lab.

"I just can't believe he could be responsible," Sophia whispered to Lucas.

"What did your threat spell say?"

She shook her head and looked pointedly at the group of people already eating breakfast. "Too many people around who hate me to be able to differentiate one from the other. All I feel is major threats surrounding me."

Lucas nodded, and they grabbed coffee and something to eat. He nudged her away from a few of the available offerings, and eventually she noted that he was steering her toward food others had taken and eaten. While she wanted to say it was overkill, two people had died of poisoning. There was no reason to make it three.

They ate quickly, off to one side, with their backs as close to the wall as possible. She hated acting so paranoid. She hated even more than it was necessary.

Though Sophia wanted to go to the Vault next, Lucas led her to his office instead. "I know you said the person who pushed you was disguised, but not all disguises show up on video," he explained as he sat at his desk. "And we might be able to follow them back to their room and ID them."

"Didn't you say that they had gotten into the security system before and erased footage?" she asked as she stood by his shoulder so she could see the monitors.

"I did," he confirmed, "but everyone slips up sometime. This could be that sometime."

They had an exact time, which should have made it easy, except the cameras in the entire Athenaeum went down a minute after Sophia left her room, and had remained offline until a few minutes after she'd called Lucas. Which meant they had nothing.

"Damn," Lucas muttered as he closed down the program, then turned his chair so he could draw her down onto his lap. "I swear to you, Sophia, I will find out who's behind this."

"I know you will," she told him, and she meant it. She just wasn't sure he'd find out before she was gone—either with her tail tucked between her legs, or her ashes in an urn.

Sophia had Olivia meet her in Lucas's office, which suited him just fine. She tried to move off his lap before the new head curator arrived, but he wrapped his arms around her waist and grinned. "Not ashamed to be sleeping with an underling, are you?" he teased.

"No, but it isn't very professional!"

He chuckled and nipped at her ear. "We're not a corporation, love. We don't have to be professional. Besides, you're just sitting in my lap in front of one person, not stripping down and fucking me in the dining hall."

She wrinkled her nose. "Which will never happen, just to be clear. I'm not into having an audience."

"Duly noted." Not that he'd actually have considered it anyway. He'd never been a possessive man before, but the thought of anyone else seeing her delicious body made him murderous.

Before he could dwell on that, there was a knock on the door. "Come," he called. And though he kept his arms around Sophia, that was the most he did. Teasing her might be fun, but he didn't want to actually make her uncomfortable. Little did she know that this display was more likely to ruin his reputation than hers. While he didn't pay much attention to gossip, he was well aware that he was thought of as stone cold, as befitting a gargoyle. And he could be, absolutely, especially when he was actively protecting someone. But while he had a stone form, he was also a man, so if anyone in the Athenaeum didn't like him paying attention to the woman he loved, they could kiss his rock hard ass.

Olivia opened the door, paused when she saw them, then stepped in and closed the door. A little smile played over her lips as she said, "This explains a dream I happened across a while back."

Sophia groaned and turned her face into Lucas's shoulder. "Do I want to know?"

"Probably not." The words were more cheerful than Lucas had ever heard from Olivia. Interesting. He had to wonder just what the dream had been about. If it was one of his, there had probably been a lot of nudity and moaning. "What can I do for you, though?" she asked as she dropped into one of the empty chairs.

"Two things," Sophia said, leaning slightly away from Lucas. His lips twitched, but he allowed her the illusion. She was still on his lap, still where he could keep her safe, so he was content. "First, were you able to get into any of the dreams I asked you about?"

"I was," Olivia confirmed, arching a brow as she looked at Lucas, then back to Sophia. "I take it he knows?"

"He does," Sophia confirmed. "About this and more that I haven't told you about. Yet."

"There's more?"

"Unfortunately. And we'll get to that, but let's focus on the dreams for now."

Olivia nodded slowly. "First, there were a lot of nightmares last night, but that's become the norm over the last week or so. And I mean a fuckton. Almost everyone in the Athenaeum had one as far as I can tell, and I'm very good at what I do."

That didn't surprise him, not with multiple deaths, attacks, and whatever the hell was going on with Lachlan.

"And the ones I asked you about?"

"I managed to get into Jericho's dreams, and your mom's, and they were...weird."

"Weird how?" Lucas asked.

She hesitated, tapping one gloved finger on the arm of her chair. "Dreams tend to be unique. Everyone has different experiences, different knowledge, so their dreams tend to vary a lot. Not just in subject but style. Some people dream in black and white. Some dream only about mundane things. Some have dreams that make it seem like they're dreaming on LSD. There's a huge amount of variation, but the point is that dreams are kind of like fingerprints in how they are from person to person."

"I take it Jericho and Heather's dreams weren't unique?"

Olivia shook her head. "Yes and no. The dreams themselves were different. Different styles, different scenarios, all that, but they were both chaotic and fragmented, which is not normal. In my experience, that means something's seriously wrong."

Sophia leaned forward, elbows resting on the desk, her brow knit with concern. "What kind of wrong?"

Olivia shrugged. "Could be illness, could be some kind of mental manipulation. It could be a lot of things, and I'm not a healer or shrink to be able to tell you for sure. But I can say they're not alone. Those nightmares I mentioned? Most of them were the same way, just to varying degrees."

Sophia looked back at Lucas before she asked, "Could you wager a guess at how many?"

"Shit. Um...maybe two-thirds of the Athenaeum?"

"That many?" Sophia rubbed her hands over her face as she slumped back against Lucas. "Okay. Just try to get into the other dreams tonight if you can. And if you come across any that are...concerning...let me know?"

"I can, but I want to know why," Olivia said firmly. "You were vague yesterday, and while I know something's going on, dreams are personal. Not only that, but people can't always control their dreams and I don't want to invade people's privacy and tell you someone's dreaming horrible things when I don't know the whole story. More than that, I won't. People may think nightmares are immortal, terrifying creatures, but we're still people and we have standards." She paused a beat. "Most of us."

Sophia hesitated now, and Lucas gave her a reassuring squeeze. She had decided to trust Olivia, and he hadn't seen any reason for her not to, so she needed to trust her instincts.

"Lachlan's been infected by something. It's what caused his outburst. So have others, though to a lesser extent, it seems. It's causing them all to act out, though it seems directed solely toward me. For now."

Olivia pursed her lips as she took that in. "Infected by what?"

"We don't know. Sergei hasn't been able to identify it, other than to say it's magical in nature. And we think it has something to do with several other...concerning incidents, going back a few months."

The nightmare went still for a moment, then her eyes met his. "My poisoning?"

Lucas saw the fury and fear in hers and sympathized. Based on what Erasmus and Sergei had said, she'd come closer to dying than she knew. It was pure luck that Suni had managed to create some of the long-lost antidote not long before Olivia had been poisoned. "You know I investigated that as well as I could and came up with little, but yes, we think it's connected. We're just not sure how everything connects just yet."

"You said several incidents," Olivia said, looking back at Sophia. "What else? And before you brush me off, remember that you are the one who made me head curator."

"I did, and while that was due to the reasons I gave you before, I only made the offer now rather than later because you don't seem to be one of the infected. Just in case you were wondering," Sophia said.

"Good to know, but what other incidents?"

"Agatha's death. Dion's death. Someone putting a cursed book where I'd touch it. Someone stealing both Agatha and Dion's bodies. Someone pushing me down the stairs and threatening me to leave," Sophia listed, her voice as impersonal as she could make it. And when she paused, when Olivia might have responded, she added quietly, "And Erasmus's death." Lucas was surprised she'd mentioned that, but supposed at this point it couldn't hurt. Besides, if they were going to trust her, if they were going to hope she could help, then she needed to know what they were dealing with.

Olivia looked more and more grim as Sophia spoke, but the last three words had her going pale. "It wasn't illness?"

"No," Lucas answered. "Erasmus knew more sorcery than any of us and had two of the best healers try to help him. From what we can tell, he was poisoned by the same thing you were, but in his case, we didn't find out soon enough for the mithridate to help him."

Silence reigned for a full twenty seconds, then Olivia shoved to her feet as she delivered a string of curses that would have made a sailor blush. Or so he assumed, because most of it was in multiple languages even he couldn't understand. The intent behind them was clear, though. It would be amusing if he didn't feel the same way.

Sophia blinked and cocked her head. "Did you just cuss in twelve different languages?" she asked, a trace of awe in her voice. "I think I counted twelve, anyway."

The question stopped Olivia mid-pace and turned her attention back to their aspida. It also seemed to drain most of the rage from the other woman. "Thirteen, actually." She sank back into her chair. "What can I do to help? Besides the dreams. I'll check the last three tonight."

That was just further proof of how loved Erasmus had been within these walls. Wherever the man had ended up, Lucas hoped he knew just how much he'd affected those who had known him.

Sophia patted Lucas's arm before she rose from his lap and walked around the desk to kneel in front of Olivia. "I know it's a shock. Trust me, it wasn't any easier for me. And we are going to find out who's responsible. That's why I asked you to join us."

"You've got a plan?"

"Sort of. There's not a lot to go on. Video has been deleted, disguise spells used, and there's been a whole hell of a lot of deception. But everyone knows the Vault is filled with a lot of rare and powerful stuff."

"Tell me about it. I've been dying to get in there for years," Olivia said with a weak smile.

Sophia grinned and patted Olivia's knee. "Then today is your lucky day, because I want you and your head full of languages to come with us and help us find something to fix all this."

Olivia's smile firmed and widened. "When do we go?"

Lucas rose to his feet. "Now. And we don't let Sophia out of our sight until we've found the answer."

Olivia nodded firmly. "I'm in. Let's catch this bastard."

Chapter 23

Sophia shot a text to Sergei just so he'd know where they were if something happened, then they went deep into the Athenaeum to the doorway she'd only entered once. Except when they were there, she hesitated. "I know it should go without saying, but you can't take anything out of here, and I'd rather you didn't talk about anything you see in here with anyone else."

"Understood," Lucas assured her.

"Of course," Olivia added.

Sophia lifted her hand to place on the palm plate, then paused and frowned. "I know there's an inventory of stuff, but does that include things in the Vault?"

"There is," Olivia told her. "At least from what I've heard, but it's not digitized like the rest of the Athenaeum. Couldn't be, since no one's been in there for a long time but for Erasmus. The aspida has more important things to do than add texts and relics to a database."

That actually made Sophia feel better. She just wished she knew where the inventory was. Could be that it was inside, which would be handy. "Okay." She had her palm scanned and entered her PIN, then opened the door. "Try to remember to breathe," she teased them before she stepped inside. After they'd joined her, she shut the door, making sure it latched firmly.

"Holy shit," Lucas said, and Sophia noted that his gaze had landed on the Armor of Achilles, just like hers had.

"This is amazing," Olivia breathed, and her eyes couldn't seem to settle on any single item. "I don't even know where to start."

"Preferably with the texts that aren't in English, Greek, or Latin," Sophia said with a smile. "I can't honestly say I've been through every-thing in those languages, but I had to bypass most of the others just because I couldn't read them. And I browsed through the relics, but there are hundreds here."

"Then I'll start with the relics if you want to start with the texts," Lucas suggested to Olivia.

"Fine by me."

Sophia nodded. "And I'll see if I can find an inventory list." She trusted them—though Lucas more than Olivia—so figured divide and conquer was probably their best bet.

Going through relics was hardly a hardship for Lucas. It had been one thing for Sophia to mention some of the things she'd seen, like the armor and Heracles's club, but it was another to see them for himself. And while it was tempting to pick up the club and give it a swing, he resisted. It was cool but wouldn't help them find a murderer or cure Lachlan and the others.

The piece of Yggdrasil was equally fascinating, and while it could help restore life, he doubted it could resurrect the dead. Especially since Erasmus and Thomas had both been cremated, and Agatha and Dion had been stolen.

Forcing himself to focus, he made his way down the shelves, awed by the things in this room. No wonder Sophia had had so much trouble when she was in here before. Some of the relics looked ordinary, but others drew the eye. There was a single golden colored feather that he almost passed by until he spotted the card that labeled it as a phoenix feather. A little further down on the shelf were several dragon scales. Dragons! Even with all he knew, Lucas had thought dragons were extinct and phoenixes mere myths. The former might be true now, but the latter clearly wasn't.

"Is this the antidote that saved me?" Olivia called from a few rows to his right.

"What's it called?" Lucas asked.

"Mithridate."

"Yep. Erasmus helped Suni get the formula, so she gave it to us, along with some of the antidote. Sergei's got that."

"We have some? Has he tried it on Lachlan?"

"Yes," Sophia answered from his left. "Didn't seem to do anything, so whatever it is, it doesn't seem to be a poison."

"Gotcha."

Lucas continued to wander, skimming the cards beside each relic. He paused by the tyet, something about it teasing his mind, but he couldn't figure out why.

"Found the inventory list!" Sophia's voice was excited and he smiled. That was the tone she should have all the time.

"See if anything on there could help us?" Olivia called back.

"I'd also check to see if anything on there could be responsible for the things we're seeing," Lucas added. "If they were able to get into level six, then they might have been able to get in here."

"Are you shitting me?" Olivia snapped.

"Wish I were, believe me."

A few minutes later, Sophia called, "Keep an eye out for a replica of the Helm of Invisibility. They could be using that."

"Will do," he responded. He kind of doubted they would have bothered with that relic, not with sorcery that could do the same available to both guards and venatores. The same spell he'd used when he went flying with Sophia.

"Holy fucking shit!"

Lucas wasn't sure if Olivia's exclamation was good or bad, and quickly tried to judge where she was so he could get to her quickly, but Sophia called out first.

"What's wrong?"

"Nothing!"

His shoulders relaxed, but he was curious as to the cause of her outburst. "Then what is it?"

"We've got one of the Tablets of Destinies!"

"Yeah, I saw that the other day. Wasn't sure what it was," Sophia admitted. "Can't read cuneiform."

"Four tablets that hold prophecies and spells. Legend says if someone gets all four that they can rule the world. This one is the Kings Tablet."

"Kings tablet?"

"One of the tablets was given to the Sumerian kings. It was kind of crucial to their rule. Not sure how we got a hold of it, but I'd love to see what it has."

Lucas's lips twitched. "So read it. If it helped them rule, then it might have a spell we can use."

"Good point."

If they were lucky, it would. Ruling as a king back then couldn't have been easy, but it wasn't really all that different from ruling the Athenaeum. The population was a hell of a lot smaller, but a lot of the same issues were still there. He would have said aside from war they were all basically the same, but it kind of felt like they were at war now. They just didn't know who the enemy was or why they were fighting.

Though he was careful as he made his way through the relics, he wasn't seeing anything that could help them. The armor could be useful if they got into a fight, and the phoenix feather might help if someone was near death and Sergei couldn't help them, but nothing helped now.

Wait, there was. Backtracking, he found the tyet again. It was about five inches tall and made of gold, the shape reminding him of a person with their arms at their sides. There were hieroglyphic symbols carved onto what he thought of as the legs.

The card for it was unhelpful, stating only that it was the original tyet. His Egyptian lore wasn't the greatest, and he didn't speak or read the language. "Need someone who reads hieroglyphics over here. Preferably someone who also knows Egyptian lore."

"Olivia, you still reading the tablet?" Sophia asked.

"Yeah. Do you read hieroglyphics?"

"Enough to get the gist. I'll holler if I can't figure it out. On my way, Lucas."

He didn't touch the relic while he waited, more aware even than Sophia of just how dangerous some of these items could be. And with this one not having a description of what it could do, he was wary. It might not even have any powers, like the club, but he didn't want to take chances.

Sophia peeked around the edge of the row, then smiled when she spotted him. She had a rolled up scroll in her hand as she made her way to him. "What'd you find?"

"A tyet."

"Oh, the original? Yeah, I saw it the other day."

"Did you read the inscription on it?"

She shook her head. "No. Why? Something catch your attention?"

"Maybe. Egypt isn't my area of expertise. I'm better with the cultures around the Arabian peninsula, like the Sumerians and Persians, but my mind keeps coming back to the tyet. Could you read the inscription, see if it's more helpful than the card?"

"Sure. You can look at the list while I translate. I'm not as fluent in it as I am ancient Greek, but I can probably muddle through," she told him, offering over the scroll.

Lucas unrolled the scroll but kept glancing at Sophia. He wasn't really worried that she'd touch the tyet and get hurt, he was just worried. But the list did need to be looked over and they didn't have time for him to just sit around. His gaze skimmed over the list. Several of the relics he'd seen, and some he had an itch to go check out. Not that they were important in their current situation, but because they just sounded cool or he'd heard of them. Nothing jumped out at him as something that could be used to do anything they'd encountered.

The texts were harder. While the tablets and scrolls often had descriptive names, that wasn't always the case, and books were even worse. The Tablet of Destinies was clear enough for anyone who knew their Sumerian lore, but what in the hell was the Scroll of Creation?

And who knew what a book titled *Essays on the Techniques for Excantations of Metaphysical Influence of the Anima* was about?

"If I'm reading this right," Sophia said, pulling his attention from the scroll, "this is an object of healing, which makes sense. Isn't Isis a healing goddess?"

"She is." Egyptian gods might not be his forte, but it was a stupid man who didn't learn what he could about the gods who protected his home.

Sophia nodded as her finger moved above the surface of the tyet, helping her to follow the symbols, he assumed. "It also says something about purifying blood, but I'm not positive there. And this bit," she tapped the air above one section of the hieroglyphics, "says something about protection."

She straightened and let her hand drop, a subdued but hopeful smile on her lips. "Think it could help Lachlan? I mean, I know Sergei's a great healer, and I'll never say this to his face, but doesn't goddess trump demigod?"

"Generally," he agreed. "He's said on more than one occasion that both his father and brother are better healers than him, so he's not so egotistical that he can't believe there are those who are better than him. And it might help. Won't know until we try."

"We should take it, then. If it can help Lachlan, it can help the others." She grinned. "Want to do the honors? Since you're the one who recognized its significance?"

He scoffed. "Don't know if I'd go that far, but sure." Handing her back the scroll, he gently lifted the tyet and tucked it into the pocket on the side of his pants. It wasn't perfect, but it would keep him from losing it until they could get it up to the clinic.

"Come here, you two," Olivia called.

"Think she found something, too?"

Lucas shrugged. "We can only hope."

They made their way through the shelves until they found Olivia, posed much like Sophia had been, with one finger tracing above the tablet rather than touching it.

"What'd you find?" Sophia asked as they walked down the row to the woman.

Olivia glanced over at them. "First, some good news. I doubt our guy made it down here, because most everyone in the Athenaeum has heard of this tablet, and I think they would have taken it if they could have."

"Why that over some of the other stuff?" Lucas asked.

"Because this tablet might not let someone rule the world, but it would damn sure make it easy for them to fuck over a very large part of it," she answered bluntly.

Sophia stepped closer and frowned at the tablet. "What do you mean?"

"I mean, this thing could bring the rain, cause earthquakes, and create an army from the very rocks. Among a lot of other shit."

"That's a little terrifying. And I'm glad it hasn't been stolen, but is there anything there for the current situation that won't result in the Athenaeum being flooded or buried?" Lucas asked. The look on her face was something he could only describe as hopeful dread. "What did you find?"

Olivia drew in a breath and turned to face them. "There is one thing that could help solve a lot of problems. Not all of them, since even our patrons can't, but there's a chance it could fix Lachlan and everyone else infected, and possibly help us figure out who's behind it all."

"But?" Sophia asked, and he agreed. That sounded entirely too good to be true.

"But the way to do it is by having someone channel the god Enki's powers, and there's a pretty big warning that it's a dangerous thing to do. It can kill a person."

Sophia definitely wasn't casting that spell, but Lucas still wanted more information. "Enki…god of water and wisdom, right?" he asked.

"And trickery, magic, healing, and exorcism, which is why I said it *could* solve a lot of problems," Olivia explained. "Exorcise and heal the infection, then identify the killer."

"There's no way it could be that easy, though," Sophia argued. "And no, I'm not saying risking death is easy. Does it say anything about what could help a person survive channeling those powers?"

Olivia shook her head. "Nope. I'm summarizing, but it basically says only use that spell if shit's hit the fan because odds are it'll kill you."

Sophia was quiet for a long moment. "During the casting, or after using the powers?" she asked softly.

"No!" Lucas's voice was sharp and gravelly, but he couldn't help it. The thought of her dying to save the Athenaeum wrenched his heart and weakened his knees. "You're not doing it, Sophia."

She glanced at Olivia, then wrapped her free hand around Lucas's bicep, drawing him down the aisle until they were out of earshot. He could have resisted, but he let her. "Lucas, things are getting worse, not better. You know that. I've got less than three days to find out who's doing this and stop them before they kill me. And in the mean time, pretty much everyone in the Athenaeum is suffering. Maybe they're all infected, maybe not, but they're not themselves. And four people have *died*. What kind of aspida would I be if I ignored an opportunity to fix it all?"

"And what kind of nasaru would I be if I didn't protect the person who's not only my aspida, but the woman I love?" he snapped, curling his hands into fists. It was less to prevent him from destroying something in his anger, and more to keep from accidentally hurting her with the claws that had extended. "No, Sophia. We're not using that spell. Not unless we have no other option."

She lifted her hand to his cheek and smiled sadly. "I agree. We've got the tyet now. Maybe we can try using it in conjunction with Sergei's healing and maybe the mithridate. I don't want to risk dying anymore than you do, I just don't want us to dismiss it completely."

He leaned into her soft touch and forced his voice to gentle. "Books and relics aren't worth your life."

"No, they're not," she agreed solemnly, "but the people who tend to them are."

Chapter 24

LUCAS HADN'T LIKED HER decision, but Sophia was firm that they would use the channeling spell as a last resort. She couldn't risk taking the tablet out of the Vault, so asked Olivia to write down the phonetics so it could be used later if needed. Olivia had agreed, then when Lucas had stalked off, promised her that the spell was now committed to memory.

She really did envy Olivia her memory.

They'd searched for a little longer, but the tyet and tablet had been the most promising options they'd found. Subdued despite the hope both should have given them, they left the Vault and made their way up to the clinic. The door was open, so they stepped inside, Lucas leading the way. He stopped after just a few steps and Sophia frowned and peeked around him, wondering at the sudden stiffness of his shoulders.

Oh. Sergei wasn't alone. Her mom was there, too. Her heart twisted, but she smiled and stepped around Lucas. "Hi, Mom."

Heather looked up from Lachlan and rather than the indifference she'd been showing the past few days, her lip curled and her eyes narrowed in a glare. "What are you doing here?" she asked in a tone that ripped through Sophia.

"Mom...why are you acting like this?" Sophia asked, taking a step toward the woman who had been her best friend for so much of her life. "Why are you treating me like you hate me?"

Heather arched a brow. "What makes you think I don't?" she asked coldly.

"Mom," she breathed, fighting against a sob. It didn't help the tears gathering in her eyes, but if she could maintain her composure, that would be enough. She hoped. "You don't hate me. I'm your daughter."

"Which only proves that the gods have decided to curse me for some reason."

"Heather, that's enough," Sergei said firmly. "Sophia is not only your daughter, she's also your aspida. Show her some respect."

"Respect is earned, not given, and all she's earned from me is my disdain."

"Shut. Up," Lucas growled. "Out of here, now, and without another word, or I'll confine you to protect my aspida."

A glance back at him showed that his skin had a gray cast to it, and his eyes had turned to stone as well. It must have been enough to convince Heather, because she huffed and stalked out of the clinic, making sure to keep as much space between her and Sophia as possible.

Gods, that really hurt. It helped—some—that both Sergei and Lucas had spoken up for her, but they never should have had to protect her from her own mother.

"She doesn't mean it," Olivia said, resting a hand on her shoulder. "Remember what I told you earlier."

That Heather's dreams showed something was wrong. Right. She was probably infected, just like the others. It made sense, but it didn't help as much as she might have liked.

"Olivia's right," Lucas said as he wrapped his arms around her.

Safe in his embrace, she pressed her face against his chest to hide her tears. These three wouldn't judge her for them, she knew that, but if she couldn't be strong, she needed to appear strong. Still, she took a minute before she drew back. "I know. And that's not the priority right now." As discreetly as possible, she wiped at her eyes then turned to Sergei. "We found something that might help Lachlan. Might need to use it while you try healing him, but we need to try everything, right?"

"We do," he agreed. "What did you find?"

Lucas pulled the relic out of his pocket and held it out to Sergei. "The original tyet. Supposed to be able to heal wounds and purify blood."

Sergei looked intrigued as he accepted the relic and cradled it in his hands while he studied it. "It does feel powerful," he agreed. "Divinely made?"

"Supposed to have been made by Isis," Sophia answered with a nod.

"Well, I don't know if it'll help, but it certainly can't hurt him. And combining divine healing with mine might just be enough to eradicate the infection. But one of you will need to use the relic while I heal. I doubt I'll be able to focus on both at the same time."

"I'll do it," Olivia said, her hand still on Sophia's shoulder.

Sergei cocked his head and glanced at Sophia. When she nodded, he smiled and gave Olivia the tyet. "Then let's see if we can help Lachlan."

They walked to the vampire, with Sergei standing on his left, Olivia his right. Their gazes met, they nodded, then Sergei lowered his hands to Lachlan's bare arm, while Olivia rested the golden tyet on his other arm. Sergei's hands began to glow softly, but this time it was mirrored by the tyet.

Sophia's hand found Lucas's, and he squeezed reassuringly. Bending his head without taking his eyes off the trio, he whispered, "It'll work. Just have faith."

"I have to." And she did. Not only was Isis one of their patrons, if this didn't work, they didn't have anything else they could try. Something had to start going right or she was going to get an ulcer.

Or be killed.

It seemed to take forever until Sergei murmured, "Enough," and drew his hands back. A second later, Olivia did the same.

"Did it work?" Olivia asked, studying Lachlan as she slid the tyet into her pocket. Sophia looked him over as well, but saw no obvious change.

"I think so," Sergei said slowly, like he didn't want to commit to anything, "but I want to thoroughly check him."

No one said a word as he used his magic to search Lachlan for traces of the infection. When he looked up, he was smiling. "I'm not sensing anything. I think that did it."

"Really? So he's cured? And we can cure the others who are infected?" Sophia asked, not letting herself feel anything resembling hope just yet.

"Really," Sergei confirmed. "I'm going to bring him out of the stasis, see how he feels. More importantly, see if he's back to his normal self."

"Olivia, be prepared, just in case," Lucas said, giving Sophia's hand one more squeeze before he walked over next to Sergei. "Do you still have the cuffs that were on him?"

"I do," Sergei confirmed, stepping away and opening a drawer, retrieving the cuffs.

"If he comes out of it still violent, we'll subdue and cuff him. I know you said you didn't sense anything, but for all we know, it had lasting effects."

"No, absolutely best to be safe. We've never dealt with something like this before and we don't know enough about it."

"Like how some people are insanely violent and others are just assholes," Sophia said dryly.

"Precisely," he agreed, inclining his head to her. To avoid getting in the way of Olivia and Lucas, he stood above Lachlan's head. "Ready?"

Sophia cast her shield spell just to be safe, even as Olivia and Lucas confirmed they were ready.

Sergei nodded and touched the tips of two fingers to Lachlan's temple. There was no glow this time, nor did he do more than brush his fingers across Lachlan's skin. That was enough, because the vampire's eyes opened only a second later. A second after that, he frowned.

"Do I want to know why you're standing over me?" he asked, the remnants of his original Scottish accent barely noticeable.

"What's the last thing you remember?" Lucas asked, not relaxing yet, though the fact that Lachlan was speaking instead of attacking was a good sign.

His brows scrunched together and he fell silent. "I...Lunch, I think, but it's a little fuzzy. Why? Did something happen?" Olivia scoffed, drawing his attention to her. "Something did." His gaze landed on the cuffs in Sergei's hand. "I did something?"

"You attacked everyone in the common room," Lucas said, the words blunt even if his tone was patient.

"What?" Lachlan asked, shoving himself upright, eyes widening. "Is anyone hurt badly?"

"Nothing that couldn't be healed," Sergei told him, resting a comforting hand on Lachlan's shoulder. "But that was nine days ago."

Sophia wasn't sure Lachlan's eyes could get any wider. "Nine days?" he asked, his voice a low growl of shock. She must have shifted because his gaze snapped to her and she tensed, bracing for a verbal assault—if not a physical one. "Sophia, I didn't hurt you, did I?"

He sounded so pained at the thought that she relaxed. "No, you didn't hurt me," she assured him, daring to step close enough to lay a hand near his ankle. "And like Sergei said, no one was hurt seriously." At least one of the injuries could have been considered serious if they hadn't had a healer on hand, but he didn't need to know that now.

"Good. That's good," he murmured, running his hands through his wavy red hair before he tugged at it. "I don't remember it. Any of it. Not hurting people or why I would have. I swear I don't. I don't have a reason to hurt anyone!"

Sergei looked at her, and after a beat, so did Lucas and Olivia. Great. It was up to her to tell him. Sergei might let her off the hook if she gave him a signal, but that would be the coward's way out, wouldn't it? Either way, she couldn't let him continue to beat himself up.

"It wasn't your fault, Lachlan," she told him gently.

His hands stilled in his hair and he looked at her with hopeful blue eyes. "It wasn't?"

Sophia shook her head. "No, it wasn't. Everyone agreed it was out of character for you, so Sergei did a thorough exam when he brought you back here. He found...an unidentified substance in your body. It seems to be what was making you act the way you did."

"An unidentified substance? But how would I have gotten an unidentified substance in me?"

"We don't know," she admitted while privately cursing herself. Other than checking the footage leading up to the attack, they hadn't focused on the how, just the what. They really should have, since others were being infected. For that matter, the four of them should be checked, too. If they could narrow down the source, it might lead to more answers. For now, she just told him what she knew. "You didn't have any puncture marks, so it wasn't injected, but it could have been something you ingested or touched. You know how dangerous some of the relics can be."

He frowned and shook his head, his hands dropping to rub over his thighs. "Couldn't be a relic. I haven't been in the relic rooms in nearly a month."

"Have you eaten anything unusual? Fed on anyone new?" Sergei asked.

Lachlan shook his head again. "I've eaten the same thing everyone else does. And I've been feeding on the same couple of people for a few years now."

"Who have you fed on in the last week?" Lucas asked. "Could be they got infected and you took it in when you fed from them."

"Has anyone else...attacked anyone?"

"No."

"Then how could I have gotten it from one of them?"

"Could be it affects vampire physiology differently than it does theirs," Olivia suggested. "We really don't know enough about it to guess."

"I wish I could say she was exaggerating, but she isn't. We barely were able to cure you," Sergei explained.

Lachlan hesitated, then sighed. "Penny and Melissa."

Lucas and Sophia exchanged looks at Penny's name. If she was behind everything, it would have been a simple matter for her to do something to dose him when he fed from her.

"I'll give them both a check to ensure they're not infected," Sergei told him. "But you should know that there are several people who are, and it's affecting their behavior."

"Affecting how?"

Sergei looked at the others rather than answering and smiled faintly. "Why don't you go return the tyet? I'll get him caught up and make sure he gets to his room."

"All right," Sophia agreed. "Lachlan, if you need anything, let me know, okay?"

"Or me," Olivia added. "I'm head curator now, so you can come to me, too."

Lachlan looked surprised. "You are?" He glanced at Sophia, who nodded to confirm it. "Congratulations then," he said, managing a weak smile. "You'll do a fantastic job."

"I hope so. Now you just rest up and feel better," she told him before she followed Sophia and Lucas out of the clinic, closing the door behind them.

"You two know him better than I do," Sophia began when they were far enough away from the clinic that Lachlan couldn't overhear. "Do you trust him that he's clueless?"

"I don't know him that well, but he's never struck me as a liar," Olivia said, jerking a shoulder in a shrug.

"I believe him," Lucas said, nodding. "He's an honest man. He can't even bluff right when we play poker."

Sophia looked up and down the hallway to ensure they were truly alone, then dropped her voice. "And do we think it's a coincidence that he's fed on one of our suspects recently?"

"I was thinking the same thing," Olivia admitted.

Lucas nodded. "So was I."

"You know something else that occurred to me in there? We fucked up big time. We've basically ignored the how for this infection. The what's important, sure, as is the cure," she said with a pointed look at Olivia's pocket, "but the how could tell us a lot."

Lucas cursed before he nodded again. "You're right. I think after this is all over, we need to recruit someone who has some kind of investigative experience, just in case."

"I'm all for that," Sophia agreed. "Hopefully it'll never be needed again, but it's one of those better to have it and not need it situations."

"Make it unanimous," Olivia said, crossing her arms. "But what do we do now? We already have Penny on our list, and none of us can identify this infection like Sergei can, and he'll be busy with Lachlan for a while longer."

"I'd like to check the cameras again, now that we have two people he fed on. Follow them for a few days before Lachlan went nuts. It doesn't really need two people, but after the attack, I'd really rather you not be alone," Lucas told her.

"I'd like to hear more about the attack, and Sophia promised to fill me in on everything else," Olivia said with a shrug. "I may not have stone skin, but I think I can protect her as well as you."

"True." But Lucas didn't sound like he liked it. Sophia almost smiled at his protective nature.

"We'll hole up in my bedroom and I'll keep my threat spell up," she told him, sliding her arm around his waist to hug him. "We'll be fine."

His arm came around her, giving her a squeeze as he kissed the top of her head. "I know. I just worry."

"I know, and it's fine. You just go check the cameras, and you know where to find us when you're done."

"Just no more getting attacked, okay? I can't handle it."

She smiled, but didn't promise anything. The last thing she wanted to do was lie to him.

Chapter 25

Sophia and Olivia stopped in the kitchen to grab some drinks and something to eat, ensuring they grabbed prepackaged food or made their own from the shared ingredients. They'd been in the Vault for a while, and her stomach was protesting being empty.

Once they got back to her room with their bounty, Sophia kicked her shoes off and sat on the bed cross-legged. Immediately, she cracked open a bottle of water, but after a deep drink, she dove into the sandwich she'd made. Olivia seemed to be just as hungry, because she joined Sophia and wasted no time in digging into her assorted plate of munchies. After the worst of their hunger was sated, Olivia washed hers down with a sip of Coke. "So...someone pushed you down the stairs?"

"Mmhmm," Sophia said before swallowing. "Was pretty bad. Sergei said I ended up with a concussion, some broken ribs, and internal bleeding. I hate to think what would have happened if I hadn't managed to call Lucas and a healer hadn't been on hand."

Olivia winced sympathetically as she popped an olive in her mouth. "Any idea who?"

"No, they used some kind of disguise spell that obscured their features. Don't even know if it was a man or woman. But considering everything else they've done, pushing me down the stairs and threatening to kill me doesn't seem too bad."

"Threatening to kill you?" Olivia said blandly.

"Oh, yeah, forgot to mention that," Sophia said with a sheepish shrug. "Got three days to bail on the Athenaeum or they're coming for me. Which means we're on a literal deadline."

"I'll make sure I hit the last three dreams tonight," Olivia promised. "But you said there was more going on? I know you mentioned some stuff back in your office, but if I'm going to help, I need more."

"Fair enough," Sophia said, scooting up on the bed to lean back against the pillows. "I'm going to go chronologically, as best as I can figure it, because there really is a lot."

"Just tell me, was I the first?"

Sophia couldn't keep the sympathy off her face as she nodded. "As far as I can tell, yeah. You and Thomas were first. After that, Erasmus was poisoned. They must have altered the dosage, because the entire time everyone thought he was sick, it was really poisoning."

"What the hell did they use? And were they just giving him mini-doses all the time?" she asked, her anger building.

"No, it seems like you all just got one dose, he just got a smaller one." Sophia set her plate on the nightstand, her hunger dissipating under the unpleasant conversation. "From what we found, they used a poison called Achlys, named after the Greek goddess of poisons and misery. It's a mix of toxins and magic, and seems to pretty much always be lethal without the antidote. But if you give a small dose, it doesn't kill immediately. And before you ask, yes, we found the antidote, and Sergei has a copy of the formula in his clinic."

"You think they have more?"

"I think they have a lot more. We found a sort of lab a few days ago," Sophia admitted.

This time she only heard cussing from six languages, but it was still impressive. "What was next?"

"The day of Erasmus's funeral, someone locked me in a supply closet. Which is tame, but since it wasn't a normal occurrence, it's worth mentioning. And after that, I was in the library, sitting and reading, when someone created an illusion of one of the shelves being on fire. And when I say illusion, it was a good one. My throat burned from the smoke, I could feel the heat, everything. I ran to find an extinguisher, and when Lucas and I got back, there was no trace of it, but Lucas found magic residue."

"They were trying to scare you away."

Though it was a statement instead of a question, Sophia nodded. "Seems like it. That was right before I was chosen as aspida, so I'm not sure why."

Olivia nodded slowly. "Doesn't make a lot of sense, not unless they knew you were going to be aspida."

"Anything's possible. No one's file has any notes about being a seer, but I can't rule out that they kept that power hidden like you did with yours."

"True. And if they've had this planned, it would be smart. Could also be they consulted an outside seer."

Sophia hadn't thought of that. "Also true. Next came the cursed book."

"I heard about that. You touched something on level six, right? Almost killed you?"

"Yep. But what isn't common knowledge is that the book was on a shelf rather than in a protective box, and it wasn't even in the right section. It's like someone left it there deliberately, hoping I'd touch it and die. I'm still not sure why it didn't. But we did confirm that it was sucking out my essence or whatever. Not a hundred percent on the why."

"So they started escalating after you were named aspida. Though I don't see what they could gain from killing two aspides."

"Neither do I, and I promise, Lucas, Sergei, and I have gone over that dozens of times. It makes no sense. You can't rig the choosing, and they could obviously get onto level six, so didn't need the position for that. I'm not entirely convinced they were in the Vault, either."

Olivia shook her head. "Can't come up with anything either, but I'll think on it."

Sophia smiled faintly then went on. "Then there was the shooting at Delphi. We found out they hired a sniper using my new Athenaeum account."

"Yeah, heard about that, too. Not that it was a sniper, but the shooting."

Sophia nodded. "After that was when Agatha died. I found her in her bedroom and Sergei recognized the spell that killed her as a forbidden bit of sorcery." And now was when things really got bad. Most of what she'd said wasn't really anything new to Olivia, but if she didn't trust the woman, now was when she needed to stop. She decided to trust. "After the meeting when I informed everyone of her death, Peter came to me and Lucas. Said his dad had reeked of magic that morning and had been acting weird. When we went to confront him, he seemed to attack us. Lucas and Peter fought back, and Peter ended up killing him."

"What do you mean, seemed to?"

Sophia started to tell her, then shook her head. "Let me keep this in order, so I don't forget anything." Olivia frowned, but nodded. "A few hours later, both Dion and Agatha's bodies disappeared from the clinic. Which is not something we've advertised, so keep that to yourself for now, please."

"Of course." The words were calm, but Sophia could see the anger growing on the other woman's features. So Sophia decided to just get the rest out. "Lachlan you know about, and my attack, which just leaves one more thing, and the answer to your earlier question."

"Oh? Oh. About how Dion appeared to attack?"

"Mmhmm. Do you remember how Death appeared a few days ago?"

Olivia shuddered and nodded. "Not likely to forget it. I'm not scared of a lot, but he was terrifying."

"Tell me about it!" Sophia was happy she wasn't alone in being afraid of the man. She knew everyone ended up in his realm at some point, but she wasn't eager to call that place her home anytime soon. "He was coming for something unrelated—a spell Erasmus had given to someone—but I decided that while he was there, I'd ask a favor."

Olivia blinked once, her lips curved, then she threw her head back and laughed. That wasn't the reaction Sophia was expecting, especially since it wasn't a quick laugh. Oh no, this was apparently the funniest thing Olivia had heard in a while.

After a minute, Sophia picked up one of Olivia's olives and tossed it at her, pleased when it splatted against her cheek. Not that the nightmare seemed to care. She just grinned and wiped her cheek as she caught her breath. "You asked Death for a favor? Terrifying, all-powerful Death who could kill the entire Athenaeum with a thought? That Death? Damn girl. You've got balls."

"Can't say it was that brave. Pretty sure his wife wouldn't have let him. She seems to like me."

That impressed Olivia even more. "Nice. But what was the favor?"

"To summon Dion."

Olivia sobered instantly. "I take it he said he didn't attack you?"

"He said a lot more than that. With everything that had happened, we were convinced Dion had poisoned you and killed Erasmus, but that he had an accomplice who had stolen the bodies and possibly infected Lachlan. But Dion swore he hadn't attacked us and would never have hurt Erasmus."

"He could have been lying," Olivia pointed out.

"Could have been, but somehow Death could tell and said he was telling the truth. So when all this is over, I'll be letting *everyone* know that Dion was innocent. He doesn't deserve to have his name remembered in disgust."

"No, he doesn't. And I have to say I'm happy to know my predecessor wasn't a murderous prick. Is that everything?"

Sophia thought for a minute, running through it all in her mind before she slowly shook her head. "I can't think of anything else. I mean, the infections, but you already know about that, and it seems that their anger is directed completely at me."

"Doesn't mean it's safe for everyone else. That could escalate too. Besides, if it's the same thing Lachlan's infected with, he didn't attack you. He attacked everyone near him. And it's not like Lucas, Sergei, or

I would let them attack you, which means we could get hurt protecting you."

Sophia absolutely hated that Olivia was right. The thought of any of them getting hurt because of her twisted her stomach into knots. Especially since she knew that no matter what she said, they would protect her. If not for her as a person, then because she was aspida. Sometimes she really hated that she'd been the one chosen. It was worse that she couldn't abdicate. It was be aspida or be dead. She preferred aspida, even if she now had a friend on the other side.

"I'm starting to think that none of us should be wandering around alone, and it sucks that I have to say that," Sophia said, slumping down and stretching her legs out. "This should be a safe place. Instead, it's feeling like the original labyrinth, and the minotaur is breathing down my neck."

Olivia gave her a sympathetic look and rubbed her ankle. "It'll get better. Before my poisoning, this place felt like home. Not just a job, but home. It's why so many of us live here. I mean, yeah, it's convenient, but it's also comfortable and warm, despite being underground."

"Which is really weird and cool all at the same time," Sophia said with a faint smile. "But I think I'd rather talk about just about anything but the Athenaeum right now. Can we just talk about anything else for a bit? I think I'm getting high blood pressure and an ulcer."

Olivia laughed. "Don't tell Sergei that. He'll take it as a personal insult."

He probably would, so Sophia just smiled. "What about you? I know next to nothing about you as a person, just as a curator. Seems like it would be nice if the only woman in the Athenaeum who didn't hate me wasn't a near stranger to me."

"Me? What do you want to know? I'm not really a complicated woman."

Sophia scoffed. "A woman who has the memories of gods knows how many family members isn't complicated? And that's before you add in working for a super secret magical library that dates back to the burning of Alexandria *and* being a nightmare."

"That just means I have a complicated life, not that I'm complicated," Olivia argued, but Sophia had to grin. "You're persistent, you know that?"

"What can I say? It keeps me sane and tends to get me what I want in the end."

Olivia rolled her eyes, but she smiled, too. "I really don't have much to say about myself. One of my ancestors knew about the Athenaeum, so when my parents were killed and I needed to go someplace safe, I managed to contact Erasmus and get in."

The words were said as blandly as though Olivia had said she broke a nail, but Sophia's heart went out to her. She couldn't say her own situation was the same since she had her mom and had never met her dad, but losing a parent still hurt. Except Olivia's eyes hardened, and Sophia guessed she wouldn't appreciate any sympathy from her. "How'd you manage to contact Erasmus without knowing exactly where it was?"

"I kind of did, actually," Olivia admitted. "My ancestor had been here, so I knew how to get here. The memory couldn't help me get through the labyrinth, but I was able to get myself noticed and insist on talking to the man in charge."

"How'd he take that?" Sophia asked. If Lucas had been the head nasaru back then, she knew he wouldn't have been happy about an unexpected guest. Erasmus, on the other hand, might have been amused. He had seemed the sort from her brief interactions with him.

"Oh, he thought it was funny as hell. Sure, he made sure I told him exactly how I found the place, but like you, he considered me being Ogham as an asset. He wanted to stick me in the curators, but as much as I like books and research, I didn't want to be stuck inside all the time, so I trained and became a guard."

"And later the only dual guard and curator," Sophia said, nodding.

"Yeah. Meant I could occasionally get out, see the sun, travel, all that."

"How long ago was that?"

Olivia's head cocked as she thought. "Not quite two hundred years ago. Think it was 1827 when I first showed up."

"And you think whoever killed your parents is still looking for you?"

"Hell, I'm not sure they were ever looking for me," she admitted. "But given that so many Ogham have been hunted down and either imprisoned or killed, I wasn't taking any chances."

"No, I get it. I don't think I would have taken the chance, either. But..." Sophia was hesitant to ask, but there was something bugging her about Olivia's history.

"Just ask," Olivia said, popping another olive in her mouth. "I'm not really touchy about my past. Secretive about what I am, but my past is just that."

Sophia didn't think she could ever be so blasé if she lost her mom, but nodded. "You made it sound like basically every bit of skin I can't see right now is covered in tattoos, but how? If your parents died that long ago, and it sounds like you didn't have other family to go to, how did you get them all?"

"You don't go for the easy questions, do you?" Olivia took a drink, and Sophia might be imagining it, but it seemed like she needed a moment. "They're not tattoos in the way you're thinking. The only needles that have touched my skin were those Sergei has used on me for medical reasons, though some Ogham do get their marks in that way, but I haven't."

"I don't understand." But Sophia was extremely curious, sitting up and leaning a little closer as she listened raptly.

"There are two ways for an Ogham to pass on their knowledge. The first is sort of like…gifting an apprentice with their master's knowledge. It's done with planning, when someone wants to share something they know. Like an expert in…botany…could gift their child or student with everything they know about plants. That's pretty common—or was—and parents often give their children bits and pieces that way. Partly to share stuff like family history, and partly to accustom the child to the process."

"Oh wow. Oral history has nothing on you guys, does it?"

Olivia shook her head. "We literally can't forget or misremember our history. I could tell you my family line perfectly back to the time when we first became Ogham."

"That is so cool. And yes, yes, I know," Sophia said, waving a hand dismissively, "there are downsides to it. But that's still cool. But you said two ways?"

There was some reluctance on Olivia's face, but before Sophia could tell her to forget it, she started speaking. "The other way is one done in emergencies. Like when someone is about to die. It's painful, to both the person giving the memories and the one receiving them, and it's risky, too. The more memories that are passed on at once, the more likely the recipient will either die or basically have their brain fried. Like when a TV gets a power surge. Even if they survive, it's disorienting as hell, suddenly having a shitload of memories that don't actually belong to you."

"I take it you've experienced that?" Sophia asked softly.

"Mmhmm. I got my nightmare nature from my mom, but my dad, just before he died, gave me everything he had. Every single memory."

That had to be bittersweet at the very least. She had a very large piece of her dad that she couldn't lose, but it also meant she could never forget anything about him. Then again, some people mourned when memories of those they'd lost faded. As useful as being Ogham would be, Sophia was now very happy she wasn't one.

"I don't know what to say," she admitted.

Olivia lifted a shoulder as she picked at the remaining food on her plate. "You don't really need to say anything. It's in the past and it's just fact. After that, I came here, but over the years I occasionally came across other Ogham, and we traded memories. Helps us stay alive."

"I don't know if this means anything considering the current state of the Athenaeum, but I promise that I'll do everything to keep you protected, Olivia. Same goes for if we find other family members or Ogham hiding in the woodwork."

"You really mean that, don't you? Even without knowing who's after the Ogham."

Sophia frowned and nodded slowly. "Of course. And it doesn't really matter who's after you. Like I'm going to let anyone try to exterminate or enslave an entire bloodline just because someone's scared of your power? Fuck that. If I were going to do that, then I might as well stop trying to find the person who killed my grandfather. I should just tuck tail and run like I was told. And that's just not me. I might be in way over my head, but I refuse to be that person, no matter how sick the thought of being the one calling the shots makes me."

Olivia's eyes were steady on her face for a full minute, and the way she was clearly not blinking was starting to freak Sophia out. But then the nightmare smiled, and she picked up a cube of cheese, biting into it and taking her time chewing before she nodded. "You're not doing as bad as you seem to think."

"I'm not? Sure feels like everything's going to hell on my watch."

"Maybe it is, but that doesn't mean you're not doing a good job. Sounds like this was mostly put into play before you ever arrived in Greece. How can you be blamed for that? Do you blame Erasmus for my poisoning? Or his own?"

"Of course not."

"Then why blame yourself for matters out of your control?"

"Because it feels like I should," Sophia admitted after coming up with nothing else. She sighed and fell back against the pillows. "You really think we can figure out who's behind this and put a stop to it?"

"We found a way to cure Lachlan, so I'm betting on us. Whoever's after you had better run and hide, because we're closing in. I can feel it."

<h1 style="text-align:center">Chapter 26</h1>

Sophia walked through the Athenaeum carrying a torch, which was the only thing to illuminate her path. It didn't look anything like she remembered. Instead of smooth cut walls and floors, they looked more natural, the narrow walls dipping in then spreading out, stalagmites hindering her way and causing her to walk around them. Water dripped somewhere deeper in the cave—because could it really be called the Athenaeum when it looked like it had been created by nature rather than magic and man?

The light flickered against the walls, the ridges and bumps casting odd shadows that moved like dancing predators. It certainly felt like she was being stalked, especially when all she could hear was distant water and soft crackling of her torch. And the harsh beating of her heart.

The floor sloped downward sharply and the stone beneath her feet was slick, causing her to step carefully. It became harder as the incline grew steeper, but she could see the floor below leveled out and the claustrophobic tunnel opened up. She was nearly to the bottom when her foot landed wrong on a smooth section of stone and she slipped. She slammed into the sharp edge of a rock on her way down, her body hitting the cave floor hard. The torch dropped from suddenly loose fingers and rolled away. Before she could grab hold of something to anchor herself, gravity took hold, pulling her hard toward the cavern below.

With the only source of light behind her, she slid into the dark.

Instead of slowly coming to a stop, it felt like she went over a cliff, only to land hard once again a few seconds later. The sounds of water and flame were gone, leaving only her ragged breathing as she fought to recover from her falls.

Blind, she started to push up to her knees, only to freeze when she heard something in the darkness around her. It wasn't a voice, not really, but she could only describe it as a whisper. No, whispers. Like dozens of voices were layered over one another, all while being quieter than a breeze. Except this whisper she felt deep in her chest, into her soul. Wincing, she curled in on herself, eyes wide as she tried to penetrate the darkness.

"Hello?" she called, but her voice echoed back at her, a hundred times louder than it had been. Fighting back a cry, she covered her ears.

When the sound had died off, leaving only the eerie echo, she cautiously moved her hands. Deciding it was safe, she carefully pushed to her feet, her movements clumsy in the complete darkness. Stretching her arms out, she took a single step forward, but her foot scraped across the stone. That sound, too, was amplified to a painful degree, and she had to bite her lower lip to contain another cry.

Again she took a step, very careful to lift her foot so as to avoid any unnecessary noise. It worked. Exhaling gently, she continued to move forward, but the whispers grew louder. No, they weren't louder, they were...separating? They now sounded like distinct voices, but she couldn't make any of them out at first.

Sophia closed her eyes since they weren't helping her anyway and tried to think her way out of this. She couldn't see, had no idea where she was or how she'd gotten here, and was surrounded by...things. Her elf side couldn't help her, as healing and interacting with plants and animals did no good in a cave devoid of life. The little sorcery she'd learned wasn't likely to help, either. She had no way of creating a light, and while she had learned a teleportation spell, she had a feeling it wouldn't work here. Not if it really was part of the Athenaeum. Only the gods could teleport within its walls.

But her shifter side might help. Owls had the best night vision of any natural creature and they flew silently, so she wasn't likely to create more of those thunderous echoes. And, since she'd be smaller, she could squeeze through openings her human form could never manage.

Decision made, she shifted, not really expecting to be able to see anything. Even owls couldn't see in complete darkness, but there was a light ahead, just one so dim her human eyes hadn't been able to discern it. Turning her head around, she searched for the source of the ominous echoes, but saw nothing but stone.

Her wings propelled her upward and she flew toward the light, praying to Seth and the other patrons that she wasn't flying right into the mouth of some mythical underground anglerfish.

Though she was hardly slow when in the air, the light ahead didn't seem to be growing any closer, but the whispers were getting louder and more distinct. When she heard her mom's voice, she forgot to flap her wings and nearly crashed into a stalagmite. Mentally shaking herself, she tried to focus on the voice while not losing sight of her goal. It took a minute, but eventually she was able to make out words and identify more voices.

"Sophia! Help me!" Her mom.

"We need you!" That was Josie.

"Don't let me die!" Peter.

"Sophia..." That one was Lucas, she was sure of it, but where the others sounded scared, he sounded like he'd given up all hope and had resigned himself to a terrible fate.

She faltered. It was almost surely a trap, she knew that, and it was bad enough to hear her family and friends crying for help, but Lucas? She would sooner drink Achlys than leave him to die. How could she, when he'd become her heart?

Before the thought registered, she was altering her course despite the fact that she couldn't actually pinpoint where his whisper was coming from. Like the light, she never seemed to get closer to him, no matter what direction she flew in. Yet the voices grew louder and she couldn't figure out why. She'd identified more voices—almost everyone in the Athenaeum, in fact—but they were all the same. And she could always pick Lucas's desolate voice from the din.

Her wings were tiring when the voices abruptly went silent, like something had forced them to stop calling out. Then she heard one more whisper, and this one terrified her beyond anything she'd ever felt before.

"If you want to save them, you will join me."

The voice was sibilant and dark, causing rage and fear to well up within her equally.

"Join me, Sophia. Save them all and say yes. All you have to do is say yes..."

Unable to fly any further, she landed as quickly as she could and shifted back to human, not really noticing that for the first time her clothes had shifted with her. "Why would I give you anything when you're threatening my family?" she yelled into the shadows, too angry to react to the scream rebounding back at her.

"To save them. You cannot beat me. I will take you or you will die. Just say yes." To further push their point home, whatever had been keeping the other voices silent released them, and the cavern was filled with cries for help.

This was wrong. All wrong. There was no reason why she'd be in a cave. There was nothing like this in the Athenaeum, and her mom and the others certainly weren't going to come to her to help with a hangnail, much less to save their lives. But if this wasn't right, then what was?

She listened to the voices, certain that somewhere in the swarm of voices there was a clue. Shaking her head, she dismissed her mom and cousin. Josie was just crying like the others, as was Jericho. Only Lucas sounded different, but all he said was her name.

Then she realized there were three voices suspiciously absent; Sergei, Olivia, and Lachlan. Why would those three be missing?

It was the thought of Olivia that made her realize she was dreaming. As soon as that registered, she relaxed, but not much. It might be a dream, but she knew enough of nightmares—both the type of Arcane and type of dream—to know that she just because she was asleep didn't mean she was safe. Which meant she needed to figure out how to wake up. Now.

"Sophia..."

Lucas's voice was louder, which was odd, because the others were all the same. Closing her eyes out of habit more than need, she focused on his voice. On her desire—her need—to be back in bed beside him, his arms wrapped around her.

"Wake up, Sophia. Wake up," she whispered to herself.

"Wake up, Sophia," Lucas's voice echoed.

"I'm trying." She pinched herself hard on the arm, though if the pain of the echoes wasn't enough to wake her, she doubted a pinch would do it.

"Join me, Sophia! Before it's too late to save them."

The creepy voice was growing more distant, and a moment after that, so did the whispers. She fought with everything she had to claw her way back to the waking world, to the bed where the man she loved waited.

"Sophia?" That was Olivia, not Lucas, and she sounded concerned. *"Follow my voice, Sophia. Fight it, fight it hard, and come back to us."*

Fight what? The voice? She didn't really want to fight a disembodied voice, but she was trying hard to wake up. And why would Olivia be in her bedroom? She'd gone back to her own room when Lucas had gotten back.

Confusion helped push the whispers further away, and she focused on the voice of two of the only people she could trust right now.

Dizziness hit her, making her sway so hard she stumbled, then fell, landing hard on her ass. Even once she was down she didn't feel right, and it was harder to focus on Lucas and Olivia. That was when Olivia got mad.

"Godsdammit, Soph! You wake your ass up now or I swear I'm going to kiss Lucas."

Though the rational part of her mind realized Olivia would never do something like that, it helped. The whispers faded, as did the light, until she was alone in the darkness. The dizziness grew stronger, just before she felt like she was losing consciousness. This time, she hoped she woke up in her bed.

Sophia's body went limp and Lucas looked at Olivia, who sat on the opposite side of Sophia from him. He was unsure whether he felt murderous or just scared. "What happened? What's wrong?" he demanded.

"Nothing," she promised, her hands still holding Sophia's. "She'll wake up in a minute. Just relax. It was a hell of a nightmare she got trapped in."

He nodded and looked back at Sophia's face, willing her to open her eyes. It took forever until they finally did, her brow furrowing when she looked between Lucas and Olivia. "Do I want to know why there are three of us in this bed?" she asked, looking down at her hands, both of which had been claimed. Lucas didn't let go, but Olivia did after patting it once.

"Before we get into that, why don't you assure Lucas that you're okay while I get you some water?" Olivia asked as she slipped off the bed.

"Okay...but Olivia?"

"Yeah?" the woman asked, pausing at the foot of the bed.

"You do realize you're wearing a tee-shirt and your arms are bare, right?"

Lucas blinked and glanced over, surprised. He hadn't even noticed, but her arms were exposed for the first time since he'd met her. He'd never seen any of her skin but for her face and neck before, not even when she'd been in the clinic after being poisoned. She had odd tattoos covering basically every inch of her arms and hands. One of the Celtic languages, he thought, and he wondered why she covered them up. They were definitely interesting, and absolutely unique.

Olivia smiled faintly and nodded. "I can't sleep in gloves and a long-sleeved shirt every single night. And getting to you was more important than covering up. But you take care of Lucas. I'll be back in a few minutes."

Sophia watched Olivia until she was gone, then gave Lucas a confused look. "Why was getting here more important?"

"What were you dreaming about, love?"

She frowned more deeply. "I was here, but...not. It was more like a natural cave. And..." Her hand suddenly clenched around his. "There was a voice."

He nodded, using his free hand to smooth her hair. "A nightmare," he summarized. "I had one, too. Also in a cave, also with a voice. Did it try to convince you to join it?" She nodded slowly, looking spooked. Not that he blamed her. "I managed to wake up, but you were rigid and making these little sounds..." Sounds that had terrified him. It had sounded like she was being tortured, though if their dreams really had mirrored one another, there hadn't been any real torture involved. "No matter what I did, you wouldn't wake up."

"I remember," she murmured, sitting up and wrapping herself around him. His arms surrounded her and he rested his chin atop her head, happier than he could say that she was all right. "How'd Olivia get here?" she asked.

"I don't know if she was walking through dreams and noticed the nightmare, but she walked in and just started...pulling you out of it."

"If anyone would be able to, it'd be her." Her voice was muffled since her face was pressed against his shoulder, but he didn't mind.

They stayed that way until there was a soft knock on the door. Olivia didn't wait for either of them before she opened the door, but since Lucas had glanced at his phone and saw it was only one in the morning, she probably didn't want to wake anyone. Besides, they knew she was coming.

"You both okay?" Olivia asked as she approached the bed, holding a glass of water out to Sophia.

"Confused and a little freaked out, but okay is a good word for it," Sophia answered. Though she straightened, she didn't pull away from Lucas, even when she took the glass and drank.

Lucas nodded. "Same. What made you come in here?"

"Before I get to that...were you two having a dream about the Athenaeum before it was refined into its current form, and a voice telling you to join it?" They both nodded wordlessly. "I was having the same dream," she said flatly. "It, obviously, was not a natural dream. I can normally leave a natural dream as easily as I take a breath, but I had to work with this one."

"So someone did this to us?" Lucas asked.

"They did," Olivia confirmed.

"Could you tell anything about it? How they did it? Who did it?" Sophia pressed.

"No." And she sounded royally pissed about it. "I can't tell you a damn thing about it other than when I was pulling out of it, I realized you two were stuck in the same dream."

Sophia frowned. "Just us?"

"I can't swear to it, but I think so. I was kind of caught off guard about being trapped in a dream, then wanting to get my ass here to pull you out before...whatever...happened."

Lucas looked at Sophia, shocked when she made a sound suspiciously like a growl, then shoved off his lap and off the bed. "I'm so fucking sick of this!" she snapped, pacing along the side of the bed.

"Sophia...we'll figure this out. It'll be okay," he told her, trying to catch her hand and draw her back onto the bed. He wasn't sure he believed his own words, but she needed to believe them.

She stepped away from his hand and he didn't try again, deciding she needed to burn off her angry energy. "No, it won't," she said, shaking her head. "The killing? That was bad enough, especially when it meant I only got *days* to know my grandfather. But now it feels like we're just being toyed with, and I don't like being a mouse. Owls eat mice."

"Yes," Olivia agreed before Lucas could speak. "We are being toyed with, but do you know what that tells me?"

Sophia stopped for a moment and her narrowed eyes settled on Olivia. "What?"

"Whoever's doing this is scared you're going to stop them."

"I don't know if I believe that, but it sounds good." She sighed and dropped onto the edge of the bed, hands moving through her mussed hair. "And there's not anything we can do tonight. Well, Lucas and I can't, but Olivia, you should see if anyone else is stuck in the same dream. If it's all clear, can you check those last three people? I'm done sitting around waiting for an idea to drop into my lap."

Olivia's lips curved and she nodded. "I can. And you haven't been sitting around. Like I said earlier, give yourself a break." She walked to the door and glanced back, still smiling. "Sleep well. And I mean that literally. I'll be making sure no one else fucks with your dreams."

"Thanks, Olivia."

Lucas leaned forward and scooped her up, depositing her on the bed beside him. "You should listen to her. You gave her an assignment, and it sounded like she gave you one."

"What?" she asked, her body taut against his, but she wasn't fighting to get up and pace again.

"Sleep well."

She sighed again. "I don't think I could. Too wound up."

It was his turn to smile as he rolled on top of her, pinning her to the bed with his body. "I can help with that," he promised before lowering his head and kissing her. She relaxed beneath him after a moment, then wrapped her arms around him and began kissing him back.

An hour later, she was sleeping peacefully, sprawled half atop him. Though he was content to hold her, it was another hour before he could bring himself to join her in dreams.

Chapter 27

LUCAS, SOPHIA, AND OLIVIA weren't the only ones having night-mares. Sergei had been caught in one as well, and only his divine blood had saved him. His father was mostly known for being the god of the sun and of healing, but he was also the god of prophecies, which meant his son had an easier time seeing things. Especially with the extra gift Seth had given him. Which meant he'd been able to see it for the nightmare it was and push himself out of it.

As he lie in the dark, staring up at his ceiling, he realized there had been something else about the nightmare that was bugging him. Nightmares were common enough, even intense ones, but there'd been a feel to the dream that felt somehow familiar.

It took some time before it clicked. There had been a sticky magical residue in the nightmare that had felt oddly similar to whatever had been infecting Lachlan. Had it somehow passed from Lachlan to him when he'd been healing the vampire? Or was it something else?

Climbing out of bed, he walked across the hall to the bathroom, wetting a washcloth with cold water and patting his face with it. What if it was something else? That made the most sense, considering how it had spread. Most of the people he'd noted as having the same—albeit a more mild—infection hadn't been anywhere near Lachlan. Nor had he found any traces of it in himself, Lucas, or Sophia when he'd checked. So how was it spreading? What was the common denominator between all the infected?

He bent to splash more cold water directly onto his face, hoping it would help wake his mind a little faster. It wasn't until he'd filled his cupped palms with water a second time to realize he was literally holding something that literally everyone in the Athenaeum came into contact with. Possibly the only thing other than the air.

Though his skin crawled now at having the water against his skin, he didn't let it spill into the sink. Instead, he closed his eyes and sent his magic into the water. He took his time, being thorough with the exam. The last thing he wanted to do was be hasty and miss it—if there was something there to miss.

The first thing he found was the magic that all water from the aquifer held—the spells that made it safe to drink. Though Sergei had expected to find that, he still poked at it, making sure it hadn't been altered in some way. Dispelling an enchantment wrought by the gods wasn't an easy thing, but changing it? That was slightly less impossible. It felt the same as it always had, so he moved on.

When he finally found what he'd been terrified to find, it was so subtle he almost missed it. It was like someone had added a pinch of salt to a bathtub—diluted and almost impossible to detect. If he hadn't examined Lachlan so thoroughly, he probably wouldn't have noticed it either. But was it just here in this bathroom? Or had someone gotten to the aquifer?

He dumped the water and turned the faucet off, drying his hands thoroughly. Returning to his room, he put on his shoes and grabbed a flashlight and the knife his father had given him centuries ago. Apollo might not be the most hands on father, but he did care about his children.

Though Sergei had never been to the aquifer himself, he knew where the stairs that led to it were. Since they couldn't survive without water, and given how deep the aquifer was, it had its own staircase and could only be reached from this level. And it was a very, very long staircase, but if there was one perk of being the son of a healing god, it was being in good physical shape. Still, his legs were probably going to hate him when all was said and done. It would be worth it if he found the source of the infection.

Unlike the main staircase, this one was narrow, the steps not worn quite as smooth. And it felt like it was never going to end. The aquifer was beneath every other level of the Athenaeum, so it took time for him to reach the bottom. There was a door with the same keypad as on every level of the library, but his palm and PIN cleared him through. On the other side of the door was a cavern at least two hundred feet across, and a good forty wide at its narrowest, and most of it was covered with water. The ceiling was low and the area around the door rough and littered with stalagmite and rocks. Unlike the rest of the Athenaeum, this one had been left as nature had created it as much as possible. There was a pump somewhere in the water, and he could see a pipe coming out of it and leading up to the residential level, but otherwise it looked completely natural. Also unlike the rest of the Athenaeum, this room didn't immediately illuminate when he walked in. There was some glow filtering in from the stairs, but he had to switch on the flashlight to be able to see clearly.

It was cooler here than it was back in the actual Athenaeum, but he ignored that as he stepped closer to the water. It looked innocent, beautiful even. In the beam of his flashlight the water looked turquoise, and it was quiet. Peaceful.

He didn't trust it.

Inhaling slowly, he crouched at the edge of the water and extended his hand. For several moments, it hovered above the water, then he plunged it into the chilly aquifer. Not wanting to be exposed to it for long in case he was right, he quickly shoved his magic into it, just like he had his hand. He knew what he was looking for this time, which helped. And he found it.

The levels of the infection weren't quite as diluted as they'd been in the bathroom, but it still was much less than he would have expected for the number of people infected. Then again, since it didn't leave a person naturally, every drink, every shower would add to it, bit by bit, until they ended up like Lachlan.

Yanking his hand free of the water, he wiped his hand on his pants and rose to his feet. It explained a lot, but not Lachlan himself. Not unless he'd come into contact with the infection directly. Had he been dosed with it by the same person who'd tainted the aquifer? That made the most sense, even if it still left them with the question of who.

Sergei left the aquifer, but his mind was busy as he began the trek up the hundreds of stairs.

Sophia and Lucas would be notified, of course, and Olivia, if Sophia had brought the new head curator in on the problem. They'd need to stop using water from the aquifer, which wouldn't be easy. Yes, they could drink bottled water, soda, and the like, but washing their hands? Bathing? Hard to do that with outside water unless they actually left, and it was hardly feasible to leave every day for a shower.

The rest of the Athenaeum was going to be a problem, too. They certainly wouldn't listen to Sophia, but would they listen to him? And at this point, did it matter if they did?

Sophia had expected to sleep like crap after the nightmare, but thanks to Olivia breaking the dream and Lucas's...relaxation techniques, she'd slept like the proverbial baby. It was honestly a nice surprise, even if her nighttime adventure had left her more tired than she'd have liked.

She should go to breakfast, but couldn't bring herself to go sit in a room while people glared at her. Instead, once she and Lucas were dressed, she shot off a text to Olivia before they headed to the clinic. They'd left Lachlan in Sergei's charge, so Sophia was sure he was fine, but she wanted to know everything the healer hadn't wanted to say in front of Sergei. And to make sure Lachlan really was okay.

The good news was that only Sergei was in the clinic sitting at his desk, which meant Lachlan hadn't relapsed. It was a step in the right direction for sure. The bad news was that Sergei looked like he'd just been through the wringer. Odd. She didn't think demigods—especially those with Apollo for a father—could look like that. Had Lachlan flipped and attacked Sergei? She didn't see any wounds, but that didn't mean anything.

"Sergei? What's wrong?"

He turned to face her directly, his bushy brows furrowed. "More than I realized, but I think I'd rather only go into this once. If Olivia is someone you trust, someone who's helping with this, we should get her in here first."

That sounded serious. "She's on her way. But are you okay?"

"Physically? Yes, but I can't say the same about anything else."

Definitely serious. He wasn't exactly a happy-go-lucky guy, but this was bad, even for him.

Olivia showed up just a few minutes later, then immediately paused as she saw their faces. "Did something happen besides the nightmares?"

"Nightmares?" Sergei asked, straightening, then he shook his head. "Shut the door." When she had, he cast his bubble spell, though being safe from spying didn't help him relax at all.

Sophia—who hadn't settled since she'd learned Erasmus had been poisoned—pressed a hand to her stomach in the hopes that it would calm it. No such luck. "What's wrong, Sergei?"

"I'll get to that, but tell me about the nightmares first. Who had them?"

"All of us," Lucas said. "All basically the same thing, too. The Athenaeum, but back when it was an actual cave. Something telling us to join it."

Sergei rubbed two fingers over an eyebrow, then lightly rubbed at his temple. "I had the same nightmare."

"Shit," Olivia muttered, hopping up on an empty table. "I'd thought it was just us three, but if you had it, too, then I might have missed someone."

"There's more," Sergei warned before she could go on. "After, I went to splash some water on my face. Was hoping it'd wake me up, because I knew something was off. Something in the dream felt like the same thing Lachlan was infected with. And I realized there's only one thing that everyone in the Athenaeum comes in contact with."

"Tell me it isn't in the air," Sophia said, leaning into Lucas's side. He wrapped his arm around her shoulders, which helped a little.

"No, not in the air," Sergei assured her. "It's in the water."

"What?" Lucas asked, stiffening beside her. "Someone poisoned the aquifer?"

"They did. I went down and checked for myself. It's not as concentrated as I feared, but since the body can't metabolize it or fight it off, it just continues to collect within the system. It's why those who were infected after Lachlan aren't displaying the same level of violence that he was."

"Then how did Lachlan go right to violent?" Sophia asked.

"The only thing I can think of is that he received this substance directly, rather than ingesting it in increments in the water."

Lucas frowned. "I'm going to guess that what we did for Lachlan won't help with the aquifer?"

"I don't see how it could, no," Sergei answered. "Both I and the tyet heal, but I heal a living body, not water. And while the four of us can easily stop drinking water that comes from the aquifer, I can't rule out that contact with it wouldn't infect us, which means showering or washing our hands is dangerous."

"And it's doubtful everyone else in the Athenaeum is going to stop using the water," Sophia said glumly.

"Very doubtful," he agreed.

"I hate to add to the already bad morning, but I've got more," Olivia said after no one had spoken for a minute.

Sophia cocked her head. "The dreams?"

Olivia nodded. "Mmhmm. Like I said, I didn't come across anyone else having the same nightmare we did, but I did manage to get into the dreams of the last three people you wanted me to check."

Sergei gave Sophia a curious look, so she filled him in. "I asked her to check Jericho, Heather, Penny, Josie, and Peter. See if anything there would help."

"And did it?" Sergei asked when he looked back at Olivia.

"Yep. Josie and Penny were basically the same as everyone else. Chaotic and fragmented. Peter's though..."

The hope Sophia had been holding onto, that her cousin was innocent, began to crumble into ash within her. "What did you see?"

Olivia hesitated, remorse in her eyes as she kept Sophia's gaze. "The first word that comes to mind is supervillain."

"Explain," Lucas demanded, before softening it with a, "please."

"I'm sorry, Sophia," Olivia murmured before her voice strengthened. "When I said supervillain, I wasn't exaggerating. Megalomania, taking over the Athenaeum, killing you...And there was something about Achlys that he was extremely happy about. Like full on glee. It would have been weird before, but knowing that's the name of the poison used on me...I think it's pretty much a certainty that he's the killer."

"Or one of them," Sergei muttered. "We can't assume he's acting alone."

Sophia felt like she wanted to vomit, but forced herself to look at this objectively. Or as objectively as she could. "Playing devil's advocate...why can't we?"

"The boy is smart, I'm not arguing that. He wouldn't be our tech guy if he wasn't, especially since there's no shortage of other tech savvy people in the Athenaeum. But he's young. And I'm not saying young means unskilled," he said with a faint smile, when Sophia might have interrupted. "But think of all that's been done. The Achlys, the various sorcery that's been utilized, and especially this substance that's infecting most of the Athenaeum. Any one of those things? I would say yes, it's simply him. But all of it?" He gave a slow shake of his head. "I just don't see how any one person could do that unless they'd been studying and planning for decades, and he's only a few years older than you, Sophia."

Logical, and she both loved and hated it. "So we're probably also looking for someone older and more experienced?"

"I would say it's likely, but at this point, I wouldn't put money on any answer."

"Neither would I," Lucas agreed, "but I do think we can agree that Peter is definitely involved. Whether or not he delivered the poison to Erasmus or just brewed it is irrelevant at this point. And when we have him in custody, we can get the name of his accomplice from him."

Sophia doubted it would be that easy.

Chapter 28

Sophia pulled away from Lucas and walked over to a chair, sitting down. He wished he could help her, but really, what could he say when they'd all but confirmed that Peter had poisoned her grandfather and infected almost all of the Athenaeum with some unknown magical substance? Only time could really heal that wound. That didn't mean he wouldn't be standing beside her, ready to hold her up when she needed it, or just hold her when she grieved. He wouldn't be anywhere else. He couldn't, not with the way he'd come to feel about her. That would be enough, but his gargoyle nature meant he was a protector, and it would be nearly impossible for him to leave her when she needed him—whether she wanted to admit it or not.

"So what do we do?" Sophia asked, rubbing her fingers against her eyes. "Just walk up to him, tell him we know, and put the same cuffs on him we used on Lachlan?" She dropped her hands into her lap and sighed. "Because I know I'm supposed to be the boss, but I've never dealt with anything like this. Never in a million years would have thought I'd have to. If it makes me a bad aspida to ask for help, then fuck it. I'm a bad aspida."

She was too hard on herself, but he got it. Anyone who had been shoved into her position would be doubting their abilities. If she'd been able to have time to get her feet under her before shit started falling apart, it might have been different, but Peter couldn't even give her that. Though he had liked the blue-haired tech, right now he really wanted to punch the little jerk. Repeatedly. It might not solve anything, but it would make him feel better.

"You're not a bad aspida," Olivia said, shaking her head. "It's a fucked up situation, and I think even Erasmus would have had trouble figuring out the best way to handle it."

"Maybe, but he also knew way more sorcery than I do, so probably had some tricks up his sleeve. He also had way more experience than I do and grew up here."

"Of course he did," Lucas said, because there was no arguing that. The man had been nine hundred years old, after all. "But you're not Erasmus. He never wanted you to be, and we don't want you to be anything but who and what you are. And maybe you're not trying to do it alone, but you know what? Who cares? You're not really supposed to. The aspides of the past separated people into three factions and named a head of each so they had people to rely on. Advisers or whatever you want to call them. And guess what, you've got two of those three here, and a son of Apollo to boot. We'll figure out it and get the Athenaeum back to normal, then you can make the job what *you* want to make of it. Just don't worry about what other aspides did or how they did it. Each one of them was different, so of course you are, too. Besides, you were chosen for a reason, so unless you're questioning the intelligence of six gods and the damn near sentient magic of the Athenaeum, you're exactly who's supposed to be aspida at this exact moment, dealing with this exact problem."

Sophia stared at him, a hint of shock in her eyes, but he noticed her shoulders easing a little as he spoke and the words sank in. He heard a soft chuckle from Olivia, and saw Sergei smile out of the corner of his vision, but he didn't take his eyes off Sophia. Right now it didn't matter what Olivia or Sergei thought. *Sophia* had to believe what he'd said. Said and meant. Yes, he'd absolutely help and offer advice, and knew the others would do the same, but they weren't the aspida. Beyond that, he really had fallen in love with her, and hated seeing her be so hard on herself. She was intelligent, thoughtful, a quick learner, and dammit, she was strong. But he could say it all day long until his face turned blue, and it wouldn't do any good unless she accepted it.

No one said anything as Sophia worked through what he'd said, and he could see the various emotions sliding over her face until one finally won out—resolve. She nodded and her back straightened, her shoulders no longer slightly hunched with defeat. "You're right. About all of it. Especially the part where I'm not questioning the patrons, especially considering that most of them are gods and goddesses of wisdom," she said, giving him a little smile. It wasn't much, but he'd take it.

"Good. Now, what we're going to do is, yes, have cuffs handy, because they should block sorcery as much as innate abilities. But no, I don't think we should just walk up to him, not when we know forbidden sorcery has been used at least once. Maybe it was his accomplice who killed Agatha, but we're not taking any chances. We approach him when he's alone and when we can catch him off guard. But," he added, looking at each of them in turn, "we don't wait too long."

Sophia nodded. "The deadline is coming up soon."

Darkness settled over her face. She must have realized that there was a good chance it had been Peter behind that disguise spell. Her own cousin who had thrown her down a flight of stone stairs and choked her. Threatened to kill her.

"It's not your fault," Olivia said before he could. "Sometimes we have family that are pricks. But he's not your only family. Your mom loves you and is a good woman. Erasmus fucking adored you."

"So did Dion," Sergei added.

Lucas nodded. "And once we get the Athenaeum back to normal, I promise the rest of the people here will all start feeling like family, too."

"I hope so. But let's worry about that later," Sophia decided with a shake of her head. "If we want the Athenaeum back to normal, we have to stop the person—or people—who are trying to wreck it. And find out why. Because I think we all need to know why so many people needed to die."

"We do, and we will." Lucas wasn't so certain, because villains monologuing only happened in movies, not reality, but he didn't allow his doubts to show. Fortunately, she wasn't an empath or telepath and seemed to buy it.

"Getting him alone shouldn't be too hard," Olivia mused aloud. "That boy spends most of his time in the computer room, and no one else is that dedicated, even the other ones who enjoy computer games or whatever it is he does."

"No, most of them have their own computers in their rooms or offices," Sergei agreed, motioning to his laptop that was just feet away from him.

Sophia smiled. "I've caught him sleeping in there sometimes. How do you guys feel about a late night?"

"I don't need much sleep, so it won't bother me," Sergei told her.

"I was military. I grab sleep when and where I can," Lucas answered, nearly smiling himself since it seemed like his beautiful halfling had an idea.

"And I'm a nightmare," Olivia answered as if that explained everything. And maybe it did. Lucas knew very little about nightmares beyond their basic powers over dreams, but not needing much sleep wouldn't be a huge stretch of the imagination.

"Good. Then I think after dinner, after people have started heading to bed, we monitor the computer room. Wait for a time when he's alone and has fallen asleep. Go in, cuff him before he can wake up, then we can question him and put him somewhere secure. And yes, I know there's a potential flaw. If it really is him like we suspect, then he could have set up some kind of alert or warning or something, but unless one of you has another way of telling when he's both alone and asleep..."

Olivia chuckled and lifted a hand, wiggling her fingers. "Like a nightmare who can lurk around and tell whether someone's sleeping or awake? Just call me Santa for the dream realm."

It took Lucas a moment before he chuckled. "I know what song I'm playing on repeat around you this Christmas."

She shot him a dirty look, but there was humor in her gaze and Sophia giggled, so he didn't mind.

"Fantastic. Then I think we should meet in my bedroom an hour after dinner," Sophia said. "I know this room is closer, but we don't want to give him any indication that we suspect him."

"Should we bring Lachlan with us?" Sergei asked, glancing at the bed the vampire had so recently occupied. "Not only does he deserve to confront the man who drugged him, but having a vampire's speed and strength might not be a bad idea if something goes wrong. And he's the only one we know isn't infected beyond the four of us."

Sophia chewed on her lip as she considered, and Lucas said nothing, letting her make the decision. "And you are sure he's clean of the infection?"

Sergei nodded. "I didn't sense a trace of it, and believe me, I checked thoroughly."

"Then yes, it couldn't hurt. It might be overkill, but I'd rather we go in prepared in case everything goes to hell. Could you fill him in? No one would think it's odd for you to want to give him another check after he was out for more than a week, and you can do that cone of silence thing."

"I can, yes."

"Thank you. Until then, I say everyone just do whatever you normally do. Hopefully he won't make another move until my deadline's up, but in case he does, keep your eyes open. I don't want anyone else getting hurt."

"And if possible, everyone keep an eye on Sophia," Lucas said, though he knew she'd hate it, which was why he quickly added to that. "I know you're capable and have your shield spell, but you're the one everyone's animosity is currently directed at. I have no doubt you could handle most of them one on one, but none of us can handle a crowd by themselves. Not when the crowd has access to the sorcery the Athenaeum does."

She blew out a breath and nodded. "No, I don't like it, but you're right. It's not being a coward, it's just being smart."

"Exactly." He offered her a hand and gently tugged her out of the chair and into his arms. "You could be an invulnerable goddess and I'd still say the same thing," he whispered to her. "I'm not losing you."

Her arms went around him and squeezed. "I know. And you won't. I won't let him kill anyone else. Not you, not me, not anyone." She leaned back so she could see his face, then looked at the others. "The Athenaeum is supposed to be a place where knowledge is preserved, and as far as I'm concerned, people are part of that. I intent to preserve it, no matter what my backstabbing cousin may have in mind."

Sophia's eyes met his again, and when she spoke, her voice was full of the conviction he had prayed she'd start feeling.

"This ends tonight."

Chapter 29

In an effort to do as she'd told the others and stick to business as usual, Sophia went back to her office after she left the clinic. Lucas had walked her there then reluctantly left her alone to take care of some preparations. She'd had to cast both her shield and threat spells before he'd leave, but she didn't mind. It was nice having someone who cared so much about her well-being.

Alone, she went through her emails and frowned, just like the last time she'd checked them. More retrieval groups had failed to leave on schedule. Though she shot off inquiries into it, she didn't expect to hear anything back. So far she'd only gotten one reply for the earlier groups, and it had boiled down to they simply hadn't felt like going. She groaned and gave herself a moment to just revel in her frustration. The Athenaeum was breaking down and it didn't make any sense. They might all hate her for some reason, but why avoid doing what the Athenaeum had been founded to do?

More checking showed that some new volumes hadn't been cataloged and shelved, though it was supposed to have been finished a few days before. Penny was the one responsible, and Sophia had a moment to hope that the cause was that she was the guilty party instead of Peter. She also knew it was nothing but wishful thinking.

Instead of dwelling, she sent Olivia an email, knowing the new head curator would take care of it when she got the chance. Likely not today, but that was fine. They had something much more important to do today.

Tapping a finger on the top of her desk, she debated. She knew Lucas wanted her to stay in her office where she was relatively safe, but it wasn't, not really. Even if she locked the door, most of the Athenaeum could get through it—some with magic, some with brute force. Her desk wouldn't provide much of an obstacle either, nor would her shield hold indefinitely. And if she was going to pretend like this was a normal day, she couldn't just hide in her office.

Leaving her office, she went to find Nick first, since his office was closest, just on the other side of the entrance room. She was almost past the second sphinx when she felt someone come up behind her. "Bitch," a male voice hissed before she was shoved forward. Caught off guard, she fell into the sphinx, the corner of the pedestal ripping into her thigh while the rough stone scraped her cheek, hands, and arms. She'd been right about her shield spell not lasting forever, but she wished she'd noticed it dissipating. As soon as she hit the ground she recast it, and it saved her from a vicious kick that would have connected with her kidney.

Rolling onto her back, Sophia cast a spell, flinging magic at her attacker. Joshua hadn't been expecting it and it knocked him back, but he stayed on his feet. The hatred on his face scared her more than being attacked out of the blue, and she strengthened the shield as she pulled out her phone. The crack in her screen was larger, but she was able to shoot a quick text off to Lucas. It consisted just of the letter

'Z', but she was fairly certain it went through before Joshua waved his hand and sent the phone flying.

She hadn't considered that the shield wouldn't protect against magic, which meant she couldn't stay on the defensive, not if she wanted to avoid being hurt any worse than she was. Her thigh was screaming and her jeans felt damp, telling her without looking that it was bleeding freely. With Joshua being a witch, things could get very bad, very fast. She didn't have the magic to really fight back, and he was a guard, which meant he was far better trained than her. To keep him from kicking her ass, she'd have to be smarter and more creative.

"What the hell is your problem, Joshua?" she snapped as she pushed herself to her feet. Immediately her left leg protested, and she shifted her weight off it, trying to be as subtle as possible.

"You," he snarled, sounding more like a wolf than a witch. "Nick and Carla never should have brought you here. They sure as hell never should have let you stay. And you damn sure never should have become aspida. You're a joke."

That hurt. A week ago Joshua had been friendly, though they didn't know each other well enough to be considered friends. The fact that she'd been worried about failing as aspida didn't help.

"And how am I a joke?" she asked, trying to stall while she thought of a way to disarm a witch. If she could aim a telekinetic punch just right she might be able to knock him out, but her aim wasn't that great, and she didn't want to seriously hurt him. If they were right, he wasn't in full control of his actions, and she didn't want to put an innocent man in the clinic unless she had to.

Somehow, she doubted he was Peter's accomplice. It would make more sense for that person to keep a low profile. Which was likely why

Peter was being so nice to her when the rest of the Athenaeum was pouring hatred at her.

"You're what, twenty-three? Twenty-four? A baby. And you've only known we exist for a month. Anyone who thought you were in any way qualified was stupid. You couldn't even fix what's wrong with Lachlan! You had to wait for smarter, more capable people to do it!" he screamed. On the last word, he thrust a hand toward her and, shield or no shield, she went flying back. She had no way of preventing the impact with the floor, so she twisted and lifted her hands to protect her head, hoping the shield was still in place. It wasn't. Whatever spell Joshua had used, it had dissolved her shield like cotton candy in water. Slamming into the floor had her breath quickly exiting her body and the stone scraped her side raw from knee to shoulder, but at least her head didn't crack against the stone. Small miracles.

Before she could lift her head to react in any way, she heard an enraged roar. She saw a blur of gray and looked up just in time to see Lucas collide with Joshua in the most vicious tackle she'd ever witnessed. Both gargoyle and witch went down even harder than she had. Though everything ached, she forced herself onto all fours, then painfully onto her feet.

Lucas sat up, straddling Joshua, and punched him hard enough to split the man's lip. Two more punches and the guard was out cold, but Lucas didn't stop.

Sophia walked forward because she refused to hobble in front of the ten or so witnesses—witnesses she couldn't look at right now. "Lucas." He didn't respond, just pulled his arm back for another punch. She leapt forward, wincing when the movement pulled at the cut on her leg, and grabbed hold of his arm. "Lucas!"

It wasn't her weight that stopped him—he could have lifted her off her feet easily. It was her touch. Only that could have calmed the rage he felt when he saw her fly through the air and land as she had. Lucas still wanted to pummel Joshua into dust, but there was distress in her voice that he didn't think had anything to do with physical pain. Looking up at her, her soft hands wrapped around his stone skin, he stilled. "What?" he asked, unable to make his voice anything but rough.

"He's out cold," she told him. "Let's lock him somewhere until he wakes up and then we can find out why he decided to attack me."

He was? Lucas looked down at a man he considered a friend and saw she was right. His eyes were closed, his body limp on the floor. And he was a bloody mess. No doubt there were some broken bones, too. Later he might feel guilty about that, but not until after Sophia had been healed, and he'd checked for himself that there wasn't so much as a scratch left on her body.

Two attacks in two days? They really had better end this tonight or he was going to end up losing his mind. Nothing had ever pissed him off to the extent seeing her hurt did.

Slowly, because it took a great deal of effort not to hit Joshua again, he rose to his feet. With one arm he gathered Sophia close, holding her gently but trying to take some of the weight off her obviously injured leg. With the other, he pulled his phone out and texted Sergei to meet them.

"How bad are you hurt?" he asked, shifting back to his human form, though he raked a glare around the room, noting each person who was just standing around watching. None of them had helped Joshua, but neither had any of them helped Sophia. If it hadn't been for her text, he never would have known she was in trouble. And he knew exactly what Joshua was capable of in a fight. Despite his early words, the fact that she'd lasted as long as she did against a trained witch was surprising. Impressive, but surprising.

"Not as bad as you were when we went to Delphi," she said with a sad attempt at a smile.

"How bad?" he asked again.

"I hurt," she admitted. "Leg's the worst, but basically everything aches. Still not as bad as the other night, though."

Lucas wanted to hit Joshua again, but refrained. "Did he say anything?"

"That I was a joke as aspida and that anyone who thought I could do the job was stupid," she said, her voice becoming more strained as the adrenaline began to wear off. That was when Sergei arrived. "You have good timing," she told the healer with a weak smile.

"Good gods, Sophia. What happened to you?" Sergei asked, rushing over.

"Joshua," Lucas answered darkly. "Heal her. I'm going to lock Joshua in his room. When she's good and he's secure, then you can heal him."

Sergei arched a brow and got his first look at the downed witch. He didn't ask what happened to him as it was all too obvious, especially with the blood splatter on Lucas's clothes. "Don't kill him."

"I won't." Lucas saw Ray nearby. He was shocked the man hadn't helped Sophia, but given that her own mother was against her, it shouldn't surprise him. "Ray, help me get him to his room," he ordered, relieved when the guard didn't argue. He didn't really want to leave Sophia alone at the moment, but knew that Sergei would protect her. He'd feel better if Olivia was here, too, but Sergei wasn't defenseless, despite being known as a healer.

Ray helped him carry Joshua's unconscious form down to the man's room and inside, laying him on his bed. "Leave. Sergei will heal him."

"Yeah, when he's done with her," Ray muttered, the last word said like a curse.

"Leave," Lucas snapped.

Reluctantly, Ray did, and Lucas followed him out. After closing the door, he cast an imprisonment spell, ensuring Joshua wouldn't be able to leave until the spell was undone. Sergei knew how to get past it, but few others did. It was necessary, as the Athenaeum had no cells to lock offenders in. It wasn't something that was needed often, but they did occasionally need to lock someone up, so long ago they'd settled upon sorcery.

Sergei had taken Sophia to the clinic, and by the time Lucas arrived, Sergei was finishing the healing. The blood still remained, as did the tear in her jeans, but the wounds were gone.

"She's okay?" he asked Sergei.

"She is," he answered. "There were no broken bones, just some scrapes and bruises." He smiled at Sophia, but it was tight. "You should have had your shield up."

"I did," she said. "At least I thought I did. He took me by surprise, and that's when I realized it was gone. As soon as I landed, I recast it, but something about whatever magic he used to knock me back got rid of the shield. So when I landed, I felt it all."

"You might have lost focus, or it might have been too long since the initial casting," Lucas said, pulling her into his arms. He wanted to lock her away where she could never get hurt, but knew that would never happen.

"Maybe," she mumbled against his chest, her arms going around him in return.

"Sophia!"

They both turned to see Olivia run into the room. "Gods. I heard there was a fight. Are you okay?"

"I am now," she promised the other woman. "Sergei healed me."

"Good. That's good. Was it really Joshua?"

"It was," Lucas confirmed.

She shook her head. "I would have thought that the more powerful people would be protected, but I guess not."

Lucas frowned, because she had a point. "You're right," he murmured. "Why aren't the four of us infected? Wouldn't that be playing into Peter's hands? At least me, Olivia, and Sergei?"

"I don't know about Olivia, but maybe the blessing from Seth is protecting us from it?" Sophia asked.

"Blessing?" Olivia asked curiously.

"Yeah, sorry. Not long after I was named aspida, Seth—the patron—showed up. Said something was going on in the Athenaeum, but the gods couldn't see what it was. Something was blocking them. So he gave me some gifts from the patrons. Right after Lachlan's attack, I asked him to share it with Lucas and Sergei. This was before we brought you in," she said apologetically.

Olivia waved that away. "I get it. And yeah, blessings from the gods could do it. And I'm pretty sure I know why I'm not affected, either."

Lucas wanted to trust her, and she'd given him no reason not to, but he was suddenly suspicious. "Why is that?"

She said nothing, looking uncomfortable.

"It's up to you, Olivia," Sophia said gently, "but if it's what I think you're meaning, you can trust them. They're both honorable and good at keeping secrets. They won't try to hurt you or tell anyone."

"You know what she's talking about?" Lucas asked.

"She does," Olivia confirmed. "Shit. In for a penny, right?" she asked, running her hands through her hair. "Okay, remember the tattoos you saw last night when I came to help Sophia out of the nightmare?" He nodded. "They're a mark of my family line. One of the upsides is that any kind of manipulation of thoughts, feelings, or anything like that is harder. Not saying it makes me resist the infection anymore than the next person, but I'd probably have to be infected like Lachlan was to start showing any signs."

"Sorry, but I'm a little out of the loop. Tattoos?" Sergei asked.

Olivia wordlessly drew her shirt up to reveal her stomach and the many tattoos that covered it.

"Fascinating," Sergei murmured, leaning forward for a better look. "Ogham script?" She gave a nod. "I don't know much about the Celtic families, or whatever abilities you may have, but can I check you over? I want to test your theory."

Olivia shrugged as she let her shirt drop. "Sure. You're checking for the infection, I'm guessing?"

"Yes."

"I'd rather not have that inside me, so please do. If I am infected, I'd like to know before I do reach whatever threshold and jump on the hating Sophia bandwagon. I'm actually kind of fond of her."

"Gee, don't sound so enthusiastic," Sophia teased, and actually made Olivia smile.

Sergei rested a hand on Olivia's cheek as one of the few patches of exposed skin, and it glowed faintly as he did his thing. Lucas had a feeling he knew what the demigod would find.

"You are infected," Sergei said after only a few moments, "but it is a mild one. No more than I've felt on anyone else besides Lachlan."

"Which means you can heal me? Get rid of it with the tyet?" Olivia asked. Her voice wasn't quite desperate, but she definitely wasn't happy to hear the confirmation.

"I can. As soon as you bring it—" He cut off when she reached into her pocket and drew it out.

"Considering it was the one thing—along with your magic—that could cure this thing, I didn't want to leave it unprotected," she explained.

"Very smart, especially considering the situation." Sergei looked over at Lucas and Sophia. "Would one of you care to use it while I heal her? I don't know if it'll work as well if she's the one using it on herself. It might, but why take chances?"

Lucas started to agree, but Sophia stepped forward. "I'd like to. I know I'm not as used to relics as you guys, but I need to learn sometime, right?"

"True enough." Olivia handed the tyet over. "It's just like sorcery. All about intention and will. Just need to touch it to my skin while he's healing me, and focus on it erasing the infection from my body."

"Sounds easy enough," Sophia said, working up a smile.

Lucas rubbed her back. "Just like the sundial," he murmured to her. "If you could use that, this should be a piece of cake."

That seemed to reassure her, and she gave him a genuine smile. "Good point." She stepped closer and eyed the little skin Olivia was showing. To be helpful, Olivia tugged her sleeve up, revealing enough bare skin for the tyet. Sophia rested the relic against her arm then looked at Sergei. He nodded and cupped Olivia's cheek. Again his hand began to glow, and after a moment, so did the tyet.

It didn't take nearly as long with Olivia as it had with Lachlan, but her infection wasn't nearly as advanced as his had been. Sergei checked her again, then smiled warmly. "You're all good. Just avoid the water, and you should be fine."

"As soon as we take care of things tonight, we have really got to figure out how to clean the aquifer," Olivia said, pulling her sleeve back into place.

"Absolutely. No way am I going to go too long without that fantastic shower in my bathroom," Sophia agreed. And though she could have easily kept the tyet, she handed it back to Olivia. "We should get back to things, especially since you've got someone to question, Lucas."

"I do, though I don't know that he's going to be able to give any clear answers right now," he admitted.

"Maybe not, but we have to do what's expected." Sophia turned to Sergei. "You gotten a chance to talk to Lachlan?"

"I did. I didn't tell him everything, but he'll be in your room with us. And before you ask," Sergei told Lucas, "I did another check and didn't sense any infection."

"Good." Now if tonight could go as well as Olivia's healing had.

Chapter 30

Sophia found herself unable to do more than pick at her food during dinner. It wasn't just the quality of the meal—though that had further deteriorated—nor was it a result of the atmosphere of the infected. It was Peter. From all appearances, he had no idea she and the others were aware of what he'd done—or at least what he'd been a part of. He was talking and laughing with those around them, and anytime his gaze happened to meet hers, he smiled and once again reminded her of the puppy dog she'd thought he resembled since the day they'd met.

How? How could someone be so friendly, so open and warm, and be part of truly heinous acts like he had? Though she wanted to believe they were missing something and he was as innocent as his dad was, she was trying to be realistic. There was entirely too much evidence stacked up against him, so there was no point in trying to convince herself he hadn't killed Erasmus.

Unfortunately, Joseph had given them nothing. No implicating anyone else, no clues as to when he was infected, nothing but a burning hatred for Sophia. A hatred the majority of the room shared.

They couldn't leave soon enough.

When dinner was over, Lucas stopped at his room. "I just need to grab a couple of things," he told her as he stepped inside. She closed the door behind her, sure whatever he was grabbing should be kept secret. Since the first thing he pocketed was a set of handcuffs, she knew she was right. He also added a couple of knives to go with the one he always carried, as well as a gun. It still threw her that the guards carried guns when most of the Arcane didn't. Not that she minded, it was just weird.

He hesitated, then pulled out one more knife. It was smaller, maybe a four-inch blade, and held in a black woven sheath. "I know we haven't started you on weapons practice yet, and if all goes well tonight, you shouldn't need this, but I'd rather you have it and not need it," he said as he offered it to her.

Sophia really didn't like the idea of having to stab anyone, but made herself think of all the injuries—both fatal and non—that had been inflicted since she'd arrived. Swallowing, she took it and clipped it onto her waistband, pulling her shirt to cover it. "I get it," she told him. "But when all this is done, I want to step up my training. I know if it does come to a fight tonight that I'll be the least useful person there. I want to fix it."

"We will," he promised, brushing his thumb over her cheek, along her jaw. "And we will get through this."

Part of her felt silly for being so worried about confronting Peter. He was a mer, and they weren't normally thought of as dangerous out of the water, but she refused to underestimate anyone, even her cousin.

They went back to her room, and she wondered how they were going to kill the hour until the others got here, much less the hours after that, while they waited for Peter to fall asleep. She'd never been an overly patient person, and with the anticipation pressing on her, she felt like climbing the walls.

Lucas noticed and had the perfect remedy. He locked her door—something she actually had never done since arriving—and tugged his shirt off.

"Lucas..." His name was said as a warning.

"Yeah?" he asked as he stalked toward her.

She backed up until she felt her legs bump against the bed and narrowed her eyes at him. "We don't have time. The others will be here soon."

"We've got almost an hour. Pretty sure I can make you scream before they get here."

To avoid being caught, she scrambled onto the bed and off the other side. "And if they're early?" she challenged, though she couldn't deny the idea of sex was extremely appealing right now.

"Why do you think I locked the door?" he asked, circling around the bottom of the bed.

When he reached her side, she quickly moved over the bed to the other side again. She felt a little silly, but she was also starting to feel like she was being stalked, just in a fun, sexy way. Her heartbeat picked up and heat started to gather between her legs as he came directly over the bed toward her, his eyes already stone-colored. Part of her wanted to simply give in. To let him grab her, tear off her clothes, and make her scream. But the rest of her found that she enjoyed the game. She didn't have much room to run, but it didn't keep her from turning and darting toward the bathroom. She wouldn't get far and knew it, but that wasn't the point. Anticipation and the chase made everything sweeter.

She was only a few feet from the doorway when a strong arm caught her around the waist. A squeak escaped her lips, though she'd been expecting the grab. Lucas lifted her cleanly off her feet and strode toward the bed, half tossing her onto it. She landed on her face and started to push herself up when he grabbed an ankle and yanked her to the edge of the bed, her legs hanging off the side. Her breathing was ragged as he reached beneath her and undid her jeans. When he tugged them and her panties sharply down over her ass, the force pulled her another few inches toward him.

The position should have felt vulnerable. Her pants were around her upper thighs and her bare ass was in the air, while she was otherwise fully clothed. Rather than feeling vulnerable, all she could feel was need. He hadn't touched her yet, hadn't even kissed her, but she could feel that she was already wet, already ready for him to deliver on his promise.

But when she felt him next, it wasn't his cock sliding into her, it was his mouth pressing against her. The feel of his tongue and lips feasting on her startled a loud moan of her as she arched back toward him. His hands grabbed her hips firmly, which kept her from moving like she wanted to, like she needed to. And the torment continued.

Her body was ready to combust, but she quickly realized that every time she got close to release, he changed what he was doing and backed off. After it happened a third time, she bit back a sob of frustration. "Lucas," she snapped, wishing her voice didn't sound so breathy. "Stop teasing me."

His response was to bite her ass, just hard enough to sting. To her shock, she moaned and tried to press back against him again. But he listened, and she felt him stand up, heard him undo his belt and pants. Then he pressed the head of his shaft against her and filled her in one strong, smooth thrust. With her legs pressed together and the angle he'd found, it felt like he was deeper than he'd ever been before, and it was almost enough to make her come immediately.

Lucas started to move, to pound into her while he gripped her hips. She felt the edge of his claws and whimpered, realizing just how far gone he already was. Her hands pressed against the bed and she rocked back to meet each of his thrusts, earning a growl that she felt vibrate through her. She shivered, which made her clench around him, and his claws pressed a little harder against her skin, but he managed to avoid breaking her skin.

Every time he touched her, every time he was inside her, she felt closer to him, and the care he took with her, even when he was on edge, made her love him a little bit more. She could get lost in him and forget all the shit that was happening in the Athenaeum, if only for a little while. And once this was all done, that was exactly what she was going to do, for as long as she could manage it.

An arm slid beneath her and pulled until her back was pressed to his chest. His hips never stopped moving, even when his teeth grazed her shoulder, her throat. Moaning, she hooked a hand behind his neck and turned her head until her mouth found his. It wasn't gentle or smooth, just a furious, desperate need for them to connect as much as physically possible. Yet when his other hand found her clit and rubbed, it was all over for her. The sensations exploded within her as she thrust her hips back, trying to get him as deep as she could. She whimpered his name, but the sound was nearly lost when he groaned. The pace of his hips quickened, driving her higher, though she wouldn't have thought it possible for her to feel any better than she had.

Both his arms wrapped around her, holding her firmly, but also like she was precious as he slammed into her once more and poured himself into her. He stayed like that for a minute, which was okay with her because her body was trembling and she wasn't entirely certain she could stand without his help. Never before had an orgasm left her feeling so completely drained and yet so thoroughly loved and loose.

His arms loosened, but he lowered her to the bed before he released her. A moment later, he flopped on the bed beside her, struggling to catch his breath. Sophia managed to lift her head and saw that, though his eyes were half-closed, they were no longer gray. Forcing her limbs to obey, she scooted over a few inches, rested her head on his shoulder, and draped an arm over his stomach.

For several minutes they stayed like that, saying nothing. Finally, he lifted his head to kiss her forehead. "We should probably shower before the others get here."

"Mmm. Probably." She could say they just needed to adjust their clothing, but a shower was definitely needed. Of course, before that happened, she needed to figure out how to move, because she'd exhausted her energy moving over to him.

It was another couple of minutes before he chuckled lightly and ran his fingers down her back. "We're not moving."

"Nuh uh. Trying, not working."

Another chuckle, then he pushed himself into a sitting position. "Okay, come on," he said, pulling her up with him. She wrinkled her nose, but it was the only protest she gave him, even when the next step was to get them to their feet. Together, they wobbled almost drunkenly into the bathroom. While he was able to strip without trouble, she had to lean against the wall or risk falling over. She didn't care. That had been, hands down, the best sex of her life and she would take any side-effects that came with it, even falling on her face. Especially when she realized Lucas couldn't quit smiling. It was a self-satisfied little smile, but honestly, he deserved to be a little smug right now.

The shower was full of little touches, more teasing and loving than sexual, but it did mean she forgot what they were planning on doing that night. Even when they were clean and were drying off, there was an air of carefree amusement rather than impending doom. Okay, so at one point Lucas gave her ass a playful smack, but it only made her laugh and give it a teasing shake.

When the hour was up and the first knock came at the door, they were lying in bed cuddling and talking. Sophia regretted it, but that single sound killed the buzz of satisfaction she'd felt since Lucas had first started chasing her. But if all went well, by the time the sun rose, they'd have Peter in custody, and would know why he'd done the things he'd done. And if he'd done it all alone, or if there was another traitor hiding somewhere in the Athenaeum.

Chapter 31

Sergei was the first to arrive, and he had Lachlan with him. Both looked somber, but Lucas noticed Lachlan looked both sick and pissed. Sergei had clearly explained what was going on to the man.

After they were inside and the door closed, Lucas asked, "Did Sergei tell you what we were planning on doing tonight?"

Lachlan nodded, his brow furrowing. "He did. It's hard for me to believe it, though. Peter is killing people? And the water is tainted? Erasmus was murdered?" He shook his head. "None of it is making any sense," he said, scratching his jaw.

"I've known about some of this since I arrived, and it still doesn't make any sense," Sophia told him with a sympathetic smile. "Unfortunately, we've confirmed most of it."

"Most of it?" Lachlan latched onto that. "What don't you know for sure? You could be wrong about some of it?"

"We could," Sergei agreed as he leaned against the wall, "but we're almost positive we're not."

"And the parts we're not a hundred percent on are whether Peter was working alone, and whether he's the one who actually did the deed," Lucas added. "Or deeds, I should say."

Lachlan's shoulders slumped slightly. "But no chance he's innocent?"

Sophia shook her head. "Unfortunately not. Believe me, I wish he was. You think I want one of my few remaining family members to be guilty of killing my grandfather? And his own father? Of trying to kill me? No, trust me, if I had any doubts whatsoever, I'd be happy, but I don't. Peter's involved in some way. And tonight, we'll figure out what way that is. Hopefully he's an unwilling accomplice, but if his dreams are any indication, I doubt it."

"I just don't understand how all this could happen. Or why he'd have done whatever it was he did to me to make me attack people. I'm just happy I didn't kill anyone."

"We've got good guards," Sophia said, smiling at Lucas, and though he wanted to feel proud, he wasn't sure he could have taken Lachlan down by himself that day, not without killing him.

There was another knock on the door and Lucas answered it, cracking it open to ensure it was Olivia before he let her in.

"I see everyone's here and in a crappy mood," she said as she crossed to Sophia's bed and sat on the edge.

"It's not exactly a pleasant task we're planning on embarking on, now is it?" Sergei asked dryly.

"No, but it could all be over by this time tomorrow, and that's a good thing," Olivia countered. "Yes, it sucks that we're going to arrest and interrogate one of our own, but if it means that no one else will be killed or attacked or any of the other shit he's been doing or has planned, isn't it worth it?"

"It is, but you know it's bittersweet, too," Sophia pointed out. "But yes, it'll be over tonight. What do you need in order to tell when he's asleep?"

Lucas nearly smiled at Sophia. She really had started to come into her own as aspida. He knew she'd had a panic attack right after being named aspida, and hadn't really believed she could do the job, but she was. No, she might not know as much about the Athenaeum as everyone else, but she was learning rapidly. And all things considered, she was doing a fantastic job. But he knew just telling her wouldn't do any good. She'd been told that. She had to believe it.

"Just need to lie down for a while. You can keep talking and all that, just don't touch me or you could get pulled in," Olivia warned.

"Easy enough. Get comfy." Sophia pointed to the other side of the bed, and Lucas was suddenly glad they hadn't actually messed the bed up. But by the glance Sophia shot at him, he knew she was thinking about what they'd done at the foot of the bed.

"Can do." Olivia climbed up the bed and rested her head on Sophia's pillow. She closed her eyes and a moment later, her body stiffened. It wasn't an obvious thing, but since he'd been watching her, he could see how all her muscles tensed just a little. Side-effect of dreamwalking, he assumed, because it wasn't like she was sleeping like a normal person. All magic took something out of the person using it, even if it was small enough to be inconsequential. Slipping through the dreams of everyone in the Athenaeum wasn't a small magic. There were some witches who could manage it, but no one was as good at it as nightmares except the gods.

"So we just wait until Olivia tells us Peter's asleep?" Lachlan asked as he pulled the chair out from Sophia's desk and sat down.

"Basically," Sophia confirmed.

"What do we do if he doesn't fall asleep?"

Sophia blinked then looked to Lucas. That was something they hadn't considered. He knew Peter occasionally stayed up late working on his computer—or playing—but surely he wouldn't forgo sleep entirely, would he? Even sociopaths needed sleep. For that matter, Lucas had never heard of a relic that would allow someone to stay awake indefinitely without side-effects.

"You guys know him better than me. Does he ever pull all-nighters? Like actual all-nighters where he's awake for more than twenty-four hours?" Sophia asked.

"Not that I'm aware of," Sergei said.

"Staying up late, absolutely, but I don't think he skips sleep," Lucas answered after a moment. "But I've never had reason to monitor anyone's sleep schedule."

Sophia nodded and caught her lower lip between her teeth as she thought. "Okay," she said when she came to a decision. "If he doesn't sleep tonight, then things are going to get a little trickier. I was given until tomorrow to get out of the Athenaeum or I'd be killed. Without knowing if it was Peter who threatened me or an accomplice, we can't be sure where or from where the attack will come. You guys are good, but if the same spell used on Agatha is used, I don't know that we can protect against it. Can we?" she asked, looking at Sergei, Lachlan, and finally to him.

"No," he had to admit, though he wished he could say otherwise. "Spells like that are notoriously hard to defend against."

"Even I couldn't. I don't even know of a spell that could," Sergei added.

She didn't look surprised, just nodded again. "So if Peter doesn't go to sleep tonight, then I leave." Her voice was calm, almost nonchalant, but he could see the strain around her eyes, the pain in them.

He hated the idea of her being alone, even if being out of the Athenaeum would be safer for her. But Peter—or whoever he was working with—had already tried to have her killed at Delphi, so he couldn't rule out the idea that trouble would follow her. "I'm going with you."

A sad smile crossed her lips as she shook her head. "You can't, Lucas. I know Olivia was a part-time guard, Lachlan is definitely fast and seriously strong, and Sergei's a badass demigod, but think about everything Peter has done. We need everyone here that we can to contain him and make sure we know everyone who's involved. You have to stay and see it through."

"She's right, Lucas," Sergei said quietly. "I know you hate the idea. I'm not really fond of it myself, but she's right. And she's not exactly a fragile, incapable child. She has Seth's gifts, your training, and Erasmus's brains. She'll be okay for a day."

Sophia was all those things, Lucas knew it, but she'd had less than a month of training, and much less sorcery training than he would have liked. But beyond all that, even if she was a powerful goddess he still wouldn't be comfortable with this. The threat to leave or die might just be a trap, something meant to get her away from the safety of the Athenaeum—or more specifically, from him. She might be capable, but if he wasn't there, he couldn't be sure she'd be safe. It killed him that he couldn't keep her safe here, either. Which meant Sophia was right. If they didn't stop this tonight, she'd have to leave, and he'd have to stay here to finish it.

It was tempting, so very tempting, to get a hold of Seth and ask him to take her someplace safe, but he doubted she'd go. No, she'd want to go someplace close in case she was needed. Which meant there was a chance he could lose her, and that terrified him more than anything else he'd ever encountered.

"Fine," he bit off, unable to keep his voice calm. "But if you do go, you go armed and prepared. Would I be able to convince you to get a hold of Seth and go with him? It's doubtful Peter or his accomplice could get to you with a god beside you."

"Except he's managed to ensure the patrons can't see what's going on here," Sophia reminded him as she walked to him and slid her hand into his. "Who's to say being with Seth would be safe, either? Besides, I'm sure this is all just hypothetical. Any second now, Olivia's going to open her eyes and tell us it's time."

He really fucking hoped so, because he was getting sick of seeing her scared or hurt. Especially hurt.

"Going on the assumption that Sophia's right," Lachlan broke in after no one said anything for a minute, "what exactly is the plan?"

Lucas tugged Sophia over to the bed, sat down, and drew her in against his side. "Hopefully Olivia will be able to tell us whether he's in his room or at his computer, and hopefully he's alone. Regardless, we go in and immediately cuff him. It should prevent him from using sorcery. When he's neutralized, we can get him someplace secure and interrogate him until we know who he's working with and how to counter whatever he's put into the aquifer."

"And if there isn't a counter?" Lachlan asked quietly.

"There's going to be a counter," Sophia said firmly. "We managed to get it out of you, so we're going to figure out how to get it out of the water."

He nodded slowly, then released a slow breath. "Then I've just got one more question."

"What's that?"

"What do we do until Olivia says Peter's asleep and it's go time?"

They ended up playing cards for the first two hours. The third hour they spent talking. For the fourth and fifth, Sophia picked a movie on her laptop. It wasn't ideal, but it kept them partially occupied.

It was a little after two when Olivia's eyes opened and she sat up, without any of the usual grogginess of someone who just woke up. "He's asleep."

Sophia and the other three all rose from where they were sitting or sprawled. "Do you know where?" she asked.

"We got lucky. He's actually in his room tonight," Olivia said as she slid off the bed and stretched.

She felt mixed emotions at that. Peter's room wasn't far from hers, and it was a smaller, more isolated space, but the rooms around his were occupied. True, it wasn't likely something would get through a foot of stone, but she knew what magic could do and anything was possible. Still, the chance that this could all be over in the next hour had anticipation warming her chest.

"Everyone ready?" she asked, looking from one face to another, ending with Lucas. They all nodded, but she noticed Lucas's gaze was dark and more intense than the others.

"Use your shield spell before we go," he murmured to her.

It was smart and she complied, feeling the invisible barrier go up. "Done," she told him. "But I won't feel bad if you go all stone skin before we go in his room." He didn't argue, just did as she asked. Despite knowing he wouldn't really feel it, she still ran a hand down his arm. "Thank you."

They left her room, and she wasn't surprised when Lucas stepped out front. She might be the boss, but he took his job as head of the nasaru very seriously. He was probably also the most dangerous of their group of five, so she couldn't really fault him taking point.

They stopped outside of Peter's room. Nothing was said, but Lucas gave everyone a questioning look, and it wasn't until he received nods from everyone that he turned the handle and eased the door open.

Peter was lying in bed on his side, eyes closed, his blue mohawk limp. He looked innocent, and it was really hard to believe this was the same man involved with so many deaths and attacks.

Lucas moved forward, the magic-dampening cuffs in one hand. Just as he reached the bed, Peter's eyes opened, and he looked from Lucas to Sophia. "Do I want to know why you five have snuck into my bedroom in the middle of the night?" he asked, and Sophia noted that he didn't sound like he'd just woken up. Had they not waited long enough for him to sink deep enough into sleep? Had they made some noise which woke him? She didn't think so, but it also didn't truly matter. They were here for a reason.

It seemed like Lucas agreed, because he quickly slapped the first cuff on Peter's wrist. Rather than trying to fight against the second cuff or questioning why he was being cuffed, Peter cocked his head and arched a brow at Sophia. He rolled onto his back and just watched her.

It would be so easy to let Lucas take the lead here, but Sophia couldn't bring herself to take the coward's way out. "We know you were involved in the recent deaths, Peter."

"Yes. And?"

His easy admission gave her pause and she could all but hear the record screech in her head. She'd expected him to argue, to plead that he was innocent, but instead he'd admitted to it as easily as she might agree to getting a drink of water. "You admit to killing Erasmus? Agatha? Your dad?"

"Thomas, too." His green eyes shifted to Olivia and he smiled. It was dark and so full of malice that Sophia had to fight not to take a step back. "Tried to kill you, but you managed to squirm out of that, didn't you? Don't suppose you'll tell me how, will you? Nothing but the antidote should have saved you from the Achlys."

Olivia took a step forward and Sergei grabbed her to keep her from attacking Peter.

"You actually did it? Or did someone else you're working with?" Sophia asked, realizing she was desperate to have him be a lacky, not the one who'd pulled the metaphorical trigger.

Peter's lips turned down in an exaggerated sad face. "Aww. Were you hoping I'd been led astray? That some bad guy had tricked me into doing naughty things, but that deep down I was full of remorse and trying to figure out how to get out from under his thumb?"

Yes, yes she had, but clearly that wasn't the case.

"Sorry, but that's just not the case. Besides, most people in the Athenaeum are weak."

"You have a strange definition of weak," Lucas growled. "You killed good people, and your dad was one of them."

Peter scoffed. "My dad was one of the weakest. I'd hoped he would join me, but I realized he was never going to see things how I did."

Sophia shook her head. "Dion was a good man, and he didn't deserve to have a son like you."

"Of course he didn't," Peter agreed without hesitation. "A son like me should have been born to a man with true ambition, true power. Instead, he was content to play with books and ignore all the power sitting beneath us." He leaned forward, face earnest as he rested his arms on his knees. "Do you know what we could do if we actually *used* what we gathered instead of hiding it away like hoarders?"

"Nothing good comes from wielding that kind of power, Peter," Sophia said, growing more horrified with each word he spoke. How had he fooled her so completely? Hell, how had he fooled the entire Athenaeum?

"I think I'm going to enjoy haunting your nightmares for what you did to me," Olivia said, smiling cruelly.

"No, you're not," Peter said confidently.

They were getting off track, and Sophia had to focus on what they were there to do. Peter might have half-confirmed he was working alone, but they needed more answers. "Peter, why? Why kill Erasmus and the others? Why taint the aquifer? What's the point in all this?"

she asked, desperate to understand. There had to be some reason, some *logic*, behind what he'd done. People didn't just decide to go on murdering sprees.

"Tsk tsk, little cousin," Peter said before laughing. "Do you think I'm going to reveal all my secrets? I mean, sure, you're all going to be dead in a few minutes, but I've seen the same movies you have. Monologuing always backfires."

"We're not going to die. We're taking you into custody," Lucas said, reaching for Peter.

Peter laughed again and lifted his cuffed hands. He hissed out a word that made her skin crawl and the cuffs melted away. They literally melted, the molten metal somehow evaporating before it dripped onto the bed. "No, you're not. You might want to turn around," he said, sounding much more confident than she felt.

Fear stole her breath as Sophia glanced over her shoulder and saw dozens of people crowded around the doorway and just inside it, waiting, watching them. At the front of them were Lachlan and Sergei. Despite having the blood of Apollo, Sergei was being held easily by Lachlan, who had one hand over the healer's mouth and his fangs shoved deep in his throat. That wasn't good. Though Sophia hadn't interacted with too many vampires, everyone knew they got more of a boost from drinking Arcane blood than human, and the blood of a demigod? Lachlan was about to be supercharged and was clearly not on their side. Maybe their cure hadn't worked, or maybe it had only been temporary. Whichever it was, Lachlan was now under Peter's control, just like the others.

"Lucas," she whispered when they started to move inside, filling the room and ensuring there would be no escape. And while Lucas and

Olivia were both very good, there was no way they could take on the entire Athenaeum with just three of them. And judging by the eager, bloodthirsty looks on each of their faces, none of them wished them well. Including Heather, who slunk inside with the others.

Lucas cursed and stepped back, putting himself between the crowd and Sophia, standing shoulder to shoulder with Olivia. Clearly, they were prepared to fight despite the overwhelming odds. Sophia ran through their options, but none of them were really promising.

They could fight, but eventually they'd lose. Peter might not kill them, but whatever he did probably wouldn't be pleasant.

She could call for Seth, but there was no guarantee he'd arrive, and if he did, she wasn't sure what he would do. Kill everyone? As far as she knew, they were simply under Peter's control, and she didn't want to see them die for it.

Talking wouldn't work. She knew that. Not when Peter had been so dismissive, even amused, by her concerns. It would just prolong things. They needed a solution, not a delay.

Peter slipped off the bed and stretched, still smiling like this was a party. He lifted his hands and clapped twice, drawing the attention of the crowd to him. "Kill them," he called out in a cheerful voice.

Sophia started to cast the shield spell again, this time to cover Olivia and Lucas too, but realized it wouldn't do them any good. It wouldn't last long, and everyone in the mob had some form of magic, even if it was only sorcery. It also wouldn't get Sergei away from Lachlan. What they needed was to get the hell out of Dodge. Then she remembered the night she'd spent practicing one specific spell down in the hidden aspida chamber. A spell she'd burned into her memory.

Her hands shot out, one hand wrapping around Lucas's wrist, the other Olivia's arm. Frantically speaking the words she'd worked so hard to memorize, she teleported them out of the Athenaeum, praying to Seth and every other patron that the spell worked correctly, because she'd never practiced taking anyone else with her, and never while fearing for her life.

The world around them went black and an instant later they reappeared in a room that was both familiar and not; her old bedroom in Georgia. It was devoid of furniture or decorations now, but that was the only thing she was able to notice before the strain of teleporting three people halfway across the world drew her back into the void.

Chapter 32

Lucas had been running through their very limited options when Sophia grabbed them and spoke unfamiliar words. They were yanked out of the Athenaeum abruptly, the shift in locations causing his head to spin. They reappeared in what looked like an empty bedroom. It was light out, so they weren't in Greece anymore. America, maybe? It was the only other place she was familiar with. He started to ask Sophia where she'd brought them when her eyes rolled back and she collapsed. Because of the dizziness, he wasn't able to fully prevent her fall, but he did manage to keep her head from hitting the carpeted floor.

"Shit. What's wrong with her?" Olivia asked, dropping to her knees beside them. "And where the hell are we?"

"I think she overextended herself, and I'm not sure. We'll have to ask her when she wakes up. I just wish she'd been able to get to Sergei." He was berating himself for not keeping a closer eye on Lachlan. Yes, Sergei had said the vampire had been cured, but clearly they didn't know nearly enough about whatever substance he'd been infected with.

"We're lucky she managed to get us out," Olivia said darkly. "I had no idea she knew a teleportation spell."

"Neither did I," Lucas admitted. There was nothing he could do for Sergei now, so he focused on Sophia. Her pulse was good, steady and strong, and her breathing was normal. He'd never found a teleportation spell in the Athenaeum, and since it would be a handy tool for the nasaru and venatores to use, he could only guess that it was dangerous in some way. Dangerous or used a hell of a lot of magic. He'd come across spells that used up a person's energy, knocking them out, and hoped that's all this was. There's no way she saved them, only to die from her own rescue attempt.

"Take the battery out of your phone. If anyone can track our phones, it's Peter." For that matter, he wouldn't be shocked if there were trackers embedded in the phones themselves. Taking his own advice, he got his phone out and removed the battery before putting both back in his pocket. Olivia did the same, looking just as pissed as he felt. When they got out of wherever they were, they'd dispose of the phones themselves, just to be safe.

Lucas was going for Sophia's phone when she began to stir, her features tightening as she rolled her head to one side. "Sophia?" he asked, forgetting about the phone as he gently slid a hand beneath her head.

"What happened?"

"You teleported us out of the Athenaeum and passed out."

Her eyes opened and she frowned at him before she remembered. She sat up quickly and he barely managed to pull back before her head connected with his face. "How the hell did he get so many people on his side?" she asked, her eyes full of anguish. "How did he get Lachlan? Sergei said he was clean."

"I don't know," he answered honestly. "It has to be tied to that magic infecting them, but I don't know anything more beyond that."

Sophia pushed up to her feet, not quite steady, but determined. She yanked her phone out of her pocket, only to stop, no doubt realizing they didn't know who, if anyone, was still sane in the Athenaeum.

"You should take the battery out of your phone," Lucas told Sophia. "We don't want him tracking us to...wherever you brought us."

A brief look around had Sophia frowning again. "It's my old bedroom in Georgia," she answered as she pried the cover off her phone and took the battery out. "We should leave. It's been sold, so the new owners could come home, if they're not already here."

"I can handle that," Olivia told them, grabbing their wrists and tugging them toward her. The room blurred and they appeared outside, away from the house but in the shadow of a large tree, hidden from the street by the wide trunk. It was both better and worse than Sophia's teleportation. His head didn't spin, but he did feel unsteady, like his soul was settling back in his body.

"What the hell was that?" Sophia asked a little breathlessly.

"Shadow travel," Olivia said with a faint smile. "But what now?"

"Now we get away from here in case they already tracked our phones, and figured out how we're going to get back in the Athenaeum and fix this," Sophia said, a determined glint in her eyes. She started walking, seeming to know where she was going.

"And how do we do that?" Olivia asked as she and Lucas fell into step beside her, flanking her. Lucas approved of her actions. Sophia might not be the most powerful of their group, and certainly not the most experienced, but she was the most important. She was magically linked to the Athenaeum, which meant any plan they came up with was almost certainly going to require her. The Athenaeum wouldn't recognize anyone else as the leader. Or at least it shouldn't, but then again, Peter should never have been able to influence so many into going against the aspida. That meant they couldn't be certain the rules they were used to playing with applied any longer.

"I don't know," Sophia admitted, "but I know what step one is."

"What?" Lucas asked.

"Find someplace safe and secluded, and call Seth."

Getting the gods involved wasn't something Lucas normally advocated for, but in this case? Bring it on.

Sophia didn't stop or even slow as they left the residential area and made her way down a mostly quiet street. Finally, they entered a park, and she led them to the most secluded part of it. The park was devoid of people, but since the sun was starting to set, she wasn't surprised. Still, she wanted to ensure they were away from anywhere teens might sneak out and visit. When she was convinced they wouldn't be spotted and were away from any cameras, she stopped. Now to get in touch with Seth.

Lucas's fears about their phones being tracked were valid, and Sophia didn't want to risk being discovered too soon. Unfortunately, gods tended to only hear their worshipers, and she wasn't sure she qualified as worshiping Seth. Still, he was a patron of the place she was in charge of, so she had to try.

"One sec," she told the others before she closed her eyes and silently prayed to Seth to appear.

Please Seth, hear me. We need your help and I can't use the phone. We've had to run from the Athenaeum. I'm no longer in control.

"You what?"

The male voice was accompanied by a slight tremor in the ground beneath their feet, and Sophia opened her eyes to see a furious Seth standing in front of them. He was dressed in shorts and a tee-shirt, his feet bare, sunglasses on his face, the latter of which he yanked off his face.

"We had to run away," she told him.

"Explain."

A pissed off god was more than a little terrifying, even though Sophia knew he wasn't angry at her. Still, she swallowed and glanced at her companions before she began to explain. "We've been investigating, like you knew. With Olivia's help," she motioned to the woman, "we figured out it was Peter."

That surprised Seth enough to have his eyes widening. "Peter? He killed his own uncle and father?"

"Trust me, I wasn't expecting it either. But he's also done something to the aquifer, tainted it with something that has infected everyone in the Athenaeum except for us and Sergei." Guilt for leaving him behind rolled through her, but she couldn't have gotten to him. She wished she could have. "We couldn't get him out."

Lucas rubbed her back and explained, "Peter told basically everyone else to kill us. Sophia had to get us out of there quick or we wouldn't have made it out. Sergei was being held by one of our vampires when it happened."

Seth frowned and cocked his head, his eyes going unfocused for a moment. "What else has Peter done?"

"What do you mean?" Sophia asked. Wasn't that enough? Seth knew everything she did at this point. Just to be safe, she thought quickly, but no, other than a few minor details, he knew what she did.

"I mean, I can't sense anything inside the Athenaeum. Last time I talked to you, I could. Worse, I can't take myself there, which should be impossible."

"He's blocking you from teleporting to the Athenaeum?" Lucas asked, his hand stilling on her back.

"Tell me about this infection," Seth demanded instead of answering.

"We don't know much," she had to admit. "About a week ago, one of the guards—a vampire named Lachlan—went crazy. Just violently attacking anyone who came near him. Sergei checked him out and realized he was infected by some kind of magical substance. Nothing he did was able to get it out of Lachlan, and it didn't seem to weaken over time. After that, we noticed that everyone was starting to act differently, but just toward me. Over the last week, they went from friendly to distrusting to outwardly hostile. Sergei did some checking and realized whatever this substance was, it was in the aquifer. We're guessing," she emphasized the word, "that the gifts you gave Lucas, Sergei, and I protected us. Olivia has her own protections, but it meant we were the only people not infected. We thought we'd cured Lachlan with a mixture of Sergei's healing and Isis's tyet, but...we were wrong. And we still don't know what the substance infecting them is."

Seth said nothing, just lifted his gaze to the stars above them.

"I might know," Olivia said, speaking for the first time since Seth had appeared.

"Might know what?" the god asked, his gaze fixing on her.

"What the infection is."

"How?"

Olivia looked at Sophia and arched a brow, her head tilting slightly toward Seth. Sophia nodded. "Not only is he all we've got—"

"Gee, thanks," Seth said blandly, but she ignored him and kept going.

"—but you can trust him. He's been helping me for weeks now. Besides, if you can't trust one of the divine patrons, who can you trust?"

"Good point." Turning back to Seth, Olivia said, "I'm one of the Ogham."

"That's your bloodline?" Lucas asked, at the same time Seth said, "You're a rune?"

Despite the situation, Olivia rolled her eyes. "No, I'm not a rune. And this has to stay just between us." She didn't wait for them to agree before continuing. "It's a bloodline. We can gift all of our knowledge to another of our bloodline. I'm one of the last of us, so I've received many of those gifts."

"How many?" Seth asked curiously.

Olivia hooked a finger in the neck of her shirt and tugged it down and to the side, revealing some of the many tattoos Sophia knew she had. "Each one is a gifting, and I'm tattooed basically everywhere but for my head and neck."

He let out a low whistle, obviously impressed. "So a lot, then. Go on."

Releasing her shirt, Olivia went on. "I couldn't tell you which of my ancestors I got any of my information from except for a few exceptions, but this all sounds familiar. The magical infection, the violent behavior, the mind control. Even the cave, because we all know the Athenaeum started as just a cave."

They knew that better than most alive after the nightmares they'd all shared. And while Sophia didn't have Olivia's genetic memory, when the woman put it that way, something tickled at her memory. It sounded familiar, too, she just couldn't place it. "What is it?" she prompted, everything inside her holding, waiting for the last hint to give her the answer.

"Miasma," Olivia told her grimly. "It sounds like Miasma."

"One of the primordial substances used to create the universe. The essence of violence. No," she said, shaking her head. "The violence of change and emotions," Sophia whispered.

Olivia was surprised, but nodded. "Yes. How did you know?"

"I found a scroll in the Vault."

Seth was shaking his head and turned, walking away a few steps, before stalking back. "I should have guessed. I really should have fucking guessed," he muttered. "The Athenaeum was built over the Miasma chamber."

"It what?" Sophia asked, her voice going up several steps with her shock.

Seth let out a humorless laugh and nodded. "That was the whole reason Eugenios was led to that particular cave. It was above the Miasma chamber. The gods thought it would help keep it safe from detection and protect it in case it ever was discovered."

Oh, Sophia was going to have a chat with all the previous aspides when she hit the afterlife. None of them could have bothered to mention that in the journals? Then again, they might have, and it just hadn't been in a section she'd read, but there was something in the grimoire.

"I've seen Miasma mentioned in one other place," she said slowly, deciding that trusting these three was more important than keeping everything in that hidden room a secret any longer.

"The place you've been sneaking off to?" Lucas asked, proving that even the guards of the Athenaeum weren't just brawn.

She nodded. "There's a grimoire there. A lot of the spells were terrifying and some I couldn't read, but there was one I came across. I'd forgotten about it, even after reading about the Miasma in that scroll. It's a spell to control it."

"You know how to control the Miasma?" Olivia asked.

Apologetically, Sophia shook her head. "When I read it, I didn't know what the Miasma was or why anyone would want to control it, so I didn't really focus on it. I don't know the spell. But if I could get back there..." Her gaze slid to Seth. "But if you can't get in there, I doubt I can."

"Maybe, maybe not," Seth murmured thoughtfully.

"We have to focus on what we do know, what we can do, at least for now," Lucas said, voice angry, but she knew he wasn't angry at her. She couldn't have known, and he'd realize that. "So Peter was just poking around the Athenaeum and found this chamber, decided to use it against us?"

"Maybe, maybe not. Could be he was infected by it, too," Olivia argued.

"Not if he was the one controlling everyone else," Lucas pointed out.

"I'm less concerned about whether he's infected or not," Sophia admitted, leaning back against a tree. "We don't just have to figure out how to retake the Athenaeum from Peter and the rest of the people there, we have to fight the Miasma now, too. Don't suppose either of you know how to do that? Especially when a god can't teleport into the Athenaeum and the only spell to control it is hidden in there?" she asked, looking between Seth and Olivia.

"Unfortunately, I've now exhausted my full knowledge of Miasma," Seth told her, "and the other patrons aren't any better. They're the ones who told me about it to begin with, and they swore that was all they knew about it."

"I don't either, but I know of a place that might have the information," Olivia said, though she didn't sound certain.

Seth narrowed his eyes at Olivia. "Where?"

"The Hall of Records."

"Isn't that just a story made up by some human a few decades ago?" Lucas asked.

"Not according to my memories," Olivia assured him. "He's just the one who named it that and brought it to people's attention."

"And you're certain it exists?"

"I'm certain it did at one point. It was said to have texts that were ancient when the Athenaeum was founded. Which means if anywhere has something about how to fight the Miasma, then it's there. Unless you," she looked at Seth, "know any gods who might know more."

Seth shook his head. "If there are any, they're not going to just pass out that information. But if I'm being completely honest, I doubt any of them do. Vazi is probably the oldest god still alive, and he only knew Miasma existed and was dangerous." His lips tightened into a thin line. "However, I think you're right about the Hall...and someone's been hunting for the Hall for the last month. I think you need to work together." He stepped closer to Sophia and his voice softened, gentled. "I'm sorry."

Confused and a little worried, she asked, "For what?" she asked, relieved when Lucas's hand found her shoulder. She didn't think Seth would hurt her, but the apology caused dread to pool in her belly. She really didn't need any other unpleasant surprises. She was at her limit.

The answer wasn't audible, Seth just held out one hand like he was motioning to someone beside him. A second later, with a faint pop of light, someone was there. Someone who nearly made her heart stop. Someone who made Blanche's words to her finally make sense.

Erasmus was alive.

He didn't look frail or sickly. He sure as hell didn't look like someone who'd died and been cremated.

Sophia's head spun, and she worried she was going to pass out for the second time in the last hour. She did stumble back, but both Lucas and Olivia supported her until she was certain she wasn't going to fall. "I don't understand," she said in a small voice.

"Neither do I," Lucas added, and where she was shocked and disoriented by the appearance, he sounded pissed.

Olivia lifted one hand. "Count me on the list of those who are confused as fuck."

Both Seth and Erasmus looked apologetic, and the latter was focused entirely on Sophia. "I am so sorry, louloudi mou. It wasn't supposed to happen the way it did," he said, taking a step toward her.

My flower. He was alive and calling her his flower, just like he had when he'd been slowly dying in his bed. "You died. Right in front of me. You died," Sophia said, her mind fixed on that one point. "I saw it. We burned your body, and the Athenaeum believed it. It chose me as the next aspida."

"I only appeared to. And it wasn't supposed to happen when you were there. The timing was off, but I didn't realize it until it was too late. And the Athenaeum choosing was magic from the patrons. They triggered the next choosing."

"But why?" Lucas demanded. "We all mourned for you. Why would you fake your death?"

Part of Sophia realized he didn't ask how, but Seth and the other patrons were in on it. It was probably an easy thing to do with them helping.

"It was part of a plan to figure out what the darkness inside the Athenaeum was," Seth answered. "Erasmus really did get poisoned, but after we were able to save Olivia, we knew how to save him. We hoped that by going along with the poisoner's plan, we could figure out who was involved, and how they were blocking us."

Lucas wasn't content with that. "And you couldn't tell any of us? You told Sophia and Sergei you were poisoned, so why not tell them what was going on? There's no way in hell you could have thought

Sophia had anything to do with it. How could you have suspected me?"

"No, I knew Sophia was innocent, and I was fairly certain about you and Sergei," Erasmus agreed, taking another step toward Sophia. "But before that I would have said no one in the Athenaeum could have poisoned anyone. I had no idea who was involved, and I didn't want to risk them finding out I was alive. Dead, I was free to search for a cure for what ailed the Athenaeum." Another step. "Sophia…I really am sorry. I couldn't think of another way. I just wanted to protect you. The Athenaeum, too, but I didn't want anything to happen to you." Hesitantly, he lifted his arms, clearly hoping for a hug. While she was stunned, hurt, and angry, she was also so very relieved that she would finally get to know her grandfather.

Pulling away from Lucas and Olivia, she half fell into Erasmus's arms, getting a true hug from her grandfather for the first time in her life. Though she slammed her eyes closed, it didn't prevent the tears from spilling down her cheeks. She would yell at him later, rage at him for what he'd put her through, but right now, she just wanted to celebrate that he was alive.

"I am so, so mad at you," she whispered against his shoulder, all while hugging him like she'd never let him go.

"I know," he murmured. "I deserve it. And I swear I'll do what I can to make it up to you."

She believed him, but she also knew it wouldn't be easy to truly forgive him. "We can't do this now, though."

"No, we can't," he agreed.

Sniffling, she pulled back and wiped at her cheeks. "So. We need to find the Hall of Records and figure out how to neutralize one of the primordial substances of the universe. How hard can that be?"

"Primordial substances?" Erasmus asked, frowning at her.

"Miasma, we can explain later. Right now, anyone know where the Hall might be?"

"If my memories are right," Olivia said, stepping beside Sophia, "We'll find the map in Egypt."

"That doesn't narrow it down much," Lucas said, sliding an arm around Sophia's waist. Erasmus's brows shot up at the casual gesture, but he also smiled a little. She'd ask him why later.

"Narrowing it down isn't going to help much, either. The map is beneath the Sphinx."

Erasmus lifted his gaze from Lucas's arm to Olivia. "The fabled hidden chamber? That won't be easy to get into."

Olivia shrugged. "Maybe not, but it's where we have to start."

"I'll take you to Giza," Seth told them. "I and the other patrons will give you whatever help we can, but we can't give you long to reclaim the Athenaeum. It would be bad enough if it was just someone taking it over, having access to all the relics and secrets there, but the Miasma makes things worse."

"How long can you give us?" Sophia asked.

"Two weeks."

"That's not very long."

"No, it isn't. But if the Miasma gets out, it could potentially infect the entire planet. And again, there's all the relics. I'm sure you've been in the Vault now, so you know what's down there. So two weeks is all I can give you, and even that's pushing it."

"What happens after that?" Lucas asked.

It wasn't Seth who answered, it was Erasmus. "We destroy the Athenaeum."

"The failsafe?" Sophia asked. "I didn't think to use it before I teleported us out." Maybe she should have, but the thought of using it made her sick to her stomach, so it hadn't even occurred to her.

"If possible, yes," Seth confirmed. "I can destroy most everything, but the failsafe would be best, as it'll destroy it more completely than even I can. The problem is that you're still aspida, so only you can use it, and only from within the Athenaeum."

Sophia let herself lean against Seth. If she let herself, she could almost come to hate the Athenaeum. While it held wonders, it had also been the source of the worst days of her life. But hate or not, she couldn't let Peter and the Miasma achieve their end goal, whatever it was.

There was a reason that Sophia hadn't majored in archaeology. She was, at heart, a bookworm. She wasn't equipped for field work, even when it didn't involve trying to prevent a potential worldwide catastrophe. As she looked at the faces of those around her, she could only be glad she wasn't alone. Between Erasmus's experience, Olivia's memories, and Lucas's skill as a guard, they could do this. They had to. She wasn't leaving her mom and the others to perish underground. She wasn't leaving Sergei in Peter's clutches.

Drawing in a breath, she straightened her shoulders and nodded to Seth. "Then...let's go to Egypt." She attempted a smile as she uttered words she never thought she'd ever say. "It's time to save the world."

Epilogue

Peter frowned as he strode down the stairs of the Athenaeum. While he wasn't upset that Sophia and her little friends were gone, he knew his cousin was going to try to cause trouble for him. Try being the operative word. The second she'd teleported out—and he'd like to know how she managed that—he'd cast spells to surround the Athenaeum with an impenetrable ward. Several of them, to be exact. There was no way she'd be able to get back inside, nor could the so-called patrons.

He continued to descend, further than anyone else had dared to venture in centuries. Perhaps not since the Athenaeum was first built. Cowardly fools, all of them. Most he couldn't blame, as the aspides of the past had well-hidden the existence of this chamber. It was doubtful all of them even knew of it. They were scared of it. But not Peter. Not since he'd accidentally come across this chamber a full decade ago. He smirked as he opened the secret doorway and continued downward, remembering the day he'd stumbled across this very entrance and, being a curious teen, had decided to investigate. It was the best day of his life. The day he'd discovered his reason for existing. The day he'd begun hatching a plan that would take years to come to fruition.

The day he'd first encountered the Miasma.

The stairs changed from the clean-cut ones above to a rough, sharply sloping floor. The people who had shaped the Athenaeum hadn't wanted to make this place accessible, so had left it as the universe had created it. Not that it made a difference. A determined man like Peter wouldn't let something as trivial as a short hike deter him.

He made his way down a path he knew more intimately than the lines of his own face, as he'd been this way hundreds of times since he first discovered it. When he reached the bottom, he spoke the words to illuminate the chamber.

It wasn't as impressive as it should be. The cavern ceiling was barely tall enough to admit him, and the walls were no wider than the pool just beyond his toes. And that? Was about the size of a standard backyard swimming pool, full of a swirling, iridescent emerald substance. It was caught somewhere between a liquid and a gas, appearing to be both at times. There were flashes of yellow and a brighter green, but it was beautiful. Beautiful and radiating pure power. How could those above not have ever sensed it?

Peter knelt and smiled at the substance in a way most would reserve for a lover. "We're getting closer," he whispered to the Miasma as he dipped a hand into it, shuddering when he felt its power slide over him, into him. "We can operate openly now. She's gone."

He shuddered again, but this time it was with a discomfort that bordered on pain, rather than pleasure. Words that weren't really words hissed through his mind, making him hunch in on himself. "No, she's gone. She was never a threat to us. To you. If she had been, I swear I would have killed her. I'd never let anyone undo what we've set in motion," he cooed soothingly to the sentient liquid, even as it pulled at him, until his entire arm was submerged, his face only a breath from the surface. Another jolt of pain and he winced. "Didn't I kill my father for our plans? If I would do that, why would I hesitate about killing a cousin I've known for a month? No, it's just you and me. We will finish what you started. What we started. Another month and the world will be forever changed. Then…then we'll be in control, and people will remember you."

The swirling paused for a moment, then it pulled Peter fully into it. He didn't struggle, he didn't even tense. He just smiled beautifully as he let his body be completely enveloped by the Miasma.

Closing his eyes, he floated there, at peace as dark plans floated through him. Soon, those plans would be complete, and the world would be consumed.

About the Author

Meg M. Robinson is a fantasy author who lives in north Georgia with her husband, a teenager, and a small menagerie of animals. She's goofy and a little dorky, which greatly amuses her family.

She's obsessed with crows, sea turtles, and houseplants. And, of course, books. When she's not focused on either reading or writing a book, she enjoys playing video games, archery, and baking.

www.megmrobinson.com

Please consider leaving a review for this book. Reviews are extremely important for authors, but especially indie authors like me! Believe me, we appreciate it!

www.ingramcontent.com/pod-product-compliance
Lightning Source LLC
Chambersburg PA
CBHW061337310726
48974CB00001B/77